CURSED
THE RING

MANTISSA CREED

∞CURSEDTHESAGA∞
www.cursedthesaga.com

DEDICATION

To my father and mother, thank you for forcing me to read.

ACKNOWLEDGMENTS

I would like to thank Nia May Green, for reading, rereading, re-re-reading and commenting on all the hundred versions of this story from the start, and for also keeping me entertained with the ideas and continuous arguments, especially the ridiculous speculations of the ending.

Many thanks to Momina Raza, for contributing to the revision of this story on it's final stages.

Thank you to all the members of my queue on Critique Circle, for all your feedback, extra patience, and reviews that opened my eyes to the world of writing and self-publishing.

Rebecca Roslyn Ngoo, thank you for being the youngest reviewer on the team and contributing to the development of the story.

I also would like to thank Gabrielle Ngoo, for being so annoying.

Last but not least, David Ngoo, because you were just there all the time.

An artist should create beautiful
things, but should put nothing of his own life into them.
We live in an age when men treat art as if it were meant to
be a form of autobiography. We have lost the abstract sense
of beauty.

-Oscar Wilde

i

I

You're No Creature, Sweetheart ...

Apart from car racing, nothing stimulates me more than riding my Ares Whisper in time for sunrise. My thighs clinging on the tank of the classic motorcycle and my body leaning forward, I race against the wind. This is my morning ritual, except today, I'm hoping the wind will blow the forbidden questions dangling in my mind.

Not today. Not now. Think of the consequences.

But I have to ask her. I need to know.

The road is narrow and curvy with leafy trees lining either side. I lean to prepare for the corner ahead. As always, I forgive the overhanging branches hijacking most of the sunlight.

In the distance, the morning sun peeks out from behind the mountains. Faithful as always, it brightens another one of my rides. The warmth of its rays penetrates my khaki jumpsuit, warming my skin, just the way I like it.

I'm mesmerized by its golden glow, but I must turn back home. Today's Saturday, which means a mandatory mother-daughter breakfast at exactly eight o'clock. The word "late" does not exist in my mother's dictionary.

"Tardiness is disrespectful, Alexandra," she once told me.

Mother only uses my full name when she's beyond pleased, or very annoyed.

Toes steady on the foot pegs, right leg pinned on the gas tank, hands tight on the handlebars, I lean in to take a steady turn.

One glance at the hill ahead and I smile. The motorcycle jostles over the rough asphalt. The engine cries while my body yearns for speed.

Past the sharp turn, I ride uphill. I'm aiming for the top, and through the orchards, the engine wails up the steep incline.

Another scream from the engine and I slam on the brakes. I'm at the top, gazing below. River Stills enhances the beauty of the city and the towering private estate that sits on a high hill, overlooking the cityscape of Ashbourne. The Stills residence is home to the founders of Ashbourne City, the Van-Baileys.

Though my heart prefers views of the natural world—the mountains, tranquil waterfalls, and green lands—I still appreciate the glass skyscrapers, in particular at night when the lights sparkle on the rivers.

It's downhill time—time to play with the wind. I start the engine again, ready to go. My head buzzes as I await the thrill. I roll the throttle for more speed. My heart is thrashing hard now, excitement rushing through my veins. Adrenaline flashes down my spine, my cheeks numb from the strong air current. I pull out a smile.

For a second, I glance down to check the speedometer. Staring back ahead, in the middle of the road stands a giant dog. No, it's too large to be a dog.

A shiver snaps my tendons taut, locking my joints as the dark, furry animal stares right at me. Its eyes are the color of the sunrise, and they hold my gaze as if to dare me.

I should brake. I should slow down, I must stop now, but my hands are locked rigid, my legs, numb. An inch from hitting the animal, I veer to the side, and the front wheel slams on the steel barriers, the momentum ejecting me into the air. Dazed, I come to land my head on a sharp rock.

In my mind, I rerun the accident and try every possible way to override the moment of the crash, but with each time, I end with my head on the rock.

I'm not sure which hurts most; my head or my leg stuck between the barbed wire attached to the poplar tree.

Shit! No helmet. Mother is going to kill me.

I choke and swallow a lump of bittersweet liquid. Sudden warmth trailing down my neck frightens me. I try to raise my arm, but I can't feel my fingers, or my legs. Stinging shivers arrest my spine.

Is it the scorching sun, or is my blood boiling?

A drop of blood from my nose burns my lips. The sun is too hot, too bright; I can't keep my eyes open. My heart is taking too much time to beat. When it beats, it hurts. I choke once for air before darkness swallows me.

The sound of a heart thudding brings me back to consciousness. It's my heart, and it throbs quicker and stronger than usual.

I'm not dead? Thank God.

"It worked again." I mumble, thinking of the first time, I healed miraculously.

I was nine when I accidentally burned my hand. After a moment of pain, the wound healed right before my eyes, leaving no sign of any injuries. Mother and Grandpa Henry—her father—explained that I was unique.

"A unique human being," they said.

What does a unique human being mean?

A question I've tried to ignore for a long time. The last time I asked Mother, we ended in a big row, and I had to live with Grandpa Henry in his ranch in Viennamo, Africa.

Today, I plan to ask Mother, again, but that will only work if get home in time for breakfast.

With the sun still fighting to dry the dew on my arm, I know I haven't been here for long.

There's an unusual strength in my bones. Wondering about the strange dog, I'm flexing my fingers when a weird presence triggers goose bumps all over me.

"Alexandra ..." a woman whispers. "Alexandra." The soft voice sounds unreal; it's everywhere and yet nowhere.

As if I'm not in control of my body, I spring to my feet with ease, then turn in search of she who calls.

"Alexandra."

I turn around, and a woman wearing a radiant smile stands in front of me. From the long silver robe with a gold binding, I'm sure she's not of this world.

I want to run, but her sparkling silver eyes hold not only my gaze, but the whole of me.

She stands at ease with hands together. "Fear not, child. I'm not here to hurt you."

"Who are you?" My voice comes out fainter than a whisper.

I examine her as she moves nearer. She shifts her pale arms to her side, and I notice her white ghostly hair. It flows in a smooth band, draping her right shoulder, then circles her waist like a wide belt.

Now I know who she is; the woman Mother said would appear to me.

"Nersii." The woman spreads a smile. "You've grown into a beautiful lady."

I frown. "What did you call me?"

"Nersii." She tilts her head slightly. "The Bane of the Cursed Angel."

"My name is Alexandra Joanne Watson. Nothing in that name says Nersii or bane."

She laughs. "There's the attitude that's proves you are who I say you are."

"What do you want from me?" I lower my gaze to her feet, but they are hidden underneath her robe that sweeps the ground.

"Tell Mia, your mother, I said, it's time." Before I can ask what she means, her face beams, and it's almost as if she wants to sing. "It's good to see you again, Nersii." Without waiting for my answer, she disappears.

I quiver and blink to reality, and inhale a few quick breaths.

As I examine myself, I'm thinking everything is okay until I notice the floral pattern of my heels covered in dust. I should have worn trainers. That is merely a minor regret because as much as I love speed, I love my heels.

I'm late for breakfast, but thank God for the stranger; I have a valid reason now.

However, the stranger's words make me more eager to know the kind of human I am—if I'm human at all. I like to think myself as human, I always do. To feel, to care, love, hurt, hate, that should prove me human.

I dust the sand off my legs, turn and find my phone next to my damaged motorcycle.

Home is just a few streets over, but I'm thinking the blood in my hair might scare innocent kids on the way. June is too early to play Halloween, but who cares? I can make this a trial run.

I prop the bike up with little effort and try to start the engine. It fires but shuts down at once. I try again, but nothing happens. Jamie, from our usual garage can help, but who needs the endless questions. Besides, I'm strong enough to roll this home, except I wonder how I'm going to pull a motorcycle in my heels. To remove them is not an option.

From the long, hilly road, I take the last turn on Vine Lane, rolling the bike under the usual dense foliage of trees. Sparks of sunlight penetrate through the leafy canopy while the birds twitter in the branches. Right and left, houses stand secured behind towering gates.

It would be friendly to shout *good morning* to the neighbors if not for the high fences, hedges, and acres of well-groomed gardens that separate each house.

From the distance, I see a "for sale" sign, and know I'm home.

Named and not numbered, Edward, the Georgian estate next door—a house like ours—has been for sale for over a year now.

Standing in front of Elizabeth Vine Lane, I enter the passcode to unlock the steel gates open. As I pull the bike on the paved driveway, I ignore the manicured lawn to cast my eyes on the ivy creeping outside the walls of my mother's bedroom.

My heart begins to race as I imagine her standing by the balcony, but I know at this time she should be in the back garden.

After leaving the bike in the garage, I take a few deep breaths then make my way through the wooden arched doorway of the main entrance.

The yellow-beige stone walls of the spacious foyer seem brighter with the sun beaming through the airy breakfast room adjacent to the kitchen. I'm calm enough now to take in the hunger-calling aroma of fresh scones and drip brewed coffee. Calm enough to hear the noise of my heels on the solid wood floor, so I remove them with care not to leave dirt on the hardwood.

A few silent steps and I draw closer to a butterfly palm, flourishing in an aged ceramic pot fixed in the sunny corner. Next to it is a hand carved console table reflecting in the giant mirror on the opposite wall. I stop to check for any possible marks from the accident. Apart from the blood on my jumpsuit, and in my hair, I see no visible marks or blemishes. Instead, I look better than before. My lithe body appears firmer, the high cheekbones enhancing my oval face.

If accidents enhance me like this, I should only need a couple more to fix my sharp nose.

"Miss Lexie!" Our housekeeper appears behind me.

"Marie? What a surprise." I had no idea she was due back from her leave today.

She backs off when I reach out to hug her, examining my hair. "What happened?"

"Shh." I place a finger to my lips and note the silver tray in her hand. I'm guessing she's coming from the breakfast table outside by the porch. "How do I look?"

She widens her brown eyes. "Like a ghost. You must—"

"See my mother now, right?"

She nods, still scrutinizing me.

"How is she?" I whisper.

"Your name in every sentence. And yes, *full names*. What happened to you?"

"Long story." I roll my eyes.

"That's what Phoebe says to me when she's trying to hide something."

I grin. "How's Phoebe?"

"Busy studying, like most eighteen-year-olds," Marie says.

"Tell her to drop by so I can give her some tips."

She laughs. "Like you did last time, spending two hours teaching her Grand Prix motor racing?"

"What's wrong with that?" I hold a laugh. "Who knows? She could be number two in the world."

Marie chuckles and pats my shoulder as she walks away. "I'm sure we know who number one belongs to."

"We sure do, Marie. We sure do." I smile, making my way to my mother.

This is it.

I try to compose myself.

This is going to be a miserable morning. I can feel it.

I consider showering, but I rather Mother sees my bloody hair. That will distract her from my being late.

Through the hallway, into the formal sitting room, I pause, gazing at a portrait. In it, Mother wears a delightful smile, proud of her achievements. I am proud of her too.

Below her image are the words, Maryanne Mia Watson, M.D.

In her eyes, I see the, *I know what you've been up to, Alexandra,* look. Most times I stop here to compose myself before meeting the real Maryanne.

I move into the cozy living room, and step in the sunroom extending to the open porch, where Mother sits. She relaxes by the usual corner where she gets a clear view of her Japanese garden. Knowing that I'm late, even the tranquil sounds from the waterfall are not enough to calm her emotions. I reach the French doors. Through the transparent voile curtains, I watch Mother as she adjusts her sunglasses, raises her China teacup for a sip, and continues to read the newspaper.

"Alexandra," she says.

I shut my eyes and pull the door open. On the table in front of her is a selection of her favorite breakfast essentials—drip brewed coffee, scones with clotted cream, and strawberries.

She keeps her head down, reading the paper.

"Morning." I lean in to kiss her cheek. "Did Marie tell you how radiant you look in that dress today?"

Still looking down, she ignores my comment and sighs. "I ask only for one thing, Alexandra. One thing—be here on time." She folds the paper, takes her sunglasses off to stare at me.

Mother's eyes widen, chest rising before falling as she crosses her arms. "Is this the best you could do? Adding some … what's that in your hair? Chicken blood?" She shakes her head.

"It's not chicken blood, Mother. It's my blood."

"Of course it's your blood." She tightens her crossed arms. "What did you do? Cut your hand then wipe some blood in your hair, and wait for your hand to heal before coming to meet me?"

This time I grimace. "You really think I would stoop so low as to cut my hand just to give you an excuse for being late?"

"No, Alexandra, I want you to feel that it's better for you to stoop that low than being late." She unfolds her arms and leans toward me. "I won't accept any reason whatsoever for your being late unless you're *dead* late."

"What if I had an accident? Maybe I tried to avoid hitting a giant dog, crashed, broke my neck and cracked my skull, just to wake up a few minutes later healed as—"

"You what?" She stares at me, searching my eyes then rises in haste. "Good Lord! Sweetheart …"

The cushioned, rattan chair topples to the ground as she hurries to hold me. "What happened?" Mother examines me with a doctor's gaze. The tension on her face reduces the size of her smoky brown eyes. "Are you alright?"

I resist the urge to roll my eyes. "I'm okay. It's just—"

"Come sit down." Mother takes my hands and leads me to sit by the table.

My mother is above average in height, but still a few inches shorter than I am. Her hair, dark caramel like mine, is just as long and wavy, but unlike me, she keeps hers always in an up-do.

"I'm sorry about the chicken blood, I just thought—"

"It's fine, Mom."

"Are you hurt? Tell me how it happened." She reaches for my neck, my hair, and back to my arms.

"That's the thing. I don't know." I let out a soft laugh.

"This is why I tell you to always wear a helmet."

I shut my eyes for a few seconds. "Mother, this is hardly a helmet discussion."

"You could have died!"

"I hate it when you do this. Why are you acting like you don't know what I'm talking about?"

"We are talking about the accident, aren't we?" Mother tilts her head.

I sigh. "I saw this strange woman."

"You run a woman over?"

"No!" I pause to check if Marie is anywhere close enough to hear us, then lean forward. "I mean the one you said I should tell you when she appears to me."

With a raised brow, Mother blinks at me. "You saw Lachey? How are you sure it was her?"

"She wore her hair like you said, over her shoulder and waist, like a belt."

Mother's eyes widen, her face paler than Lachey when I saw her in the woods. She draws closer to me, takes my hands and holds them to her lips. "Tell me what she said." Her voice sounds smothered.

I pause, watching her tearful eyes while she kisses my hands. "She didn't hurt me," I say, hoping that would comfort her.

"Of course, she wouldn't." Mother's voice comes out faint. "She gave you a message for me, didn't she?"

I nod. "She said 'it's time'. What does that mean?"

"She's warning me against the keepers."

"Who are the keepers?"

"You'll know later."

"Are they bad news?"

"They caused your accident." Mother seems reluctant to say more.

"Why would they do that?" I wonder.

"Part of you is still human." Mother dabs a tear from the corner of her eye. "They have been shielding you from a full transformation. The accident was a sign you've begun to lose your humanity. They think you are old enough to do as you are destined to."

"Destined? What's that? And how do accidents make me lose my humanity?"

"Not the actual accident, but the healing." She ignores my first question. "From now on, you have to be extra careful. Each time you force your body to heal, it takes a bit of your humanity. That's why you look firmer after healing."

I think about her statement for a minute, then draw in a deep breath. "Mother, don't you think it's time I know what kind of creature I am?"

Mother clasps my hands to her chest. "You're no creature, sweetheart. I told you before; you're unique. That's all you need to know, for now."

"What harm is there in me knowing?"

"I want you to have a normal life because you won't have it forever. It's not fair that you should pay for my mistakes."

"What mistakes?" I ask.

She sighs, not attempting to answer my questions.

Careful not to stir this into the row we had last time, I'm cautious of my tone. "Is it so bad for me to become immortal? I mean, I'm destined to, right?"

"Yes, but you're different, Alexandra, and believe me, I know what's best for you."

"I was hoping that maybe we could talk about that—about me. She called me Nersii."

"She can't keep her mouth shut," Mother mumbles. "Give me six months and I promise to tell you everything." She gets ready to stand, picking her newspaper again.

"The same six months, you promised a year ago to tell me about my father?"

She kisses my cheek as she stands. "Knowledge is not always a pleasant thing, sweetheart, especially when acquired at the wrong time."

"So this is it. Walking away is your answer to everything?"

"Six months, Alexandra." She squeezes my shoulder and head toward the French doors.

"Mom." I stand as I call her.

She turns to answer me with a creased forehead. "What is it again, Lexie?"

"I've decided to tell Chan, I'm not completely human."

Her eyes narrow. "What brought that on? And what will you say when he asks what you are?"

"I'll just explain things, somehow." I shrug. "We've been together for over a year now, and I'm fed up of keeping a secret."

With pursed lips, Mother shakes her head. "Don't you think it's too late now? Exposing yourself to him will not make him change his mind."

Too late? "What do you mean change his mind?"

"Is that not what you're trying …" Her eyes widen with the sudden realization. "Oh, you don't know. I assumed he told you last night."

"Told me what?"

Mother sighs. "Honey, I wish I could say, but it's not my place."

"But it's your place to have secrets with my boyfriend?"

"All I'm saying is, before you expose yourself, perhaps you should wait until you hear what he has to say."

"I don't understand. Why did he tell you before me?"

"He just wanted my approval, I guess."

"Approval? What's there to approve?"

"I can't say, honey; he will have to tell you himself."

"You're my mother, you should—"

"Lexie …" Mother blinks, then looks over my shoulders.

I follow her gaze and see Marie by the French doors.

"Excuse me, Miss Lexie," Marie says. "Mr. Channing is here.

II

DO YOU REMEMBER THE FIRST TIME WE MET?

I hurry up the grand marble stairs to the open corridor. Though I want to hear what Channing has to say, I can't let him see me in this messy state. Moreover, I don't want to explain the accident.

My room is at the far end, beyond my mother's. I reach the carved wooden door, close my eyes briefly and take a sigh, dreading the mess in which I left in my room this morning. I seldom leave my room untidy, but at the time, my thoughts were otherwise involved.

My hand on the brass door handle, I inhale and push it open. A gentle wind from the open balcony grazes my cheeks. The room is brighter with the white linen curtains drawn to the side. I turn to check the bed.

Marie. I smile.

The whitewashed cane bed I left untidy is now spruce, dressed with soft, raw-umber linen. On my work desk at the corner next to the side table, my laptop is still open as I left it, but everything around it is now organized. A picture of a joyous Chan and me, taken during prom, has been moved from the work desk to the bedside table.

From the hardwood floor, I walk toward my small sunken living area and pause on the sea grass rug. The blue rose cushions now set uncluttered on the large white sofa.

Remember to thank Marie.

I hurry to the bathroom. With the worries in my mind, it's easy to forget to appreciate the little bits that make this room my favorite. I love the exposed stone walls, freestanding bathtub, brass showerhead, and the vintage mirrors, all designed to my liking.

My heart races as I shower. The warm water pouring over my head washes the blood and dirt, but not my worries. I don't want to think of what Mother is discussing with Channing right now.

A moment later, I'm out of the bathroom. I pick out my tennis whites to wear. I didn't intend to take that long showering, but it's as though half of me is eager to see Chan while the other is terrified of what he has to say. What if he knows the truth about me?

The laughter of Channing and my mother spill in through the open windows. I'm sure she has offered him iced tea, and as usual, they converse as if they are a mother and son.

They weren't always so close. Countless, silent prayers I prayed wishing for them to get along. One day I found them in an emotional embrace, one longer than a regular hug. To me, the hug didn't look inappropriate. Instead, it appeared more as if Chan had become the child—the son she never had, somewhat replacing me. I never asked how it happened. What mattered was that my prayers were answered.

My racket bag over my shoulder, I make my way outside. I'm not looking forward to tennis today; I just want to hear what Chan has to say.

Chan sits at the table with my mother, his eyebrows raised as he explains something I can't hear. His slicked back, brown hair is flawless as usual, giving him a gentle, clean appearance.

He sees me and pauses. "Hey, you." A grin forms on his face.

"Ace." I return the smile. My eyes meet his blue pupils, and a fluttering sensation fills my stomach. After a year with him, I should be used to his presence, but no, he still gives me the butterflies.

"Now, don't get mad at me." Chan stands, graceful as always, and gives me a tight hug. He presses his lips on mine and pulls away to gaze at me with his usual warm smile. "I know there's something different about you, but I can't put a finger on it. So tell me. Is it the length or the color of your hair?"

"Perhaps it's your eyes," I tease. "Are you sure you don't need glasses?"

"No, I like the way I see you," he whispers, and we stare at each other, smiling.

I look away to hide my heart's response to his slow blink. Thoughts of my secret and losing him cross my mind, and an unexpected lump forms in my throat.

Channing frowns. "Are you okay?"

I nod and move closer to link my arms with his, before leading him away from my mother.

"See you later, Doc," Chan calls to my mother, and we leave the porch.

"So long, Chan. Be safe," Mother answers. Knowing exactly what *safe* means, I roll my eyes.

"You're not dressed for a match?" I ask Chan as we approach the driveway. He's wearing a blue outfit; a pair of jeans and a casual shirt.

"I thought today we could do something more intriguing."

"Intriguing?" Heat rises in my chest.

To cancel tennis, he must have something important to tell me, I conclude. "Now what could be more intriguing than my usual straight sets, hmm?"

He grins. "How about we spend the day at my place taking turns yelling at each other?"

I let out a soft laugh. Channing's voice is always warm, so gentle that it's almost entrancing. In our first days together, I would ask him to read to me, just so I could listen to the sound of his voice. I still do, but not as much.

"Hmm, let me see …" I tilt my head, thinking. "A glass of wine, a game of chess with you telling me how you've never met anyone like me, and thereafter you take me to bed?"

"Hmm, a glass of wine … a little passé, don't you think? I was thinking of you in my bed all-day, with me at your service."

"What's the catch?"

"No catch." He opens the passenger door for me. "Just me, giving myself to you, and I guarantee you a hundred percent kisses back if you're not satisfied."

I bite my lip as I stare directly at his, then duck in the passenger seat while Chan scurries toward the driver's side.

While pulling the seat belt, I see a large brown envelope by the dashboard. "What's this?"

"Open it."

The engine roars and the car glides toward the open gate.

I hasten and unseal the envelope. "Hurricane Auction House?" My eyes widen.

"A piece of land in the east of Ashbourne is listed for auction, next year, January the second. I thought it would be perfect for your racetrack plans."

"You registered me as a bidder? How did you do that? They're exclusive to Hurricane members."

"Let's just say I know friends who know friends who know friends who—"

"Okay, I get it." I throw a playful jab at him. "You don't know what this means to me."

"In fact, I do. That's why I went through the trouble."

Leaning over, I grab his collar and seal his lips with a passionate kiss. "Thank you," I whisper and continue on his lips. The kiss is no different, and if at all it is, it's better, more intense. So, I conclude whatever he has to say can't be detrimental.

"We're going to crash if you keep kissing me like that." He chuckles.

We stop at the traffic lights. Stealing a look at me, Channing scratches the top of his head then brushes his thumb over his clean-shaven chin.

I frown and watch as he begins whistling, his fingers tapping the steering wheel.

Closing the auction catalog, I turn to him. "No, no." I shake my head with realization. "Don't think this means you're forgiven for the unwanted generous donation because it doesn't."

He rolls his eyes. "Come on, Jo ..."

I never liked anyone calling me by my middle name until Chan came into my life. "No, you're not forgiven." I shake my head. "I told you, I have enough cash in my trust fund, and I want to do this myself, but you went and transferred hundreds of thousands to my account against—"

"Correction." He raises his hand. "Just one hundred thousand. Again, why are you so against me helping you?"

"I don't want our relationship entangled in favors like you giving me a hundred thousand dollars."

"But I want to."

"I know." I sigh. "And I appreciate you, but I want to know that every moment I'm with you, it's because I love you and not because I feel I owe you something."

A line forms on his forehead. "Or maybe you don't want anything holding you back when you decide to dump me."

I open my mouth, and for a few seconds, nothing comes out. "How could you even think that?"

His hands tighten on the steering wheel. "How could you deprive me my right as your boyfriend to help you?" His voice breaks and I'm surprised how much emotion it carries. "I feel ..." He raises his shoulders stiffly and drops them with another sigh.

"What? What do you feel?"

"Insignificant ... unneeded."

I study his face, but he won't let me look into his eyes. "So all you want is to be needed?"

"Needed by you." He eyes me deliberately.

"Pull over."

"What?" He grimaces.

"Stop the car. I need to say something."

With a puckered brow, he pulls over. The engine shuts, and I climb over to sit on his lap, my face to his. With my legs on either side, I sit up straight and stare into his eyes. "Chan, I don't need you, but I want you, and that is greater than needing you, don't you think?"

He leans closer and brushes his nose against mine. "How is that? Need is what you can't live without and want is that which you desire."

"Desire is more significant. You cannot abuse a want as you would a need. A crutch, for example, can be abused whereas something like my superfast bike is treasured."

He shakes his head, laughing. "What of sex?"

"Still, you would agree, it's better when we want it than when we need it."

"Even better when you say you need me."

I laugh. "Okay, I think you just need me to need you."

"No." He leans in to kiss my lips, pushes a lock of hair behind my ear. "I just want you to need me. That's all."

"Whatever you need or want, I love you, isn't that enough?"

"It is if you let me help you."

As I sigh, he brushes his lips against my neck.

"Okay." I concede. "You're forgiven. And I promise not to stand in the way of you helping your girlfriend."

"Good. I like that better." He raises his head to examine my eyes. "Let me start by saying I'm familiar with two names on the bidders list. So I'm sure you will find the funds useful."

"Thank you." I give him another kiss then slip back to my seat. "The land is valued at two hundred thousand. I have double that, and I'm willing to use it all if it comes to it."

Channing starts the engine, turning onto the road. He increases speed as we merge into Nightshade, a four-lane highway leading toward the main cities including Milbourne, where Channing lives.

"If you spend your trust fund buying the ranch, what will you use to build the circuit?" Chan glances at me.

"Um." I hesitate. "John De Luca secured a loan for me."

"What?" He eyes me with a creased forehead. "You accept a loan from Deluca, yet you yell at me for offering to help?"

"It's a bank loan ..."

He's shaking his head before I finish, but even as I see the creases on his forehead, he maintains that soothing tone. "Bank loan. Friend loan. Church loan. It's one and the same, Jojo."

"He's like a father to me. I couldn't refuse."

"Father?" Chan draws in a long breath. "Don't you see how he hugs you every second? A million kisses I've seen him shower on you. Without license, he teaches you to fly those fighter planes. I wonder what he will teach you next."

"Chan!" I gasp. "What's wrong with you today? It's so unlike you to be—"

"What? Jealous?"

"For lack of a better word, yes, Jealous."

"I'm sorry. I guess it's that time of the month." He laughs as I shake my head.

For a moment, we don't speak until he turns to me again. "Seriously, sometimes I wonder if he's in love with you."

"He's in love with my mother, so it's obvious that he cares about me."

"Or vice versa," Chan mumbles.

I shoot him a baffled glance, but he looks away, chuckling.

"Have you told Doc about your racetrack plans?" he asks after a moment.

"I will tonight. After the party."

Chan eyes me as he shifts the gears, and when I turn to glare at him, he shakes his head, a smile sneaking from the corner of his lips.

We arrive at Channing's apartment an hour later. Located in the North-West, the apartment looks a hundred years old, with enormous glass windows looking over the tranquil River Stills. The inside reflects a combination of ancient and contemporary designs—bright, airy, extensive and yet full of character and charm.

Under the Egyptian cotton sheets, on a medieval style bed with hand carved edges, Chan and I exchange kisses. Hands all over each other, I'm almost forgetting my troubles. His nibbles are stronger today, and his grip tighter than ever before. I'm thinking he wants to kiss the secrets out of me.

Still, I don't hold back. I give as much as I'm receiving, and I can't help but notice the desperation in his touch. His eyes burn into mine, and I refuse to acknowledge the cloud forming in them, until a tear drops on my chest.

"Chan?"

He doesn't answer, showering me with kisses. He lifts his head and fixes his eyes on mine. He's trying hard to relax his face, but it's there, in the watery eyes he won't blink.

"What's wrong?" I reach for his cheek. "Are you okay?"

He touches my cheek with renewed tenderness. "I never thought I would meet someone like you."

My nose flares, my hand by his neck, I pull him to my chest. I drown in his addictive scent; an elegant fusion of cedar wood, and mint.

"I have something to tell you," he says.

My heart pounds. Holding him closer, I inhale deeper. "I'm listening," I say.

Chan pulls me up as he sits up; a tortured expression embraces his face as he gazes at me. "I love you and will always love you. You know that, right?"

I nod. "And you'll never know how much I love you back." The drumming of my heart increases as I swallow. My thoughts mingling with my secrets, I'm thinking I don't want to hear this. Whatever he has to say, I don't want to know.

An overwhelming shiver runs through me, and I hug him, tight. Channing squeezes me into his arms as if he agrees with my thoughts, moving his fingers to trace my spine. With passion, we press our lips together, nibbling and gasping in need for more.

It doesn't take long before our kisses grow stronger. My body gives in to him. I can hardly breathe as he carries the kisses to my breast, further down to merge them with the passionate flutters in my stomach. My body follows his kisses, listening to his fingertips. Then, his ringing cell phone disturbs us.

In haste, he reaches to kiss my neck, then my lips. Looking into my eyes, he says, "I'm sorry. I should get this." He stretches to pick up the phone from the bedside table.

"Doc," he answers, then leans to kiss my cheek. Entwining our hands, he continues. "Just about ..."

"Is it my mother?" I ask.

He nods at me before frowning, his focus back on the call. "Doc, I don't think I can—"

He releases my hand, stands, and grabs his black, lustrous bathrobe to wear as he walks out to the balcony. The glass doors shut behind him.

He's talking as he paces from one corner to the other, his free hand shifts continuously from his forehead to his hair to the back of his neck.

On the marble railing his elbows drop, as if the weight of the world is now too much for his shoulders to bear.

I grab his shirt to wear and move to open the balcony doors. "Chan?"

He hangs up the phone and turns to stare at me, rushes to cup my face, and kisses me with urgency. Taken aback, I respond with wariness at first, but as desire flows through my veins, my tongue finds his. My arms around his neck, flows into his hair, just as his hands slide below my waist.

Without breaking the kiss, we stagger past the glass doors and back in the room, one hand grabbing my thigh while the other on my back secures me by the wall. He groans as I pant with desire, but questions in my head turn my blood cold.

"Chan, stop." I break of the kiss. "What did my mother say?"

"Uhm …" He shakes his head as if to clear a frenzied daze from his head. "She wants me to introduce her to my father."

"What?" I grimace. "I don't get it. She knows you haven't spoken to your father in years, why would she—"

Channing releases his hold on me. "She's just doing her job as your mother." He walks over and throws himself on the bed. "I told her I'll try to call him some time," he says, clasping his hands behind his head.

"I don't understand why she's bringing this up again. Is she—?"

"Hey," he extends his arm to me. "Can we not talk about this now? That shirt looks better on you than me."

I exhale, dropping my shoulders as I stare into his soft eyes.

"Please." He extends both arms.

With a sigh, I give in and proceed to sink in his arms, feeling almost complete as he holds me close.

"Will you tell me what you wanted to say before my mother disturbed us?" I whisper.

"Do you remember the first time we met?"

I scoff. "You really think I'd forget that?"

Without warning, my thoughts take me back to that moment, and I smile. "I was late for the assembly, looking forward to meeting the student president, and there you were making that 'save the world' speech. I thought your voice alone could save the world."

He lets out a hearty laugh. "I looked at you, and I thought you were …"

"As faultless as the sunrise, you said."

"You remember?" He pulls me closer. "I know it's crazy, but your hair is the color of sunrise and your gray eyes are like cloud patches within it."

"I'm trying to tell myself that's a compliment." I look into his eyes, smiling.

"It is," he says. "Nothing mattered from that moment, nothing but you."

Rising to his feet, he walks to his closet, comes back with a small jewelry box. "This belonged to my mother. I wanted you to have it from the day I met you, but I didn't want to scare you away, so I kept it hidden, until now."

"Oh Chan, it's beautiful," I cry, admiring the brown woven bracelet as he secures it on my wrist. It has three carved jade stones on it. "What's the occasion?"

"Have you forgotten it's your graduation party tonight?"

"Still, this is, so ... It's your mother's, I can't ..."

"Believe me; she would have loved you to have it." He kisses my cheek. "The jade will keep you from harm."

I stare at him for a moment, then lean in to kiss him. "I love it, thank you."

"Whatever happens, I want you to know nothing will ever change the way I feel about you. Remember that." He draws closer to me. I'm waiting for him to speak when he holds me close, and kisses me once more, with the same desperate need. "Don't be too hard on your mother."

I want to protest, but the stern look in his eyes makes me concede. I nod. "Will you tell me everything?" Admiring the bracelet on my wrist, I snuggle in his arms. "Everything about your father and this thing you told my mother. It's as if you're now trying hard not to tell me."

He chuckles. "I know you're smart, Jo, but please let me off this time. I promise to tell you when I'm ready." He shuts his eyes as if in a prayer, and then opens one to see me inches from his lips. He smiles as he steals a kiss from me. "Will you kiss me like the last time you saw me was six months ago?"

I giggle. "I don't know how that feels, but I'll try." I brush my lips over his skin as I crawl on top of him.

"Let's extend that to a year," he whispers.

I shake my head, and smile, removing my shirt as Chan reaches to unhook my bra.

My mind drifts to his conversation with my mother. I reckon she said something to stop him from telling me. *But, why would she do that?*

Maybe now is the time to confess.

"Jo." Chan reaches for my face.

"Hmm." I blink and stare into his eyes.

"Not that your body isn't enough to hold my attention, but I need your mind here too. What are you thinking?"

My rising chest stops for a second as I stare into his blue eyes. "How much I love you."

With one hand entwined with mine, and the other tracing my collarbone, he whispers, "Show me. Show me how much."

III

Your World And Mine Are Different ...

It's 10 PM. In our open entertainment area—the largest room with triple French doors, leading to the back garden—guests fill the gallery, dancing and laughing in melody.

Decorated with cream voile, sculptured garden statues, and congratulatory ornaments, the outside flourishes with glamour. Circle-shaped lanterns float on numerous cypresses and the flowering Yoshino trees. Lights tangle and cluster around to give the surroundings elegance and warmth.

Completing the party atmosphere is the typical light, classic music merging with the voices, whispers and laughs of the guests as they sip champagne.

Everyone is here, except for mother and my boyfriend. I don't know whose arrival I anticipate more; mother's or Channing's.

Channing dropped me home around four, promising to be here in time for the party, but it's been an hour since the party started and yet he's not here. According to Marie, Mother, and John De Luca, left to get gherkins.

Who needs gherkins?

I'm eager to hear what mother has to say about her conversation with Channing.

From the corner of the room, a hand waves to me. I don't need binoculars to see who it is—Emily Fair, my best friend.

I watch as she swings toward me, and already I'm fighting a smile, watching her blowing me kisses as she approaches.

"Ouch!" She holds her delicate chest as if in utter pain. "Cinderella in piercing Van-Bailey couture and yet … prince charming is nowhere to be found."

"Not in the mood, Millie." I shoot her a warning glance.

She stares at me with her vivacious emerald eyes, positioning her face closer as if to remind me how beautiful she is. Her sandy blonde hair styled, like always, in a messy chignon. She has a daffodil hair clip on the side, a result of her love for flowers. At 5' 6, she is a little shorter than I am, slender with a subtle appearance that often contradicts what comes out of her mouth.

"Don't think I didn't see you in the kitchen." Emily raises her brow, grabs two glasses of champagne from the waiter and hands one to me. "Ah-ah, don't frown," she says waving a finger at me. "You were in there, eyes closed, hand over your heart, just like you do when you're thinking of him."

"What are you now? My shrink?" I swallow a mouthful of champagne while Emily rolls her eyes.

Peering over Emily's shoulder, I frown. "I thought he was your 'ex'. What's he doing here?"

Emily turns to follow my gaze, looking past the wide doors to the garden where Clive is laughing with his best friend Jay. "Wanted to remind him of what he had, but no longer has," she sings, then draws closer to me. "Now don't change the subject, Lexie. Where's Chan?"

I shrug. "Don't know. He's not picking up my calls."

Emily searches my eyes for a moment, then sighs, the playful expression replaced by a thoughtful look.

Earlier over the telephone, I explained to her what's going on with Channing, and my mother. "I'm sure if you give him a few minutes, he'll be here," she says.

"Right." I almost snort. "I've been giving him a few minutes for the past hour now."

"Maybe if you stop counting."

I give her a sideways glance. "You think it's possible my mother has been pretending to like Chan. Perhaps she wanted to find his weakness and to use it against him?"

"Ha-ha!" Emily laughs. "Seriously you need to stop thinking like you work for the FBI. Pretending for a whole year? That's absurd, don't you think?"

"Hm." I agree. "So what is it, then? What do you think he wants to say?"

"If he's hesitating then I'm guessing he most likely wants to pop the question."

"Propose!" I laugh, just to stop the laugh too soon. *What would be my answer if he proposes?*

"What is it?" Emily asks.

"Why would you warn your girlfriend if you want to pop the question?"

She smirks. "Testing the waters, they call it."

"Nah." I shake my head. "I wonder where he is right now."

"Making out with your mother." She laughs.

"Why must everything be a joke to you?"

"You think too hard about everything."

"I just like things to make reasonable sense. Is that too much to ask?"

"Well, not everything should make sense; the moment of conception, for example."

Shaking my head, I stifle a laugh. "You should learn to pay attention. I said reasonable, *reasonable* sense."

"I made you laugh, didn't I?"

"You keep it up, and I promise to marry you someday." I roll my eyes as she laughs again.

Emily and I have been friends since primary school. She is the only friend who knows I'm unique. Odd, since I don't remember telling her anything.

When we met, we were two strangers living in Ashbourne and studying in Milbourne. At the age of nine, Emily lost her mother. Since I don't have a father, I guess we are alike in that way. Back then, we dreamed of our parents getting together so we could be sisters, but even now, I can say we are closer than sisters would be.

"Lexie!"

I turn to the voice of my mother coming from the doorway. She's not with Chan, not with John De Luca either, but she wears the same old sweet smile that she always wears on events like today.

"Honey, you look stunning. Fuscous gray is perfect for your skin tone and the lace ... nothing goes better with your curls." Mother inhales with approval. "Do you like what I did with the garden?"

"I do. Thank you." I force a smile. Tonight, she looks more graceful than usual in a lace band plum dress, detailed in opulent beads. Her hair is in an elegant up-do.

I keep still as she hugs me. When she pulls back, I hand the empty champagne glass to a wine waiter and turn to her again. "Mother, what did you say to Chan when you called him this afternoon?"

"Nothing." The excitement in her voice disappears. "Did he say I said something?"

"It's obvious you said something. You spoke to him for five minutes, at least."

"This is no place or time to discuss such matters, sweet—"

"Don't sweetheart me!" I fight to repress the rage creeping on me.

"Alexandra." She grabs me by the arm and drags me toward the hallway. The sound of our rushing heels adds to the loud music as she leads me to the kitchen.

On entering the kitchen, she releases my arm and stares at me with fury. "There are over sixty people out there who are here for you and I won't have you make a scene," she hisses.

"I just want to know what's going on." I hiss back. "What did Chan tell you?"

"Are you saying he hasn't told you?"

"Are you pretending you don't know he hasn't told me because you told him not to?"

"Honey," she sighs. "If he didn't tell you, he must have changed his mind. You have nothing to worry about."

"Exactly, I have nothing to worry about, yet I worry. Do you know why he's not here yet?"

"Honey, how would I know where Chan is? You speak as though we share your boyfriend."

"Because I feel as if we do, Mother."

She opens her mouth, releasing a light gasp. "I have no idea where Chan is, sweetheart. The Van-Baileys closed Stills Lane. It's traffic maybe."

"Traffic does not stop a phone from ringing." I hold my rage.

"I'm sure he's safe." She rubs my arm. "Before the party ends, he will be here, and you will wonder why you were even worrying in the first place."

"I just find it hard." My shoulders stiffen as I begin pacing. "I mean what if he's dead somewhere? And I'm here doing nothing, getting mad at him."

Mother shakes her head, disagreeing as I struggle to keep my voice from breaking.

"I would never forgive myself if …"

Click. Click. Click. My mother and I stare at each other in silence, listening to the sound of heels drawing nearer.

Rebecca Finchley appears with her blonde hair in a tight ponytail. Emily and I call her 'The Diamond Lady'; diamonds in her ears, diamonds on her neck, on her wrist, fingers too—and forever engaged to John De Luca, Marshal of the City of Ashbourne.

The same John De Luca who is my mother's best friend, and whom I think should have proposed to her, not Rebecca. Not only is he one of the best-looking, middle-aged men in uniform, but I also think he is in love with my mother. To me, the two are so close the attraction between them is not hard to miss, but Rebecca Finchley has perhaps missed the obvious, or maybe chooses to be blind to it.

"Is everything okay?" Rebecca asks.

I glare at her, and keep my lips sealed.

Rebecca shifts her gaze between my mother and I. "We were all wondering where you two had disappeared to."

"Thank you." I sneer. "I was also wondering why you are wondering where we are. If everyone out there wonders like you wonder, Rebecca, I wonder if this kitchen would be large enough for all of us."

"Alexandra!" Mother stares at me with disapproval.

"What?" I puff out a sarcastic laugh, turning to grimace at my mother. "I'm sure you were wondering the same, Mother."

Without looking at Rebecca, I head for the door, leaving my mother with Rebecca in the kitchen.

Who would have thought a smile can be difficult to display. I'm back with the crowd, looking for Emily, but end with another glass of champagne.

"I asked Robert to do the honors." Mother, from behind me, startles me as she whispers by my ear. She refers to Robert Fair, Emily's father, who's also a family friend.

I nod and turn to watch Robert on the stage holding a microphone, then frown. "When?"

"When what?"

"When did you ask Robert? How did you know Chan wouldn't be here?"

"I didn't." She gives me an awkward smile. "We needed someone to receive the guest, and I asked Robert."

I nod again, an apologetic nod this time.

First taking a long breath, my mother kisses my cheeks, then mingles through the crowd toward Robert.

"Ladies and gentlemen," Robert announces. "Miss Alexandra Joanne Watson."

This is the second heat of the party, time to extract more smiles. Chan is still not here, and I don't feel like smiling to anyone. I have called him so many times now, but my calls go straight to voicemail.

Champagne glasses clink in a musical harmony as the guests cheer, toasting to my successful life. Sweet, soft and placid music breezes through the garden. Tight hugs and kisses I give to those closest to my heart—not that they are many. Most of the guests are from my mother's charity organizations. Soft and warm hugs, I reserve for a few friends from school.

Friends I prefer to call acquaintances; they hardly know the real me. I don't think they care either, as long as I live in upper east Ashbourne.

Halfway through the party, the music stops. It's time for the embarrassments. I need Channing now, but he's not here.

Customary to all graduation celebrations in Ashbourne, I, the host, relax and watch as the guests do what they call, 'How did she or he do it?' acts. They take turns mimicking my outstanding and or embarrassing high school moments.

Jay, a natural comedian, is imitating my frown on the stage when Emily comes to sit with me by the front row.

"The Heartless are playing in Milbourne December twenty-sixth and tickets are selling fast. Last chance to see them turn into wolves," she mumbles.

I shoot her an incredulous look. "Seeing them? Yeah, except they don't turn into wolves, Millie."

"Of course they do, Lexie Watson." She has her hand on my shoulder now. "I'm sure you don't want to miss that."

Shaking my head, I lean to sing in her ear, "*Grizzly tales for gruesome kids.*"

She rolls her eyes.

Emily has this notion that Ashbourne is a city of vampires. According to her grandmother Carol Fair, the Van-Baileys are the leaders of the vampire nation. They not only feed on humans, but also kill werewolves that dare to show themselves in Ashbourne.

Yes, of course, they must be vampires, the way they seem to possess everything. Talk of their arrogance. Nonetheless, the only thing I believe they suck is people's cash and not blood. They seem a hundred percent human to me; walking in the sun, no fangs, no pale skin.

"Who in Ashbourne has ever been attacked by a vampire or any other supernatural creature for that matter?" I ask.

With a faint moan, she eases her back on the seat. "I know you're in a bad mood because of Chan, so I will just buy the tickets and we'll talk it over when the time comes." She gulps the remainder of champagne in her glass and forces the empty glass in my hand. Then, in high spirits, she swings to the stage.

I sit and listen to Emily's jokes for a few minutes as it was her turn to make fun of me on the stage.

"My name is Alexandra Watson, and when I finish high school, I want to be a nun," Emily says, and everyone laughs. "'What are your hobbies?' Ms. Peters asks, and the future nun replies, 'car racing'." The crowd laughs again. "I'm sure you'd all agree it's hard to imagine a nun behind the steering wheel of a race car." There's uproar in the crowd. "But I'm happy to say it all changed." She grins at me. "Oh no. Not all. Just the nun bit. She changed her mind when her eyes fell on the student president." Emily bites her bottom lip as she stares at me. "Channing, oh, Channing," she sings. "Thou art cursed for depriving us of Grand Prix World's number one nun. Miss Alexandra, the great, everyone!"

A loud noise of applaud, whistles and cheers erupt from the crowd. I shake my head at Emily and close my eyes, forcing a smile as my thoughts take me to Channing again.

I can't take it anymore; sitting here smiling and laughing. After a few laughs, and when the music begins playing, I see the crowd is not paying so much attention to me. I slip back into the house, upstairs to get my car keys.

With the keys in my hand, I make my way to my mother's room so I can write her a *don't wait up* note. By the vintage dressing table, I scribble the words on a notepad, but when the ink runs out, I pull the first drawer to get another pen. There are no black pens. With frustration, I force open the second locked drawer, and there I saw a pale blue envelope.

From the handwriting and the two letters, 'Jo', I know who wrote it. I pick it up with hesitation, my hands shaky as a series of questions with no answers fly through my mind.

Why is this letter here? When did it get here? What is it saying and does my mother know? If she does then, why did she not tell me?

Jo Darling.

I begin to read the neat cursive words etched on the pale blue pad. It takes me a few lines to understand what it means. As I read on, most of the questions I asked earlier, receive answers. Furious tears blind my vision before I finish reading. I can't believe what I'm reading, and I want the message to change so much that I read again, hoping something somewhere along the lines can tell me it's all a joke.

Jo, Darling,

You're probably reading this letter because I couldn't bear to look at you and say goodbye. You've always been better than me when it comes to goodbyes.

I wanted to tell you at the right moment, but the right moment never came. You must know that I didn't intend to leave you heartbroken. In a normal world, I wouldn't dream of being away from you—not for a single second, but not everything is normal, Jo. There are things about me that you don't know. I should apologize for being a coward and not saying anything earlier.

I'm sorry, and I love you ... never doubt that. There is no one else, never will be, you should know that. If you wish, you may be angry, sad, and unforgiving, that is fine; but please don't make me think you believe I never loved you. I want you to be happy. I already spoke to Doc, and she agrees that I should go. Your world and mine are different, and I think you're better without me.

Love you always,

Channing.

In a daze, I grab the letter and storm out to the corridor, down the stairs to the entertainment room, and out to the garden still full of guests.

They are dancing.

The beat of the music carries my feet with so much rage; it's as if the god of war wrote this moment in the unrighteous books of hell.

"Alex?" Emily is the first to notice the hurricane waiting to burst out of me.

"Where is she?" I tremble.

"Who?"

"My mother. Where is she?"

Then I see her coming. My chest rises and falls, faster and faster as I watch her.

"Lexie?" Mother blinks.

"My own mother," I hiss with fury. "The enemy of my heart."

Her eyes flicker to the letter in my hand. All at once, blood vanishes from her cheeks, leaving her face a shocked ashen. Her mouth opens, but nothing comes out, except in her eyes, a cloud of emotion begins to emerge.

She swallows hard as she grabs my arm, pulls me away from the curious crowd. She leads me back in the house, at the end of the hallway in the study and shuts the door behind us.

"He did what he had to do, honey. It's the right thing to do ... for you."

"For me?" I bark. "How is breaking my heart the right thing for me? How can you be this heartless?" I inhale a sharp breath. "You told him, didn't you? You—"

"I told him nothing!"

"Then why this?" With a trembling hand, I raise the letter to her face. "Tell me why he would do this to me? And you approved, I guess?"

"He's supernatural, Alexandra!"

"What?" I freeze, searching my mother's eyes. "He's ... how do you know?"

"I found out. And when I confronted him, he didn't deny it."

He had a secret. I'm tempted to believe my mother, to believe that Channing is supernatural. A sudden excitement embraces me.

"Like me," my voice struggles to rise above a whisper. "He's like me." I motion toward my mother and hold her hands. "Mother, isn't this the best thing ever? He's leaving because he doesn't know we are alike. I can still stop him."

I start for the door, but Mother grabs me by the arm. "Now, listen to me, sweetheart." She cups my face. "No one is like you. No one. And no one should ever find out who you truly are. That's why Chan has to go."

"Huh!" I let out a loud broken breath. The truth etches in my mother's unblinking eyes, but I have to ask. "You asked him to leave?"

"No." She takes a step closer to hold me as my hands tremble, but I shrug her off.

"But you gave him enough reason to leave, right?"

"That was his choice."

My stomach heaves and I'm struggling to breathe. I need more air. No, I think I'm thirsty. I crave for something, something I can't identify. My breathing quickens and I feel hot. "I'm such a fool." I burst into sobs.

"Sweetheart, I know this is hard—"

"No, you don't!" I raise my finger at her. "You have no idea what you've done to me. Where is he?"

"Lexie, listen …"

"Answer me, Mother!"

"It's too late, Honey. His flight is for eleven forty—."

"Flight? My God! What flight?" I sniffle.

"No. No." She shakes her head. "I won't allow you to go after him."

"Okay." I laugh, sniffle and cry at the same time. "I could stay, and you tell me what I am, or you let me go after Chan. Which is it, Mother?"

Her face screws tight with emotions, and with trembling lips, she whispers, "Flight A7 Pannonia, eleven forty-five."

"So predictable," I mutter, heading for the door and slamming it on my way out.

"Here!" Emily, who must've been eavesdropping behind the door, hands me the car keys and my wallet. "Let's go get him."

I thank her and ask her to get a bottle of water for our journey. She skips toward the kitchen while I rush out of the door to the driveway, and speed away without her; I want to be alone right now.

In silence, stereo off and windows closed, I race with determination toward Ashbourne airport. It seems the world is empty.

At the airport, I rush through the counters, skipping the barriers, my guts in my throat as I hear the last call, for the flight he is to board. Through the departure lounge, I plunge through the crowd as I rush for the counter.

"Pannonia, eleven forty-five, please." I pant.

Inserting my credit card into the reader, the red-haired woman at the sales desk goes on to recite the flight details to my impatient ears. Then, she pauses. My fingers anxiously tapping the counter also pause, acknowledging the look on her face.

"I'm sorry, but payment has been declined."

My heart sinks, and for a second the red-haired woman appears in the face of my mother. "No." I yell, unable to breathe. "No, don't do this to me!" The woman's eyes change, from sympathetic to fear or possibly shock, then I realize. "Please, try again," I say in a calm voice this time.

"I have—"

"Just do it!"

She tenses. With pursed lips, she shakes her head; hesitating. "Would you like me to try another card?" she asks.

I draw in a quick breath and try to pinch myself out of this nightmare. I raise my head toward the glass walls behind the sales desk, and I see his back.

"Chan!" I head toward the departure lounge.

The attendants at the gates stop me. "I just need to speak with him, please." I wipe tears.

The doors begin to shut, and my heart shuts with them, but then I see him. I see his face out by the doors with the flight attendants, pleading to come back to me, but they say something I can't hear.

"Channing!" I cry.

He stares at me. "I'm sorry," he mouths. "I love you, always."

"I need you," I say through a hiccupped sob. "I need you, please."

His face screws as if to stop himself from crying, then he disappears behind the doors. That's it. He's gone.

On auto pilot, I turn back, sniffling while numbly making my way back to the parking lot. It takes me a while to find my car, and when I do, I struggle to compose myself.

In the dark and deserted highway, I drive in silence heading back home.

Halfway on the road, my phone rings—my mother again. I press the silent button and throw it on the passenger seat. I don't want to talk to anyone, especially my mother—not now.

Emily calls and I tell her everything is fine. I want her to go home. If she stays, she risks becoming collateral damage because I intend to declare war on my mother. Tonight my mother will reveal all that she knows and when she's done I will declare my future without her.

I turn onto an empty, quiet Vine Lane. The streetlights appear brighter as if to pity my cloudy eyes.

I'm a few yards from the house when all of a sudden, something within unleashes. Something I cannot explain. It begins as a faint headache. Within a few seconds, blood is boiling inside of me, heat blazing out of my skin as if I'm the sun.

I fight with my bones as they ache to expand. My heart is pounding hard and deep, only once a minute. Through my watery eyes I see more than I want to see, everything appears in high definition.

"Aargh!" I hit the brakes, and arch backwards coiling in deference to a sharp pain striking my spine. I attempt to reach for my phone, but the pain is unbearable. One more try, and my fingers just about reach it. I press number two, but I can't hear; they are too many voices disturbing me.

"Mom," I whisper, stretching for the phone. "Mother."

IV

THE RING. THE CURSED. THE WHITE BLOODS

Abarrage of pain rains over me. It slams me to my seat without mercy. From my eyes, it claims all the waters I can give. I give it all … until a pain in my head interrupts the bitter moment. My chest tightens and with a loud scream, I arch forward.

"No! No!" Blood trickles out of my nostril and over my lip.

I rub it off with a quick huff, but it keeps dripping. The blood on my hands turns from red to silver. My eyes widen.

I must be hallucinating.

From where I am, dying, I see the iron gates of my home, only two houses away.

"Alexandra!" With the confusing voices, I still recognize this one—it's my mother's, and it's coming from my phone. "Honey, are you okay?"

"Mom." I lean closer to the phone on the edge of the passenger seat. I'm not sure if my voice is loud enough.

"Ouch!" I shriek at another sting on my spine. My muscles stiffen, my racing heart sending burning blood through my veins. I want to speak again, but my jaw tightens and saliva fills my mouth.

I'm thirsty, but not for water. My throat is cracking with a craving I cannot explain.

Two quick jerks and I slump on the seat. As well as my weak heartbeat, I sense everything. It seems I feel a connection to all that is around me. I hear voices from people I can't see, some voices are familiar while others strange.

On the road, I can see the tiniest part of the asphalt. The leaves on the trees breathe with me as if they and I are the same.

Just when I think it's over, cold blood tracks my veins. I quiver. Heat stings my skin as it breaks the frozen blood. There's a war emerging from my marrow. Something inside wants out. It's a battle between hot and cold, but what I need now is lukewarm. A tingling sensation vibrates through me, the pain abates, but the shock of the pain remains.

The beep from my house gate squeals in my ears. I compel my eyes to stay open and push my head above the dashboard. It's opening; the gate is opening. With stiff fingers, I find the gears and slide my foot on the gas.

I just need to get to the intercom.

Jerking, the car moves forward. The closing signal from the gate beeps. In a panic, I push harder on the accelerator, tires screeching as I take an abrupt turn into the driveway. Blinded by the lights shining in my eyes, I hit the brakes. The engine stalls and I stay seated.

"Lexie, honey …" That's the voice of my worried mother. She rushes from her car to me and pulls my door open. "Oh God, Lexie, what happened?"

Relief replaces my terror, but anger rules and I ignore my mother as I step out of the car. She's calling in panic, but I'm not answering. It seems I'm dreaming.

My knees weakening, I stumble and fall on a pot of butterfly weed, the orange scent flooding my nostrils. My mother's arm by my shoulder startles me, and I shake it off as she tries to help me up.

I push the front door open and squint at the bright light—it's too bright. The hallway appears larger, so does the stairs. My heavy legs weigh me down as I struggle to walk.

An arm caresses my back, and I turn in fright; it's my mother again.

"Alexandra, please talk to—"

"Don't!" I let out a ragged breath. "You're not my mother."

"Lexie, wait!" She hurries to stand in front of me. "He asked me not to say, and—"

"He's not your son!" I roar. "I am your daughter, and it is I, I, you're meant to …!" I break off, my body acknowledging a sharp pain running down my spine. The intensity is almost unbearable—almost. "Aargh!"

"Lexie!" My mother rushes to catch me.

I can't see her clearly. The excruciating pain in my head won't let me look at her. My chest tightens and I can't move. The aches and heat are unbearable. My blood burns, my veins rejecting the heat. Mom, I want to say, but my jaw refuses to move.

"Oh God, Alexandra!" Mother screams just as my knees give way.

Right there in the hallway, my hands touch the ground. The world around me moves in an endless motion.

"Shall I call for an ambulance, Doctor Watson?" Marie calls.

"No," Mother voices, her voice sounds stronger this time. "No ambulance. Let's take her to the living room. Breathe, sweetheart," she whispers in my ear as they lay me on the large couch. "You'll be okay, I promise."

"John, please pick up." Mother pleads on the phone a few seconds later.

Blinking hazily, I fight to see her. She stands not far from me, pacing in frenzy with the phone by her ear. "I need you," she gasps. "It's Alex. I think it's happening. She's boiling ... hot as fire and her veins, everything ... God, John ..."

She pauses for a moment, sobbing on the phone, and only responding with nods and hums.

Little by little, everything begins to fade; I can barely hear John De Luca's voice as he enters the house. A moment later, he scoops me in his arms and carries me to my room, placing me carefully on the bed. I'm drifting in and out of consciousness as he checks my eyes, ears, and feet. I feel the prick from a needle as John runs a line into my veins. The last thing I see is my mother hanging an I.V. bag next to the bed before I drift into darkness.

⚜❈⚜

I open my eyes and realize I'm still in bed. The room is dim, and I'm dressed in the miserable, white, cotton nighty that I hate.

I.V. bags are still hanging beside me, but the lines are no longer in my veins. The beaded linen curtains are shut, no lights on, except for the two side lamps. To my right further down by the wall, on my whitewashed work desk, I notice my laptop is no longer there and in its place sits what looks like a heartbeat monitor. I also notice the sensor on my finger.

Back on the monitor, green, steady white and blue wavy lines move across the screen. Apart from the faint beeps from the machine, silence rules. Five past four, the clock on the screen reads.

My thoughts wander to my mother, and there and then, I hear her speaking. She is not in my bedroom, but her voice is as clear as if she's next to me. I hear John too.

"Is she going to be all right?" Mother asks.

"I can't say." John sighs. "We'll have to wait and see; her heart beats like human. It's just her blood is still burning, and her eyes ... they're still silver."

I try to sit up, to look at the silver eyes in the mirror beside the monitor, but every part of me feels heavy, including my fingers. On top of that, my head aches.

"You think she's—?"

"No!" John doesn't wait for Mother to finish. "She was about to, but it stopped now—hopefully."

"You're not sure?" Mother's voice sounds troubled.

"Well, I am, but she's changing every day, Anne, and I hate to say it again, but we need the Ring." John whispers the word ring. "Once we have it, we'll never have to worry about her transforming like she almost did tonight." He sighs. "If only—"

"You don't have to worry about that anymore," Mother says. "I have it sorted out."

"How?" John's voice sounds skeptical. "You do know it's virtually impossible to get that Ring?"

"Yes, I do, and—"

"No! No, you don't understand," John states. "It's in Pannonia, Anne, and they keep it in the Great Vaults. We both know which kind can get in there—talk of the blood. It won't work without the white blood."

"I know!" Mother replies. "It's all good. All done. I found one of their kind."

"You found a white-blooded vampire?" John almost yells.

I try to sit up again, but my movement distorts my hearing, so I lie still. The less I move, the clearer I hear.

"Not a White Blood," Mother explains. "But he's going to help us get the Ring."

"Do you realize how dangerous this sounds? Where did you find him? Who is he?"

"I promised not to tell, that was his condition."

"Don't tell me, you told a total stranger about ah ..." He pauses, before adding, "Alexandra."

"I trust him completely, and you know what else he told me?"

"What?"

"He knows the angel—the Cursed Angel," she whispers. "And he promises to do all he can to make sure the angel never gets close to Alexandra."

John snorts. "And you believed him because ...? It's so easy to identify the Cursed Angel? What if he's lying, Anne? I mean ... he could be mistaken. Now that you let Channing go, she will be more vulnerable. Who knows if the next boy she meets is the one—the Cursed One."

"He said the cursed one is in Pannonia. I have this under control, John. I swear, you have nothing to worry about."

"Like how you had it under control when you asked Chan to leave?"

"Why does everyone think I asked him to leave?" Mother moans. "He was like a son to me, you know, and it was his choice to leave, not mine."

"I know you, Anne; you have a way of getting what you want and still look like a victim."

"If I could do that, I would have you."

John doesn't respond straightaway, but after taking a deep breath, he speaks again. "Come here. I wish the same, but you know why we can't."

It's silent again until my mother speaks. "Where's the ring I gave you? Don't tell me, you gave it to Rebecca."

"An ancient ring for Rebecca?" John lets out a cackling laugh.

Mother joins in, and for a moment, they are both lost in laughter.

My mind drifts back to Chan, and my heart responds with an ache.

"So when did your mole say they would bring the Ring?" John asks a moment later.

"Six months or more. He needs a White Blood."

"Of course, and I assume he knows what he's dealing with." John concedes.

I don't hear either of them speaking until my mother asks, "What do we do now?"

"I think you should double her dose while we wait for the Ring, and hope nothing like this happens again before then. Just be sure not to aggravate her. Any kind of trauma will trigger the transformation."

"I love you," Mother breathes.

John sighs as if in relief. "Not more than I love you."

"You think she will ever forgive me?" Mother whispers.

"She—"

Their voices go quiet. It seems my supernatural hearing has vanished. A moment passes and I hear my mother thanking John, but she sounds as if she's just outside my room.

The door opens, and I shut my eyes. I don't want to talk to her, not now.

Mother plants a soft kiss on my forehead, and reaches for my wrist. She injects another dose of whatever it is in my veins. A small part of me wonders if I'm a vampire. I'm hoping she'll whisper to tell me, but all she says is, "I love you".

As the pain subsides, sleep draws the curtains of my eyes, and slowly I give in. Mother nestles me in her warm arms. I try not to think of Channing, but the mind has a sense of its own. He remains the focus of my mind. It reminds me that he has abandoned me. He is gone, and I miss him.

I still smell his lingering scent and yet my heart has frozen. 'He is gone,' says my heart. I doze and yet the words in his letter continue to haunt me.

Your world and mine are different.

His words haunt me the next day, the next week, and the month that followed.

Apart from the usual *"how are you feeling"* from my mother, and the same *"fine"* from me, my mother and I haven't discussed what happened. I still replay what happened the night Channing left. I still smell the pale blue envelope, the blood from my nose and the grass, the green leaves and the scent of oak trees and butterfly weed. My stomach heaves each time my mind flashes back to the moment the doors shut on Channing.

The Ring.

The Cursed Angel.

The White Bloods.

Vampires.

A Curse.

On top of the issue of what I am, these are the things that have kept me glued on my laptop, on the Internet, seeking to know more, but they still remain a mystery to me.

I have questions for my mother, but if asking will risk her knowing that sometimes I'm blessed with supernatural hearing, then I risk never hearing secrets again. Perhaps the hearing was just a one-off, but then again, maybe it wasn't.

I haven't abandoned my plans. The plans I had when I left the airport, the plans I intended to put into action that night. It might be a month overdue, but today is a good day to let Mother know how I feel.

I haven't been on my bike for weeks now. I don't feel like riding, but I'm tempted to maybe *accidentally intentionally* hit something and trigger the hearing again. Only the sun and I are not the friends we used to be.

Outside through my closed balcony doors, though it's already 8AM, the sun seems to hide behind the clouds. The clouds spread all over, swallowing the sun's rays and yet again, a gloomy blanket covers me. A blanket I now desire more and more each day.

I sit on the chaise, by the wide window, facing the morning sun. Since Channing left, it has replaced my morning ride. I call myself the sun watcher.

Today is the day; everything is working in accordance with my decision.

Emily trimmed my hair last night; it feels a lot lighter, thanks to her.

Marie is off.

The sun is not shining.

Mother had a night shift; I expect her home by 9:30AM, about an hour from now. I can still pursue my dream in Pannonia. All I need is to find a home, and build my dream while looking for Chan.

Emily is what holds me back. *What would I do without her?* She will be heartbroken, but she is better without me; I'm nothing close to a friend nowadays.

It's nine o'clock, I have to go before Mother comes, but the ticket is not here yet. I pick up the bags I packed earlier; one small suitcase, the essential makeup bag and my wallet. I wear my indigo jeans, a pair of the orange heels, a navy Ashbourne polo—tight to my skin, and then cover it with a tan leather jacket. With my hair in a loose ponytail, I make my way down the stairs to the entrance hall, ready for the courier.

From my purse, I pull a letter I received from college two days ago and place it next to the telephone table, where she can see it.

"This should be enough to break her," I whisper just as the intercom rings.

I press the enter button and rush for the door. I don't wait for the courier guy to speak, before grabbing the envelope, sign on the electronic reader and thank him.

The ticket now in my hands, I'm ready for my mother.

They say revenge is sweet, and I agree. I want to get back at my mother for how things ended between Channing and me. I want to see her as flabbergasted as I felt when I discovered she had betrayed me. I crave to bruise her unwavering heart, so she feels broken and as betrayed as I feel.

The muffled beep of the intercom alerts me of her arrival. Earlier I contemplated leaving without saying goodbye, but to miss the look on her face would be like dying just before the applause to my masterpiece.

In the lock, a key turns and the door opens. I see a smile on her face, and her hair is atypically down. She's in a happy mood. Shrugging the coat off her shoulders, she doesn't notice me at first, but when she does, she gasps.

"Good lord, sweetheart, you almost gave me a heart attack."

"The little things that startle your heart, Mother." I snort, fold my arms and lean by the wall a distance from her.

In silence, she hangs her coat by the rack and then pauses, eyes on my bags. "Going somewhere?"

"Pannonia." I pick up my handbag and refuse to look into her eyes, but I feel them on me.

"College begins soon. I don't think running after a boy who left you is a wise thing to do."

"I'm not going to college, Mother. I don't want to."

She pauses; mouth open as she frowns at me. "You're not going to college?"

"Nope."

She nods and inhales as she raises her hand to her forehead. She begins to scratch her head, but ends up placing both hands on her waist, aghast as she stares at me.

I expected anger in her eyes, anger or rage, but all I read now is disappointment. Now I'm confused. I've forgotten my next line. I have to think of one that goes with the disappointment in her eyes.

"Remember that motor racing dream I told you about?"

"No!" Her voice breaks. "I will hear no more of this! I can't let you destroy your future." With trembling hands, she tears the letter I left on the table earlier. "Couldn't you at least talk to me first?"

"Can't I keep one secret to myself? You sure keep a lot."

"So this is revenge, huh? Because if it is, I'm not having it." She's back to her normal self, sniffling as she moves her hands on the telephone table, arranging things that are already in order. "There's no way on earth I'm allowing you to drop out of college. Not for racing and certainly, not for a boy."

Then the war of words begins. She's telling me I'm going nowhere, and I'm telling her I will go. She threatens she will do all she can to stop me, but I remind her I am her daughter, after all.

"What are you going to do this time? Tie me to the Yoshino tree or perhaps you prefer the traditional *freezing my funds* style?"

"If I have to, Lexie, I will. You will have not a dollar to spend." She picks up her phone and begins dialing.

"You're so predictable, it hurts. I've already withdrawn enough cash and no last-minute tickets this time." I take the ticket out of my purse and flip it so she can see it.

She gasps, and holds her chest as tears well up in her eyes. "Lexie, please don't do this to me."

Here comes my sweet revenge, I tell myself as I stare at her tortured face. I've been waiting for this moment. I wait for the pleasure, but it doesn't come. I should be celebrating her wet cheeks. I'm sure her heart is trembling now, just as I wanted, but I'm not happy. Instead, I force a smile which should come naturally if I were truly happy.

Where is my sweet revenge? She wins, yet again, but I'm not going to show her how her tears move me.

I shake her hands off and grab my bags as I head for the door.

"Alexandra, I said you can't!" The strength in her voice shakes the determination in my feet, and I stop halfway to the door.

"You can't control me anymore, Mother," I hiss.

I take a step forward. I don't hear or see my mother, but she snatches the bags off my hands. With empty hands, I turn to find my bags in hers. I scream in frustration. Chest rising and falling, I struggle to get the bags back, but she's stronger, yanking them off me each time I grab one.

"You know what?" I yell, clutching my wallet in one hand. "You can have them! Let's see if they'll be your Alexandra!"

I march with anger toward the door, but something stops me. The door is ajar with nothing blocking the way, nothing but air, yet I can't move past it. It feels as if I'm pushing against a balloon.

I turn to my mother. Her hand is up, extended toward me with the palm raised at me.

"What's happening? What are you doing?" I ask, forcing my way through the door. "Stop it!" I bawl, gasping as hot-air tingles through my skin. She puts her hand down, and I break through the door, and drop to the ground. The last thing I see is darkness.

V

The Sun & I

"Why won't you leave me in peace?" I groan at Emily.

I'm having my morning shower and Emily nags me to hurry up. I'm not giving in to her; it's not as if we're going anywhere.

She has been doing this for the past six months. I hoped once she started college she would leave me alone, but I was wrong. She still comes, either in the morning for a walk in the garden, or late afternoon to keep me company on the balcony.

Yesterday was Christmas, and she was here with her father, Robert, trying to convince me to forgive my mother.

"Christmas is a time for forgiveness, Alex," Robert said.

Yeah, right. Try being me for a minute, I remember thinking to myself.

"The bathroom is not your refuge, Lexie. Get out!" Emily voices. "And it's time for a haircut," she adds, then mumbles, "I don't know how you even shower with hair that long."

I glance at the wet hair clinging below my waist and force a smile.

We were going to start college together; Emily studying fine arts while I take forensic sciences, but my mother and I are playing the waiting game. She waits for me to tell her I've changed my mind and would like to start college this year, while I wait for her to tell me she is willing to sponsor my racetrack dream. I wonder how long this will go on.

I come out of the bathroom and find Emily packing my stuff in a wooden storage box. "What are you doing?"

"I'm taking everything that is Chan's, everything that has anything to do with Chan. I'm taking it to my house until you start putting more effort into getting out."

I stare at her with a frown. "Way to go, Millie."

I move to the mirror, to dry my hair. "And while you're at it, please make sure you also pack my dreams of him in there, pack his scent that haunts me every night and I think you will need a strong net to catch the sly memories; they can be heavy at times."

She doesn't laugh as I expected, but stands upright and stares at me with teary eyes.

"I'm not going anywhere, Alexandra," she utters in a pained voice. "If that's what you're aiming for, so you can run to Pannonia without me, that's not happening." She slams the box shut.

I drop my shoulders, step closer and give her a hug. "I'm sorry," I whisper. "I promise if I ever decide to leave, it won't be without you. I love you."

"I love you, too." Sniffing, she pulls away from the hug. "See what you made me do. I can't remember the last time I cried."

"When Clive fell off the bridge." We laugh and reach for her hands. "Crying is good too, right?"

A moment later, Emily has finished cutting my hair. She didn't cut it short; it's still hangs below my shoulders. *I would never know what to do with hair above shoulder length.* We head outside to my balcony. With icy glasses of freshly squeezed tropical juice by our side, we rest on the padded loungers, Emily out in the sun while I stay in the shade. The crisp breeze blowing through brings with it memories I'd rather forget. For the past week, the sun has been kinder to me. Though it still causes me to itch, it doesn't burn as it did before.

"Your mother got you a new bike," Emily says, adjusting her sunglasses.

"Did she?" I continue reading the Ashbourne Grand Prix magazine.

"It was meant to be a surprise, but—"

"But she told you to pretend and spoil the surprise to see how I'd react, huh?" I give her a sideways glance. "She never runs out of surprises. Did she tell you she stole my ticket and passport?" I put my magazine down.

"That was months ago. She worries about you, Lexie."

"She has nothing to worry about. She has everything under control. I lost my boyfriend, don't know my father, and I don't know what I am. I'm at her mercy, aren't I?"

"Maybe we should go and have fun at the Orange City. The weather is beautiful."

"And the sun?"

"What about the sun?" she asks.

"Nothing," I say in a dreamy tone.

"Lexie, it's so sunny out there and—"

"I hate the sun. You know ... the sun and I used to have a good rapport; rising as I rise in the morning, shining on me when I ride. And when night comes, I'd watch it give way to the moon."

"Lexie, I don't—"

"Wait, I haven't finished." I grab her hand and turn to stare at her. "What I don't understand is that now, even as I lay here, Millie, the sun still shines. It knows I can't ride, I haven't done that in a while, but it still shines, and I'm sure it sets beautifully without a care if I'm watching. So what happened to the connection? There was never a relationship, was there? The sun doesn't care if I'm alive or dead. I miss the sun, but it doesn't miss me. And so it pities me. I hate pity. Pity is for the weak."

"I know you do." Emily answers as if she's talking to a five-year-old. "Let the sun go, Lexie. There's always the moon and the stars, right?"

I sigh. "Some nights I feel I should let go. But then I think if I let go, if I let him go, I might never love again. Don't you think so, Millie?"

"Grandma Carol once told me there's more than one kind of love. The universe is full of souls waiting to connect with us. If we open our hearts and let go of what is no more, only then will we grow to another level."

"And you believe that? Do you think it's true? Some mornings I wake up and I think my heart is not my own. I want to forget, to shut off this pain, all these memories, but it won't let me. It's as if love is the only food for a soul. Once that's gone, it can only feed on memories, regardless how choking those memories might be. What if I don't want another kind? I don't want the moon or the stars. I was just fine with this sun."

"Your mother has been crying because you missed the Christmas Minutes and spent Christmas in bed—"

"Let her cry. She refuses to tell me what I am. By the way, did you ask your grandma about the Cursed Angel?"

"She won't tell me anything. She says I'm playing with fire and made me promise never to speak of it again."

I take in a deep breath. "He's never coming back. Is he, Millie? It's been six months now, and I've not heard a word from him. No letter, no phone call—nothing. He's truly gone."

"Usually miracles happen when we stop expecting them to happen."

"He said his world and mine are different. What did he mean? Does the sun not shine in Pannonia? Or does it rise from the south instead of east? Does love in his world feel almost like hate as I feel it now? Why do I love him just to hate that I love him still?"

Emily doesn't answer this time.

"I wonder if he watches the sun with as much resentment as I do." I exhale.

I just want you to need me, he said.

"Why are you smiling?" Emily disturbs my thoughts.

"Nothing." I give her a lazy smile.

She eyes me warily.

"What?" I ask.

"I miss you," she whispers.

"I'm right here."

"And yet you're not. Chan took you away, and I've been waiting for you to come back for too long. Come back. I miss my best friend."

I stare at her for a moment and look away to hide the tears clouding my eyes. Suddenly, I realize how she has been nursing my emotions and yet I gave her nothing in return.

I stare back at her. Now I see what I've done to her. The sparkle in her eyes is not as visible as it used to. It seems she has been trying to save me from drowning, and I have done nothing but to pull her down with me. I still don't feel like going out, but at least I must show her that her efforts are not in vain.

"Do you still have tickets for The Heartless? Let's go out tonight." I squeeze her hand.

She sits up, a brilliant smile displayed on her face, and it seems the glow in her eyes is beginning to show. "You mean that?"

I wink. "I guess I'm back."

"Oh God, I love you." She pounces on me, circling her arms around my neck. "Shit!" She rises. "I have to go home and get the tickets."

"It's only ten minutes away."

"I know. Just didn't want to disturb Dad." She snuggles next to me. "Besides, I still have to drop off that box full of Chan's dreams, remember?"

Chuckling, I link my arm with hers. "So tell me. How did you manage to escape from your dad this Boxing Day?"

Her face brightens with delight, her eyes mischievous as she bit her lips. "I told my father there was no way I could spend Boxing Day without Alexandra." She laughs.

"Seriously, Emily, I hope he's not lonely with you here."

"Dad wanted to spend today with his new girlfriend, Laura, and I wanted to spend it with you, so it was a mutual agreement."

"And your grandma?"

"In Rome with Grandpa."

"Those two lovebirds," I sing.

"I swear to God, Lexie, I am going to find love like theirs."

"There's no love like that anymore. It died during your father and my mother's generation. I'm living proof. Google my heart and I swear you'll find it broken."

"Awww," she moans as she turns to me. "Come for love," she says, and forces a hug on me. "Don't worry, I promise to find you another Chan."

"Find out what I am first." I sigh, pulling her closer.

It's eight in the evening. While Emily takes a shower, I stand by the balcony watching my mother drive off in her executive Saloon V3. As the car disappears behind the hedges, I sneak to the garage to see the new bike.

It's dark and quiet, but darkness is my friend now. Not wanting to turn the lights on, I struggle to find the bike. I proceed past the Aero Whisper and find the sleek machine resting in the corner.

"A Black Mamba," I whisper. "She got me a Black Mamba. "Ha!" I stifle the excitement, my trembling fingers gliding across the glossy tank.

The Black Mamba is the latest motorcycle, the most powerful in the world. I stoop to admire its sturdy built, loving the color; gunmetal silver.

Without warning, the garage lights flash on. I rise to see my mother standing by the doorway. My heart pounding, my chest rises.

She smiles. "I knew you would love it."

"Mother, what are you doing here? Shouldn't you be at work?"

She steps to the bike. "I know this can't replace Chan, but, honey, this is me saying I'm sorry."

"Sorry for what? Refusing to tell me what I am? Refusing to talk about my father? Or is it for the two hours I can't account for that day I tried to leave for Pannonia?"

"For everything. It will all make sense one day. I promise." She looks at me, waiting for an answer, but I say nothing.

"Please, Lexie."

"You hurt me."

"I know, and I'm sorry. I want us to talk. I miss breakfast with you. You may not believe what I'm about to say, but I swear to God, I loved Chan like a son, and I miss him, too."

I stare at her watery eyes for a moment. I don't think she misses him as I do, but in that instant, as I stare at her, I believe she does miss him in her own way.

With a strained voice, I begin to talk. "He said he wanted me to need him, you know, and I ..." I try to compose myself, taking in a deep breath. "I argued with him, Mom. I argued and argued and told him I didn't need him. How could I be so insensitive?"

"Hey." She takes me into her arms. "It's all right to cry, you know."

I hate crying, but her words make me burst into tears.

"It gets better with time." Mother cups my face and smiles. "I have something to show you."

"What is it?" I dab tears as she tugs me toward the second garage door.

She stops at the steel door, her eyes unable to hide her excitement. "It was supposed to arrive yesterday as a Christmas present, but I managed to sort the documents—"

"Mom! You're killing me with suspense."

"Sorry." She opens the door, and a scent of calla lilies floods my nostrils before I see over a dozen bouquets in front of me.

I gasp at the beauty of the petals, then pause to catch a breath again when I notice what's behind them; a silver Theta Scorpii, Chan's exotic car.

"Chan?" My stomach flutters. "Is he here?"

"No, honey, he's not here." Mother pulls my arms to her chest. "He's not coming, but he wants you to have this." She hands me a postcard.

Wish I were there with you.

Merry Christmas, Jo.

Always, Channing.

I turn the card over; there are no more words, no address, but a picture of the Great Pannonia Cave—a magnificent cavern made of milky limestone.

My eyes well up and Mother sets me on the bench by the wall. She remains quiet and rubs my back as I compose myself.

"Lexie," she begins.

I look up into her eyes.

"About your plans to take a gap year, I want you to know I've thought everything through, and I would like to help with your motor racing dream if you still want to make that happen."

I sit up, blinking away tears as I stare at the affection in her eyes.

She reaches out for my hand, squeezing it a little. "I love you, Alexandra. All I want is the best for you. I want you to be happy. And if racing will make you happy, I'm all for racing."

I sniffle, dabbing tears off my eyes. "Maybe you and I can bless the track when it's done, huh?"

"Don't push it, Lexie," she warns, smiling.

"Thank you," I say, and we embrace quickly before I rush to my Theta Scorpii.

At the dinner table, Emily, my mother and I are enjoying my mother's divine panna cotta while discussing the auction coming up in the New Year. We talk about the Theta Scorpii, Chan and the lilies, but nothing to do with what happened in the last month. After a quiet moment, Mother begins on another story from her silent partner—the daily newspaper.

"Guess who's moving next door?"

"Your hospital?" I chuckle.

"If it were possible, I would do it for you, Lexie." Mother chuckles as she shifts in her seat a little. "Listen to this." She clears her throat and begins to read.

"David Deschanel, founder of the Deschanel luxury car manufacturer based in Pannonia, has denied claims he will be moving into one of the most expensive streets in the world—Stills Lane, stating he preferred the less flamboyant Vine Lane ..."

"Our Vine Lane?" I grimace.

Mother nods quickly and continues reading.

"And rumor has it Mr. Deschanel will be moving into Edward as it is the only property on sale on Vine Lane."

"Next door?" Emily gasps. "I heard he has two boys. One's nineteen and the other's twenty. Lexie, just when I thought there was no hope for you."

I shake my head at her, bored with the new boyfriend talk.

Thoughtful, Mother turns to Emily. "You think that's true? We've never seen their faces on TV or the newspapers."

"They say David, paid the media never to publish photos of his family," Emily answers, then swallows another spoonful of her dessert.

"They must be more than wealthy," I mumble.

"Very close friends with the Van-Baileys, they are," Mother adds.

"So?" I snort.

Mother folds the paper and looks at me. "So, nothing. They're friends with the Van-Baileys, that's all."

"I'm sorry, but why do people use the Van-Baileys to measure everything?" I grimace. "Why must everyone speak so highly of the Van-Baileys when all I see in them is arrogance? Zachary this, Zachary that. I'm sick of it."

"What is it with you and Zachary?" Mother moans. "You don't know him, and I guess if you were to meet him out there you wouldn't recognize his face, yet you hate him so."

"Well, forgive me that I don't make it my business to study the faces of the obnoxious, rich, and famous." I turn to grab a napkin and wipe my mouth.

"And where do you place yourself? Amongst the poor?" Emily intervenes.

I roll my eyes. "*Obnoxious*—obnoxious, rich, and famous, I said. Pay attention."

"Why do you hate—"

"I don't hate him, Millie," I voice, and then move my eyes to my mother. "Like you said, I hardly know him. It's just that I despise those who think money can buy any ..." I break off, frowning as my mother and Emily begin laughing. "What's funny?"

"She sounds better, already, doesn't she?" Mother comments.

We remain quiet for a while before Emily nudges me to continue with a conversation we'd discussed earlier.

I hesitate, then clear my throat. "Mom." I look into her eyes. "Can Emily and I go and watch The Heartless?"

"A concert? Alex—"

"Please. They're playing in Milbourne. Tonight is our last chance."

"Tonight? What did I say about random outings? Honey, you can't ..." Her brow furrows. "You didn't just plan this today, did you? Tickets are sold in advance, right?"

"I bought them." Emily confesses with a nervous smile. "She didn't want to go at first, but I got one for her."

Mother moves her gaze to me. "So what changed your mind?"

"I need to test drive the Theta Scorpii."

She sighs. "Speed, speed, speed. Like father, like daughter." She shakes her head.

"I won't speed! I promise."

"I hear … I've heard those exact words before from your father, so I know what they mean coming from his daughter."

The father I don't know. I draw in a deep breath.

Then she nods. "Go and have fun," she says. I lean to kiss her cheek, then sit back.

Speed, here I come. I stare at my mother, smiling.

Rising to her feet, Mother plants a kiss on my cheek. "Keep your promise, Alexandra and I'll keep mine. Drive safe."

As she disappears down the hallway, I turn to give Emily a soft high five, whispering, "If I don't see any of them turn into wolves like you promised, Millie, I swear—"

"You'll forgive me, of course." Emily shrugs and forces a spoonful of panna cotta in my mouth.

VI

THE FOURTH, VAN-BAILEY ZACHARY

At midnight, Emily and I cruise down Tuberose Lane in my new love—the Theta Scorpii. With windows closed, classical music melting my heart and the car flying against the wind, I feel I'm on my way to a better me.

We are on the way to Milbourne, to watch The Heartless. Tuberose Lane—my favorite highway— is not a favorite of many as they prefer the new and wider Nightshade Expressway.

Curvy and hilly, Tuberose meanders along various trees and colorful, almost fading, wild flowers.

Though autumn now gives way to winter, the trees still hold color; the few healthy leaves sway in the trees while the majority covers the flowers below.

The splash of color merges with the bright streetlights. It's here that I turn the music off and roll the windows down. The sound of the wind in the trees and the river running beneath the bridge situated a few yards ahead of us is music I like to hear.

As usual, the road is quiet. The drivers who use this route are those like me who strive to test the speed of their machines, away from the public view.

"So you are serious about your secret immortality investigation?" Emily asks.

"Never been this serious." I glance at her briefly. "It's about the three: the Ring, the Cursed Angel and vampires. From what I heard John telling my mother, it seems vampires exist, but to imagine myself as one is unreal. If they do, are they in Ashbourne? Are there even any supernatural creatures in Ashbourne? Then there are the White Bloods."

"There are two explanations. Either you got your immortality from your father or your mother. Since Doc appears human, I can only conclude the answer lies with your father."

"I used to think so, but after what she did to stop me from leaving for Pannonia, I'm not sure she's ordinary. Then again, she's my mother. She can't be ... I'm more confused than ever."

"What about Grandpa Henry. Can't you ask him?"

"He hates lying to me. *'Listen to your mother, butterfly'*, that's all he says."

Emily sighs. "How about we leave the immortality talk until after the fun? Right now, I want to talk about how we are going to attract the attention of those Deschanel boys coming to live next door."

I laugh. "Are we still in kindergarten that we should have boyfriends living next door?"

"My gut tells me, they *shall* be good-looking. If not, they should *at least* be well-mannered."

"Rich, powerful boys don't do manners."

"Channing did."

"Whatever. I'm not interested. Besides, I can't date humans or else they will turn into another Channing. I can't date creatures either in case they are enemies to my kind. Can't you see, I'm cursed?"

In silence, Emily stares at me for a while. "Still, it doesn't mean you can't have fun."

"True." I grin and toss the gears. "This is fun. Now hold on tight."

"Not this kind of fun! Lexie, slow down!"

I ignore her and speed along until a light flashes from behind us. A quick glance in the rearview mirror and I reduce speed. A black sport car tails behind us.

"Is that a Zetra Zeus?" Emily's eyes widen. I know she's just as trilled as I am, to be that close to such a phenomenal car.

"A car after my own heart." I bite my lip, and slow down to let the car pass. The driver reduces speed and remains behind us.

"What's wrong?" Emily looks back.

"He's following us ... I think."

"Who the hell is he?"

"Don't know." I sit up straighter and adjust my seat a little.

For a moment, neither of us disturbs the silence. We approach a red light, and I hesitate before pressing on the brakes. My car stops and I wait for the car behind.

The Black Zetra Zeus driver pulls his car parallel to mine, stopping in the lane of oncoming traffic.

Emily and I turn to look at him. He looks back at us with a cheeky grin, his fists drumming the steering wheel. He seems to be nodding and humming to music playing in his car.

I shake my head. "What does he think he's doing stopping in that lane?"

"Lexie, I think I know him."

"He's handsome. Should I let him know you fancy him?"

"I dare you to tell him." She grins.

The Zetra Zeus driver honks. I turn and stare at the driver again. He flashes an audacious grin, the engine of his car daring as it roars.

I shrug at him. "What's that for?"

He returns the shrug, the passenger window spontaneously gliding as he leans toward it.

"Ladies first." Without warning, my heart flutters. His deep, mellifluous voice makes me warm inside.

The light flashes from amber to green. Intending to speed off and leave him behind, I press heavy on the accelerator, but he speeds along, racing with me.

I simper, enjoying the chase. "Okay, here we go, honey. The time is now."

"Let him go, Lexie." Emily stares at me with worry. "This is dangerous."

I ignore her, concentrating on the race. I want to win because I know he thinks he can beat me because I'm a girl. An ordinary girl, maybe, but I'm far from ordinary. "Boys," I mumble, shifting the gear, "who needs them?"

The nose of his Zetra Zeus edges past my Theta Scorpii, and I shake my head at the smug grin forming out on the driver's face. The key is not to panic, and so I shift to sit up, firmly holding on to the steering wheel while my foot nudges the accelerator further. It only takes a few seconds, and I'm flying past him.

He glances at me and shakes his head while my lips curl up with delight.

"How's that, Millie? You feel the buzz?" I laugh.

Emily doesn't answer. Her face pales as she clings to the seat.

"Millie?"

"God, Lexie … I … I'm going to puke." She heaves.

Without thinking twice, I slow down and turn to her. "Millie, are you all right?"

"Stop, Lexie. This isn't funny!"

I don't pull over until we pass the white bridge. Silence rings in my ears as the engine dies. I turn to Emily who wears a screwed face.

The Zetra Zeus driver stops next to us. "Is she all right?" he calls out.

I give him a quick glance. "She will be."

It takes a moment before Emily calms down, and I decide to give her another five minutes to make sure she's okay.

"She looks hot," he calls again.

This time I shake my head, and answer without looking at him. "You want her number?"

Millie elbows me. "Haven't you done enough?" She hisses then pushes the passenger door open and begins to throw up.

I rub her back gently, pass her a box of Kleenex and turn back to the boy in the Zetra Zeus. "You still want her number?" I ask in a mocking tone.

He laughs. "No, I meant your car. She's beautiful."

I marvel at him and shake my head. He thinks he's funny. "What gave you the impression it's a she?"

He shows off his even teeth. "She's beautiful like the owner…"

"Ha," I snort. "You got that right. The owner is beautiful. *He* is beautiful."

"I knew that." He runs his fingers through his hair. "Only a gentleman like me would know how to treat a lady like her."

I stare at him, then shoot a glance at the bottom side of his car with disapproval.

"What?" he asks.

"Doesn't look like it from where I'm sitting."

"What do you mean?"

"She's got a dent."

"You're kidding me!"

"I'm not the type to joke about such abuse." I curl my lips and watch his brow furrow.

In haste, he dashes out of the car, mumbling something that sounds like curses. As he steps around, I follow and join him to see the look on his face after discovering the truth.

As fast as my heels touch the ground, I sense his dazzling presence over me, full of authority, but surprisingly engaging.

He's tall; perhaps the same height as Channing, with the same elegance, but there is something different about him—something divine, yet coated with a supercilious, or perhaps a theatrical feel. Adding to his oval shaped face, is the long layered dark-brown hair with an off-centered parting, giving him that extra measure of charm.

It's not just the way he looks, but also how he holds himself – head cocked, smiling sarcastic eyes, arrogant eyebrows. He stands with legs almost rooted to the ground as if he owns it. Moves as if the earth is his, made especially for him, and the rest of us are mere extras privileged to stand in his presence.

Apart from the stylish yellow scarf around his neck, he wears all black— skinny jeans defining his sturdy legs, a black Ashbourne polo shirt, and a vintage-like leather jacket.

His eyes stare at the lower side of the car, and playful creases form on his forehead. He now knows I tricked him.

He shakes his head. "It's not only that you succeeded in fooling me, but I can't believe that I believed you, just like that."

I hold a smile, watching as he bites his lip while casually kicking the wheel of his car.

"Be gentle with her," I tell him.

He laughs, a hearty chuckle that makes me chuckle too. We stare at each other, smiling for what seems to be a long while.

"In fact, it's a *he*," he speaks again, staring at me with a side smile, "and he enjoys the kicks sometimes."

Behind me, the car door slams. I turn and see Emily holding a bottle of water, washing her hands.

"You do racing, right?" he asks.

"As a hobby, yeah."

"You should think seriously about taking it on as a profession because you're..." He shrugs and then adds, "Crazy."

"I'll take that as a compliment." I stare into his eyes again.

He's got glistening brown eyes that pierce deep as if to freeze anything that dares to question them. Though his posture reflects grace, his manner still appears arrogant.

As I gaze at him, I notice that already, he has displayed about seven different smiles; a lower tight-lipped just before he answers a question, a standard closed while he listens, and a side smile when he feels caught up, reserving the wide grins, and the radiant smiles for the humor.

"I could give you my card if you want to try pro training. I'm opening a racetrack soon ..."

I laugh.

"What's funny?"

"I intend to do the same, soon ... I hope."

"You do?"

"Uh-huh." I nod.

"I see," he says. "Still have my card in case you need help or—who knows?—I might need ideas, too."

"Of course," I say, and drop my gaze to the card. My heart pounds. "Zachary Van-Bailey?" I gasp quietly. "You're Zachary?"

He grins, extending his hand to me. "Fourth, Van-Bailey Zachary."

With my hand shaking his, I open my mouth just to shut it again, not knowing what to say.

The car door slams again, causing me to jump. It's Emily. This time she rushes toward us screaming with glee.

"I knew it," she cries. "I knew it was him." Continuing to scream, she jumps on Zachary, her hair in chaos.

I'm watching Zachary's response, and I'm surprised he doesn't flinch at Emily's embrace. Instead, he gives her a warm hug with what appears to be a sincere smile.

"Oh, my!" Emily sighs. "Can you believe it? Finally, I can say I've met Zachary Van-B in the flesh." She kisses his cheek, and I wince, thinking of the vomit.

Zachary says nothing, but smiles as he returns the kiss on Emily's blushing cheek. I resist the urge to shake my head while I watch Emily, rubbing Zachary's chest too.

Then, she takes things further than I imagine. "Would you like to join us? We're going to see The Heartless."

"Emily, no." My eyes widen. "I'm sure he has better places to go."

Zachary stares at me for a moment without saying anything, and sighs. "I'm also a fan of The Heartless, but I've heard their concerts are too dangerous. You can meet a lot of heartless beings there."

"We'll be fine," I say, a bit uneasy. "It was good to meet you, Zachary. Emily, let's go."

Emily leans over to embrace Zachary again while I roll my eyes and turn to walk back to the car.

"So I'm not going to get a hug?" Zachary says out of the blue.

I turn to him, and for a few seconds, I imagine his arms around me. My heart skips. "You got one from her," I say and continue to the car.

"It's a shame she's not as tough as I thought," he calls to me.

I pause, grimacing as I turn to face him with exaggerated slowness.

For a second, he mimics my frown. Then quickly it disappears. "The Theta Scorpii, I mean," he adds, appraising my car.

I walk back to him. It seems he wants a challenge. "I can tell you now, she is way tougher than he is, and unlike him, she has a lot to offer. What can he give, apart from …?" I pause and step closer to his Zetra Zeus.

Examining it with judgment, my finger glides over its contours. "Mm ... arrogance? Security? And comfort, perhaps?"

He laughs. "I agree she's way better in looks, appears adventurous, powerful and sturdy enough to bring any man to his knees, but here is where things get exciting." He shifts his weight from one foot to the other, a smirk growing on his face. "She's not built with the same degree of resilience as he is. He's almost invincible, if not totally. She lacks the summer fun, and her engine sounds numb, if not frozen."

He blinks, a smug blink as I frown with disapproval—disbelief maybe—and for a second, I feel I have known him all my life. He places his left hand in the pocket, and raises the other, ready to explain as our eyes remain locked.

"Are you two still talking about cars?" Emily interrupts.

"Yes!" We both voice at her.

Emily raises her brow and flings her hands at us before walking back to sit in the car.

I stare at Zachary again, but this time he's not smiling. His eyes search mine and the more I stare at him, the more I forgive his arrogant eyebrows.

He steps closer, reaching for my hair. My heart throbs, reacting to his proximity, and I remain frozen as he gently brushes a few strands off my face.

Breathing in and out, he swallows and leans in to whisper by my ear. "He's an 1800 A.D. Immortal machine, been there, seen it, done it and conquered."

"1800 A.D. Immortal?" I struggle to find my voice. "I never heard of that. He's sure getting rusty."

He bites his lip again, fighting the smirk I see already creeping on his face. "Now that you laughed at him, I'm going to put you to shame," he says. "Come on, let's go."

"Where?"

"On the green light," he calls, walking back to his car, to the driver's side. "We race up to the main junction."

A shiver of excitement rushes through me. With a growing smile, I rush back to the car. As I take my seat, I look at Emily, and as soon as our eyes meet, she sees what I'm pleading for.

"No, no, Lexie. I can't—"

"It's just a five-minute race. Come on, you're the one who said I should have fun."

"Don't twist my words, Lexie."

"Okay." I raise my hands. "I have a ticket for the Gossip Flower Show. It's yours if you let me."

Emily turns to me with raised eyebrows, but soon displays a smile. "You're kidding."

"Cross my heart. No kidding."

She nods, and I turn to secure the seat belt, not that I need it, but it's become a good habit.

I wait for Emily as she secures her belt before I turn to Zachary again.

"Ladies first," he calls, roaring the engine.

I stare at him, sticking my tongue out. "I don't see any gentleman here."

Zachary stifles a laugh.

I start well ahead of Zachary, but as we reach halfway, he draws closer and closer until he zooms past me. Trailing behind him, I try all I can, all the tricks I know, including the dirty ones, but nothing works; I just can't catch up with him.

"Bad boy," I mumble. "He was holding out on me the first time."

"Slow down, Lexie, there's no need," Emily warns. "You can't catch him now, anyway."

"No. It's not over until I win." I increase speed and watch as the speedometer nudges to the top end, the car flying almost like a space shuttle.

Soon, I catch up with Zachary. He salutes me, laughing, and I roll my eyes and keep a straight face.

In another second, he's ahead of me again. I feel the strain now, but I'm not giving up.

We approach a curve, about five miles to the finishing point. Zachary is ahead but not far from me. All of a sudden, a loud, grinding noise howls from the Zetra Zeus; Zachary brakes.

Thinking of nothing, but winning, I seize the moment and increase my speed, maneuvering to the left to overtake him.

As our cars remain parallel, we stare at each other—amused—as we enjoy the thrill.

Zachary seems determined to keep me behind, but I'm not having it. I glance at him; he's looking at me too, grinning. He looks ahead. Then his face drops, the smile vanishing in an instant. I'm following his gaze, when Emily screams.

"Alexandra, watch out!"

VII

STRANGER THAN FICTION

I *want to see The Heartless. I want to hear their uplifting music, to dance to the tune of their crazy guitars, and drown in their raspy voices.*

Those were Emily's words before we left home, but what I wanted was to see them phase into the wolves as she said they would.

"Alexandra, watch out." Emily screams.

"Shit!" Beaming lights—blinding headlights—barrel toward me.

Matching the beat of my heart, I slam on the brakes.

It all happens in what seems to be a long time, but is only a few seconds. Tires screech, a horn blares in distress as I cling on the steering wheel. The brakes lock and the wheels skid, but the distance between the bright lights from the oncoming vehicles and me keep shrinking.

A disturbing whiff of burning rubber engulfs my nostrils, and though Emily's cries are almost like a dream, they remind me why I have to be brave.

The lights become brighter, closer. I can't look any more. I can't witness the moment of collision. The moment I become a murderer, the accident killing my best friend, cutting Zachary's life short, including that of the strangers in the other vehicle.

Glancing at Emily, I hear my voice saying "I'm sorry".

What if I'm not strong enough for this? I could die too.

Thoughts of Chan mingle with the deafening horns, the shrill and ear piercing sound of metal crashing. With a trembling hand, I find the gears again.

In the midst of the lights and the noise, a foggy image of Zachary appears, standing still in the middle of the road, eyes closed with his hands together as if in a prayer.

"No!" I gasp as my foot fumble to find the brakes again. I can't move. "Zachary, No!" I'm screaming, but nothing seems to come out of my lips.

Boom! My body arches forward just to slam back and rest on the seat. I hit a tree, I realize as my eyes blink through the deployed air bags.

Another slow blink and I open my eyes to see Emily's eyes shut, her head slack on the air bag.

"Millie?" I call. "Millie, come on!" I force my door open, intending to run over to Emily's side, but then stop, cringing at a loud bang, followed by the excruciating sound of an engine whining.

I glance around, and on the road behind me, I see an eruption of fire. A car is on fire, but it's not Zachary's.

"Emily!" I scream, rushing to open her door. "Emily, please!"

"Calm down, Lexie," she moans, her hand rubbing her neck. "I'm fine."

I sigh with relief, then help her out. "Call an ambulance, and keep away from the car," I tell her before hurrying toward the burning vehicle.

It's my fault. I'm not going to sit and watch an innocent person burn. After all, what is the point of being immortal if I make no use of it?

Staring at the size of the fire, I know this will not be easy. The pain will be unbearable—at least for a few minutes before healing, but that's nothing compared to the misery the poor being must be enduring in that fire.

The smell of gasoline makes me hesitate as I approach the searing flames. Intense heat triggers my blood to boil. The vehicle is upside down, and that seems to feed the rage of the flames.

From the driver's side, a man appears to be struggling. I close my eyes as my hand reaches for the door handle. Then I scream in pain, yanking the door open. I don't want to stop and measure the pain, so I continue and lean in to pull the stranger out, but I'm too late. In a flash, from the other side—the passenger side, someone grabs the stranger and yanks him out.

"What the …?" I mumble, rushing over.

I hurry faster than usual, but not fast enough to catch the two figures as they speed away, disappearing into the darkness. It's not just their speed that confuses me, but the man I thought to be burning in the car seems unharmed and on his feet, escaping. Regardless, why run away?

"Lexie, are you okay?" Emily asks as I approach her under a streetlight.

I nod, tensing at the burns on my hands as they heal.

"I never get tired of watching this," she says, studying my skin as it renews to heal the scars.

I look away as she takes my hands; I don't want to see it.

Though the idea of immortality is intriguing, seeing the healing manifestation makes me wonder more about my nature and the possibility of being some kind of creature.

"Are you okay?" Emily squeezes my hands. "Did you help them?"

"There was no one inside. They probably escaped before the fire."

I pull her closer to give her a hug. "I'm sorry. I almost killed my best friend." My eyes lose the battle against tears.

"As if you have any other." She sniffles and hugs me tighter.

I pull away from the embrace with a loud gasp. "It's too quiet."

"What do you mean?"

"Where's Zachary?"

I don't catch Emily's reply; my mind is rewinding to the vision I saw earlier.

Oh God, No! No noise was bad news; the dead don't make noise. Tears blind my eyes as I think of him dead. I'm not sure if it's the guilt eating me up, but I can't have him dead.

I ask Emily to wait underneath the streetlight, where she would be spotted easily by the ambulance and faraway from the smoking car in case it caught fire.

She tries to stop me, but I don't listen.

"Zachary?" I call out. The tire marks lead me to his car on the side of the road. It rests against a hearty evergreen that flourishes in contrast with the yellow and orange leaves falling from the surrounding trees. "Zachary!"

"Over here." My heart skips at the sound of his weak voice. I hurry over to the other side and find him on the ground, his back resting on the front wheel of his car with hands clasping his right ankle. His jacket is missing.

"Are you all right?" I rush to kneel beside him.

He stares at me as if in amazement and gives me a faint smile. "I'm good. I think I twisted my ankle. No big deal. Are you girls all right?"

I nod and turn to examine his ankle. I don't have any clue what to do, so I just rest my hand on it. I feel his eyes on me, and I turn to look at him. His lips curl into an easy smile.

I drop my gaze to admire the black polo shirt clinging to his lean muscles. My eyes come back to meet his, and a warm tingle fills my stomach. I look away, not knowing what to say, and indulging in the comfort of his being; he is still alive, still here and he seems okay too.

"Why are you looking at me like that?" He frowns and I realize I'm still staring.

"Did you pull the other driver out of the fire?" I ask.

"Fire? No." He grimaces. "Where? Is he hurt?"

I shake my head, then extend my hand to help him up as I rise. "No. Someone or something pulled him out. Like the speed of light, and when I say speed of light, I literally mean speed of light—blink of an eye, they vanished."

"Just like that?"

"Just like that; right in front of my eyes."

"Stranger than fiction, huh?" He leans forward to fix his shoe.

"My thoughts exactly."

"At least now we know we didn't kill anyone," Zachary adds, now standing in front of me.

"Where's your jacket?"

"Um ..." He runs his fingers through his hair. "Don't know. When I heard the loud bang, I got out of the car, fell in that pit over there." He looks back to point at the pit. "That's how I twisted my ankle, blanked out. When I woke up, it was silent until an angel came along."

"An angel?" I blink, narrowing my eyes.

"Yeah." He tilts his head as he rubs an eyebrow with the back of his thumb. "An angel with striking gray eyes, caramel locks and a brilliant smile. If only she smiled more often."

My face warms. I want to smile, but my thoughts take me back to the fire, and I shake my head. I cuddle myself with sadness, thinking everything over.

All at once, an avalanche of mixed emotions showers over me and I struggle to hide the tremor of what just happened.

"Are you okay?" Zachary staggers a little, stepping closer to me. "Is it something I said?"

"Uhm, I thought ... uhm ..."

"Hey." He pulls me to his chest, patting my back. "If you start crying, I will too, and I don't think you can handle that."

"I'm sorry." The comfort in his arms is surreal. If he weren't a stranger, I would have stayed in them for a while.

"No need to apologize." He whispers, wrapping his arms tightly around me. "My compliments don't often make people cry, but I must tell you, this feels really good."

I pull away from the embrace and stare at him. "I was apologizing for the accident, for the stranger who vanished, for my best friend, and for you ... your twisted ankle, not for crying or your compliments."

"Ohh." He nods, hand still on my waist. "That's what happens when you meddle with fate."

"What are you saying? What fate?" I stare at him with a frown.

Tongue in his cheek, he stares at me. "All I asked for was a hug. You refused, and this happens. We almost died, and in the end look where you ended up—right in my arms."

I blink, absorbing his statement, then breathe with indignation as my eyes track his, but he's not brave enough to look at me. I turn to walk away.

"Wait! Come back!" He rushes after me, steps in my way and then reaches for my hand. "I'm sorry; that was a joke," he sighs. "You fooled me the first time and I—"

"And you thought now was a good time to even up the score?"

He is already shaking his head. "No," he says. "I realize I was out of order, and I apologize."

I pause, biting my lip as I gaze at his raised eyebrows.

"Did anyone tell you, you frown a lot?" he asks, closing the gap between us.

At once, my forehead relaxes. I look away fighting a smile, and the next moment I stare up, his face is inches from mine. Yet again, my heart throbs, my chest almost betraying me with the rapid movements.

There's something about him that makes me vulnerable, and yet at the same time I feel powerful.

Staring into my eyes, slowly, he works his fingers into mine, entwining them with caution. Something happens to me, something I can't explain. Heat travels through our fingers, and mysterious, strange images begin to flash in my head. I see Zachary, and I'm kissing his lips, with measured intensity at first, and then faster, and faster. He returns the kisses with greater enthusiasm and as the passion increases, my mouth waters and, no, it's not for the kiss. I feel the urge to bite him, to bite his neck, break his bones, but he bites me first.

"Arh!" I snatch my hands away from his, ending the vision.

"What's wrong?"

"Nothing," I say, staring at him with a pounding heart.

From a distance, a siren rings. "The ambulance is here," I say.

"You called an ambulance? I thought you said you two were fine."

"I didn't know if you were okay."

"Awww." He raises his hand to touch his chest. "I'm touched." He laughs.

Zachary's mechanic arrives about half an hour after the ambulance leaves.

I stand still, watching as they secure my Theta Scorpii on the truck. I guess it's clear who won the race. Zachary's car escaping without a scratch and mine damaged.

"He said it's not as bad as it looks." Emily puts her hand on my back as we watch the driver, towing it away.

"You think this could be a sign?"

"Sign?" Emily frowns. "Sign of what?"

"He's never coming back, and he and I are as damaged as that car."

"This has nothing to do with Chan." Emily stares into my eyes. "You could have avoided the accident by not racing with Zachary."

I nod. "I'm sorry."

"Why don't we forget The Heartless and celebrate our survival … well, at least mine, with eight rounds of X2s?"

With my car damaged and my heart and senses shaken, all I want is to go back home and soak my nerves in a warm bath. But, I can't deny Emily whatever she wants, not after I almost killed her.

The drink is her way of coping, and I can't refuse her that relief. Besides, I'm not ready to face my mother right now.

"I know just the place." Zachary intervenes and hands me a Deschanel Motorcars card. "Mike will bring your car before the New Year's Day. I made him promise."

"Thank you," I say.

"So," Zachary begins again, this time leading us to his car.

In the car, he goes on and proposes to take us to a place he knew to be safe—Club Flash. But, he receives a phone call just as we arrive at the club.

He parks closer to the entrance and answers the call. "Dad …" he says after a listening quietly for a moment. "I'm too far from the airport. I could tell Maxx to—" He pauses, pressing his forehead. "Yes, I hear you," he says in a low voice and hangs up.

He stares at me and sighs. "Can I have permission to find you?"

I frown.

"Though I really wanted to have a drink with you, I have to do something for my father right away."

A sadness clouds over me. I can't ask him not to go. He's a stranger, the *obnoxious* Zachary.

"I know friends who will take good care of you," he says and offers to let us use his car, stating that he would pick it up the next day.

I thank him but refuse his offer. Before leaving, Zachary arranges for a chauffeur to drop us home afterwards. He introduces us to Paul, the manager, who lets us in without the ID hassle.

We step in through the steel doors. The sound of heavy bass and a spine-tingling melody fills my ears. Designed in a ring shape, Club Flash appears stylish. The dance floor is set in the middle, surrounded by the bar all around, only broken by two exits; the main entrance and the back door.

The dimmed spotlight on the ceiling gives the place a cozy atmosphere. A few people swings on the dance floor, some cavorts about in the center, and the others relax on leather settees, with a few loitering around the bar.

I can't say I feel intimidated, but they come across as one large family, calling each other by nicknames, waving and passing drinks to each other.

Being here for the first time, I feel more like a recently adopted family member. However, Paul helps to make us comfortable.

I choose to sit by the bar while Emily skips away to the dance floor.

The music is like I have never heard before. No vocals—only instruments, and so many playing at the same time and yet forming into a titillating unison. Guitars moan gently, the piano keys merging with the lucid harps, and the drums—vivacious. I can't help nod along like everyone else.

An hour of filling my belly with nonalcoholic drinks, I've had enough and want something that will sting my tongue. Since Emily appears intoxicated, the thought of leaving her vulnerable again, delays my thirst.

The music continues blasting. I smile at Emily flirting with a blond haired boy on the dance floor. Across the bar on the other end, I see a familiar face.

"Channing?" I gasp quietly. *Did he color his hair?*

He sits away from the crowd with a glass of what seems to be a cocktail, wine colored that he swirls around.

My heart pounding, I stand and surge through the crowd making my way toward him. "Hey," I tap him lightly.

He turns to face me, and immediately, my heart tightens. "Sorry, I thought you were ..."

"Let me guess ... Ashton?" Appraising me with his blue eyes, the stranger raises his eyebrows.

"No." I shake my head, wondering if I'm losing my mind. "No, I'm sorry."

"Hey wait!" he calls as I walk away. "I could be that somebody you thought I was."

I force a smile. "Thanks, but no." I walk back to my seat at the bar.

Whether I want to think about Channing is debatable, but at least I can say I don't want to think of him. Images of our last time together bombard me. I smell his scent, hear his chuckle, and feel the seductive strength of his lips. I can't breathe.

"Double X2s, please." I turn to call on the bartender.

He doesn't respond, but grabs a white cloth, and begins to wipe the counter. I'm thinking he's wiping it to get ready for the ultimate presentation of my drink, so I wait.

He's a short man, hefty, late twenties perhaps, with a masculine look, and spiky jet-black hair. At the top of his right shoulder, I notice a vampire fangs tattoo.

He turns sideways and pauses to chat with another customer, totally ignoring me.

Louder this time, I try to get his attention again. He shoots a scornful stare at me, shakes his head and continues to wipe the counter.

"Excuse me, did you not hear me?" I ask.

"ID, please." His harsh voice voids the *please.*

I grimace. "What?"

"If you look under twenty-one, I have a right to ask for an ID before selling any alcoholic—"

"Have you lost your senses?" I fume, arising. "How do you think I got in here? They check IDs at the entrance, don't they?"

"Well, that's the entrance, sweetie. This here is the bar, and I'm the bartender."

I stare at him for a minute and place both my hands on my waist as I struggle to hide my rising chest. Something stirs inside me, an unexplained rage. "You're going to have to stop me." I leap over the counter and grab a bottle.

"Whoa! You're going too far, lady!" The bartender grabs me by the arm.

"Take your hands off me!"

He grabs both my arms, secures my wrist behind my back then pins me to the wall. My cheek burn against the brick wall and I groan in fury, wanting to free myself.

"Lexie!" Emily cries.

I can't answer. My bones have stiffened, and overwhelming strength swells up in my veins. With little success, I fight to suppress the anger, blood pumping through my heart with sheer fury.

I spin up in the air in a flash. I'm not in control of my body, twirling with precision then thrusting my right foot on the bartender's neck. With a loud grunt, he plunges to the ground. I pounce on his chest and lean in to his face.

The crowd gasps, but they don't matter. Right now, there's an excitement inside me. I want to go on, to choke him by the throat until he begs for mercy.

My mouth waters and I hold my jaw tight, realizing it's my mouth that is ready to attack and not my hands. I fight to keep my jaw clenched. I'm drawn to his neck, but the fear in his eyes distracts me. A hand touches my shoulder. I flinch; it's that Channing lookalike.

"Are you out of your mind?" he hisses, grabs both my arms, and pulls me toward the back door behind the counter.

Am I out of my mind? I shudder, staring back at him with tears rolling down my cheeks. I'm as shocked as everyone else. I've never attacked anyone before, and certainly not for something as minute as a drink.

"Lexie, are you all right?" Emily comes over to hug me.

"Give us a sec, please," the boy says, pulling me away from Emily. He drags me into a side room, an office, shuts the door on Emily, and turns back to face me. "You could have killed him!"

I open my mouth to answer, but Emily pounds on the door and yell for the boy to open up.

"Emily, I'm fine." I want to make her stop.

"So?" the boy asks.

"I swear to God, I don't know what happened … I don't know what came over me. That has never happened to me before." I tremble.

He shoots me a weary gaze, studying my expression, then pulls me to his chest. "You can't show yourself like this."

"What are you talking about?" I pull away to look in his eyes.

"To the humans. You can't …"

"I can't what?" I frown at him, thinking if he knows I'm more than human, he probably also knows what I am. "You know?"

"Know what?" he asks, seeming as confused as I am.

"What are you?"

He pauses before whispering, "That question is forbidden."

He takes my hand and leads me back to the bar. With eyes on us, including a glaring pair from the bartender, the boy holds me by my waist, guiding me to take a seat by the bar.

Emily who's talking to Paul, the manager, waves at me. I wave back, smiling nervously.

The blond stranger orders two X2s and sits me down to drink with him.

"This place belongs to those who want to have fun without fear of exposure." He begins to explain. "We like to enjoy the entertainment, drink a little, no drugs, no sex behind doors." He lets out a soft laugh as he continues. "It's all to do with making friends and not asking questions. More like a *hear no kind; see no kind* club."

"So you believe we live in a supernatural city?" I ask, sipping the X2 that stirred the uproar in the beginning.

"Don't you?" His eyes glitter as he eyes me.

"Vampires?"

He nods.

"Werewolves?"

He nods again.

"Ghosts?"

"No." He frowns. "I can't ever say I've never seen one."

"Anything else?"

His smile grows. "Angels too, gorgeous."

"Did you just call me gorgeous?"

"Yes, any objections?"

I shake my head, laughing.

Like Channing, he has blue eyes, except his are large. The short layered blond hair complements his golden skin tone. Even seated, I can tell, he maybe a little shorter than Channing. Dressed in dark-brown skinny jeans, a loose T-shirt protruding from under a high-fashion sweater, cord necklace with a matching bracelet, he appears to be the easygoing type, with panache.

"You've seen an angel before?" I ask again, unable to hide my enthusiasm this time.

"Of course. I think my best friend is one. If you met my brother, Ashton, you'd be forgiven for thinking he is one too."

"Are you one?"

He eyes me cheekily. "If you keep asking, I will be forced to lie to you."

I grin. "Sorry."

"I know you're trying your luck, but what I want to know is why you're so eager to know?"

I bite my lip, taking a deep sigh. "I just want to know how you can tell who is what just by looking at them."

"You don't." He swallows a sip. "Some you can smell, but with most you have to watch and learn. Like they say, by their fruits you shall know them."

"Can you tell what I am?"

"Are you something?"

"If I say I am?"

"Then, I would say give me two weeks to figure you out."

"Or, is the two weeks to get close to me?"

"Maybe." He chuckles quietly, brushes his hair off his face. "You're a beautiful lady, after all."

"I know." I raise my brow, and stare into his eyes. It seems I have found the key to the answers I long for, and so I lean in to kiss him.

He responds as I expect, holding back at first, but the kiss gets stronger in the end, and I pull back with a smile.

"Surprised?" I ask.

"It's not every day a beautiful girl kisses me like that."

"Why not?" I stare at his smiling eyes. "You're a handsome boy, after all."

He laughs.

Another quick glance at the clock and I signal to Emily it's time to go. I swallow the remainder of my drink and plant a goodbye kiss on the face of the familiar stranger before heading toward the door.

Call me. Call me. I say as I walk off, and ...

"Hey, wait!" His voice stops me midway. "I don't know your name," he says.

I turn around laughing, and stretch out my hand to touch Emily who staggers toward me. "Nor do I," I say to the stranger.

"Sean!" He rushes to me. "My name is Sean."

"I'm Alex, and this is Emily, my best friend."

"I could give you my number, and instead of attacking the bartender, you could call me when you need a drink," he whispers.

"Sounds like a plan," I whisper back.

From his pocket, he brings out a smart phone, and we exchange numbers.

He plants a kiss on my cheek before I turn to tighten my grip on Emily's waist as we head toward the door. Outside, we cross to the parking area where the chauffeur waits.

"What was that about?" Emily asks when we are seated in the car.

"I gave him a cupcake."

She stares at me with wide eyes. "You kissed him? Why?"

"You mean besides being attractive and funny? He reminds me of Chan, kind of a wild Chan, plus the dimple on his right cheek ..."

Emily arches her eyebrows. "Is that a *but* on your lips?"

I sigh. "The kiss ... I mean there was nothing to it. Don't get me wrong, he's a fantastic kisser, but ..."

"No butterflies."

"Nope." I purse my lips. "No butterflies."

"So why are you leading him on?"

"Good question." I shift to face her with a serious face. "When he stopped the fight, he asked me not to show myself to humans, and when he realized I had no idea what he was talking about, he backed off. He must know what I am, and I intend to keep seeing him until he tells me."

Emily shakes her head. "You will stop at nothing, Lexie, I see that now."

"Not till I find out what I am."

As Emily shuts her eyes with exhaustion, I pull her closer to rest her head on my lap. I give in, and my mind drags me back to Zachary Van-Bailey and those images.

VIII

GOING ONCE, TWICE, AND DEAL

The silence is killing me. On days like today when my mother chooses to hibernate in her room, to hide the hurt she thinks I can't see, it makes me feel helpless.

I have no idea what is wrong with her.

In casual, dark-brown skinny jeans and a mustard cashmere sweater, I stand by the window in the breakfast room, my hands hugging a steaming cappuccino mug.

With Mother still in her room, the TV off, it's quiet except for the sound of the coffee machine.

I stare at the flower baskets hanging outside by the porch swing and take a sip from the mug. The warmth from the steam and the comforting smell of the cappuccino seems to be just what I need.

Outside, the wind sings through the trees, and the leaves dance as if to rejoice, giving thanks to the heavens for the promise of heavy rain. It seldom rains in Ashbourne, and though every sign points to the cloudy skies, I doubt we will actually get a shower.

A week has passed since the accident, and we celebrated New Year's Eve yesterday. Apart from the arrival of my Theta Scorpii from the garage today, I also look forward to the Hurricane Auction. I'm bidding for the land I need for the racetrack.

The thought of how close I am to my dream fills my stomach with a warm sensation. I smile, imagining the future.

An all-girls Grand Prix motor racing...

The music coming from my mother's room distracts my pleasant thoughts. Six days in a row it's been *Mozart Andante* every morning. "Not again," I murmur.

Yesterday, Mother offered to accompany me to the auction, but after considering her current mood, I told her not to worry. Channing, before he left, arranged for me to meet a friend to guide me through the auction procedures.

Bidding begins at 2PM. I have already prepared for the joys of celebration—champagne with Emily at the famous Nair Saif, in the heart of Ashbourne City. Of course, with every celebration there has to be success first; I must return home with my name on that property.

Perhaps I could use the celebration as an excuse to invite Sean.

Four days ago, I sent him a *hello* text, and that worked just as I intended; he wants us to meet next week.

Mug to my mouth again, I swallow my last sip. Then I see my mother, still in her cream robe, crumpled pale blue tissues in her hand. She walks past the hallway heading toward the kitchen.

"Mom!" She hasn't gone to work for four days now. I wonder if it's the almost fatal accident causing her to behave in such a manner or perhaps something else.

I place the mug by the telephone table and rush after her. As soon as she turns, I force a hug on her. "I'm sorry, and I mean it. It will never happen again, I promise."

She pulls back to cradle my face. "You don't understand, do you?" Her voice comes out muffled. "You don't know how important you are to me. You are my life; the only part of your father I have left. I lost him, and I can't lose you too, Lexie, so stop trying to expose yourself. Do you understand that at all?"

I nod, tears welling up in my eyes. She has said this over and over in the last seven days, so yeah, I understand her, just as I did the first time.

I link my arm with hers and lead her toward the breakfast room. I pull out a chair for her. "I'll get you coffee," I say and rush to the kitchen.

"John is asking if you could accompany him to the jewelers next week." Mother says as I place her coffee on the table in front of her.

"John De Luca?"

She nods and scoops two brown sugar cubes into her coffee.

I know it's John De Luca. I just had to say his name in full; everybody does, except my mother. It seems his first name and surname can't be separated.

Leaning on the wide windowsill, I cross my arms, waiting for her to answer.

"He wants you to find a gift for Rebecca for their wedding."

I hesitate for a moment, understanding now why she's distressed. John De Luca and Rebecca are getting married. "So, they set a date at last?"

I watch her, wistful as she stirs the teaspoon in her cup. Then I cough.

She blinks back to the real world. "What was it you said?"

"Why me?" I say.

She looks at me with a frown, confused.

"John De Luca and I, we speak cars and jets, not diamonds," I state. "So why choose me to help with her gift?"

I know John De Luca is fond of me, and I like him too. But, as Chan once pointed out, the extra kisses he always showers on my forehead makes me a bit uneasy.

Apart from that, I love his company. It's normal for us to spend an afternoon at the Ashbourne Air Force parade. Either to talk about cars or I'd watch John fly the fighter jets."

"You might not adore diamonds as much as Rebecca does, but John seems to think you know what she likes," Mother says.

I want to shake my head, but instead, I watch my mother. With sorrowful eyes she stares out the window, her thoughts absorbed with a sickness I know too well.

"It gets better in time." I hold a smirk.

A soft smile forms on her face. "You are so alike in so many ways."

"Whom do you mean? Me, and Rebecca, or John De Luca?"

She blinks, then widens her eyes as if she's just come out of a trance. "You and your father."

My father. I frown.

"The way you behave sometimes reminds me of him. He drives me nuts just like you do." She laughs as if to pity herself.

"Drives?"

"Hmm?" She grimaces and then realizes her mistake. "Oh, I can never think of him as in the past, can I?"

Channing comes to my mind, and though he's not dead, I can still identify with my mother's thought process.

"What exactly drives you nuts so I can do it again?" I steal a look at her, a smile tugging at the corners of my mouth.

She glowers at me playfully, then sighs. "Your passion," she says. "You are like him. When you feel passionate about something, you don't give up. It scares me, sometimes."

I want to ask more questions, but I fear that might stop her from saying more now that her eyes are close to tearing. She never speaks about my father. I wonder what's happening with her, and if now would be a good time to ask to see a photo of him.

"Don't ever do anything like that to me, Alexandra. Do you hear me?" She tries to put strength in her words.

And just like that, we are back to the accident talk again.

No, it's not a good time, I conclude, stepping closer to her. I lean to press a gentle kiss on her cheek. "I hear you, and I give you my word, Mom. That won't happen again—I'm sorry."

"Good." She kisses my hand by her shoulder. "Now, let me have the keys."

"Keys?"

"Give me the keys to the Theta Scorpii."

"Mom, please. I promi—"

"Give me the keys, Lexie." She raises her voice. "I'm not budging this time."

I cast my eyes to her open palm. I want to object, but I have no grounds; actions have consequences. Shoving my hand in and out of my jeans pocket, I drop the keys into her hand.

"I'll lock the bike and the car in the garage. You won't have them back until I feel you deserve them." She stands to leave.

"Mom, please—"

"I love you too, honey." She kisses my forehead and walks off, disappearing down the hallway.

Guilty?

Yes, I am in every way. What I did that day, putting Emily and Zachary in danger, was unacceptable. I'm wrong, and this time I can't blame my mother.

❧

With no car or bike to drive to the auction, I opt for the common means—a taxi. As it arrives, I glance at the clouds again; they seem darker than before.

I think of Emily, how she wanted to come, but because of recent events, her father prepared a busy schedule for her, a schedule that doesn't have me in it.

Turning into a quiet country lane, the taxi driver slows down, driving with caution through the stony road. He follows around the curves and increases the speed gradually. Through the sunken lane, we come out into the fields of Hurricane Auction House and there I gasp. I had no idea such ancient buildings still existed.

Located in the countryside, toward the border of the resort City of Hurricane, Hurricane Auction House stands on the hilly lands of a Country Club, surrounded by manicured grounds, has a green forest of pine trees, and a glorious botanical garden. Gothic looking with tall towers, gables crickets, pinnacles and rose windows, the building resembles a cathedral.

"Keep the change." I give the driver double what I owe.

My bag on my shoulder, I cross toward the huge building, climb the stone stairs and arrive at the entrance door. The bronze Cuenca doors make me feel smaller than I am as I walk past.

A pleasant gentleman in a classy, vanilla colored suit, white shirt without a tie, opens the second door for me. Adjusting a hair strand back to merge in his side curled pompadour, he smiles at me. "Miss Watson?"

I nod.

"I'm Spenser, a friend of arh ... of Channing."

"Alexandra." I curl my lips into a soft smile, extending my hand to shake his. "You can call me Alexandra, or Lexie."

"This way, please, Alexandra or Lexie." He grins as I smile, directing me toward the wide open doors. "You're beautiful, like he said, and surprisingly ..." He scratches his head.

"Surprisingly ... what?"

"Surprisingly, elegant. Almost too fragile for fast cars, I'd say."

I want to smile, but my frown deepens.

"Forgive me, I don't mean to sound rude. It's just that when I heard about your love for the track, I expected you would be more like—"

"A tomboy?"

"That's not the exact word I would use, but I can say, yes, that fits it well."

We smile at each other.

Spenser pushes through another set of wooden doors to reveal a large reception area.

A tall, red-haired, glamorous lady stares at me with a wrinkled brow as she scrutinizes my membership card. I read the name badge on her chest – Eden. Her pink lips spread to form a tight smile.

"A Dainty? Spenser, come on."

"Watch your mouth, Eden," Spenser says. "Channing's Joanne, Alexandra."

"Joanne Alessandra?" Her accent changes to Italian.

Spenser nods.

Now she stares at me with a different look; one full of admiration, if not envy. "I'm honored to meet you, Alexandra." She hands the card back to me and signals Spenser for my bag. "Safekeeping until the ball or whenever you like."

"Ball?" I ask Spenser as we move on toward the foyer looking for door number eleven. "I'm having no ball. And what's a Dainty?"

Spenser smiles, but doesn't answer as he continues walking.

"Where are you going?" I ask, slowing my pace to stop in front of a thick wooden door with iron hinges. "This is it. Door eleven."

Spenser turns to face me. "You might want to change into something more fitting. It is customary for guests to dress—"

"Customary? Not for me." I move ahead and push the doors open.

"My God." I freeze, staring at the guests.

It's not just the polished, glamorous appearance of the faces staring back at me, not the smell of their expensive perfumes, nor the priceless heavy, corset-like costumes that cling on their bodies, but also the room—the fortress in which they stand.

Huge granite pillars, gothic style walls with large stained glass windows. Ribbed vault ceiling above the magnificent arches. It's breathtaking. There are no formal seats, just random antique stools set in semi-circular lines facing the richly carved podium.

"Alexandra?" Spenser whispers.

"Hmm?" I go to him as the crowd mumbles; possibly talking about my rather casual outfit.

"Don't worry. They're probably talking about your beautiful hair." Spenser extends his arm in a gentlemanly fashion.

"How come no one told me there was such a theatrical dress code?" I complain as Spenser shuts the doors again and we step back into the corridor. "I mean, did you see what they're wearing? They look like they just came from an ancient era. And wherever did they find those gowns?"

Spenser stifles a laugh. "We have gowns here. I tried to tell you, remember?"

I remain silent, and he shakes his head, leading me to the last room down the corridor. The room is full of exquisite outfits, just like the ones I've seen the guests wearing. The costumes are displayed on various mannequins.

"Oh, these are artistic. Can I try some on?"

Spenser chuckles. "You are free to do as you wish, Alexandra."

My eyes pause on the colorful exotic birds in cages further at the corner of the room. I smile and walk toward them.

If I were a bird, I would fly away and find Chan. There are ten birds, all unique in color which includes yellow, deep blue, green and electric-blue.

"You have twenty minutes. Pick what you like. Meanwhile, I'll register your interest on lot … twenty-one, right?"

"Right." I turned to thank him and he leaves, shutting the door behind him.

A few minutes later, I pause to admire a gorgeous costume; long and designed with delicate fabric. Enchanted by subtle beige, exquisite embroidery and layers of lace, I pick it as my choice, and exhale when I find it's my size. It's soft, but heavier than my usual outfits. I turn to glance in the mirror positioned in the middle of the room, and I smile, loving the elusive lace covering my chest and arms.

I hate new shoes, so I settle for the vintage heels on my feet, and thank God, they match. Before leaving I stop to say goodbye to the birds.

In one of the cages, the yellow bird is stuck—its leg tangled in moss and thin twigs, and I'm thinking I can't leave it like that; I have to set it free. Hand on the hasp, I turn it, and as it opens, an alarm rings.

"No, no," I whisper, trying to shut the door, but three birds fly out before the door closes.

From a distance, I hear urgent footsteps and panicking voices drawing closer. With the birds now flying and twittering around the room, I realize I have lost control. I sneak out, but I'm not the only one to succeed—the birds do too.

In my dreamy dress, I begin to chase after them. In front of me the double doors open, letting in a flood of light. A calm breeze cools my flushed skin; two men in black uniforms also rush in.

"No!" I cry, watching the birds flying outside above a breathtaking garden. The garden has thick hedges, and a long parallel line of dwarf conifers set amongst colorful foliage of flowers.

"Get her!" one of the uniformed men says.

"No! Please." I struggle as they grab me, securing my arms behind my back. "I will pay whatever the cost. I need to be in the auction room right now."

They say nothing, pulling me back through the doors.

A phone rings. The man with a mustache releases his right hand to fish the phone from his jacket pocket. He speaks in Italian as he answers the call. When I hear the name Van-Bailey, I grimace.

He hangs up, and communicates with his partner in Italian, and mentions the name Van-Bailey again. I flinch as they drag me outside, to the garden.

"Spenser knows me! Call Spenser." My breathing quickens, my chest rising and falling erratically.

I'm preparing to fight when, all of a sudden, they release me and begin to apologize, in English this time. I shoot a harsh glare at them, flexing my stiff wrist.

"Apologies Ma'am," they chorus and walk away.

I take a deep sigh and examine myself, making sure my costume is still presentable. Gazing into the skies, I see the birds. They fly in circles; wings floating in a steady motion.

"Hey, beautiful." A grinning Zachary startles me as he appears beside me, hands behind his back.

I return the smile. "Hey, knight."

"Knight?" He moves his gaze from the birds flying in the sky to my eyes.

"Apart from saving me from those angry officers, you look like a knight in that outfit." I drop my gaze to admire the coat of arms pinned on the front of his snug fitting, buttoned up jacket. The matching dark-brown, skinny pants tucked in the knee-length boots, makes him fit in with the crowd inside.

"You like knights?"

"Only the knight-errant."

Zachary chuckles and takes a step closer to me. "What do we do with the free birds?"

"We fly after them," I say, cautious about the distance between us. He looks different today with his neat, wavy hair combed back.

"They will come back." Zachary takes a sigh. "They always do." After a moment, he turns to study my expression. "I was just thinking about you before you invaded my privacy." He comes nearer again, our hands almost touching.

I hug myself to avoid his hand. "Is that so? What exactly were you thinking?"

"That you never told me your name."

"You never asked."

He leans to whisper in my ear. "Alexandra …"

My heart explodes. I can't tell if it's his soft laugh or the sound of his voice in my ears. His saying Alexandra sounds to me as if he has given me a brand new name.

"You know." I inhale lightly. "So why do you ask?"

"I didn't." He smirks. "Give me your hand, let's take a walk."

"No." My lips curl into smile, but I stop them, and walk away from him, heading toward the arched garden path.

"You enjoy me chasing you, right?" he calls to me.

"I think you enjoy chasing me."

"I'm not the one running."

My back to him, I skip around playfully to face him. "I just like the speed, it doesn't matter who's chasing whom."

"Is that so?" He bites his lip marching toward me. "Maybe you should start running faster."

I'm already running, giggling as I speed along the gravel path with him chasing after me. I accelerate toward the colorful, elongated, pergola engulfed with climbing roses and green vines. I'm tempted to stop and indulge in the earth smell of old stone and roses, but I think Zachary chasing after me is more fun.

Halfway through columns, I slow down and look back. I don't see Zachary; he's gone. I pause, guarded as I look everywhere, but he's nowhere.

"Zachary?" I call in a whisper at first. "Zachary!"

No answer.

I turn and take a few steps back, a little worried. In a flash, Zachary startles me from behind, clutches my waist as I scream, and while I struggle to free myself, he holds me to his chest.

Laughing as he lets go of me, I turn and throw him a playful punch. From deep in his chest, I hear him laugh, his eyes delightful as he pulls me closer again. My arms almost circle his neck, but end up on his chest. The flashing images come back; the same images of us kissing and the biting. I pull back.

"What's wrong?" Zachary's eyebrows knit together.

"The auction! What time is it?"

He looks down at his watch and swears. "It started fifteen minutes ago. Come." Reaching for my hand, he holds me, and we rush back to the building together.

"One hundred and ten thousand ... One twenty ..." the auctioneer calls as we sneak in.

"Alexandra." Spenser rushes to whisper in my ear. "I've been looking everywhere for you. He's calling your lot. And here ..." He passes me my bidding card.

"Thank you," I say.

"By the way, that dress looks amazing on you. Good choice," Spenser adds.

I smile at him and move toward Zachary at the back, who's gesturing for me to join him.

"That's my lot." Zachary and I turn to whisper the same words to each other as I sit beside him.

We laugh, but following the laughter are the baffled frowns. We are going to bid against each other, and we begin arguing while the bidding goes on.

"Zachary, I'm sure you can get any other property you want. You must leave this for me," I argue.

"Must." He laughs. "Did you say must?"

"One forty," the auctioneer calls.

Zachary raises his card, and I roll my eyes.

"Okay, please." I place my hand on his free hand.

He glances at my hand on his, and smiles, interlacing our fingers before raising them to his chest.

"One fifty at the door," the auctioneer calls again. "One sixty?"

Zachary raises his card again. "I'm sorry." He kisses the back of my hand. "I need it for the racetrack I told you about."

"So do I," I almost scream. "Zachary, please, this is my life." I raise my card, bidding for one seventy.

He raises his card again to bid for one ninety. "Tell me why I should leave this for you. It's also my life."

"Well," I hesitate. "Because you, like a knight-errant, would do the honorable thing and not compete with a lady."

Zachary shakes his head and laughs in silence.

"Two hundred?" The bidding rises. "Two hundred, anyone?"

I raise my card.

"Maybe we should team up," he suggests. "Your beautiful ideas with my irresistible pocket. Together we can build passion, speed, and whatever else you like on our new racetrack." He raises his card to bid on two twenty.

"That way we both win." I flash a smile at him and raise my card for two- thirty.

"Exactly," he whispers.

There's murmuring in the room, and I realize we are now the only two still bidding on lot twenty-one.

I shake my head. "No. I'll accept if we split halfway on everything, half my pocket, half my ideas and the same for you."

Zachary raises his brow at the same time the auctioneer calls for two-forty. "An equal partner, I see." He nods, smiling.

He bids two-forty.

I raise my card for two-fifty, still waiting for his answer.

"Fine." He gives in at last and raises his card for two-sixty.

I raise mine for two-seventy. "You mean that?" I ask, unable to hide my excitement.

"I do. Completely." Delight is etched on his face as he stares into my eyes. At the same time, he raises his card, bidding on two-ninety.

"One more thing," I say, and he frowns a little, waiting for me to speak. "We must enroll girls for racing."

"As you wish, beautiful." He smiles. "Deal?"

"Deal." I seal it.

Smiling, the auctioneer turns to me and calls three hundred. He calls once more, but I shake my head.

"Will take two nine five?" He tries again.

I stare at Zachary, wondering if I can trust him. He winks. Again I shake my head at the auctioneer.

"At two hundred and ninety thousand," he calls once, twice, and slams the hammer on the third; lot twenty-one to Zachary Van-Bailey—to us.

Zachary takes my hand as the crowd cheers, and plants a kiss on my cheek. "It's good doing business with you. Two-ninety is a bargain."

I agree. My hand still in his, I fight to suppress the flashing images, but they keep coming. In the end, I snatch my hand from him.

This time he turns to me with a frown. "Are you going to tell me why you keep pulling your hand away from me?"

"They are my hands, not yours."

"Or is it the heat, you can't handle?"

"You feel it too?" My voice comes out fainter than a whisper.

He takes my hand again and stares into my eyes with a mischievous gaze. "Is that all you feel?" He quizzes, fiddling with my fingers. "Does your heart not beat as hard as mine?"

"This isn't funny, Zachary."

※

Drops of rain begin to fall as Zachary and I take a stroll down the garden path an hour later. Pushing the glass doors of Hurricane café, we enter a warm area with old wooden chairs and couches. We choose seats by the small, wooden table next to the windows, where we can see the rain as it continues kissing the ground, one drop at a time.

"So how does it feel to be Zachary Van-Bailey?" I ask after ordering a cappuccino.

Zachary takes a sip and smiles at me. "There is no one like me out there—only one Zachary Van-Bailey IV, and I get to have a drink with Alexandra." He swirls his mug a little.

"Oh come on, as if …"

"You think it's no big deal?" He pauses with the mug halfway to his lips. "Tell me this. If I were anyone else and invited you for a drink, would you have said 'yes,' or 'no'?" He swallows a mouthful as I contemplate my answer. Before I can give it, he adds, "You would have said 'no' without thinking twice, wouldn't you?"

"Not if *anyone else* had given me the race of my life, saved me from some psycho security guards, and agreed to be my dream partner."

"Dream partner! I like that." He grins. The light in his eyes fades; replacing it is a hint of sadness.

"Are you alright?"

"I almost killed you that night."

"If you were pointing a gun at me, I didn't see it."

He smiles, eyeing me with emphasis. "If you were a book, you'd be written in Japanese."

"Why? Because you can't read Japanese?"

"No." He breathes in, resting his head on his fist as he watches me. "The letters appear the same, but when you search closely, you'll see that each symbol is unique."

"Um, I see …"

Relaxing in his seat, he glances toward the counter. "Hey, you want a cupcake?"

I nod with the mug to my lips. "Sure."

"What flavor would you like?" He's already on his feet as he asks.

"Any. Surprise me."

He leans to position his face inches from mine. "Let me see if I can translate this Japanese," he teases, his gaze shifting from my eyes to my lips. "There," he whispers, stroking my blushing cheek. "I think I got it," he smirks and makes his way to the cake counter.

When he's back, he places a small box of red velvet cupcakes on the table in front of me.

"My God! I love these," I sing.

"See?" You're not that hard to read after all."

While we enjoy the warm drinks, I listen and laugh at Zachary's intelligent humor, smiling and giggling, acknowledging his hand rubbing mine now and again.

It's no longer raining when we decide to leave. Without thinking, we take the long way back to the auction house where I'm to collect my bag and take a taxi home.

It looks as if it's going to rain again, but that doesn't bother me. We take our time sauntering down the pathway, discussing fast cars. This time he's asking me questions about motor racing. How I fell in love with speed.

After a while, we don't speak but stroll side by side. Beneath the leafy pergola, Zachary pauses to hide from the rain that's begun to fall again.

"Let's give it a few minutes." He squeezes my hand.

The rain doesn't stop, but comes down harder. We try to run, but it's all in vain. When we reach the end of the garden path, we are already soaked. My wet dress feels heavy with the rain. We give up in the end and stroll in the rain as if it's sunshine.

"Aren't you going to change into something less um … wet?" Zachary comments as I pick up my bag from Eden. "I've been trying so hard to stop my eyes from lingering in the wrong places, but now it seems everywhere is wrong."

I watch as he tries not to smile, but eventually I see the twinkle in his eyes. "I mean; we could change into something comfy and find a place to eat lunch while waiting for the rain to stop," Zachary says.

"I'm under curfew since the accident. I must be home by six," I confess. "Besides, I love the rain."

"It's a good thing, I love rain too." He smiles.

We walk out into the rain and head to the taxi waiting area. Zachary is not talking as much as he was before. Then he goes silent, holding on to my hand. I'm trying not to panic as the flashing images disturb me again. Now they seem to blend in with the flashing lighting and the heavy rain.

The taxi arrives, and Zachary holds my hand tighter.

"So this is it?" I lean to speak into Zachary's ears, and step away.

He nods but says nothing.

I force a smile and wave at him sheepishly, the rain dripping on his face.

"Alex." Zachary rushes to open the taxi door for me and turns to give me a tight hug.

The noise from the rain is deafening, so we speak in the other's ears.

"So it's my birthday... Saturday the twenty-eighth of April …" Zachary breathes in my ear, his hands on my waist. "Maybe you could show up and make my day."

I sigh, pull back to look up at his brown eyes. "You do realize that's four months from now?" I say in his ear.

"I know." He rubs my waist a little, stirring my pounding heart. "I'm just booking my date on your calendar before others do."

I stifle a laugh, my mouth still by his ear. "Why not? Send me an invitation."

"Yeah, why not?" he replies in a low tone. "I'll call you."

"You don't have my number."

"Don't worry about that. We are dream partners now, remember?" He takes a deep breath and lets it out with measured slowness. "I'll find your number, your house, and I'll find you."

Our cheeks touch as I pull away. He holds me back with urgency and kisses my cheek. I'm electrified, and moisture floods my mouth as he lingers just above my lips, his right hand moving to my wet hair. He stares into my eyes and leans in again, but I step back; scared of the flashing images becoming a reality.

"What's wrong?" he asks as I gasp. "I was just going to kiss your other cheek and you ..." His eyes searching mine, he trails off.

I drop my head; nervous. With his index finger, he tilts my chin up, forcing me to look at him. "You thought I was going to kiss you like this ..." Softly, he leans to brush his warm lips on mine. He pauses for a second watching my reaction, then continues, urging my lips to part, and they do. I want to pull away, but my knees go weak, plus the butterflies—a fluttering sensation within my stomach paralyzes me. I return the kiss, surprisingly more intense than I intended. He closes in the slight gap between us, his hand surging in my wet hair while the other pulls me to his chest as he intensifies the kiss. We are both breathless, but we don't stop. I think of pushing him off, but my hands are doing the opposite.

"I'm charging for this!" the taxi driver beeps his horn.

I open my eyes, and realize my hands are still pulling Zachary's soaked jacket toward me. I drop it in an instant.

"Charge all you want!" Zachary refuses to move, his eyes on mine, and one hand still holding onto my waist. "Let me take you home." He offers as he rubs my waist lightly with his thumb.

I shake my head. "No, I'm good." Carefully, I remove his hand from my waist and duck into the taxi.

"Alexandra, wait!" Zachary brings out a few notes and passes them to the taxi driver.

"What do you think you're doing?" I grimace.

"You wouldn't let me take you home. At least let me pay for the taxi."

I don't have the strength to argue with him and so I nod, my eyes avoiding his.

"Bye." Zachary leans over to the window and touches my hand, smiling.

With every breath, I fight to stop my heart pounding. Bit by bit, as the taxi drives off, my heart becomes stable again. I stare back at Zachary and watch him standing still with hands in his pockets, and the rain still dripping through his hair.

"Shit!" I close my eyes and slam my head back.

How did I let this happen? What will I tell Emily ... and my mother?

IX

I Don't Think I've Told You This Before ...

Knight: Favorite season?

    I smile at the text message from Zachary. I saved his number as Knight in case of prying eyes.

Me: Autumn. It's 6am, in case you don't know.

I'm in the kitchen. It's Monday today. Marie is off, and so I thought to prepare breakfast for my mother. I hate cooking, but this is something I have to do today. Yesterday, I received a call from my mother's lawyer, telling me she will be calling my mother to confirm the contract details this morning.

It's been over a week since the auction, and I still haven't told my mother about the partnership with Zachary. I only told her I won the bid. The celebration didn't happen.

I'm still finding the courage to tell my best friend how I ended up locking lips with the man of her dreams.

Knight: Autumn Reigns, it is then. Were you dreaming of me?

I giggle at Zachary's response and continue making the sandwich for my mother.

The aroma from the brewing coffee reassures me I'm doing something right. On the other hand, the loud music—*Eine kleine Nachtmusik* by

Mozart, tells me my mother is running late. She plays it most mornings; something to do with the music helping her speed up and yet at the same time feeling in control.

What is stopping me from telling my mother about the partnership? I place the sandwich in the toaster and turn it on.

After all, it's not as if I have done anything wrong. Out of the ordinary, yes, but not criminal.

Fear of the unknown. It does that to people.

How can I explain doing something so unpredictable, and serious, like agreeing to a partnership with Zachary—a stranger? When it comes to my mother—I always hesitate.

What is it, really? Is it the beating of my heart before spitting the words out? Or perhaps it's my mother's *unpredictably predictable* reaction?

The music goes down. It's low, but I can still hear it, which makes my heart beat faster.

"Alexandra!" Mother calls from upstairs.

"This is it," I mumble. From the tone of Mother's voice, the word from the lawyer must have reached her ears.

I remove the black apron and make my way upstairs. A quick knock on the slightly open door and I enter her bedroom. She doesn't give me a chance to say good morning before she begins her rampage.

"When were you planning to tell me, Alexandra?" Her face is creaseless, but I can see the storm in her eyes.

"Umm … I don't know what you mean."

"Partnership with a Van-Bailey?" She sighs, staring at me. "How? Why? I don't understand."

I wipe my hands on my silk yellow robe. On TV, the Ash News anchor concluding on the six o'clock news disturbs my thoughts.

"Say something!"

"It was either that or I'd lose everything, Mom."

"What do you mean lose everything?" Her eyes flicker to the top of my head. "And what did I say about fixing your hair in the morning?"

"Mother—"

"You're still young, sweetheart. Partnership with a Van-Bailey is nothing, but ludicrous." She stretches to pick a pair of earrings from the dresser.

"Mom—"

Her pager beeps. She pauses to read it. I drift off, admiring her in the pencil black dress; how it shapes her hourglass figure.

She looks up at me. "I do everything to take the eyes of the world off you, but what do you do? Exactly the opposite."

Her speed almost in tune with the orchestra, she pins her hair into an elegant up-do, stumbles as she shoves the right foot then left into the silver heels. At the same time, she hugs her leather purse and folders to her chest and rushes past me, out of the room to the landing.

"I'm disappointed in you, Alexandra."

"I'm sorry ..." I rush after her as she speeds down the corridor.

"And that's the same Zachary who almost killed your best friend the other day, isn't he?"

"I know this sound crazy, Mom." I skip in front of her, to look into her eyes. "Zachary and I met at the auction. We realized we were bidding on the same property ..."

She opens her mouth just as she widens her eyes, but I refuse to give her the opportunity to interrupt me.

"We thought it best not to bid against each other, so we teamed up."

She wrinkles her nose as if what I've just said is disgusting. "Good Lord, what's burning?"

"Oh!" Inaudibly, I swear, my feet almost conforming to the tautness of the music as I hustle down the marble stairs to the kitchen.

I've never been a good cook, but to burn a sandwich ... That's the last time I'll try.

As my mother enters the kitchen, I hand her the brewed coffee. She shakes her head, laughing. "Very thoughtful, sweetheart, but I wonder ..."

"What?" I suppress a smile. "What do you wonder?"

"Is it your conscience making me coffee or your fear?" She stares at me over the mug on her lips. "Fear of the unknown. It does that to people."

I stifle a laugh, resisting the urge to roll my eyes. "I'm trying to be a good daughter, and here you are wondering."

Placing the folders aside, she raises the mug to her lips. "I'm still trying to figure out how this happened. I thought you hated the *obnoxious* Zachary." Her hand rises, two fingers quoting *obnoxious*.

"And you were right," I admit. "I didn't know him then."

Pursing her lips, she shakes her head. "And now you do? You spent two hours with Zachary and you think you know him?"

"Three, actually." I move closer to her, and with a sigh, I take her hands into mine. "Forget Zachary, and look at it this way ... If things don't work out, at least I haven't exhausted my trust fund."

"So you agree there's a chance this might be the biggest mistake you've ever made?"

"I was just indulging your lack of faith in me, Mother."

She sighs. "Lack of faith in the partnership, not in you, sweetheart."

"Two heads are better than one, you once told me."

"It's what's in the second head that worries me. Why did Zachary agree to this partnership?"

"He thought it would be a good idea to add a feminine touch to his concepts, that's all."

"Okay I can accept your tummy was perhaps, full of the butterfly effect when you decided to believe such a lame excuse, but for you to think I can believe that too ... that's madness, honey."

"Okay, okay, I didn't care about his reasons. I focused on what I wanted."

"Well, it's clear to me he also focused on what he wanted—you."

She stares at me, waiting for my response, but I'm only thinking of what I want from her, and that does not include upsetting her. She remains silent for a while, studying me as she finishes her coffee.

"With your blessings, by tomorrow I would be a proud co-owner of Autumn Reigns." I steal a look at her.

"Autumn Reigns?"

"Yes, that's what we named the racetrack."

She rolls her eyes then pauses to look into my eyes as if she's searching for my soul. "Fine," she says. "I said I would support you in this, and though you went behind my back and did this thing with Zachary, I will keep to my word."

Biting my tongue and kissing her cheeks, I thank her.

"You can call in for lunch if you get bored," she says, returning my kisses.

"I'll be fine. I have a date."

She raises her eyebrow. "With Zachary?"

"My God, Mother, no, with—"

The beeping pager interrupts us, again.

"I should rush, honey." She grabs her folders. "Don't even think of stealing the keys for the Theta Scorpii. I noted the mileage," she warns and heads for the door.

I follow her and wave as she drives off. "Yes!" I clench my fists with joy.

The weather appears calm, but lacks the brightness and spirit of the sunshine. Inch by inch, the clouds drift along in gray batches, but they appear too light to shed water. Nonetheless, the brisk winds have succeeded, declaring today a dull and dreary day.

I have a date with Sean; that's what I wanted to tell my mother before her pager interrupted us.

Sean and I will meet at the Nair for lunch, but that's after a visit to the beauty salon with Emily. I dread facing Emily to confess about my meeting with Zachary.

Since it's six thirty, I treat myself to another hour of slumber on the large couch in the living room. With my mother's Mozart off, the house is quiet.

I hope Emily will not turn up too soon. She has been complaining I'm avoiding her, and it's not a lie. My excuse, however, is that she has started college, and I don't want to distract her.

While I relax on the couch, half-paying attention to the breakfast show on TV, nostalgia swallows me, and I dream of Channing.

"Say it as it is, Jo," he would say in his soft voice. *"There's nothing to fear."*

Giving in to the soporific television, I close my eyes, relaxing my head on the soft cushion, just to rise again in haste. The noise of the intercom wakes me. Emily, I conclude, staggering to the intercom.

"Hello," I say in the handset.

"Alexandra, it's Zachary."

"What! Who?" I rub my eyes, glance at the front gate through the video intercom, and there he is.

It's him, Zachary, in his Zetra Zeus. I press enter and put the receiver down.

Without a moment to think, I skip to the mirror in the entrance hall to see what needs fixing. Staring at my reflection in the mirror, I give up. Everything needs a fix; bed hair, the sleepy eyes, the yellow robe and the bare face.

A quick moment of composure, then I pull the door open.

Our eyes meet, and we instantaneously grin at each other. In a gray military-style shirt and a pair of trendy, dark-blue jeans, Zachary stands still with both hands in his jean pockets.

"You found me." I laugh.

He remains silent, staring at me.

I replace the smile with a frown. "Is everything all right with Autumn Reigns?"

He chortles. "You make it sound as if we have a child together."

He comes nearer. I should say something like *come in*, but with him so close, it seems my thoughts are no longer mine, my eyes hypnotized by his. I blink slowly, imagining how ridiculous I must look in the bright yellow robe, with my tousled hair. If only I listened to my mother. I turn away from his gaze.

Then I hear him speak. "I don't think I have told you this before, but I believe I have repeated it in my head hundreds of times ..." Slowly, he steps closer.

I raise my head to look into his eyes. "What is it?"

"You are beautiful, like really beautiful ... I'm just being honest."

I search his eyes to see if he means it, but all I see is his brown pupils piercing mine. His eyes are brilliant white with a glistening chocolate iris.

He blinks, rubbing his jaws as his gaze drops from my eyes to my lips. Heat flashes on my poor, pale face. I feel I need to turn away, but before I can hide the blush, his fingers reach out for my cheek.

My lips tremble, going against my senses, but not against my heart. I close my eyes as he leans in to press his soft lips on mine, my heart exploding as our lips mingle. And, of course, the butterflies. His kiss is different this time, more like a need for satisfaction rather than an exploration. Touching his nose with mine, he plants tender kisses on my cheeks.

"Aren't you going to invite me in?" He laughs breathlessly over my ear.

I lead him to the informal living room. At first, we both seem overwhelmed and can't say or do anything apart from smiling at each other. I offer him a seat, but instead of sitting, he strolls toward the picture hanging on the wall.

"Is that you and your sister?"

"That's my mother." I step to stand beside him. "And that's Grandpa Henry, and his late wife, Grandma Catherine."

He smiles. "I see where you got the hair from."

A moment later, I carry a photo album as we move to the kitchen. I offer Zachary breakfast, hoping he would say no, but I'm wrong. While I think of what simple meal to prepare, Zachary's eyes pause on the burned sandwich. I pick it up in haste and throw it in the bin.

"Was that your attempt at cooking?" He begins to laugh.

"Will you stop laughing?"

"I'm not …" He screws up his face, trying not to laugh, I guess. "Why don't you sit down and tell me about yourself, while I make us breakfast?"

"You can cook?"

"Of course." He snickers, folding his sleeves, ready to begin.

I show him where the pans and utensils are. While he prepares eggs and creamy mushrooms, I browse through the photo album.

With every photo, I tell him a story, screening what I don't want him to know. However, I tell him how I'm an only child and live with my mother. In return, he tells me about his sixteen-year-old brother, Maxx, and his eighteen-year-old sister, Scarlett, who apparently, prepared soggy cereal for him earlier.

The breakfast is ready. While making cappuccino, he asks me to serve the eggs and mushrooms. As he adds the cream on top, he tells the story of how his uncle, Oliver Van-Bailey, owner of the famous Nair Saif restaurant, showed him the secrets of making a head-buzzing cappuccino.

We sit at the breakfast table, facing each other. Zachary stares at me with curiosity, waiting for me to take a sip of the cappuccino. I tease him at first, taking a sip and keeping a straight face.

"Don't you like it?" he asks as I frown, swallowing.

"Hmm ..." My frown deepens.

His forehead creases, then I grin. "Absolutely buzzing," I sing.

He rolls his eyes.

Zachary eats but not as much as I do. Instead, he watches while I eat from beginning to the end, asking all sorts of questions. I confess about how pathetic I am at cooking, and how I can't do without a cappuccino. He tells me a story about how his mother made a banana cream pie, years back, and how he fell in love with the pie.

"I don't eat bananas," I say.

"Allergy?"

"No, I just don't eat them. I tried once, but it didn't work; they're tasteless to me."

Zachary nods with a slight crease on his forehead. "Now I know not to eat bananas before kissing you."

I drop my gaze. "I don't think that's going to happen again."

"On your end, you make sure you don't eat Marmite because I hate Marmite." He chooses to ignore my previous statement.

"I don't like Marmite either, Zachary."

"There." A smile crinkles his eyes. "So you will kiss me again?"

I shake my head, turn to finish my cappuccino in silence.

"What are you thinking?" he asks after a moment.

"Why you are here?"

Wiping the corner of his lips with a napkin, he draws in a deep breath and stares into my eyes. "I figured since we're now working together, it would be a good idea if we can get to know each other."

"By kissing?"

He smirks. "No, I just can't help myself. Each time I see you, that's all I think about." He claps his hands together. "What's your excuse?"

"My excuse?"

"I mean if you don't want to kiss me, you can say no. But, if you find my presence leaves you tongue-tied, you are free to use your hands and push me off."

My mouth opens as I stare at Zachary, but nothing comes out.

"See, tongue-tied again." He stifles a laugh.

Without thinking, I pick the bottle of whipped cream from the table, stand and spray some on his face, and watch as his mouth opens.

"Look who's tongue-tied now," I giggle.

Zachary freezes for a few seconds, calmly rubs his eyes, wiping some of the cream off, and then …

"You!" He hisses at me playfully and rises to his feet. My eyes are on his hand as he shakes the bottle of whipped cream. Watching as he boldly steps toward me, I back out of the kitchen, laughing.

He grins. "You're dead!"

Giggling, I run into the hallway, toward the stairs with Zachary chasing after me. Up the stairs I speed, skipping two at a time. Behind me, I hear him breathing. I turn to see how far away he is, but then trip as my foot touches the landing.

Zachary catches me before my hands touch the ground, laughs as he lays me down, and with extra caution, he moves on top of me.

"Zachary, please!" I cry with laughter, struggling to break free from under his arms. My efforts are futile. I give up, blink my eyes open to meet his, and plead for mercy.

"It's payback time!" He sprays the cream on my face and neck.

I moan as he chuckles, still trying to spray more. Thank God, the bottle seems empty now. He releases me and lies beside me, then turns to whisper, "Do you want me to lick it off?"

My heart explodes. I shoot him an incredulous look. He mimics my expression and we begin laughing. We stay on the floor for a while, our eyes blinking at the ceiling while our hands, inch by inch draw closer to entwine.

I try to control my breathing when the flashing images come back to haunt me. This time I see myself in his arms, eyes drained, veins protruding, and my lips blue-black. There are no bites anywhere, no physical pain. The pain is within me. I see it in Zachary's eyes, too. I'm dying.

I blink out of the vision, and see Zachary's eyes on me. I force a smile at him, and he does likewise. We stare at each other for a while before I break the silence. "So do you have more getting to know you questions?"

"No." He displays a faint smile. "Getting to know someone isn't a matter of what they tell you, but about being with them over time. Maybe months or years, and during that time you get to know the real person, by observation, silently—no questions asked."

"Really?"

"Really."

"So I guess we won't know each other for that long since you're asking questions rather than observing me."

"It's not that at all." He reaches out for my eyebrow, wipes the remaining cream off, and then slowly, his smile disappears, eyes on my lips again. "I can be impatient sometimes." He sighs as he gets up, offers me a hand to help me up, but I shake my head.

"Go on. I need a moment to clean up," I tell him.

He disappears down the stairs, and I cross to my room. While wiping the sticky cream off, I take a minute to reflect on the flashing images. They terrify me, but I'm more curious than frightened. I want to know what they mean, and why I see them whenever I touch Zachary. If I ask him, I could scare him off. *Maybe I should ask Sean later.*

I don't understand this desire I have for Zachary. I miss Chan. I know he's probably never coming back, but I can't give up on us. Whatever it is I'm feeling for Zachary is nothing but infatuation; it will fade away.

"I like your hair messy like that," Zachary comments as I walk into the kitchen. He has cleared the table, and now he arranges the dishes into the washer.

"Is that why you came so early? To see Alexandra un-cut?" I cross to help him switch on the dishwasher.

"No." He side smiles. "I hoped to meet your mother, and when you opened the door with your hair like that, I said to myself, I'm going to forget that girl I kissed in the rain because this one looks better."

I nudge his shoulder playfully. "Now I know how quickly you dump your girlfriends."

"No, it's not easy to find beautiful girls, you know," he smiles. "Usually it takes me a century."

"A century, huh?" I eye him. "How charming."

"Is that all you think I am—charming?"

"I mean, like, really charming."

He cracks up, laughing. "Honestly, I expected you are going to come up with a profound word to describe me. I'd probably need a dictionary to find the meaning, but ... charming? Am I that dull?"

"Come on, Zachary, I'm a lady, remember?" I smirk at him, rinsing my hands.

He washes his hands too and stares at me after turning the tap off.

"And?" he prompts.

"Ladies don't reveal their feelings too soon," I say then tell him, still. "You expect me to tell you how I'm utterly blown away by your eyes?" I smile as he bites his bottom lip with delight. "How you're the only person who's managed to melt my heart since ...?" I want to say Channing, but I don't want to give him an opening to a story I prefer not to discuss.

"Since what, Alexandra?"

I fix my eyes on his then look down, shaking my head. "Nothing.

He eyes me with suspicion and turns to pick up a tea towel. He dries my hands first and then his. "What are you doing today? Let's go celebrate our union."

"I have a date." I fold my arms over my chest and rest my back against the worktop.

"Oh." He blinks. "I thought, now that you've found me, you don't need dates anymore."

"You're funny, Zachary."

"With whom?" he asks.

"What?"

"Who are you going on a date with?"

"A friend."

"Boyfriend?" He moves close to me.

"Potential boyfriend."

"Call him and cancel. I was here first."

"You're here without notice."

"You didn't ask me to leave." He moves closer, his face inches from mine.

I pause, smiling at his smug face. "Maybe I should."

"I don't think you could. Even if you wanted to."

"You sure about that?"

"Maybe you would do it just to prove me wrong."

I look at his lips and back at his eyes.

He studies my face, and grins. "Yeah, I want that too."

"What?" I grimace, confused.

"I see you want to kiss me."

I push him off and turn away to hide my flushing cheeks. "Okay, you win."

"You want to kiss me?"

"Yes—I mean, no."

He laughs.

"I meant okay, I'll cancel the date," I explain.

The smile on his face tells me what I already know. He has won on both points. We stare at each other in silence. My heart races as I imagine him close to me.

"I have a feeling you always get your way." I decide to break the alluring silence.

His lips curl up. "Believe me, if I had my way you wouldn't be standing."

"What's that supposed to mean?"

"Don't know." He scratches his head a little. "Did I say that aloud?"

I give him a light punch on his chest while he laughs.

Later, away from Zachary, I call Emily to postpone our date, and I don't tell her about Zachary. As I expect, she's not happy and accuses me of neglecting her, but I know she will support anything to make me forget Chan. In the end, she demands a name, and the first name I think of is Spenser.

Sean, who answers my call with excitement, agrees to a rain check, but from the tone of his voice, I can sense the disappointment. To compensate for the sudden change of plan, I offer to spend a whole day with Sean on Saturday. I still need to know what I am, so keeping a healthy relationship with Sean is crucial.

In the hour that follows, Zachary and I talk about the plans for our racetrack and agree to use the same contractors he has worked with over the years. We compare ideas, and after a few disagreements, we agree on the infinity shape. Autumn Reigns will be the longest racetrack in Ashbourne.

"I want the other end also over the hill," I say as Zachary and I study the track plan.

"Hill to hill? Alexandra, that's dangerous."

"Are you saying this because girls are involved?"

He eyes me and smiles. "Fine. I'll see if we can get it past the building regulations."

"Thank you." I kiss his cheek.

Outside, Zachary flings his car keys to me and strides over to the passenger side. For a few seconds, I stand still, my brain processing what I'm about to do.

With caution, I sit in the driver's seat, my nose taking in the leather scent. Pressing on the ignition button, I glance at a grinning Zachary, my ears inclining to the sound of the engine.

"You hear that?" I say in a low voice. "Mouthwatering."

"I hear," Zachary whispers. "16-cylinder monster."

"A thousand and one horsepower. Naught to a hundred in a blazing five point seven seconds. Plus, it's weighs next to nothing." I breathe in appreciation.

"You know your stuff." He winks. "Now drive. First time in the passenger seat, so I expect nothing but a smooth ride."

I smile, and drive away.

According to Zachary, Van-Bailey Speedway was his first project, something he started two years ago when he was seventeen. He intended to keep it for family fun, but as extended family members, friends and friends' friends expressed their interest, he then decided he needed a larger, longer track. That's how we ended up meeting at the auction, and now he wants to show it to me.

"So you can tell me what you think we should incorporate into Autumn Reigns," he explains.

We arrive at the Van-Bailey Speedway in less than an hour. Situated in the east of Ashbourne, it's about half the size of Autumn Reigns. To my surprise, the track is clear, no cars racing, and no crowd, apart from a few individuals, in yellow traffic jackets, whom I guess are working on the tracks.

"We're closed today, and I thought it would be a great time to show you how things run here," Zachary says.

Designed in the shape of a Z, Z for Zachary, I guess, the wide tracks seem rough, but with a sturdy texture. The track is surrounded by a myriad of tiered seating, and it appears more like an arena. It's impressive, but a little too dense for my liking. I like things to run free and wild.

"I have a surprise for you," Zachary whispers as we push the glass doors open, making our way to the open office space.

"What is it?" I whisper back.

He turns to stare at me and chuckles. "Like I said, it's a surprise."

"Boss!" A young man calls from behind us. "I'm sorry, I—"

"It's fine, Danny." Zachary answers. "Is everything ready?"

"All done." He nods.

"Alex, this is Danny, my friend. He's in charge here. Danny, meet Alex, the new partner I told you about," Zachary says, just as Danny and I shake hands.

"It's lovely to meet you, new Boss," Danny says.

"You too, Danny."

Danny is a tall young man who appears to be the same age as Zachary. With the broad shoulders and a clean military haircut, he holds a confident appearance.

"There it is," Danny steps toward the glass walls, looking out to the open field.

I follow his gaze and turn to Zachary with a frown. "Is that—" I'm saying when Zachary takes my hand and smiles.

"A hot-air balloon, yes. With that, we can get a clear view of this track and fly toward Autumn Reigns. What do you say?"

I'm speechless. "Is this really necessary?"

"Believe me, from up there, it's a completely different view." He pulls my hand and drags me to the hot-air balloon.

In a moment, we are in the air. It's cooler up here and the air a bit humid. Regardless, it doesn't detract the breathtaking views of the large Z shaped track, the natural grounds, and the river curving along various thick trees. Heading toward the hilly Autumn Reigns, miles away, we follow along the River Stills.

"Zachary?" Lost in the moment as I marvel at the world below, I turn to find him sitting behind on the padded wicker chair. "Zachary, this is amazing ..." I take in a deep breath.

"I know," he mumbles.

"No, you don't. Come see." I look back and catch his eyes on me. "Come!" I extend my hand to him, urging him to join me.

Taking a deep breath, he stands and steps over to hug me from behind. He holds me close as we check out the views. I rest my head on his chest while he relaxes his head on my shoulder.

"Oh, I see it now." Zachary nuzzles into my neck.

He kisses my shoulder, the warmth of his lips triggering my heart to beat faster. I pull Zachary's hands closer around my waist, entwining our fingers, tight.

"Are you looking at the view or looking at me?" I ask, watching his eyes on me.

"Which do you think looks better?"

I open my mouth to answer, but stop as his cell phone vibrates. He releases his hand to pull it out of his pocket, presses the red button and without a word, shoves it back.

"So, what's your answer?" He places his hand back in mine, by my stomach.

"I don't want to be full of it like you, so I choose not to answer."

"Ouch!" he cries. "Full of it. That hurts."

"Shut up." I scowl at him playfully.

Without warning, he grabs my waist and swings me around to face him. While I open my mouth to ask what he was doing, our lips meet. His scent refuses to give me a moment to think. My hands crawl up around his neck as my heart races. I give in to him, allowing his tongue to mingle with mine.

The balloon descends and so does the speed of our kiss, coming to an end with a breathless gasp from both of us, and followed by silent laughter.

"She kisses me again," Zachary whispers in my ear.

"Did she? I wonder what she was thinking," I whisper back, dropping my head back on his chest. "She can't be trusted, you know."

"Neither can he." Zachary sighs as he circles his arms tight around my waist.

I force a smile and rest my head on his shoulder. My mind drifts to Channing, my thoughts somewhere between letting go and holding on. Letting go because I feel I have betrayed him, and on top of that, even if I try, I don't think I can stop. It feels like I have broken my pillar of strength and left myself vulnerable to Zachary.

Later, we are back in the Zetra Zeus, Zachary dropping me back home. In the entrance hall, Zachary kisses my cheek as he prepares to leave.

"Are you always this nice?" I ask.

"No." He grins. "Only when I want to win a heart."

"What happens when you lose?"

He smirks, scratching his head as if what I've said is inconceivable. "Losing to me doesn't exist." He bites his bottom lip. "But, just to feed your curiosity, if I lose, I will be forced to steal."

"You would steal my heart?" I tease.

"If I have to, yes." He doesn't smile.

"Leaving me heartless?"

"Not heartless." He comes closer and links his little finger with mine, our noses almost touching. "I'll leave mine with you." He steals another kiss from my lips and backs off toward the door.

"Knight," I call.

Acknowledging his nickname, he pauses and stares at me with raised eyebrows.

"I had a lovely time, today." I say with a serious face. "Thank you."

His eyes widen as a dazzling smile forms on his face. "Me too." He salutes and turns to walk out, shutting the door behind him.

❧❦❧

"Oh, my God, Lexie." Emily screams over the phone later that night. "I think I just spoke to my next boyfriend."

I smile. *At last, she's forgotten about Clive.* "Who? You mean your ex-boyfriend is going to be your next? Impressive."

"Shut up, Lexie," she groans. "I just spoke to Zachary Van-B. He called me a few minutes ago."

I sit up from my bed. "Zachary called you? Why? Where did he get your phone number?"

"Hey, calm down," she sings. "No need to be jealous, he asked about you too."

"What did he say?" My heart begins to pound.

"Well, it was clear he wanted to ask me what flowers I like. So, he asked for your favorite flowers."

"And?" *Why is my life so complicated?*

"He wanted to know if I liked the same." She says and I listen as she goes on about the possibilities of Zachary asking her for a date.

X

New Neighbors

"Two weeks, Lexie. You've been so quiet for the last few days. When we finally want to get together, you decide to meet Spenser instead?"

"Emily, I had the track to attend to, papers to sign. Besides, I didn't want to distract you from college. Is that not what a good friend would do?"

She rolls her eyes. "Yeah, right."

In Emily's house, I stand next to the windows of her bedroom as I try to explain myself.

Situated at the corner of Park Street, the town house is a ten minutes' drive from my house. On entering the house, one thing that stands out above the rest is the beautiful stripped wooden floor in the entrance foyer. It leads into the main hall and a bright sitting room.

Carrying on the wood theme, the wide stairs lead to three bedrooms upstairs. Emily's is the last at the end of the passage.

I'm here to pick up Emily for a day of body pampering at Fruity Beauty & Spa. Since I spent yesterday with Zachary—Zachary, that I've temporarily given the name of Spenser—I decided to reschedule the pampering for today.

Now she asks many questions. Questions I can't answer.

So, what have you been doing with Spenser?

How is the racing going with Spenser?

Do you think Spenser might be your perfect rebound?

I have never lied to Emily, and this is getting uncomfortable. Even the cheeks I try to hold up have begun to fall; I'm tired of forcing smiles. I can't do it anymore.

"What's wrong with you?" Emily asks. "You're making me tense pacing with your shoulders tight like that."

Emily removes her robe and makes her way to the closet to dress up. She disappears behind the doors while I throw myself on her comfy bed. I bounce twice before coming to rest, then open my eyes to the white walls of her bedroom. They are the only thing white in this room; everything else is colorful; the striped cushions, ethnic bed covers, and the matching heavy curtains.

"I'm waiting," she sings from the closet.

"For what?" I ask.

"You're going to tell me what's bothering you, aren't you?"

I stand and move to the window. Everything appears calm; the leaves are still, the birds flying in silence and the sun's rays fighting to shine through the white clouds.

"Have you ever trusted a stranger?" I ask, now leaning by Emily's closet door. She is standing by the mirror in a cream dress.

"It depends if the stranger is sexy, like Zach Van-B, otherwise, no. Speak now." She prompts, going back to the question I've been trying to avoid.

I know I have to tell her eventually, but a lot has happened with Zachary in such a short time.

"You don't really want to go out with me today, do you?" Emily places her hands on her waist, studying me.

"I do. It's just that …" My fingers find refuge in my hair.

"It's just … what?"

"Uhm …" I let out a soft laugh.

She eyes me with raised eyebrows. I look away, unable to hold her condemning gaze.

"What did you do?" Her frown grows deeper.

I sigh, hoping for luck as I change the subject. "So, you didn't tell me. Are the boys in Stills College as fine as your fine arts?"

She rolls her eyes. "Now that you're hanging with Mr. Auction guy, I think I could do with an upgrade." She taps my cheeks and turns toward the mirror. "I think I like this." She turns sideways to admire the light sage dress then looks back at me with a creased forehead. "What are you not telling me, Lexie?"

I part my lips slowly. "We've been invited to a party?"

"Now that's music to my ears. But, whose party is that, that makes you bite your tongue?"

"Well," I clear my throat. "We kind of met the other day at the auction, day before yesterday, and we—"

"I'm sorry, who is *we*? You and Spenser?"

"There is no Spenser ... Actually, there's a Spenser, but I just used his name. It's Zachary. It's been Zachary all along."

"I'm sorry. I don't get you."

"Everything I told you was true, except I just replaced Zachary with the name Spenser."

"So you're in partnership with Zachary and not Spenser? But why would you hide that from me?" She frowns, then her eyes widen. "No, it can't be; you and Zachary?" She stares at me with her lips slightly parting. Her mouth widens by the second. Then she lets out a broken breath. "All along it's been Zachary?"

"It happened so fast, I didn't mean to hurt you."

"Hurt?" Her voice cracks. "Hurt ... why do you think this would hurt me?"

"I thought—"

"Thought what? That I'm so into Zachary. Just because I admire Zachary doesn't mean I want him. I'm not a stupid girl."

I grimace. "Are you calling me stupid?"

"Do you want him?" She eyes me with blazing pupils. "Because if you do, you're the most ..." Her face scowls as she holds her breath in frustration, "stupidest, selfish friend, I've ever seen."

"Millie ... I didn't plan for any of this to happen."

"So how did it happen?"

I remain silent; truly thinking of how it happened.

"Go on; tell me exactly how this happened."

I hesitate, spelling the apprehension in her wet emerald eyes. "We had a chat over coffee."

"And?"

"I, he kissed—we kissed."

"Why would you kiss Zachary Van-B, knowing it would lead nowhere? Why do you always fall for the heartbreakers, Lexie?"

"It was raining!" I snap.

"So? Since when do we kiss people because it's raining?"

"After a very warm cappuccino; you know during the sweet, sorrowful goodbyes."

"Give me another reason. That one is madness!"

"He's the first guy ever to guess my favorite cupcake."

"So you kissed him?" Her brow furrows. "You kissed him because he guessed your favorite cupcake?"

"All right!" I give in. "I kissed him because I wanted to kiss him. There you have it. Now go on pop the chardonnay and let's celebrate how you always win every argument!"

Emily snorts with exaggeration, marches back to the closet, and returns with a pair of white heels. "He's no good for you." I can hear the pain in her voice as she speaks, pointing at me with one shoe. "He probably has twenty girlfriends, talk about wannabes."

"Wannabes like you, you mean."

She pauses. "Now that's hurtful. You don't talk to me like that."

"But you get to talk to me as if I'm not good enough for Zachary?"

"I'm talking like he's not good enough for you, Lexie!"

"He's not good for me and yet last night you were telling me how he's your next boyfriend?"

"That was yesterday."

"So, why the third degree? It's as if I've stolen your boyfriend."

"You think I'm jealous?"

"You can't deny you wanted Zachary even before we met him and you can't stand that he chose me."

She glares at me and coughs sarcastically. "You're so unbelievable!" She runs to the bathroom and shuts the door. Then she begins to whimper.

With a trembling hand, I squeeze my forehead before following her to the bathroom.

"Millie?" I call. "Emily, come on. I didn't mean it like that."

She remains silent, but I hear her sniff.

"I don't even want Zachary. We're just having fun." I try again.

She opens the door and speaks in a ragged breath. "Like Shakespeare, tragedy is your idea of fun."

"Millie, lis—"

"I just need you to be quiet right now!" She picks up a tissue to blow her nose. Tilting her head from side to side, she begins to mimic me. "I miss him, Millie. I can't date anyone, Millie. He's never coming back, is he Millie?" She shakes her head as if disgusted. "How quickly you have forgotten Chan."

For a second, my heart stops beating, then a flash of fresh anger embraces me. "Quickly? You call seven months, one week and two days, quickly? How dare you!" My face burns. "What do you know about how I feel? How it feels to live every day without—"

"Calm down—"

"No, I won't calm down! I fight every morning not to think of him! I wake up some mornings feeling like I will never love as I love him. With every second, I hope and pray he will come back to me. Other mornings I wake and resent him for leaving. And the worst mornings I feel numb—no emotion—then I wonder, is it because I miss him so much or maybe because I'm some creature. I'm not human. One day I'll wake up and feel nothing for anyone. And that includes you, Millie." I take a breath and start for the door.

"Lexie wait!" she calls, but I don't stop, slamming the door on my way out.

Eight o'clock and I'm home helping Mother set the table for dinner. Tonight, we have dinner with the new neighbors.

The papers were right when they reported the famous Deschanels moving next door. I have not seen them yet, but Mother tells me about them. As always, I guess she intruded into their still strange home and indirectly forced a dinner invitation into their hands. Poor souls, they must think we're nosy neighbors.

"It's so we can break the ice and get to know them better," she says.

It's time for my shower, and I take time to play with the warm water while trying not to think of Emily. When I'm done, I pick out one of my favorite outfits – a yellow cap sleeved mini dress, embroidered with beaded lace. I check my curves in the mirror and smile as they please me. My dark caramel curls flaunt on one side of my shoulder, exposing one of my pearl earrings on the other. I glance at my feet and think the gold sandals look virtuous.

Every part of me reflects beauty, confidence, and perfection—as it should be. It's not that I have done anything to enhance the way I look, but it has something to do with the way I feel. Something is happening inside. The glacier that froze my heart for so long has broken at last. It has melted into the unknown, allowing my heart to pump life through my whole being, and bringing out a brand new me—a better me.

I smile, staring at my gray sparkling eyes then stroke my cheeks with a shimmering blush.

"Did you see Zachary again today?"

I jump, then realize it's Mother. "Mom, you scared me." I take in a deep breath, looking at her reflection through the mirror. "And no; I didn't see Zachary. I was with Emily."

She smiles, the kind of grin that says, tell me more. "I saw your eyes when you spoke of him last night. I'm glad you're dating again."

"I have no idea what you're talking about, Mom. All I said about him was concerning the racetrack, so where are you getting this dating idea?"

"It's good to see you over Channing—moving on."

"I'm not!" I pause, suppressing a rush of emotions rising in my chest. "I'm not over Channing, and I'm fed up with everyone telling me so. Let's not talk about Zachary again, please?"

I motion toward the balcony to check the driveway. "They are here," I say, watching the neighbors arriving at the small gate. "You said he has two boys. Unless I'm losing my sight, those two, look like girls to me.

"Humble enough to come on foot," Mother mutters as she joins me by the window. "I'll go get the door." She moves closer to adjust the shoulders of my dress before she leaves.

I grab my phone and call Emily. It's picked up by the answering machine.

"Millie, we both said some nasty things to each other so get over it."

I pause, thinking my statement over.

"Okay, the question is – should we allow an obnoxious boy to come between us? I say no. I know somehow I hurt my best friend, so if you find her, please tell her I said I'm sorry, and I love her."

As I hang up, I hear voices - high-toned voices. I peek out of my door to listen, and yes I hear them; the exaggerated tones and lurid laughs strangers do when they first meet.

"Lexie! Honey, they're here!" Mother calls.

I wait until the voices fade before making my way downstairs. The doorbell rings again. "Millie?" I mutter a quick prayer, and rush to get the door.

My hand on the handle, I pull the door open, and there I gasp. "My God! What are you doing here?"

"Alex?" Sean in a black outfit with a dark mushroom colored waistcoat stands at the door. "What are you doing here?" he asks.

"Well, I live here."

"I'm here for dinner."

"Are you insane? Who invited you?"

"Doctor Watson, of course." He frowns. "Wait a minute. Are you her daughter?"

I stare at his eyes, and collude he's trying to be funny. "This is no time for jokes and certainly not ..." I trail off, concentrating on the sound of heels I hear. "Leave, please ... just leave." I press the door to shut it, but he holds it open.

"What's going on?" Mother appears behind me and steps forward to Sean. "Lexie, why are you telling our guest to leave?"

My mouth opens, and for a brief moment, nothing comes out.

"Please come in, Sean," Mother says.

"Thanks, Dr. Watson," he says. "And these are for you." He hands her a bouquet of colorful tulips.

"How sweet." She leans over to hug Sean. "Thank you, and please call me anything else apart from Dr. Watson. I get enough from work every day."

Sean smiles. "Doc, it is then."

I frown at Sean, who smirks at me before directing his gaze at Mother again. "That smell is mouthwatering. I can't wait to eat."

"Such a gentleman, aren't you?" Mother laughs. "I hope you like fish. Sea bass, Lexie's favorite. Come, let's join the others," she says, picking up her pace. Sean and I follow.

"Sean, I'm so sorry. I—"

He is already shaking his head before I finish. "Nothing to apologize for. You look gorgeous, by the way."

"So do you." We smile at each other, making our way to the entertainment room.

Mother introduces me to David Deschanel, Sean's father, who shakes my hand politely. David, a little taller than Sean, has polished gray hair and a smile that reveals the care taken in trimming his stubble beard. In addition to his confident and calm look, his blue eyes ooze with warmth and compassion.

I exchange hugs with a blonde-haired Victoria, Sean's sister, the eldest in the family. She has a sharp look, straight and long hair, and she is dressed in a tight asymmetrical white dress with pointed edges on the shoulders. Her mysterious violet eyes stare at me as if to find a secret.

Megan floods my nostril with the scent of strawberry shampoo from her jet-black curls as she hugs me. She holds me for longer than Victoria before pulling away, staring at me with her warm hazel eyes. She kisses my cheeks, standing beside me.

David shifts his gaze between Sean and me. "You two know each other?"

"No," I say at the same time with Sean, who says, yes. "I mean we don't, like really know each other, but yes we met the other night," I add.

"Oh, my God," Megan exclaims. "Is she Alex? I didn't know she lived next door."

Sean scratches his head a little.

"Which Alex?" Victoria asks.

"Alex who beat up the bartender," Megan answers with excitement.

My mouth opens as I turn to Sean. "You told them about the bartender?"

"I was just—"

He doesn't finish as Mother interrupts. "You were drinking, and you attacked a bartender?"

"Just one glass and I—I didn't mean to attack anyone. It just ..." I sigh.

"I'm sure she didn't mean any harm." David draws Mother's attention away from me.

As David turns, asking Mother about a safari painting hanging on the wall, Sean draws nearer and whispers into my ear.

"I'm sorry," he says.

"You owe me."

"Just like you owe me a date?" He raises his brows as I smile.

At the wooden, rectangular dinner table set in the formal dining room, we take our seats, ready for Mother's cooking. Sean sits on one end opposite David, who is on the other end. Mother, who's in the kitchen, will sit next to David on his right.

I've offered to help her serve the food, but she refuses, determined to do it all on her own.

On David's left is Megan, who rests her head on Sean's shoulder. She's facing me. Victoria is to my left, at the corner of the table.

David asks about college. I explain how I'm taking a gap year and will be back in college by the end of the year. He moves on to ask about the Theta Scorpii he saw the other night, asking if it's mine. My blood warms as we start talking about Deschanel luxury cars.

"Dad." Victoria turns to her father. "If you want to tell Alex, you made the Theta Scorpii, go ahead. Just don't beat around the bush."

David laughs.

"I already know." I smile at David. "I'm honored to finally meet you."

"The honor is mine, darling. To see someone, as young as you, enjoying my work is a delight."

"The Zetra Zeus is my favorite, though," I add.

"You've driven that one, too?"

"A friend let me drive one for a few hours. It was nothing, but phenomenal."

He swallows a mouthful of his wine. "Sean, maybe you should enroll Alex in our gold membership, so she can get more than just a few hours on a Zetra Zeus."

"Sure." Sean grins at me.

"I don't know what to say." I turn to David. "Thank you."

"Can we talk about anything else apart from cars?" Megan moans.

Sean turns to Megan with a thoughtful look. "What else is there to talk about? Oh, yeah, we could talk about how many calories are in a cucumber?"

We all laugh and Megan punches Sean teasingly. In the same moment, Mother walks in with a tray set with the starter in small plates.

"What's everyone laughing about?" she asks, smiling.

"How Alexandra frowns like her mother," Sean says, and again, we laugh.

"Poached salmon and lemon zest crème fraîche, topped with king prawn." Mother smiles. "This is my Monday special. Tell me what you think and be honest."

We begin eating. One at a time, we express our thoughts on the starter. Soon David and Mother drift into their own conversation. From the little I hear, they are discussing work.

While they pour more wine in their glasses, Sean and his sisters tell me about their absent brother Ashton.

"He's younger than Victoria but older than Sean, and, of course, I'm the last born." Megan tells me.

"Strength; you can never know what he's thinking," Sean says.

"And his greatest weakness?" I ask.

Victoria's face beams. "He's the kindest of us all."

I smile and turn to Megan as she says, "And he's better looking than Sean, that's for sure."

"He must be an angel." I stare at Sean. "Sean is very handsome."

He grins and scratches the side of his stubble beard. "Thank you, gorgeous." He turns to his sisters. "How about that girls? You're starting to wish I wasn't your brother now?"

"Is he always so self-absorbed?" I quiz the girls.

"*Always,*" the sisters echo in response.

Unexpected, David intervenes. "Ashton is the man behind all the car designs we've created over the years. Your Theta Scorpii, Alexandra, was his first. It's been almost two years now since he left, and we haven't launched any new designs since."

"Where did he go? Is he in college?" I look around the table for an answer.

"No, he stopped college, stopped everything really, after the death of my wife, Lynette," David explains.

"I'm sorry to hear that," Mother says.

"Thank you." David appears to force a smile. "I think her death affected all of us in a different way, but him the most. They were very close."

Sean scoffs, but David ignores him.

"He's got his kind soul from his mother." David swallows a sip of wine before continuing. "Always trying to put things right, to heal every soul."

"He didn't tell you where he was going?" I ask.

David swallows hard. "No, he didn't. I woke up one morning, and he was gone, leaving a note for us not to look for him."

"Is that all, Dad?" Sean's lips twitch. "Why don't you tell them exactly what he wrote in that letter?"

"I don't think that's necessary, Son."

Mother stands. "Perhaps I should bring in the main." She sighs, before heading for the kitchen.

For a moment, everyone at the table remains silent until Sean turns to his father.

"Say he's your favorite, and I swear I won't cry, not that my tears would move you, Dad." He mumbles the last line.

"Sean, come on." Victoria tries to calm him down. For a moment, the creases on his forehead disappear, until David speaks again.

"Son, I understand the memories can be upsetting at times, but—"

"Memories?" Sean's voice is scornful. He puffs a sarcastic laugh and leans toward me. "You want to know what upsets me, Alex? Lies upon lies." His tone grows louder. "He speaks of Ash as though he's Christ. You would've thought he's learned by now, seen his true nature, but no; he still sings his praises. My brother, who abandons his family and chooses to search for a witch. Ha!" He shakes his head. "Ask me why he needs a witch, Alex, and I'll be glad to tell you."

I want to ask. I want to know why, but the tension around the table dries my mouth.

"You don't have to answer that, Alex," Victoria whispers just as Mother walks in with a silver trolley. On it, sits carved wooden bowls carrying steaming hot water, with one leaf that's similar to basil.

"I hope you will all find this comforting," Mother says, gauging the tension at the table. "It's our way of welcoming guests."

She places a bowl on the table, next to David, and does the same for the rest of us, taking her seat, smiling. "Alexandra and I want you all to know you're welcome on Vine Lane, and we are happy to have you as our neighbors."

Resisting a frown, I stare at Mother. I have never heard of this tradition before, and I wonder what she's up to.

We all dip our hands in our bowls, rinsing our fingertips as Mother demonstrates, except for Sean.

He wears a scorned expression as he stares at the steam from the bowl. "I'm sorry. I'm not doing this."

The table goes silent as we stare at Sean.

"Umm, I'm sorry." Mother breathes. "I didn't realize. Did I offend you—?"

"No." David almost yells. "You don't need to apologize, Doc. You've done nothing wrong." He turns to Sean. "Son, I'll not accept that kind of attitude toward Dr. Watson. I'm sure you won't lose anything by washing your hands."

"Dad, this is not a *fucking welcoming* gesture, and you know it. She's—"

"Watch your mouth, son!" David rises.

Sean pushes the bowl to the center of the table. "Apologies, Doc, but I'm not touching that water." He draws the chair to stand. "I think I'm done here. Goodnight and thank you for the starter."

Mother's mouth opens, staring at Sean as he storms out. Victoria goes after him, and soon after, both Megan and David apologize for Sean's behavior and stand, ready to leave.

"My apologies once again, Doc." David walks out of the front door with Megan behind. "I'll make this right. I promise."

The door shuts. With arms crossed, I turn to glare at Mother. "What *welcoming* custom was that, Mother? It looked more like a ritual to me."

She smiles. "Nothing more than a little something to protect us, honey." She gives me one of her long hugs, and kisses my cheek as she pulls away. "Sea bass with creamed spinach for two by the porch?" she calls as she sails toward the kitchen.

"Why not?" I step into the kitchen to help her. As always, she isn't going to tell me anything.

Beep. Beep. The night is here. I'm relaxed in my bed, my mind rerunning the events during dinner with the neighbors when I receive a text from Zachary.

Knight: Today was a bad day.

"Tell me about it," I mumble and begin texting back.

Me: You didn't eat a banana, I know.

Knight: Yeah, that too, but that's not what I mean.

Me: Now you're waiting for me to ask what you mean.

Knight: Yes, go on and ask.

Me: ~~What do you mean?~~ Why should I ask when it's obvious you can't wait to tell me?

Knight: ~~Alexandra hangover. Tried black coffee, it's not working, but I know what will.~~ You still don't want to ask?

Me: ~~Tempted.~~ Nope.

Knight: ~~A kiss from Alexandra.~~ As you wish, Beautiful.

I smile.
The intercom rings. I ignore it, knowing Mother will answer.

Me: Night, knight.

Knight: Sleep well, beautiful.

Another moment, and there's a knock at my door.
"Lexie, honey, Sean is here to talk to you," Mother says, standing outside my bedroom door.
In a rush, I pick up my robe and advance toward the door.
"Hey," Sean runs his fingers through his hair as Mother leaves. "Sorry to disturb you, but I couldn't sleep without apologizing to Doc, and you."
I cross my arms and lean by the doorway. "It's a good thing you came. I don't entertain boys who disrespect my mother for whatever reasons."
"I'm sorry. Can we talk in private?"
"Sure. Come in." I step aside to let him in.
He hesitates. "Maybe we should go outside, in the garden?"
Garden, at this time? I shoot a curious look at him. "Okay," I say and tighten the belt on my robe.

We make our way out. In silence, we head toward the back garden. I lead him to sit on the bench Chan and I used to sit on.

For a moment, we say nothing. Sean cracks his knuckles one by one. I elbow him to stop. He laughs nervously, stopping with a sigh, and turns to me.

"I'm sorry you had to see that earlier. What a way to impress a girl." He seems to force a smile. I cross my arms.

"Talk of true colors." I say.

"Beautiful like a rainbow, huh?"

I let out a faint laugh. "Very funny, Sean."

There's a mixture of a smile and a frown on his face. He goes silent, staring at his fingers again. "Is our Saturday date still on?"

I think of saying, no, but change my mind. "I was going to ask you the same thing."

He shoots me a cynical look. "I figured maybe after the way I acted, you would—"

"Cancel it?" I shake my head. "Not without giving you a chance to explain yourself."

"You're beautiful inside too. Lucky me."

The corners of my lips curl into a faint smile. "I can't believe you are a Deschanel. And you live next door."

"Does that make me less attractive?"

"No, it's —"

"So *convenient*?" He grins.

"I was going to say ..."

"Destined is fine, Alex."

"Sean!" I moan.

He laughs. "Do you believe in love at first sight?"

"Love no, but attraction, yes."

"Attraction is good, too."

I stare deep into his blue eyes. Then nudge his shoulders. "So tell me. Why did you refuse to dip your fingers in my mother's welcoming bowl?"

"Because it wasn't welcoming," he says.

"How do you know that?"

"Because my mother used to do the same."

"Of course, she would. It is a welcoming custom after all."

"No, it isn't." Sean cocks his head. "It's a protection spell. Any supernatural being that dips their fingers in that water will be stripped of all their supernatural abilities each time they step in your house."

"What?" I rewind his words. "How is that?"

He shakes his head. "Now I see why I can't figure you out."

My heart throbs. "What do you mean? Why can't you?"

"Your mother probably cast a spell to hide your scent and delude others of what you really are."

"What are these spells you keep talking about? I grimace.

"Come on, Alex. Don't pretend you don't know what I'm talking about. It's a well-known fact that witches cast spells to disguise the immortal identity of their family members, especially their kids."

"*Witches*?" I turn fully to face him. "Are you saying my mother is a witch?"

"You telling me you don't know?"

"Mother is not a witch. If she were, she wouldn't have allowed you back in here, especially after you refused to wash your hands."

"She didn't."

"What do you mean?"

"As part of my apology, she made me wash my hands."

I stare at him, dumbfounded. *This makes sense though.* That's how she stopped me from leaving for Pannonia.

"Like I said, my mother was one." Sean stands. "I know these things."

"Wait! Where are you going?"

"Home," he says. "I've said too much."

"No! Don't go." I pull him to sit back. "Tell me more."

"About what? Your mother probably has a million ways to punish me for telling you this."

"I promise not to tell her anything. Now tell me everything. The vampires, the White Bloods, and—"

"*What are you searching for*? And who have you been talking to?" He panics. "White Bloods are sacred. You don't just talk about them as if you're talking of the weather."

"Then tell me. How are they sacred? Where do I find them?"

He pauses, studying me for a while. "Why do I feel that if I tell you everything I won't get to see you again?"

"Sean, please. I'm begging you."

"I'm going to make this easier for the both of us. I like you, like, really, really, like you. I'm not sure if you feel the same."

I turn away from his gaze for a brief moment.

"I'll trade my information for time with you. I know I'll win your heart soon enough." His honesty comes out as sharp as a two-edged sword and right now I feel wounded with guilt. "Shall we shake hands to that?" He extends his hand to me.

"Umm, I ..."

"What are you scared of?" He places my hand between his palms.

"I'm not clear what 'time with me' means."

"Getting to know you better. No commitment, if that's what you fear."

"That sounds fair?"

He smiles. "I always try to be fair.

"You are naturally kind, aren't you?"

"Still trying to be selfless like my brother, Ashton."

"From how you reacted at dinner, I got the sense you don't like your brother."

"I don't hate my brother, but I despise how my father favors him. Everyone knows he prefers him to me. Even Ash agrees with me."

"I'm sorry you feel that way." I squeeze his hand.

He tightens his hold on my hand and brushes it with his thumb. "We're very close, actually, Ash and I. At least we were before he left. Now I have no clue if he's dead or alive."

"You miss him?" I watch his inner eyebrows rise.

He nods. "We all miss him, so much that his coming back is only second to that of Christ."

"Lexie!" Mother calls.

Sean leans in for a hug. "See you Saturday."

"No, wait," I moan as he kisses my cheek and rises to his feet. "Let me talk to her and come back."

Sean chuckles. "She's not calling you, Alex. She's telling me it's time to leave. Goodnight."

I drop my shoulders and hug him again. "Night."

XI

THE LOVE OF HIS LIFE

"I like Megan better than her snobbish sister." Hands on wheels, Emily glances through the side-view mirror. "I think we've lost them." She reduces speed and sighs. "Why do people always think a slow driver is a better driver?"

I smile. "I'd love to hear someone answer that."

Emily eyes me playfully. "Not that I'm saying they should speed and kill their best friends, but—oh, there they are." She picks up speed as soon as Victoria and Megan appear behind us.

They are following us in Victoria's silver Theta Scorpii—a newer version of my car.

Earlier, this morning, they arrived at my house asking if I can show them the Village Mall. I didn't want to, but Mother insisted.

They want to find costumes for a masquerade party. I know where to take them. Lost Closet is one of the world's finest department stores, and I'm sure they will find what they need.

"Did you see how she sits looking around as if she's heard it all?" Emily adds. "As if there's nothing in the world she hasn't heard before?"

"I think she's just reserved." I try to defend Victoria. "You like Megan because she's opinionated like you."

"Admit it. She's easier to talk to. Victoria just sits and stares, her violet eyes and blonde hair like a breathing statue. She's cold."

"That's what you said about Chan the first time you spoke to him, remember?"

Without speaking, Emily stares at me, smiling. "She speaks of Chan without the sad eyes. Yay!"

I roll my eyes.

After ignoring me last night, Emily arrived at my house early this morning, and we've made up. I've apologized for lying, and she admitted she was maybe a 'teeny-weeny bit' jealous.

"If he makes you forget Chan, even for a minute, go ahead and have fun," Emily said at the end.

It took me over an hour to update her on "dinner with the neighbors" drama, how Sean is Sean Deschanel. I also mentioned part of my conversation with Sean, keeping the witch revelation to myself.

"Emily, that hurts!" I moan as the clutch burns for the second time.

Too excited to see her earlier this morning, I ended up making unrealistic promises and allowed her to drive my car.

"You do it again, and I'll drive."

"Stop being mean. At least give me a chance to get used to it." Emily moans.

"We might not have a car for you to get used to at the end of the day."

She shifts the gears with extra care this time, and I smile at her, admiring the little daisies pinned to her hair.

"So, how was it, then?" she asks after a moment.

I grimace. "How was what?"

"Did he close his eyes?" She cranes her neck toward me, her eyes wide and dramatic. "Did he hold you tight or let go too soon? Who pulled off first?"

"Eyes on the road, Emily!" The frown on my face disappears as I turn my face away from her, trying hard not to smile. "And who is that you speak of?"

"Come on. Why is it you don't want to talk about him? Did he say he's going to kill you if you tell anyone? Who knows, perhaps he's a serial killer—*Zach the ripper*, that sounds familiar."

I hold a giggle. "Don't know about the eyes, but I pulled away first."

"Well, that answers one question—your eyes were closed. That's why you don't know."

I laugh, and without warning, my mind takes me back to the kiss in the rain. Just like that day, a fluttering sensation fills my stomach. In my mind, I replay everything as it happened, all the kisses in order, and now his scent is all I can smell. I want more.

"Are you day dreaming?" Emily asks.

"I don't know, but when we kissed, it felt right. You know like that moment when you see the light on red, and instead of racing past, you brake gently."

"Lexie," Emily shakes her head. "How can you liken a kiss to driving a car? Please," Emily moans. "Anyway, the last I heard about doing something right, was about Africa and poverty; not about traffic lights or kissing someone."

"But you understand what I mean, right?"

"What I understand is that he's poisoned you."

"No, he hasn't," I say with a quiet voice.

I don't want to think about this. If I feel anything for Zachary, what do I feel for Chan? I hardly know Zachary, and yet I feel as if I have known him all my life.

"Yes, he has. And God help you because I think his venom is as deadly as Chan's. Look at you; you can't even speak."

"You are so wrong ..." I break off, interrupted by my phone ringing. "It's Zachary."

"Talk of the snake."

"Shh." I shoot her a playful scowl as I place the phone by my ear and say, "hello."

"Hey, beautiful," Zachary says in a less enthusiastic tone than normal. "Can we meet ASAP?"

"*Why?* Is everything okay?"

"Yes, our daughter Autumn Reigns is fine, only missing her mother." He tries to joke as usual, but I still hear a hint of sadness.

"What about you? Are you alright?" I ask with caution.

He lets out a heavy sigh. "I'm meeting a friend at Lost Closet in an hour. Can you meet me there?"

"I'm approaching the Mall right now. Call me when you get here. I'll be in—"

"I think I'll find you," he says.

"Zach, wait!"

"I'm here."

"Business or ... Personal?"

"Does it matter?"

"A little."

"Both," he replies, and I feel him smiling. "And, Alex?"

"Yes."

"I, um ... never mind. See you soon."

"Okay, soon."

❦❧❦

"How about this one, Lexie?" Emily asks, but I ignore her. She wants me to give my opinion on her costume, but I'm still waiting for what I asked her to do five minutes ago.

We are now in Lost Closet. After familiarizing Victoria and Megan with the store, we stop at the 11th floor, the Peeling Back Centuries department.

It's enormous, with vintage costumes dating back to the sixteenth century. The aisles are organized by century with a range of private changing rooms at every corner of the floor. Emily and I are in one of them.

Unlike the usual high street shops, the changing rooms are not cubicles, but spacious rooms decorated with soft furnishings. They also come with a personal shopping assistant, except Emily and I choose not to have an one.

While the girls shop for the masquerade costumes, Emily and I decide to indulge in the fun of trying on different outfits.

There's a huge mirror on one side of the walls in the changing room. I stand behind a burgundy fabric covered screen, changing while Emily is concealed behind a cream one.

I have tried on six costumes, and I think the fun has just begun as I slide into the seventh—a blackberry corset costume, off-shoulder style, with tight bodice and detailed beading on the edges. It slides down my hips, and I sigh when it settles perfectly.

"Lexie, one last time. I won't bother you anymore," Emily pleads.

"I'm still waiting for you to lace my dress up," I tell her.

"This is the last one, and I'll do your dress. I promise."

Admiring my reflection in the mirror, I sigh and carry my heavy costume to her screen. "My God," I gasp at her curvy fish tail gown. "You've stepped back centuries."

"You like it?" Her eyes light up.

"Yeah, but you look like a widow in black." I drag my lengthy dress and walk back to the costumes hanging on padded hangers by the antique-like mobile clothes rail. "How about light green, butter-cream or bronze, maybe." I raise a bronze costume.

"Oh God!" Emily skips with excitement. "I know just the color and where to find it." She kisses my cheeks and rushes toward the door.

"Where you going?" I call after her, but it's too late; she's shut the door.

I go back to the mirror and close my eyes as I realize, yet again, Emily didn't fasten my costume.

A moment later, there's a knock at the door. I drag my dress to the door. Certain it's Emily; I turn the knob and walk back, annoyed.

"I'm not looking at you until you lace me up," I say.

"No problem." That was a reply, but not from Emily.

"Zachary?" I turn in haste, my heart pounding from both his sudden appearance and the excitement that he's here.

"Miss me?" He raises an eyebrow but keeps his hands behind his back.

"You're early," I say, breathing in a scent of fresh calla lilies.

"Couldn't wait to see you." He grins.

I eye him with suspicion; he's holding his hands behind his back. I tilt my head to the side. "What are you hiding?"

"Nothing special," he says, playfully mirroring my head.

With a deliberate slow pace, I take one step after the other moving toward him. Matching my speed, he backs off and stops when he's closer to the door. His face beams with excitement as I pause inches from him.

He looks overly smart today, dressed in a pair of black satin pants and a crispy, plum, checkered shirt with smartly folded sleeves.

"How did you find me?" I breathe by his lips.

"I saw Emily at the desk."

He searches not only my eyes, but my whole face—from my eyebrows, then to my nose, goes to the top of my head and down to my lips. "She said I'd find you in here," he whispers, dropping his gaze to my dress, then releasing one hand to reach for my open back. "You need help to fix this?" His fingers trace my spine.

I catch a sharp breath, resisting the urge to shut my eyes. "Yes." I swallow, placing my hand on his chest.

I measure the excitement in his eyes and smile. "But how will you with the other hand behind your back?"

I'm waiting for him to speak, but he stares at me, his face beaming. It widens into a grin as if he's just had an epiphany. "Guess what I have for you?"

I roll my eyes. "I can smell them, Zachary."

"You just spoiled the surprise, Alexandra. Couldn't you pretend, at least?" His shoulders slump as he flashes the bouquet in my face. "White, as you like them."

"Calla lilies? Someone has been reading my résumé," I tease and drop my head to smell them.

"I swear; favorite flowers are not part of a résumé." He wraps his arms around my waist, and mine with the flowers circle his neck.

"Aren't they?"

"No." He shakes his head, smiling.

"So how did you know? You went through all the trouble, huh?"

"I just know you, beautiful." A side smile grows on his face.

"Tell me the truth, and I'll give you a thank you kiss, right here, right now."

The corners of his lips curl into a smile. I'm staring at his lips as he stares at mine. Our eyes lock again. I turn, walking away, but Zachary clutches my waist, tosses the flowers aside and brings me to his hold.

Not that I want to, but I'm still thinking of how to protest when he impatiently seals his lips with mine. Our lips move in harmony, the same excitement binding me to his hold. I have my hands around his neck when he breaks the kiss.

"That's the truth," Zachary whispers, and steps behind me.

Exhaling, he slides his arms around my waist. I shut my eyes as he kisses my cheek, brushes his lips past my neck to trace my collarbone. As my breath quickens, he stops and begins pulling the laces of my dress to fasten them.

There is a long silence before Zachary speaks again. "Tighter?" he asks.

"Just right." I clear my throat. "It's perfect like that."

We say nothing for another moment; Zachary fastening the laces. I breathe at every movement he makes. As he ties the last knot, my mind wanders.

"So, why does the knight bring me flowers?"

Zachary leans in to touch my cheek with his, then sighs. "Perhaps he seeks forgiveness."

"Time for confessions, huh? What's there to forgive?" I hold his hands on my belly closer, lacing our fingers.

"Betrayal of trust, it looks like."

"*Looks* like?" I turn around to face him. "And how was trust betrayed?"

He closes his eyes, reaches for my hands, and plays with my fingers. "Alexandra, I don't know how to say this, but ..." He shakes his head.

"Tell me!" I cup his face and force him to look into my eyes. "Is it so bad that you—"

"It's complicated. I don't—"

"Zach!" A familiar voice calls from outside the room.

I frown. "Is that ...?"

"I have to go." Zachary plants a kiss on my cheek before dashing out.

"*Sean?*" I murmur, wondering if I heard right.

A moment passes, and I drag my lengthy dress out of the dressing room to find Zachary, but he's gone.

I meet Emily by the eighteenth-century section. She looks dazzling in a dusky pink ball gown.

"Did you see Zach Van-B?" Emily asks. "He was looking for you."

"Did you see Sean, anywhere?" I ask.

"Lexie, are you all right?" She stares at me as if I have gone mad.

"Forget it." I shake my head and turn toward the dressing room, but Emily tugs my arm, and drags me toward the shoe section.

"I need your opinion."

"*Really?*" I shoot a questioning gaze at her. "Did you lace my dress as you promised?"

She embraces me. "Come on, the job is done, so why dwell on the past?"

We meet Victoria and Megan in the shoe section. They wear long masquerade costumes; Victoria in a midnight-blue, mermaid styled dress and Megan in a revealing electric-blue, mini dress with a matching feathered mask. We stop to complement the two girls, and thereafter Emily pulls me toward the colorful shoe section.

"Now, stripe or polka dot," she asks as she models in polka dot five inch heels.

I frown; she has too many striped heels. "Polka—Ouch!" A yellow shoe, flying from the isle behind, hits my head before landing on the ground.

"What was that?" Emily asks. "Are you okay?"

I nod and pause to listen to the rumblings and stifled laughter coming from the isle behind.

Annoyed at their laughter, I march toward the next aisle.

"Lexie, wait." Emily follows. "What are you going to do?"

"Deal with the moron who dropped a shoe on me." I freeze, refusing to believe what I was seeing. "My God!"

Emily, now beside me follows my gaze. "Well, well, if it isn't the venomous snake," she mumbles, staring at Zachary. "And the antidote, thank heavens," she adds, referring to Sean, who stands beside Zachary.

Sean, looking smart in a pair of brown chinos and a cream shirt with two brown strips along the buttons, laughs with Zachary.

Zachary nudges him, and grins as he hands a shoe box to a dark-haired girl who receives the box with a pleasant smile.

"Please tell me they're not brothers," I whisper.

"They're not brothers." Emily turns to me with a smirk.

I roll my eyes.

"Now don't turn pale on me, Lexie. It could be they just met, and they …" She shakes her head as the two boys exchange a complex hug. "No. I don't know what to think. Oh I know." She links our arms and pulls me toward the boys.

"What are you doing?" I whisper.

"Pretending like we don't know them."

"*What?* No. How?" I try to resist as she drags me forward.

"Don't worry. Nothing rude."

Zachary is the first to notice us as he turns in our direction. Our eyes meet, but he looks away in an instant.

Sean is about turning to look at us when Zachary moves his hand over his shoulder and drags him further away.

"Wait," Sean complains to Zachary and walks back. He stops when he sees Emily and me. His frowned face instantaneously melts into a beaming smile. "Alex? Emily."

He's about to say something—possibly, hello—when Emily interrupts him. "Who dropped the shoe on us?" She crosses her arms over her chest.

Sean frowns, but I can still see a smile on his face. He turns to Zachary with a mischievous smile and elbows him. "Was it you, Zach?"

Zachary scratches his head. "Don't know. Was it you, Sean?"

"I think the shoe fell on you," Sean answers, and the two boys chuckle.

"You are saying you didn't drop the shoe?" Emily asks again.

Sean leans to whisper at Zachary, loud enough so we can hear. "Can we still be proud gentlemen if I say yes?"

"No." Zachary shakes his head and smile.

Sean stares back at us with a smug look on his face. "We dropped the shoe, yes, but, not on you."

As the boys laugh, I shake my head and lean toward Emily, whispering, "*Romeo and Juliet; Act 1, Scene 1.*"

Sean moves closer to hold my hands.

My mind runs to Zachary, and without warning, my heart picks up the pace.

"We dropped the shoe on you. It wasn't intentional, but still it dropped on you, so … I'm sorry," Sean says.

Conscious of Zachary's eyes on me, I try to free my hands from Sean, but he holds them tight, his eyes tracking mine.

I don't want to look at his face. His blue eyes haunt me.

It seems I can't think properly. My eyes are now looking at Sean's hands, holding mine.

"I'm sorry, have we missed something?" Zachary breaks the silence. "Have we skipped the rest of the scenes because I can see you two confessing your undying love?" He laughs, but I can't tell if it's a sarcastic laugh or not.

Again, I try to free my hands from Sean, but he keeps holding them tight.

"Sean, don't forget the intros," Zachary says.

I frown at him, wondering who needs the introductions. Is he pretending he doesn't know me? *Why?*

"She makes me forget things." Sean chuckles.

He pauses to give way to a couple passing through. They have several shoe boxes in their hands.

Sean turns to Emily and me. "Alex, Emily, meet my best friend Zachary. He's more like a brother to me. Zach, meet Emily, and Alex, the girl I told you attacked the bartender."

My mouth opens. I'm not surprised Sean told Zachary about the bartender. He is not aware I know Zachary, and Zachary is playing along.

"You didn't lie; she's beautiful." Zachary extends his arm to shake my hand, then Emily's. "Only you didn't tell me her best friend was just as beautiful. It's a pleasure meeting you, girls."

"You too." I force the words out, and Emily echoes the same.

Emily glances at me and we both turn looking at Zachary, who says nothing apart from displaying a pleasant smile.

My heart is still humming as I stare at him. He holds my gaze for a few seconds, parts his lips, but nothing comes out. A crease forms on his forehead.

"So what do you say now that you've seen her?" Sean turns to Zachary, who seems absent-minded.

"What?" Zachary asks.

"You think Mimi will approve of my new neighbor and friend?"

Zachary's jaw clenches. He swallows as if preparing to answer, but Emily speaks before him.

"Who's Mimi?"

"My best friend, who's also the love of his life," Sean says, facing Zachary this time.

His words fall on my chest like a heavy brick. I try to suppress my emotions, but cold air blocks my throat tight.

"Zach has a *girlfriend*?" Emily asks.

Sean frowns. "Of course. Did you wish …?"

"No." Emily shakes her head as if the thought never crossed her mind. "I've always thought he would have *girlfriends*, not just one."

Zachary's face stiffens. Lips pursed, he turns to Sean. "Sean, we should go," he utters.

He can't look at me, and now he wants to leave.

"Sean!" he calls again.

"Wait! What's wrong with you?" Sean shoots him a curious look before turning back at me. "Join us for an early dinner at Nair. Mimi is coming, so you get to meet her—and the girls are coming, too," he says, referring to Victoria and Megan. "What do you say, Zach?"

"Um, sure. Why not," Zachary stammers.

"Are you all right?" Sean asks, staring at my tight face.

I was fine until he asked. Now, all the tight air inside of me, shoots out of my chest at once. I feel as if I'm choking.

Sean holds my hands. "Alex, what's wrong?"

"Um, I'm fine." I try not to gasp aloud. "I'm thirsty. I need some water or maybe it's the heels."

With my hand to my forehead, I take in more air. "I'm sorry. I should go free myself from this tight costume ... some *idiot* fixed it too tight. It's suffocating."

XII

I Might As Well Hold It Against Myself ...

In the dressing room, Emily and I argue. She's going on about the "I told you so" topic, and I don't want to hear it.

"Hurry up. I can't breathe," I say to her.

"It's not the dress suffocating you, Lexie. It's the truth." She takes her time unlacing my dress.

"Truth sets people free, not the other way round," I mumble.

"I said it, he's bitten you, forget him. Sean, the antidote is available. Match made in heaven. Blue eyes like Chan, fate brought him right next door to you. Plus you picked him first, remember?"

"You know I picked him for other reasons, nothing to do with how I feel."

"So you agree you feel something for Zachary."

For a minute, my eyes rest on the jade bracelet on my wrist. "I just need this costume off."

With our costumes now off, Emily and I change into the dresses we wore from home; colorful high-fashion dresses accessorized with fancy bracelets and earrings.

We take our bags and head out of the changing room. A cool breeze from the air con above blows on me as I close the door. For a moment, I shut my eyes, trying to calm the uneven rhythm of my heart.

Twice, Emily forces a cough. I turn around and see Zachary in front of me.

I stare into his brown eyes, and rage fills my chest. It spins into a tight ball that rushes up my throat. My nose flare, but I'm not going to give him the joy of seeing me cry.

I turn, walking the other way. Zachary grabs my arm. "Don't run away from me, please."

"Let go of me!" I shrug him off and stumble backwards.

"Alexandra, please don't make me chase after you—not now."

"You need to go, Zachary." Emily takes my hand.

Zachary clenches his jaw, blocking my way as he turns to yell at Emily. "You need to back off. This has nothing to do with you!"

"No, *you* should to back off!" I stand between him and Emily.

"I need to talk to you," he whispers.

"I don't need to talk to you." I turn, following Emily, but Zachary blocks my way. "What do you think you're doing?"

He doesn't answer, holds me by the waist and drags me back in the dressing room. We struggle as he takes the keys from me and shuts the door on Emily's face.

"Talk to me!" He breathes as he pins me to the wall and restrains me between his arms. "What's wrong with you?"

"Wrong with me?" I push him off, snorting. "You're the one who has a girlfriend."

"And what's that got to do with you?"

My face heats up and I shake my head. "I can't believe you have the guts to ask me that question. If it's nothing to do with me, then why do you need to talk to me?"

"Well, I just need to see you are okay."

"Now that you've seen I'm okay, I can go home, right?" I start for the door.

"Okay!" He runs after me and takes my hand. "Mimi and I were together. Some time ago, we broke up, and she left." He inhales, continuing with a mollified voice. "She came back yesterday. That's what I wanted to tell you earlier, but I couldn't."

I yank my hands out of his hold and stare into his piercing eyes. He doesn't blink, and I wonder if he's telling the truth.

As I fight to suppress my anger, my chest tightens. *I wonder why this bothers me.* I expected someone like him would have a girlfriend, if not girlfriends. Maybe, deep down, I hoped he didn't.

"Sean is a good guy if you get to know him," he says in a low voice.

"Great." I puff out a sarcastic laugh, turning my back to him. "So you are now passing me to your best friend. Is that what you two have been discussing? Talking about me as if I'm your Zetra Zeus?"

"Alex, you know I could never do that."

"No, I don't!" I swing around to face him, challenging his unyielding eyes. "I'm just seeing exactly who you are now. I don't really know you, Zachary—do I?"

His brow furrows. "So you're putting all this on me?" He moves his left hand to his waist. "From beginning you knew what you were doing, Alex. As far as I remember, we never said we were dating. If you think I'm going to apologize for anything, I'm not!"

"We *were*?" Heat flashes over me as I laugh in anger. "Did you say we were?" I stare at him with arms crossed. "Tell me this. When did we become the past? Did you not give me lilies an hour ago?"

"It happens. A boy can give a girl flowers at random, just like you kissed Sean."

"What?"

"Yes, he told me, if that's what you want to ask."

"Is that what this is about?"

Zachary shakes his head and opens his mouth to speak again, but I'm faster. "That was once, the night of the accident. It meant nothing."

"Well, he seems to think it means something." He runs his fingers through his hair and turns away from me.

"That didn't seem to bother you when we kissed earlier."

"I speak not for myself, but for Sean. He's my best friend." Zachary faces me again.

"Ha!" I blow out a disgusted sound. "You are such a player, aren't you? And never use that tone on me again, Zachary."

"What tone?" He grimaces.

"You know what I mean. That formal Van-Bailey voice, 'I speak not for myself blah, blah'."

He almost laughs, but in the end, a smile molds on his face. For a moment, we remain silent, staring at each other.

"I'll find a way to tell him about the racetrack. He doesn't know about us, and I say we should keep it that way. He told me yesterday about how he met this incredible girl, and soon I realized that girl was you. I can't hurt him."

"Really?" I shake my head. "Is that why you didn't tell him, or you didn't want your girlfriend to know what you've been up to?"

"What do you want me to say, Alexandra? I said, I'm sorry."

"No, you didn't," I yell. "All you did was to give me reasons why you are so smart, and I'm such a fool!" I turn away to hide my clouding eyes.

"Okay, I'm saying it now. I'm sorry. I never meant to hurt you, and I still want you as my dream partner—please."

I turn and stare at him with a sigh. He holds his breath as if waiting for what I have to say.

I don't know what I'm fighting for. What do I really want from him? Why am I so upset?

"Would you hold it against me if I say I really like you—more than Sean?"

He catches a quick breath then hurries to pull me to his chest. "I might as well hold it against myself," he whispers. "It's my fault. I'm sorry."

He pulls back to look into my eyes. With measured slowness, he reaches for my face, his fingers tender as they brush my blushing cheeks. Focused and unhurried, his face draws closer to mine, our noses touch, and we both exhale heavily.

My mouth water as he moves his lips from my cheek, stopping just above my top lip. In breathless anticipation, I inhale his scent and move my hesitate lips to touch his.

He kisses me once, but I back off. "I'm sorry, I can't. I mean, it's just ..."

"It's okay. I understand." He swallows, then smiles a little. His smile disappears, and as if in a hurry, he presses his lips passionately on my forehead. He pulls me into a tight hug before heading for the door.

I take in a couple of sharp breaths, hugging myself as he pulls the door open.

All of a sudden, I feel cold. It's as if my heart has been plunged into an avalanche. I can't let him go. I hate that he deceived me, and yet I want him.

"Zachary, Wait!"

He turns, gazing at me with eyebrows raised.

"Um ..." I stutter, wary of the open door. "I ..." The beating of my heart increases as I stare at him. With every breath, I battle to control my erratic chest.

"What is it?"

I part my trembling lips, try to speak again, but the only language they express is silence.

Zachary rushes to hold me and seals our lips. Scrambling for air, we wrestle, scuffle and gasp as our tongues intermingle, our bodies coiling to each other with desire.

His lips slide to my neck, and I let out a faint gasp, not only from the shivers that his warm kisses shoot over my body, but the flashing images. The visions are back, and this time he's kissing my neck. I see fangs flashing from his mouth, ready to puncture my neck.

"No!" I pull off breathlessly.

"I'm sorry," he whispers, touching his forehead to mine.

I don't answer, but lean in and bury my head in his neck. We stay like that for a while, then I hear Sean calling him. "Zach!"

Zachary lets go of me, fixes his shirt in haste while I wipe traces of the kiss off his cheeks. Turning for the door, he clears his throat and walks out, bumping into Sean just outside the door.

"Is everything okay?" Zachary asks.

"Yeah." Sean's gaze moves from Zachary to me. He narrows his eyes a little. "Is everything okay?"

"I was asking Alex if she and Emily need a parking reservation at the Nair. You know how the bridge—"

"Yeah, the walk over the bridge can be a nightmare, at times." Sean agrees. "So, we are good? Everything sorted out?" Sean stares at me and Zachary.

"Um, I don't think I can make it for dinner. I really need to go home. My mom—"

"Alex, please." Sean stares at me. "Emily said she's coming." He turns to look at her sitting at a distance, by the waiting area. She smiles and waves as we stare at her.

I sigh, wanting to say no, but before I open my mouth, Sean says, "thank you, see you at six."

In unison, the boys kiss my cheeks and wave goodbye. I watch their shoulders bump into each other as they walk away.

At ten past six, against the boys' advice, Emily and I step on the arched stone bridge. Big mistake; the bridge is too crowded. We hustle through the crowd of visitors who always come here to admire the Nair's glorious lines of water fountains. The walk is not as straightforward as I hoped.

"I told you, we should take the car," Emily complains while we struggle to avoid rubbing shoulders with strangers.

"Why should we drive all the way around the Mall when we can just cross over here?"

"We—shit!" Emily bumps into a man carrying a box of cream doughnuts. "See—that is why," she adds, and we exhale, stepping off the bridge.

Ahead of us stands the grand, glossy entrance of the restaurant. Its wide, glass doors and windows are glazed with gold.

Two door attendants bow slightly and smile as they greet us. They pull the doors open, and we walk through. We're greeted by the delicious smells of broiled steaks and brewing coffee.

There are stairs and lifts to the right. To the left, guests fill the room as they dine on spaced round tables, surrounded by mirrored walls.

I have been here before with Mother, but not on the private floor where Sean instructed us to go. Past the brown, sleek, earth colored walls, we head to the elevators, going up to the twenty-first floor.

We come out of the elevator and enter the imposing lobby of a high-ceilinged room with glass walls throughout.

The sound of our heels tapping against the mosaic tiled floors is subdued by the tinkle of laughter behind the chalky brick wall in front of us. A guitar plays lazily as the laughter fades, and a male voice sings.

"Is that Sean singing?" Emily whispers.

I shrug. "Sounds like him."

A few more steps and I pause, watching Victoria, Megan, Zachary and another boy who looks like Zachary, snuggled on the fluffy, cream sofas. They are listening to Sean, who sits upon a stool, singing as he plays a guitar. *Where is she? Where's Madeline.*

Not far from the circular sofa, and closer to the glass walls, is a long rectangular table, already set, dressed in white and metallic bronze. Fluttering colors of gold and purple from the city's night-lights and the fountains outside penetrate through the glass wall, creating rippling patterns on the trendy dinnerware.

Sean is the first to see us. He hits the last note on his guitar and smiles in our direction.

"They're here! We can eat now!" Megan skips to embrace Emily and me.

More hugs follow, mixed with joyful hellos from the others. Zachary makes no attempt to hug me, but introduces his brother Maxx, who looks almost identical to him.

With shorter black and wavy hair, Maxx stands as tall as I am. His shy, brown eyes make him appear softer than Zachary. However, the Van-Bailey arrogance still shows through his tight smiles and the stiff shoulders.

He is a little shorter than Zachary, and more patient in his manner of speech.

Soon we move to the table. Sean takes the seat at the end, backed by the city views. He pulls me to sit next to him on his left, opposite Megan. Beside me is Emily, facing Maxx. Zachary sits at the other end of the table with Victoria on his right and an empty seat on his left.

The mood is merry with Sean, who's finding every excuse to make everyone laugh. Victoria keeps whispering into Zachary's ears, and Maxx is quiet, like I am. He's observing everyone, including me. Our eyes meet, and we both smile at each other.

"They're too loud," he says.

"*Too*, too loud," I reply and we both chuckle.

From the other end of the table, Zachary draws attention to himself. We all turn to him, waiting to hear what he has to say.

"It gives me pleasure to see all of you *my people*, dashing about for my sake – for my birthday," he teases.

There's grumbling at the table, complaints about Zachary's choice of words, *my people*.

"Oh, before I forget ..." Sean turns to me. "Zachary said I should give you and Emily invitations to his birthday party, April 28. Will you go with me?"

"Sean, I ..." I trail off.

"Six weeks are enough for you to think about it." Sean reaches for my hand under the table. "Let me know when you decide."

I nod and slowly pull my hand from his.

"The theme is a masquerade," Sean continues. "I suggest shopping early. That's why Vee and Meg were shopping for their costumes today."

"Masquerade?" I ask.

"Van-Bailey style. You will love it. I promise." He smiles.

"Whose empty seat?" I ask, staring at the seat next to Zachary.

"Oh, that's for Mimi," he says.

"Zachary's girlfriend?" The words almost choke me as they come out of my mouth.

Sean nods.

Why exactly am I here?

The starter is served. White wine bottles poured one after the other, and yet the seat next to Zachary is still vacant.

Later, the waiters bring the entrée placing each dish in front of us as ordered.

With everyone else involved in small conversations, I turn to Sean. I ask him how long he has known Zachary. He tells me since the day he was born. The Van-Baileys and his family have been very close friends since back in Pannonia.

As I continue chatting with Sean, I catch Zachary staring at us every now and again. He continues to check for time.

Minutes later, he wipes the corner of his mouth with a napkin, draws his chair back as if to prepare to stand and turns to stare toward the elevator.

I follow his gaze, and there she is, swinging toward him. Zachary's eyes light up as she leans in to kiss his cheek.

He stands and embraces her with affection. Holding her close, he kisses her on the lips, his eyes shut. I see how he adores her. Until now, I've never doubted my good looks.

Her skin is silk ivory, the opposite of my golden. Her platinum-blonde hair, sharply cut like Victoria's, shines with health. As if her curvy shape is not enough to make my heart ache, she has a warm smile that brings cheer, and her presence is captivating.

I watch as she greets everyone with an earnest hug. She has something to say to everyone—about everything, something to make everyone laugh.

It's my turn, and I watch as she comes. With her blue eyes on me, she opens her arms. I want to hate her, but how can I when she squeezes me so warm and tight as if I'm her long- lost sister.

She walks back to sit next to Zachary. I pull out my chair to sit and think of reasons to belittle her, but find none.

"That's Madeline Cruz," Sean whispers. "We call her Mimi. She and Zach have known each other since they were babies. Best friends at first, but after helping Zachary through some tough times, I knew they would end up in love," Sean explains as I watch Zachary and Madeline whispering to each other.

"What tough times?"

"I can't really say much because he wouldn't want me to tell you, but he wasn't himself for a very long time."

I turn to Zachary. He's laughing with Madeline. Soon after, they excuse themselves and leave the table. Zachary doesn't even look at me as he leaves.

Earlier, I've asked myself why I'm here, and now I understand. I've wanted to see Madeline, to see her and compare her to myself. Now I have, and my stomach ties in knots. The sight of the two of them leaves me cold. If there ever a time I felt inhuman, it's now. I want to stand and scream, but I don't want to be the obsessed 'side-girlfriend'.

"Are you alright?" Sean disturbs my thoughts.

"Yeah." I nod and stare at him for a while before deciding to tell the truth. "Actually, no, I'm not alright. I need to go home."

Emily, who's laughing with Megan and Maxx, turns look at me with an understanding.

Abruptly, I stand, excuse myself and rush out toward the lifts. Emily follows, together with Sean, and I'm surprised to see Maxx next to me.

"Did you drive? I could drop you home if you like," Maxx says in a gentlemanlike manner. His offer makes me smile a little, and I feel a tiny guilty for leaving dinner as I did.

"Thank you, Maxx, but ..." I glance at Emily, and she nods. "We'll be fine," I say to Maxx with a pleasant smile.

"It's nice meeting you," he adds and leans in to hug me. He holds me so close as if he's known me for a long time. He hugs Emily too before turning and walking back toward the table.

"Is he always such a gentleman?" I ask Sean as we walk out of the elevators heading for the exit.

"Maxx?" Sean smiles. "Wait until you know him. Not to say he's not a gentleman, but he's fun to be around."

I remain silent, waiting for Emily, who's hugging Megan goodbye.

When she's done, I say, "You can stay and have fun if you want. You don't have—"

"Only if you give me permission to pour wine on his face," she says, referring to Zachary. But, I can't let her get so involved.

"You want me to drive you home?" Sean asks as we cross the road to make our way to the bridge.

"No, thanks, I think we'll be fine."

"Are you okay, Alex? Do you feel unwell?"

"Yes, sorry for spoiling dinner. I do feel a little sick."

"Don't be silly." He plants a quick kiss on my cheek. "I'm glad you came," he smiles, and we say our goodbyes.

"Slow down, Lexie." Emily says.

It's been about ten minutes of silence since we left the restaurant.

Driving away from the city lights, I turn onto the highway that takes us home. The road is free of traffic. In the light of today's events, I feel relieved. The bright orange streetlights, however, reminds me of the night I first met Zachary. I'm aware it's not that long a time, but to me, it feels like a century ago.

"You told me so, right?" I push the gear forward, holding the steering wheel with one hand while I rest my head on the other by the window.

"I'm so sorry, Lexie," Emily says.

I force a smile, briefly glancing at her. "Are you, really?"

"Really." She reaches out for my arm and rubs it gently. "I know how much you liked him."

"Liked?" I cough out a sarcastic laugh. "I still do."

Emily withdraws her arm and turns to stare out her window in silence.

"You know ..." I pause to swallow. "I'm the one who warns you against boys like him, but I failed to caution myself." I shake my head, laughing. "I'm such a fool. How could I ... I mean, how did I even consider him and me?"

"Take time to know someone, you always say."

"That's why I won't forgive myself." I stop at the traffic light on amber. "How could I even blame him when I betrayed myself?"

The light flashes green, and we are on the move again.

We get home around half past eight. The note by the telephone table tells me Mother has left for work. She adds a few extra lines reminding me to set the security alarm.

Emily offers to sleep over. She thinks I might go back to my melancholy days, but I'm stronger now.

After a shower, I wrap myself in my favorite coffee-colored silk dressing gown, and lounge with Emily on the couch in the informal living room, watching a movie.

"I could really do with a cappuccino," I sigh, and turn to Emily, hoping she would offer to make one for me.

She ignores me, and it's clear she has a troubled mind.

"I won't go if you don't want me to, you know," she says, going back to my decision not to attend Zachary's party next month.

"Go and have fun," I tell her. "Seriously, I'm fine with you going. You don't want to miss a chance to meet someone new, right?"

"Why won't you come? I mean, you still have to work with Zachary, so you will talk to him at some point."

"I know, and I don't have a problem talking to Zachary. I just can't watch him with her."

We remain quiet for a while.

"She's beautiful," Emily says in a dreamy tone.

"Thanks for reminding me. I almost forgot," I say in a sarcastic tone.

The buzzer rings. Emily and I stare at each other.

"You're expecting someone?"

"No." I stand to check the video intercom. "Nair delivery. It must be from Zachary or Sean. If it's from Zachary, I don't want it."

Nair Saif, the restaurant, is known for twenty-four seven delivery service, so it's not unusual for them to be making a delivery this late.

"I'll go." Emily hurries to the door while I walk back to the couch.

As the door opens, the aroma of rich cappuccino fills my nostrils, grazing my throat to sit in my caffeine-craving belly.

The door shuts, and after a few seconds, Emily appears from the hallway. In her hand is a small cupcake box, decorated with lavish stripes of light-blue, pink and lime, tied in style with a chocolate brown ribbon with a laced edge.

"It's for you." Emily passes the box and cappuccino to me.

I open the small card attached to the ribbons and grimace as I read it.

Alexandria,

I'm sorry.

Love, Zachary.

I draw in a deep breath, ease back on the couch, and turn up the TV volume.

After a minute, Emily passes me the cappuccino. "It will get cold, unless, you don't want it."

I hesitate before extending my hand to take the cappuccino.

"I'll just have a sip," I say, but one sip turns into two, three and more.

"You haven't opened the box yet," Emily prompts.

I say nothing, staring at it. "He thinks a mere cappuccino, and a box of stupid cupcakes can fix everything." I grumble and continue sipping on the cappuccino. I slide the box to Emily. "Throw them away. I don't want them."

She opens the box, picks up a red velvet cupcake and raises it to her mouth.

I stop her. "Okay, I'll have it," I say.

She laughs and picks up one cupcake before passing the box to me.

"This does not mean I'm going to the party, get that straight." I reach for my cappuccino again.

"It's not me you should be saying that to." Emily relaxes her head on my shoulder, and we turn back to the movie, but I'm not watching. My mind is too full of Zachary to focus on anything else.

XIII

DON'T MAKE ME SING THE SONG

"I hoped to call you *dad*, one day," I say to John De Luca as we stand in one of the Union Square's gold-plated elevators.

John, in his usual black pants and a black shirt, turns and frowns at me. "You can call me dad if that's what you want."

He adjusts his favorite blazer, rich caramel in color with minimal armor details by the shoulders. The color brings out his silver-like eyes.

"You will soon be Rebecca's husband," I say, and raise my arm to remove my lemon cardigan. It's not noon, yet the weather is growing warmer; summer's approaching.

"And who said being someone's husband stops one from being a dad?" John asks.

"John, come on." I nudge him. "I'm sure you know what I mean."

The elevator stops on the fourth floor. The doors open and a rush of rich perfumes floods my nostrils.

In a gentlemanly fashion, John offers me his arm, and like during our usual walks, I place my hand on his arm. We stroll past the glossy jewelry shops steeped with glamour and gold.

We are heading for *Timeless*, the jewelry store where John is to pick up the ring we chose for Rebecca earlier this morning. John wanted it engraved. The jeweler said it would take them an hour to work on it, so we decided to take a stroll while waiting.

"Now I see it was just a fatherless girl's wish." I continue trying to force an explanation out of John.

"Alexandra," John says in his pay attention low, but imposing voice. "Father, stepfather, dad, daughter, they are merely names. What matters is the relationship. Like you and me, we are father and daughter, aren't we?"

I shrug. "Like I said, I don't know how it feels to have a father, so, I guess—"

"Are you guessing about me? *Us?*" He shoots me a questioning glance. "What is it you ever wished from a father I didn't do for you?"

I drop my gaze, and now I wish for this conversation to end. "Nothing," I say.

"In my eyes, you will always be my daughter." He pulls me closer and presses his lips on my forehead. Letting go, he offers me his arm again.

I accept with a smile, and we walk ahead.

"Tell you what." John glances at me with a smirk.

I try to scowl, but a smile creeps out of my lips. "What?"

"Already, I'll have booked, um ... what's the name of that designer you like?"

"VEGA?"

"VEGA, yes." He rubs my hand as we start walking again. "I told him to do the tuxedo that I'd wear on your wedding day, when I give you away."

I laugh.

"And the other part of me told me to prepare some super-bonding glue I'd apply to my hand. When you place your hand in mine on that happy day, we'll be stuck together, so I won't ever have to give you away."

"And who said I want to marry?"

"Do you mean you want to have children out of marriage? Because I know how much you want to have children, someday."

I pause to think for a moment. "Can I still have children, even after I become immortal?"

He stops with a frown. "Your mother and I are working on that."

"You care so much for me and Mother, yet you are marrying Rebecca."

With a tight jaw, he remains silent. His brow creases, and I almost regret asking. "Sometimes in life we don't always get what we want. There is one thing greater than love, and that's sacrifice," John explains.

We cross the busy high street and walk into Timeless. The gentleman who served us earlier, smiles as he sees us and without waiting for us to speak, he unlocks a glass cabinet behind the counter and presents it to us.

John checks if everything is as agreed, and soon we are back on the street, sauntering to the place where we left our car.

I turn to John, as we drive back home. "Can I ask you something?"

"Anything you want," John says in a lowered voice.

"It's about a boy." I sigh.

"Let me guess. Zachary Van-Bailey?"

My forehead creases. "Is it that obvious?"

"From the day your mother told me about the partnership, I knew there was something more."

I smile, contemplating whether I should continue.

"What's your question?" John glances at me.

"Uhm." I gaze down at my fingers, then look up at John. "I kissed him."

"That's not a question."

"Aren't you surprised?" I stare at his eyes.

"No." He smirks. "He's not the first boy you've kissed, is he?"

"What if I say I see things when I kiss him?"

The car slows down. "Things?"

"Strange, flashing images of him and me." I draw in another deep breath. "I suspect Zachary is a vampire, and since his father is your best friend, you would know if they are vampires, right?"

His mouth opens, but I speak before he does.

"And don't tell me there are no supernatural beings in Ashbourne because I know there are."

"Whom have you been talking to, Alexandra?" John asks.

"Since you and Mother chose to keep everything a secret, I decided to seek the truth from elsewhere."

"And where exactly is elsewhere?"

"New neighbors."

"Sean, of course. I should have known." He shakes his head. "If there were a heaven for telling the truth that boy will be first to enter, only he will regret it. With all of us in hell, I can't help thinking how lonely he would be."

I laugh.

"Glad I can still make you laugh." John rubs my arm a little.

"You didn't answer my question, though."

He glances at me briefly. "Didn't Sean tell you? His family and the Van-Baileys are very close, whereas I'm more of a worker than a best friend to him."

"He said it was against the rules," I explain.

"At least he remembers to keep within the rules," John taunts.

"You know about the rules of the Supernatural?"

John laughs in disbelief. "I am the Marshal of this city, after all."

"And the answer to my question?"

"You have answered the question yourself. It is against the rules. I work for the city, work for the Van-Baileys. I can't break the rules."

"Even for your daughter?"

A smile crinkles his eyes. "You sure know how to cuddle my heart, don't you?" He pulls me closer to kiss my cheeks, then sighs. "It's dangerous, especially when you are moving around with the Van-Baileys and the Deschanels. Never tell anyone about your nature, Alexandra. You never know who turns out to be your enemy."

⁂

"Too revealing," I mumble, holding the dress against myself in front of the cheval mirror. "I don't want to give Sean the wrong idea."

Too late now, Alexandra, the damage is done. He already thinks you want him.

"Too formal." I fix the shaft, black dress back on the hanger and pick a light green outfit. "Too covered," I sigh. "He might end up thinking I want him to unveil the veiled."

Undecided, I sit on the bed again. Then I stand, pacing as I contemplate.

It's Saturday, and I have a date with Sean. At least, I'm anticipating that until I hear voices downstairs by the entrance door. I step out of my room and tiptoe to the landing to listen.

"Sean!" says Mother.

"Afternoon, Doc," he replies in delight. They seem to have sorted their differences.

"And you brought friends!" Mother adds. "Zachary and ..."

"Madeline," she answers.

I close my eyes and grumble quietly. "Why? Why? Why?"

"Wait ..." Sean says. From the closeness of their voices, I can tell they are in the hallway now. "You know Zachary?"

"Of course," Mother replies.

"Who doesn't know me?" Zachary interrupts and quickly adds, "Where's your younger sister?"

"Oh stop it, Zachary. I'm not that young." Mother laughs before calling, "Alexandra!"

I wait until I get back in my room before calling out, "Coming!"

Two minutes later, I'm in a vintage floral smock dress with my hair braided into a fishtail. Through the windows of my room, I see Sean holding hands with Madeline. Zachary walks behind Mother in the garden. She's taking them on a tour of her Japanese garden.

A touch of blush on my cheeks and I close my bedroom door, heading to the garden.

I meet everyone standing by the porch. I greet the boys and Madeline with hugs and a warm smile, and we take our seats by the breakfast table.

"I love your perfume, Alex. What is it? Nuante?" Madeline asks, tilting her head a little as she gazes at me.

"Breathe, by Nuante. Floral."

"I figured." She nods. "I'm more into the fruity kind, but I love the one you're wearing."

"Thank you." I take a seat next to Sean.

"Lexie, honey, did you know Madeline is the daughter of Thea Cruz?"

"Really?" I stare back at a smiling Madeline.

"I was just telling her, how her mother and I have worked together for years now." Mother explains, then turns to Madeline. "You have to tell your parents how much we, at the hospital appreciate the funding and their support."

"Will do." Madeline smiles. "We should be thanking you. All the hard work doctors do, keeps that place running, right?"

"Very right." Mother nods, and turns to Zachary, who seems distracted. "Zachary, what's your secret?"

Zachary's eyes widen just as my heart picks up the pace.

We all turn toward him, waiting for an answer.

"My secret?" He laughs nervously, running his fingers through his hair. "What secret?"

Mother smiles. "This coffee is perfect. You have to tell me how you brewed this one."

There is laughter around the table while I stare at Zachary and back at Mother. "He did coffee for you?" I ask.

"You should let him tell you his secret, Alexandra, honey, that's all I can say."

I briefly glance at Zachary. He winks, and I look away, resisting the urge to roll my eyes.

"Invite me again and I will show you exactly how to make it even better," Zachary adds.

"Don't make that mistake, Dr. Watson." Madeline shakes her head. "He will end up here every day. Zachary likes the attention."

"*Loves*, you mean?" Sean emphasizes before we all stand to leave.

"Pay them no attention," Zachary says. "Just to let you know, I cook, too. I can do massages ... I can even do your taxes!"

Mother laughs while we all grumble at Zachary.

"This is cute!" Madeline sighs with excitement and stares at Zachary. "We should double date all the time."

"We should, shouldn't we, Alex?" Zachary smiles.

"Yeah, we sure should." I try to raise my voice, but it comes out muffled.

In an open-air, thatched-roof restaurant, adorned with rustic furniture, we are sitting on padded, thick sea grass chairs surrounding a cherry slab table, one of many tables in the restaurant.

Soon to be launched, Maxx's restaurant sits on a beach, shaded by palms and secluded by the surrounding lush country scenery. Though a distance from the restaurant, the view of the calming, clashing movements of the beach waves seem to have hypnotized me.

"Hey, are you okay?" Sean whispers with his palm on my cheek.

"Yeah, I just feel a bit off," I reply and reach to brush back a few strands of hair off Sean's eyes. "But I'll be fine, don't worry."

"You need to learn to stand up against these bullies, Alexandra. If you don't want to go out, tell them, or else they will force you to go everywhere they go," Madeline campaigns. "Especially, this one." She turns to Zachary and kisses his cheek. "He won't stop until he gets what he wants."

"Sean, you are dressed-up smart today, trying to impress someone?" Zachary asks.

It feels as if he's trying to change the subject.

"Why are you guys always out to embarrass me?" Sean moans as Madeline and Zachary laugh.

From the kitchen, Maxx is coming toward us with another circular ceramic plate, similar to the ones already on the table. A white apron with the letters, VB, printed in gold hang around his neck, over his black outfit. As he places the plate on the table, he whistles a tune that sounds like a song.

Taking his apron off first, Maxx pulls up a seat between Sean and me. "You're ready for me to sit with you, of course." He laughs. "This is just great, isn't it—Zachary, Zandra and friends. Zandra." Maxx turns to me. "You don't mind me calling you Zandra, do you?"

"Of course not," I reply.

"I have to say you look gorgeous in that dress." Maxx holds my hand and kisses it gently.

"Oh, thank you, Maxx." I smile at how theatrical he looks.

Maxx's gaze flickers around the table and stops on me. "Thank the lord it's not raining today, otherwise, how would we ride the hot-air balloons? He lets go of me and with a grin, turns his gaze toward Zachary, who tightens his jaw.

"How does that even make sense?" Sean asks, directing his question to Maxx. "Who's planning to ride a hot-air balloon?"

I drop my gaze, hiding the reality of how it all makes sense to me.

"Don't worry," Maxx answers. "Zach knows exactly what I am talking about. Don't you, big brother?"

Zachary flexes his jaw, staring at Maxx. "Just know when we get home, Mom is not going to be there to protect you."

I want to laugh, but my heart is beating faster, scared of what Maxx is going to say next. *How much does he know about Zachary and me?*

"That seriously hurt, Zach. Don't make me sing the song." Maxx shakes his head and begins to whistle the same theme he was whistling earlier.

"Maxx, what are you singing?" Sean asks the question I was about to ask.

"Yes, Maxx. What are you singing?" Madeline drops her fork, wipes her mouth with a napkin, then turns to stare at Maxx.

"Nothing, nothing, just a song I can't seem to remember the lyrics to." Maxx turns to Zachary, a smirk forming on his face. "But if you want to know where I got it from ..."

"Yes." Madeline frowns. "Where did you hear that song?"

We all pause, waiting for Maxx to speak.

"I heard Zach singing it in the shower." Maxx bursts out laughing.

Sean and Madeline laugh the loudest while I smile, but Zachary remains frozen.

"I remember the lyrics to the song now," Maxx interrupts the laughter. "I remember now! Here, it goes ... *Kisses in the rain, kisses in the rain. I kissed her in the rain and then she left in a taxi,*" Maxx sings, pitch perfect.

Fighting not to widen my eyes, I turn, staring at Zachary, who glares at his young brother with a flushed face. "You made up the last part: I don't even sing that far out." Zachary's voice sounds defeated.

"So you don't deny singing these lyrics in the morning, afternoon and night," Maxx asks, leaning closer to Zachary.

"I don't deny singing, but—"

"Who did you kiss in the rain?" I shoot my gaze at Zachary. This was my chance to get back at him. "What foolish girl would ruin her hair for you?"

"So true, Alex." Madeline laughs and high fives me. "That definitely wasn't me."

"It's no one. She's nothing," Zachary says in a deep voice.

I pick up a bottle of red wine to pour a drink for myself, but Sean takes it and pours it for me.

While I gulp half the glass, Maxx stands up hastily, rushing to the kitchen.

There's whispering at the table. Sean and Madeline are arguing with their lips inches from each other.

I catch Zachary's eyes watching them. He looks back at me, but quickly looks away. Then he grabs the same bottle of wine I picked up earlier and pours his glass full.

"Where's the guitar?" Madeline hisses.

"I told you I forgot it and no, I'm not going back." Sean shakes his head.

"It's important for Maxx. I'm sure Alex won't mind missing you for fifteen minutes." Madeline smiles hard, waiting for Sean's response. "Please, I'll do anything you want."

"*Anything*?" Sean smiles at Madeline.

"Anything." Madeline nods.

"Okay, but ..." Sean turns toward me, but Zachary speaks before him.

"Alex will be just fine with me."

I jab his leg with my heel underneath the table, but he doesn't flinch.

"Lexie?" Sean turns to me.

I nod. "Go on, Sean. I'll be fine."

Zachary and I watch as Sean and Madeline leave. Sean's arm circles Madeline's waist, Madeline's around his shoulders, her head leaning toward him. At the door, Madeline gives Sean a kiss on the cheek.

I'm almost tempted to ask if Zachary and Sean share a girlfriend, but I don't want to start a conversation with Zachary.

"So ..." Zachary turns to me after a moment. "My phone calls don't mean anything to you."

I cross my arms against my chest. "Sorry, I don't think I have your number. Apparently, I am nobody ... a no one, right?"

"Alex—" He tries to speak again, but I'm already on my feet.

"It's cold here." I stare at Zachary. "Don't know if it's the breeze or the heart of the knight." I turn, heading for the kitchen to talk to Maxx.

I swing open the wide, stable doors and enter an enormous kitchen. With exposed brick walls, a burning brick oven, cove-vaulted brick ceiling, slate-tile flooring and large ceramic work tops, the kitchen appears more homey than commercial.

Maxx has made different pieces of dough, and he's now arranging them in the refrigerator.

"Hey, Maxx."

He turns in haste. I think I startled him.

"Zandra—my God! ... See what I did there." Maxx grins. "What happened? Did you forsake my brother?"

I struggle to smile. "I got bored, and thought you could perhaps, teach me how to cook?

Maxx's forehead creases before it relaxes. "You got bored, eh—aren't you feisty?" Maxx tilts his head, and nods. He grabs my arm and checks the time on my watch. "Sure, we've got some time. It would be my pleasure. What do we start with? Pizza or steak?"

"Steak," Zachary answers as he enters the kitchen.

I turn to Maxx. "No. I'll try pizza."

"Reverse psychology. It always works for me," Zachary comments.

I glare at him. "Whatever, Zachary. Now get out of the kitchen."

"I was just trying to help, beautiful. It's what friends do."

Maxx coughs aloud and clears his throat.

I stare into Zachary's eyes. "I don't want you as my friend anymore. Don't call me beautiful. Besides friends don't …" I pause remembering Maxx who now stands beside me, holding a large glass bowl with a flour mixture.

"While you two burn your passions, Zandra, mix the dough." Maxx places the bowl in my hands. "And, Brother, remember the fire extinguisher is to your right by the door."

"Wait!" I call on Maxx. "Where do you think you're going, leaving me with—?"

"It's fine," Maxx answers. "Zachary knows his status in my kitchen. I'll be back in five. I need to make a few quick calls."

XIV

YOU JUDGE ME TOO QUICKLY

I wait until the doors close behind Maxx before turning to Zachary. "Friends don't kiss, lie to, or hurt each other."

He remains silent as I turn back on the work top. I wash my hands, and start to work on the flour mixture. Soon, my hands are sticky.

"May I?" Zachary reaches over to scoop some flour from the glass jar.

"Go away, Zachary. Go and help Madeline."

I wash my hands and bring them back to the dough. It's stickier than before. "Shit!" I knead harder, hoping the mixture will stop sticking to my hands, but it gets worse.

Zachary laughs.

"I said, get out, Zachary! I will decorate your smug face with flour."

He laughs harder and steps forward to wash his hands before seizing the mixture from me.

"You need a little flour on the board, like this." Zachary sprinkles flour over the work top, some on the now sticky dough and a little on his hands. He works his fingers into the dough. Like magic, the mixture begins to form into a smoother consistency.

Zachary rinses his hands and dries them with a dish towel. "Here." He dips a table spoon into the flour jar. "Give me your palms."

I do as he says. He dashes flour into my palms. Then he steps aside so I can work on the dough.

I follow what he did earlier, and it works. It's almost fun working my fingers into the mixture.

After stretching over to wash his hands again, Zachary stands inches behind me. My heart throbs and my stomach flutters, acknowledging his proximity. With caution, Zachary places his hands on my waist. I gasp quietly, wary of the strength his touch draws out of me. My knees weaken as he pulls me closer to his chest, tighter, wrapping his arms around me as his head nestles my neck.

The right thing to do is to push him off, to tell him never to touch me again, but I choose to close my eyes.

"I'm sorry." His voice comes out softer than a whisper, and his lips on the back of my neck, touch my skin as gently as a butterfly.

I open my eyes and meet his gaze in the reflection from the mirror in front of us. He tilts his head and with each breath, his lips trace the length of my neck, once, twice, and again.

Emily was right when she said he is a snake, except he doesn't kill his prey, but bites and blows.

His touch had pleased me before I knew about Madeline. Now that he is like a forbidden fruit, it's as if my senses have been heightened—every fingertip, every brush of the lips, his breath escaping into my ears, the strength of his arms around my waist, all pouring in triple fold.

"I'm sorry," he whispers again.

This is nothing but lust, infatuation. One day, I will wake up and find myself immune to your touch, Zachary. I promise you that.

I move my hand to grasp a handful of flour, turn in a flash, and throw it in Zachary's face.

"Aargh! What's that for?" he moans.

"What do you think?" I bite my bottom lip.

"Is that what I get for apologizing?" he complains, wiping his face with a napkin.

Sneezing, he grabs a few serviettes and pushes the back door open, heading outside.

I smile, trying to clean up the mess, but as Zachary continues sneezing, I follow him outside to see if I can help. I find him sitting head down on a rustic bench.

"Are you okay?"

"Does it ..." He sneezes again. "Does it look like I'm okay?"

I brush back a few strands of hair from his face then take his hand as I sit beside him. "Sorry." I sigh.

He sneezes once more, and after a moment, it stops.

His face is red when he looks at me. "And you call me *evil.*"

"I never said I was a saint." I give him a sideways glance, and we both shake our heads and gaze toward the cloud-like beach waves far ahead of us.

In the distance, I stare in awe of the terra cotta sunset seascape. Hoping to get another glimpse of the visions, I thread my fingers with his. This time, I'm focused. I want to take note of every flash.

Zachary looks at me with a frown, but still kisses the back of my hand before placing it onto his chest.

No images are coming, but the warmth is deeper than before, and it's not just in my hands, but moves up my arms, too. Zachary doesn't move, only squeezes my hand lightly.

"Zachary."

"Hmm." He gives me his full attention.

"We could tell everyone the truth, and you and I can be more than dream partners ... if you want."

In an instant, Zachary's face changes, from soft to cement hard with a crease-patterned forehead.

He releases his hand from mine. "No, I can't. I can't do that to you."

"What do you mean?" I try to weave our hands again, but he rises to his feet.

"I just can't. It will lead nowhere," he says, pacing at first, then advancing toward the white sands. "You're not the one for me. You and I are not ..." The winds blow away the rest of his words.

I hurry behind as he begins to walk faster. "What are you scared of?" I say as I catch up with him by the dark, wooden beach cabana. I reach for his hands, my eyes searching his, looking for his soul. "We can just date and see where it goes. It's not as if I'm asking you to marry me." I laugh nervously.

He looks into my eyes for a few seconds and shakes his head. "No, Alex." He turns his back to me.

"What is wrong with you?" I skip in front of him again. "Why are you so adamant we won't work? Is it because of Sean?"

Nothing has prepared me for the anger that flashes on his face. "I said No! Alexandra! Can't you get that? I don't want you!"

I want to run, but shock has frozen my bones on the spot.

"Look at me." He grabs my face between his hands. "I don't want a relationship with you. I have her, and she's all I ever wanted," he tells me, but his eyes seem to say, I'm all he ever wanted. *Maybe my desires have clouded my vision.*

"You can't make me fall for you," he adds. "You're nothing, but a fantasy."

I let out a juddered breath, a chilling breeze grazing my cheeks as Zachary lets go of my face.

Then rage takes over. "How dare you?" I raise my hand, aiming for his cheek, but he stops it midway, his hand clasping my wrist.

My chest rising erratically, I stare back at his eyes. My heart hardens as he drops my hand. There's an ache inside my guts. Blood rushes through me, not with excitement, but anger, and rejection.

He stares at me as if it is I, who has wounded his heart. His face tightens, and all I see in his eyes is pain. He walks away, heading back where we came from.

I quicken my pace and grab his arm. As soon as he turns, I reach to cup his face. I don't wait for him to speak, pressing my lips on his. He doesn't react, leaving my lips working on his, stroking his chin, and down his neck. Then move to whisper into his ears. "Tell me to stop if you don't want me, or you can push me away if you're tongue-tied."

He groans, and his lips catch mine as he squeezes my waist with a burning desire. One hand slides and secures my back while the other reaches for my thigh. Stretching the kiss, he shifts me up above his chest. My lips never leaving his, I rush my hands into his hair, my body coiling to fit in his arms. His tongue mingles with mine and we groan, breaking the kiss in sharp breaths.

As if we aren't close enough, Zachary brings me closer into his chest. He slides his hand under my dress to grab my thigh.

"Don't." I pull away and search his eyes.

With sultry eyes, he stares at me in silence, his fingers caressing my skin.

"I give you two minutes to make up your mind," I whisper.

He narrows his eyes and speaks in a raspy voice. "About what?"

"Me or Madeline. Unlike you, I know what I want, and that's you. I admit you are irresistible, but if you choose her, I swear to God, I'll make it my business to make you remain faithful to her, even if it means bleeding my heart dry during the process."

The light in his eyes disappears. He shuts his eyes for a brief moment then stares at me. "I chose you weeks ago."

I scoff and move away from him. "You mean you chose me as the one to dump, huh?"

"No, Alexandra." His voice comes out tired. "You judge me too quickly."

"I say I judge you too late. Emily was right. You're a snake."

"So you hate me now? Or is this loving hate?"

I glance at my watch. "You have one minute left."

He runs his fingers through his hair, once, twice, thrice and again, but says nothing.

"Ten seconds," I breathe, my heart pounding in anxiety as I wonder. It's not whom he chooses that scares me, but if he chooses not to answer. "Five. Four."

In a flash, Zachary tightens his grip on my waist. Then he elevates about an inch above the ground. With my hands clinging to his chest, he speeds away. It all happens in half a second. All I see is speed, and when I blink again, we are back in the kitchen. My back is to the brick wall, and my body secured in Zachary's arms.

He's a vampire. I tremble. While I'm still trying to figure that out, Zachary strokes my cheeks gently, and whispers, "It's Madeline." Without waiting for my response, he heads for the door, slamming it shut as he walks out.

My eyes well up with tears, my chest tightening as I digest what's just happened as well as Zachary's response. Then I wipe a teardrop by my cheek.

"Zandra?" Maxx rushes in.

In haste, I turn my back to him and dab the tears from my eyes.

"Did you miss me that much?" he asks with a worried voice.

"I'm fine," I force my voice out.

"Or is it the pizza? If I had known that mixing the dough would cause you so much pain, I swear I wouldn't have asked. It's just I didn't know you were one of those girls who cry when food gets in their nails—"

"Oh, God, Maxx. It's not you." I turn to face him. "I'm just ..." I pause when I see a smile on his face. "Sorry, I messed up the dough." I try to laugh, but it comes out like a dry cough.

"You should talk to my mother; she thinks she can make a chef out of anyone. She could help you if cooking gets you down."

"Oh, really?" I force a laugh.

"Apart from my sister who's just doomed; no one can help her," Maxx adds, disregarding my sniffles.

"Really?" This time my voice breaks.

"No. I was just trying to make you feel better." Maxx sighs, and drops his shoulders, coming toward me. "He didn't mean to hurt you, you know."

I grimace. "You were listening?"

"Let's take a walk, I'll explain to you this complicated creature we call Zachary Van-Bailey." Maxx pulls me out of the kitchen.

Not wanting to face Sean and Madeline with my red eyes, I welcome the idea.

Maxx grabs a black coat before we step through the back door, heading back to the sandy beach. As we reach the bench that Zachary and I sat on earlier, Maxx places the coat over my shoulders, and we continue walking.

The sun is still a bright orange and the breeze so refreshing that I inhale and breathe the tension out.

"The two-legged creature occasionally resides in that house over there." Maxx points to the other side of the beach. "If you have any questions, please feel free to ask."

"He lives there alone?" I ask.

"Madeline lives with him—if that's what you mean."

I want to swear, but I stop myself. The house is too far away for my eyes to see clearly, but it stands alone, kind of whitewashed.

"It's the best place to be during the summer. You should come for his birthday. He's holding the after-party there."

"I'm not coming, Maxx. I'm sorry."

"Way to get a boy down. I rarely get to see you, and now you want to remove those rare moments from my life. You should be sorry," Maxx complains. "Look into these innocent eyes. Do they deserve to be punished because of my brother's stupidity?"

"Well ..." I trail off, noticing the likenesses of his eyes to Zachary's.

"Actually don't. They might remind you of him." Maxx laughs, and so do I.

"I know about you and my brother," he says after a deep sigh, offering me his arm in a gentlemanly fashion.

I link my arm with his, and we continue ahead. "He told you?"

"Of course, we keep no secrets. When we were young, we made a blood pact; witches were present, wolves, and angels. He sacrificed a life, and we now have this everlasting bond."

"Maxx, come on." I grumble.

"Yeah, I'm kidding. I saw you in the rain, at the café, and the hot-air balloon," Maxx says in a serious tone. "I'm not a stalker or anything. I just happened to be in all those places for very good reasons, which I'm happy to explain if you wish to know." He nudges me, laughing.

I smile but fail to hide my blushing cheeks. "And all this time your brother didn't tell me he had a girlfriend."

"Because that would have been a lie, he didn't have a girlfriend. Still doesn't."

Aghast, I shoot a look at him. "What do you mean he doesn't? What about Madeline?"

"I rarely take his relationship with Mimi seriously. He ended it with her a long time ago. In fact, she's still trying to convince him to take her back."

"You mean she's not his girlfriend? Does he always kiss girls who are not his girlfriends?"

"I don't know. You tell me." Maxx raises his brows.

"I know what you're thinking," Maxx says as we begin walking again, the salt of the beach brushing past my nostrils. "They look and behave as if they're together. That's how their relationship is, and always has been. They break up and make up like children in kindergarten."

"Why did they break up the last time? They seem so together."

"Zachary said he needed some space." Maxx spreads a lazy smile. "And by space, he means ..." Maxx pauses, seeming reluctant to say more.

"He means ...?" I urge him to continue.

"Time to hunt for his long-lost love."

"Long-lost love? Zachary had a girlfriend before Madeline?"

"I know how you feel, Alex. The competition never ends, does it?" Maxx teases. "But remember, settling for second-best isn't bad." He points at himself, and we laugh.

"Who is she?" I ask after a brief moment.

"A century ago Zachary fell in love and never fell out."

"A century?"

"That little drama earlier with my brother?" He glances at me. "That was his way of showing you that arh ... we are more than humans. I don't see why he had to do it. It was obvious. I mean, look at my jaw line!"

I punch him impishly and with a heart pounding, I wait, praying for him not to ask me what I am.

"There is a girl destined for Zachary," Maxx continues. "The books say when the time comes, she will find him, and he will forsake all others for her."

"Books? Which books?"

"Books my parents like to keep under wraps; the sacred books of the Van-Baileys. They speak about our roots and our future." Maxx runs his fingers through his hair, just like Zachary does.

"Does Madeline know about this girl destined for Zachary?"

"Madeline knows about our family. She helped Zach throughout his glum years, when he couldn't get over his lost love."

"And she's okay with him finding this girl?"

"She kind of takes him as he is, you see, but most of all, she trusts my father will be successful in making sure the girl never crosses the borders into Ashbourne."

"I don't get it." I grimace. "If the girl is destined for Zachary, and he longs for her, then why stop them from finding each other? That's what he wants, isn't it?"

Maxx stares straight into my eyes, then adjusts the coat over my shoulders. "She is his death, and a hybrid," he explains. "Ashbourne is the only city that welcomes supernatural beings, but like every other city, my father—for the sake of my brother—put down a law that commands every hybrid to be killed once identified."

I think about his words for a moment, trying to understand his point, then sigh. "And why are you telling me all this?"

He smiles. "One: because I've got a rare gift which I refuse to tell anyone about since it makes most people uncomfortable around me. Two: I've never seen my brother so happy like when I saw him the night after the auction." Maxx smiles and begins to laugh.

"Why are you laughing?" I smile at how he holds his chest like Zachary does when laughing. It reminded me of the time Zach chased after me at the auction house.

Maxx calms down and clears his throat. "He wrote a song for you that night and sang it in the shower, morning, day and night." Maxx laughs again while I shake my head.

After composing himself, he continues with a serious face. "For the first time in a hundred years, from his finger, my brother removed the ring given to him by the girl before she died."

"She's dead? So how is he looking for her?"

"Years ago, the bright star revealed that she was born into the world again."

"Like a reincarnation?"

"Kind of, but this one is direct and definite. She's probably born to the same parents, who have to be supernatural or immortals."

"How will he recognize her? She probably looks different from before."

"They say when they meet, the moon will pass through the sun and earth, concealing the sun, and darkness will fill the earth—total eclipse."

"You think she will be more beautiful than Madeline?"

"Most definitely, but I doubt if she'll be more than you are."

I elbow him as I smile, but soon the smile disappears as I imagine the unimaginable. "How will she kill him if or when they meet? Do you know?"

"No. No one knows, but I think you can stop him from looking for her."

"Me? How?"

"Like I was saying, he changed from the day he met you. He even canceled his trip to Dacia where he believed a witch would help him find the girl."

"How do you know he did that because of me? Maybe he just thought—"

"He is my brother, Alexandra. I've known him for centuries. Besides …" Maxx pauses, holding my gaze to make sure he's got my attention. "I was with Zachary, teasing him about you, him, and the hot-air balloon when an excited Sean burst into the room. He told us how he almost lost his chance with the girl next door after messing up dinner. After a moment of laughter, my brother asked, 'What is her name? And which street did you guys move to?' 'Alexandra. That's the girl I told you attacked the bartender in Flash the other night,' Sean explained, and that was it. Zachary sank back to his old self again. After congratulating Sean on finding a new girlfriend, he gave him the notepad with the lyrics to the song he had written for you. 'Sing it for her. I'm sure she will like it,' he said."

"So he just gave up on me because of Sean?"

"Sean only made Zach's decision to leave you, easier. There are other reasons and I've told you the ones I think you should know about."

I pause for a moment, trying to make sense of everything. "Now that I know, what do you want me to do? It's obvious he cares about Sean, Madeline and his long-lost love. I don't have a place in his life, do I?"

"I say he cares about you more than anyone else; me included."

"If he cares about me, then why did he pick her over me?"

"Mimi is like his pillar of strength. He feels safe with her, whereas you are new to him, and most of all—think of what would happen if or when he finds his lost love. He's scared of hurting you, Zandra. He feels he'd rather hurt you now than later."

"Did you hear what he said to me? 'I don't want a relationship with you. I have her, and she's all I ever wanted.'"

"He's doing everything he can, to keep you away. You are his dream partner. You guys are Zachary and Alexandra. 'Zalex!' he said to me when I asked. Be that or anything else, but don't hate him. Don't shut him out of your life."

I remain quiet, watching the water washing the sand away.

"We should walk back now." Maxx disturbs my thoughts.

"You go ahead. I just need a minute with the ocean."

Maxx leans closer and kisses my cheek. "Don't drown," he whispers and starts jogging away. "And Zandra!" He pauses and turns to look at me.

"Yes?"

"I'll tell you another secret if you come for my brother's birthday party. And Sean will sing the song." He winks, and I give him a faint smile.

The road is quiet as Sean, and I drive home. Besides my confusing interactions with Zachary, lunch has been entertaining. One thing I've learned is that a combination of Sean, Madeline, and Maxx means loud talking, screaming and running around at times. In the end, Sean and I found a common interest—tennis.

"Sexiest mixed doubles tournament is coming up next month. You want us to sign up?" Sean bites his bottom lip.

"I don't get why they do that, really. What's sexy got to do with playing good tennis?"

"My blond curls blowing in the wind," Sean utters and wiggles his eyebrows. "Actually, I'm surprised you're still playing hard to get when it's clear we get on so well."

"I'm not the girl next door who falls for blue eyes, though I admit yours are seductive."

"Wow, I almost blushed." He checks his face in the rearview mirror. "You are the girl next door though, at least next door to me."

"There is a girl on the other door to your right. She's a blonde like you."

"I've seen her. She's not my type. You are. I'm still thinking of what I can do to impress you. Maybe I could bring you a wild bouquet of roses and wear a bow tie, write a short note in black ink, tied with a neat ribbon like they did in the eighteenth century, mm?"

I laugh. "Maybe you should do that. I would love to see you in a bow tie."

"And my hair, do you want me to gel it and make a wide off-centered parting? And maybe add a jet-black mustache?"

"You're crazy." I giggle. "But yes, bring lilies."

"Lilies?"

"I like lilies, not roses."

"It's good to talk. I was going to get twelve dozen roses for you."

"*Twelve*? Why twelve?"

Sean returns my gaze. "My father says each dozen for each month throughout the year, and a girl will remember you throughout the year."

My lips curl into a smile. "Your father is a wise man."

He grins, and we remain silent for a while before I open my mouth to confess.

"Sean."

"Yes." He glances at me briefly, shifting the gears.

"I have a confession to make."

He grimaces. "I'm all ears."

"Not that you are not desirable—because you are, believe me your chest can drive any woman insane, but—"

"Wait! What was that you said about my chest?"

"You heard me! Stop bragging."

He chuckles, and I laugh with him. Something about his laugh makes me nostalgic.

"As I was saying," I begin again. "When we first met, I had no intentions of getting to know you. All I wanted was information about the supernatural Ashbourne, and I hoped you would tell me what I am."

"I know. I'm not stupid." Sean's eyes twinkle. "I did not intend to tell you anything, but to lure you to my bed." He grins.

I shake my head. "And now? Do you still want to lure me to your bed?"

"Hmm ... not that I don't think about it, but I would say I'm more eager to know you better."

"Do you ever lie?"

Sean kisses my cheek, glances at my seat belt before increasing the speed. "Lie sprints, but the truth runs a marathon."

XV

THE PARTY

"Zachary's father locked him out of the house in the rain? A day before his birthday?" Emily stares at me through her gold and green feather mask.

Dressed in masquerade outfits, we are in a Drop-head Coupe, one of the classic ceremonial Deschanel luxury cars. I'm driving to the Van-Bailey residence. Sean arranged a chauffeur for us, but I decided to seize this once in a life time chance and sit on the driver's seat of this rare motor.

The feeling is surreal; the twilight breeze blowing through the peacock zephyrian, feather mask on my face. In the same costume I tried the other day in Lost Closet—blackberry corset-like, and off shouldered with a tight bodice and intricate beading, I feel I belong in ancient years.

"Who would do that to their own son? Why?" Emily continues.

"You know Sean. He would rather keep quiet than lie," I shrug.

"Did you not ask Zachary?"

I pause, acknowledging how my heart longs for him. "Apart from the good morning and goodnight text, we don't really talk," I tell her.

Zachary doesn't know I'm coming, and part of me wants to see the look on his face when he sees me. However, with the masks, I doubt if I'll find him.

"I thought you went to check on the racetrack the other day. Didn't you see him?"

"Nope." I draw in a deep breath. "I always check with Danny first, to make sure he's not around before I go there. It's easier that way."

"You still want him, don't you?" Emily tortures me with this question every day, and the answer never changes.

"It's not as if I can just shut my feelings off. God knows, I wish I could."

"Perhaps you should channel your feelings to Sean." She teases, and I eye her with annoyance.

7:55p.m., we arrive at the security gates leading to the Van-Bailey Stills. VBS Lane, as most people call it, is a long private road that leads to the Van-Bailey residence.

Apart from the river behind the house, it's the only way of getting to the house. Arriving at the Stills Lane gates, we stop and show our invites.

Though Sean gave us a note to avoid security checks, the four guards who stand in black and gold Van-Bailey suits insist on scanning us.

The drive through the Lane is like reading a heart-warming short story in ten minutes. It's a two-lane curvy, hilly road, with dense trees curving inward as if bowing for the cars as they drive past. Like overexcited wedding guests throwing confetti, the thick branches let the colorful leaves fall on us as we drive along.

There's a champagne vintage car behind us and another far ahead of us. It's already meandering up the hill to the Van-Bailey residence.

Vintage, always reminds me of Chan, and just like that, my mind drifts to him.

"And so Mimi wins?" Emily asks.

I take a few seconds to understand what she's talking about, and then answer. "The war was never between Madeline and me." I glance at her briefly. "There's a fine line between me, fighting for Zachary, and throwing my miserable self at him. A lady must always know when to walk away." I say it with so much passion as if to convince myself.

Emily turns to me. I can't see her expression through the mask, but, from her parted lips, I'm guessing it's surprise.

"And you have to understand Madeline shares history with Zachary. I can't beat that, can I? Besides, she is really a nice person," I explain.

Emily's mouth opens wider. I stare at her with a smile.

"True! She is," I add. "Zachary is in good hands, so I'm taking your advice to channel my feelings to Sean."

"Just like that? Don't you think you're moving too fast—from Zachary to Sean?"

"Come on, Emily. Make up your mind. You're the one who said I should. Besides, the two weeks I've spent with Sean on the tennis courts have been fun."

Emily takes a moment, staring at me. "Yet you sound so sad."

"I never had to fight for someone before, so yeah ... of course, that makes me sad."

"There's a first time for everything." Emily leans to kiss the bottom of my cheek. "Welcome to my world."

I reduce speed as we reach the wrought-iron gates.

"Selfish bitch mother of the devil! This place is amazing," Emily whispers as we drive onto the motor court.

"Who have you been hanging with in college that has succeeded in plastering your tongue with such profanity?" I mumble, marveling at the estate.

In the style of renaissance architecture, the four-story estate stands perched by the River Stills. The mansion is well-lit by not only rich indoor lights, but also copious illuminating garden lamps popping from mature trees and emerald lawns.

There's a feeling of serenity, an atmosphere that almost compels one to keep still. Despite the brisk air blowing from the river behind, the palm trees, and tropical flowers are as still as the statues and sculptures.

With a smile, I thank the attendant, who directs us to an open parking bay. I quiet the engine, then turn to Emily with a forced smile as I try to hide the beating of my heart; the thought of meeting Zachary makes me anxious.

Once out of the car, Emily and I adjust our costumes, making sure they are presentable. I pause to look around, and yes; the guests are here. They arrive in luxurious and lavish glossy black, cream, white and metallic cars. Like us, they also park in a designated parking courtyard close to the entrance. Some cars are driving off, one after the other as the passengers get down.

The guests look flamboyant and incredibly comical in the designer, masquerade outfits. The colors and style vary, but, like a perfect, luxury Christmas tree, they all blend in harmony; deep reds, rich gold, purple, blue, crimson like Emily's.

Some guests are in hysterics while others are smiling. They curtsy with exaggeration before heading toward the doorway.

A balmy breeze embraces me as Emily and I proceed past the double entry doorway, stepping into a two-story foyer.

Decorated in a palette of cream, white, and gold, the hall oozes with Italian styled ornaments and furnishings.

A lady dressed in a crimson costume, and wearing no mask, receives our birthday gifts and places them in the room to the side. I hoped to use the birthday present as an excuse to see Zachary and now that opportunity has been taken away.

Maintaining the elegance stitched into our costumes, Emily and I follow the usher, heading toward the alluring melody of an orchestra. The classic sound of champagne glasses clinking rings in my ears, soothed by the gentle laughter from the guests.

The voices draw nearer as we get closer. By the wide opening, the usher gives us a friendly bow, gesturing us to step inside.

With Emily beside me, I take a few steps and enter a swarming, grandiose ballroom. A few guests turn, staring at us with their ostentatious masks, just to ignore us altogether, as if we are nothing, but a mere addition to the already dazzling room.

With a line of elegant round-headed arches on either side, the room oozes with charm. Several luxurious chandeliers hang down, adding to the grand theme and welcoming atmosphere. Gold and rich textured draperies hang beside the large square windows. Some tucked to the side, giving way to the crafted wall lights.

It's not just the spellbinding music jubilating from the orchestra musicians assembled on the mezzanine gallery that draws my attention, but also the guests. They dance to the music in unison as if they all went to the same school of dance. Divided into two groups, the musicians play as if in conflict of each other and yet in harmony.

I'm waiting for the waiters, carrying silver trays with champagne glasses to come closer when I sense someone staring at me. I sense the stare from the mezzanine, where the musicians are. I glance up, my eyes flickering from right to left, away from the musicians.

My heart pounds when I pause on a man who isn't dressed for the occasion; no mask and no masquerade outfit but a pair of straight-leg officer's pants and a classy shawl-collar pullover.

It's not that he seems to be focusing on only me that make my heart beat faster, but he looks almost identical to Zachary. His hair is the same—chin length—only in black waves instead of brown. He looks older too, with stronger features; the jaw line is more defined, the brown eyes, however, are not as glistening as Zachary's.

His stance reminds me of the first time I met Zachary with his "I own this world" presence. I drop my gaze, hoping it's possibly not me that he looks at, but when I glance up again, he gives me a tight smile. It looks to me more like a warning smile rather than a friendly one.

"Did you see that?" I nudge Emily.

"You are brave," Emily whispers. "Very few people get to look him in the eye for that long."

"Why? Who is he? He was staring at me like—"

"That's Zachary the third, Lexie; the man who kicks his son out in the rain. You don't even know your boyfriend's father?"

"He's not my boyfriend. Get that right."

"Whatever. Your dream partner's father, then, if that makes you happy." She sighs. "He holds the city in his hands, and you don't get to look him in the eye."

"Why? And how do you know all these things?"

"Jeremy Capello." She lets out a soft laugh. "That man can report on family history and current affairs, better than the history channel and CNN put together."

Emily picks up two glasses of champagne from a waiter's tray and passes one to me. "To you and me." Her lips curl up as she raises her glass.

"And our future princes and knights." I return the smile, and we cross our arms as we gulp the champagne. Then I spot two boys watching us from the doorway.

"Who are they?" I elbow Emily.

"Can't wait for the after-party," Emily grumbles as she scrutinizes the boys. "How can I see a prince when they are all covered in these costumes and masks?" She moans.

"Try talking to someone," I say.

"I'm telling you, Lexie, if I don't end up with a decent guy after this night, then I'm going for a boob job."

"You're just saying that." I give her a lazy smile, knowing she doesn't mean it.

"Or, possibly a butt job. Don't you think my butt is too small?" She swings around to face me.

I chuckle. "In that costume, I say your butt is too bulky. Besides, you and I know the best boys don't love you for your butt or your boobs."

"Be honest, Lexie Watson." She brings her face close to mine. "You seriously think if we didn't look this sexy, we would be here tonight?"

Trying not to laugh, I press my lips together. "I give up on you, Millie."

I scan the room, looking for the birthday boy, Sean and Maxx, but I don't see either of them. However, I notice Victoria in the midnight-blue mermaid styled gown. She's dancing with a man who looks like her father, David.

It's not long ago when I finished a glass of champagne, and yet I feel thirsty. So thirsty, I can barely stand it. No waiters seem to be around. I don't want to hunt for a drink, and so I wait patiently for a waiter.

My eyes flickering around in anticipation, I spot a waiter, but he only has one glass on the tray. He's coming closer, and already my throat is pulsating with excitement. The waiter comes directly to me. I smile with gratitude as I pick up the glass, and take a deep breath.

With eyes closed, I raise the glass to my mouth. It's at that moment that someone snatches the glass from my hand.

"Millie?" I turn to her, then realize she is not the culprit.

"What did I do?" Emily frowns.

I don't have time to answer her. I need to find my glass of champagne.

I look around, turning in every direction, to see who has the glass, but I see no one. Then I see a hand raising the glass up in the air, above the heads of the dancing guests.

Swaying my gown to the side, and holding it up, so I don't trip on it, I mingle through the crowd, following the hand with the glass.

Emily calls, but I ignore her, swinging past pillars and couples dancing until I reach the glass doors leading into the foyer.

Moving further away from the crowd, I hesitate at the silence.

When the figure appears a distance down the hallway, I grimace at a familiar face behind the mask, then smile as he grins. I can recognize that curbed smirk in my sleep. Even the warrior-styled costume; rich black pants matching the military jacket embroidered with gold buttons and chevrons over a collared, glacier white shirt with an oversized ribbon tie is not enough to hide that theatrical posture.

More eager than before, I rush toward him, follow him up the grand marble stairs to the landing. About five doors away from where I stand, he stops, raises the glass as if in a toast, and takes a sip.

I consider turning back, but the desire to chase is greater than my reasoning.

Standing with pride, like a knight, his smile grows, encouraging me to follow him. Daringly, I strut toward him. My eyes focus on his, as he swirls the champagne in the glass while watching every inch of my movement.

I'm a few feet away as he takes another sip, opens a door and walks in.

Once at the door, I pause and slowly walk through. One foot inside the door and I'm in his arms. With the speed of lighting, he twirls with me in midair for a few seconds before putting me down to rest my heel on a fluffy cream rug laid on the parquet floor.

We stand in a large bedroom with triple French doors leading to a shaded balcony. I don't get a chance to study the room as Zachary lifts me up and traps me in his arms by the balcony door. The twinkle in his brown eyes makes me smile. My heart throbs from a mixture of fear, excitement and the feel of his touch.

"Mistletoe!" He pulls a small plant from his back pocket and dangles it between our heads.

"It's not Christmas, Zachary." I ignore the gold and red swirls on his half white, half crimson mask covering his upper face and aim for his eyes.

"It feels like Christmas hearing your voice again," he whispers.

"Then it must feel like heaven with Madeline," I say. I look down, realizing how much I missed him.

"Is that what you think?"

"Am I wrong?"

He remains silent, his eyes on me as if to explore every feature of my face.

I step away from him. "Why did you bring me here, Zachary?"

"I didn't. I should be asking why you followed me here."

Shaking my head, I hasten to pick up the now half-full champagne glass and drain the contents at once. "Happy birthday, Zachary," I say, starting for the door.

"Wait!" Zachary moves at vampire speed and stands in front of me. "I see you got me a present." From his pocket, he brings out the little box I gave to the lady at the door earlier.

"It's ah ..." My face warms, remembering how I struggled to find the perfect gift for him until Maxx showed me a bracelet he said he would love.

"Can I open it now, with you here?" He smiles cheekily.

"It's nothing, really." I rush to stop him. "Come on. What could I get for a guy who seems to have everything?"

Zachary sways to the side and continues to open the wrapping of the box. Eyeing the bracelet, he laughs.

My face drops. "You don't like it?"

"No. I mean yes, I like it. It's just I was thinking even if the case were empty, I would still like it."

I smile.

He looks up to my eyes. "I like it a lot. Thank you." He moves closer to me. "Do you mind?" He passes the bracelet to me, so I can help him put it on.

I take the brown leather cuff bracelet from his hand and aim for his wrist. Zachary steps closer; close enough to drown my nose in his virile scent.

Fighting the urge to pull him into my arms, I circle the bracelet on his left wrist. The silence between us is singing songs about hidden desires. I'm done, but I keep my head down. I need air in my lungs before I can stare at his eyes again.

"Thank you," Zachary says with a sigh and pulls me to his chest.

Every nerve within me responds with a thrilling desire, but I quickly pull away from him. "Is this why you led me up here?"

He gazes at me for a moment before shaking his head. "No. I think we should talk. This business of texting once every morning and every night, it's not working. Kids pick up on these things."

"Kids? What are you talking about?"

"Our daughter? Us not communicating. Guess who suffers? Autumn Reigns."

I fight a smile. "Okay. We're talking now, so I guess we're good, but next time, try not to steal my drink." I take a step toward the door again.

"Alex, wait!" He grabs my hand, and we stare at each other. "I miss you." He reaches for my mask and removes it with care, stroking my cheek as he stares into my eyes.

As Zachary leans in, my lips part in an instant, but before his lips touch mine, I push him off. "I meant what I said, Zachary. You made your choice, and now..." I step back, struggling to breathe. The desire in me makes me shudder. "I don't get you. What's wrong with you? What is it that you want, really?"

"You don't understand." Zachary's voice comes out strangled.

"Then help me understand," I plead, taking his hands in mine. "I know about your lost love, so you don't need to hide that from me."

"Wait." He backs away. "How did you ... *Maxx?* Maxx told you?" Fingers steepled against his lips, he shuts his eyes for a moment. "Welcome to the family, Alexandra, but I'm going to kill him." He heads for the door.

"Zachary!"

"He had no right!" Zachary fumes.

"At least he trusted me enough to tell me the truth, which I can hardly say about you. You could have just told me the truth, instead of lying that you have a girlfriend."

"Oh, yeah? Did he tell you why he trusts you? Did he tell you about his precious gift?"

"What about the gift?" I grimace.

"Ask him. It seems you two have become close friends now, haven't you?" He heads for the door again.

"Zachary, wait!"

He turns and stares at me with a creased forehead. "I don't care if it's my birthday. I'm going to deal with that new friend of yours and teach him never to interfere in my relationships."

I rush to the door to block the exit. "No, I won't let you."

"I'm not asking for your permission!"

"Of course that would be silly, wouldn't it?" I cross my arms. "You asking permission to go hurt your brother, who had the guts to tell me the truth."

Zachary pauses for a minute, then sighs as he turns his back to me, hands on his waist.

With caution, I rest my hand on his back, rubbing it gently. "I'm not upset with you, and I—"

"I don't need your pity, Alexandra!"

"Look at me." I move in front of him, remove his mask and track his gaze until our eyes meet. "I don't pity you. I care about you, and as your dream partner, I'm here to help you and make your dreams come true, regardless of how ridiculous they may seem."

He searches my eyes for a moment, takes my hand and leads me to sit on a tete-a-tete chaise lounge next to the window. "Even if my dream is to find her?"

I raise my hand to rub his right eyebrow, and then exhale. "If that's what you want, yes, as long as we are truthful to each other."

"'Truthful' truthful, or 'keeping a couple of secrets' truthful?"

I force a smile. "I want to be truthful, so I say 'a couple of secrets' truthful."

He takes in a deep breath, and I watch as his eyes narrow, eyebrows knit together. He stands and steps to the French windows.

I follow him. "Zachary, are you okay?"

In silence, I stand by his side, and through the floating voile curtains, I vaguely marvel at the tropical garden. It's divided into sections; the hedged area with swings and benches and footpaths paved with quarried flagstones. Following the pathway through the arched, rubble gateway, there's a large swimming pool.

"You want to know why I chose Mimi?" Zachary asks without looking at me.

I hold my breath for a second before answering. "If you want to tell me."

He holds my hand, leading me back to the chaise lounge. With my hand between his palms, he stares into my eyes. "You and I are different. You're human, and I ... I'm not. One day, I'll find this girl I'm looking for, and ... I don't want to hurt you."

"You worry you're going to hurt me. What about Madeline? Aren't you going to hurt her?"

"She knows. We talked about it, and she understands."

I grimace. "You think I don't understand? You gave Madeline the choice to accept your situation, but you won't do the same for me?"

"Not you," he says with a condemning voice. "You will never accept there's someone else for me." He pauses, thinking. "You believe you can sway my heart and keep me for yourself."

There's truth in his words, but I'm not going to let him know he's right.

"What makes you so sure that's what I think? I ask.

"I feel it here." He places his hand by the side of his chest. "I think about you all the time. And sometimes when I look at you, I think you and I can conquer the world."

I smile as he squeezes my hand.

Then he adds, "Maxx thinks you are the key to me forgetting Jo, and part of me hates that he could be right."

"Who's Jo?"

"Not Joanne like your middle name. It's just Jo, and she's the love of my immortal life." He lets out another low laugh. "Madness, isn't it? To be in love with someone for a century."

"No, it's not." I rub his arm. "I think it's love as it should be."

"You make it so easy for me to open up my heart out to you," he breathes.

"So, why do you hate that Maxx could be right? Do you think I'm not good enough for you or … what is it?"

"It's everything, Alex." He looks into my eyes. "It feels as if everything is against us, even the stars. There are many things you don't know, things I can't tell you. You and I against the world, we will probably win, but against my father." He shakes his head and inhales.

"Go on." I rub his hands. "Tell me about your father."

Zachary clenches his jaw. "My father is one of the reasons I gave up on us. He despises dainties."

"Dainties?"

"Humans, we call them dainties." Zachary's frown grows deeper. "I could go against everyone else, but not my father. You have no idea how dangerous he is, Alex. He can kill anyone just by channeling his anger into their brains."

"He *what*?" I gasp, ready to stand, but Zachary grabs my hand, restraining me.

I catch a breath. "My God, Zachary. I saw him staring at me earlier. And Emily is downstairs. She has no idea."

"Hey." Zachary reaches for my face. "He won't hurt you. You think I would allow you here, knowing there's a chance that he would hurt you?"

"How do you know he won't? He was looking at me like—"

"My mother made him promise not to harm you, your friends or any of your family as long as you and I remain just business partners and nothing else. I know he will keep that promise if I keep mine. Nothing is as crucial to my father as his word." He pulls me in a hug as I battle to control my erratic chest. "I won't let anything happen to you. I promise."

"You knew about this, yet you agreed to a partnership with me?" I ask as I pull away from the embrace.

"I'm sorry." His eyebrows rise. "I hoped you would be something more than human. I hoped maybe if he sees you, in person, he would like you as I do." He sighs. I don't mean to scare you, but I need you to know so you can understand my choices."

I pause for a moment, staring back into his frozen eyes. "Does this mean there's no hope for you and me?"

Zachary leans closer and pulls me to his chest. "There." He kisses my forehead. "It's better I lose you to my best friend, than to have you absent from this world."

In haste, I pull my head off his chest to look into his eyes. "What if I'm not—?"

Zachary is already shaking his head. "I would literally lose my mind to know that I caused your death. So don't—"

"Listen!" I grab his hands in mine. "What if I become something else other than human, a vampire, maybe, like you?" I ask, knowing soon I'll be immortal.

Zachary frowns. "You would become a vampire, just to be with me? Are you in love with me?"

I blush. "Of course not. It's just a hypothetical question. Silly, knight." I elbow him.

"She calls me knight, again." He grins. "Now that's the best birthday present I could get from you."

"How about you answer my question?"

"I'm not trying to dodge your hypothetical question, if that's what you think." Zachary smiles as he tucks strands of hair behind my ears. "Hypothetically, if you were immortal, I would go down on one knee and ask you to be my girlfriend. And if you said yes, I would take you to the Van-Bailey Manor in Pannonia. There's a vineyard where we would squeeze grapes to make wine, and play hide-and-seek."

I laugh, biting my bottom lip at the beauty of his vision. After a moment, I inhale and exhale deeply. "So what becomes of us, now?"

Zachary raises his brow. "Friends? Dream partners?"

I reach out for his collar as I gaze into his eyes. "If this is going to work at all, we need to set up a few rules."

"Rules?" Zachary frowns.

I rise, hiding the sadness creeping on me. "Since we kind of, already crossed the 'just friends' line, we need to remind ourselves on what being just dream partners means."

Zachary extends his arms to me so I can help him up. "Can I kiss you before you tell me the rules?" He side smiles.

I turn around and move to rest my head on his back. "No, you can't."

"But it's my birthday." He turns to face me and moves behind me, as I did, pausing to inhale the scent of my hair. "That's what you give a guy who seems to have everything."

I swing around to face him. He closes his eyes as I brush his hair back and plant a soft kiss on his cheek. It almost feels like the last time. "Dream partners should not kiss ... especially on the lips."

"If the dream partner didn't intentionally tempt me with her seductive gray eyes, then this wouldn't be a problem," he teases.

"Come on, Zachary, you flirt the most."

"Liar." He bites his bottom lip.

"You're always touching my hair. That should stop."

"Alex, the last time your hands were all over my hair," he voices.

"Then we just take our hands off each other."

"Oh, so you don't want hugs from me anymore?" He laughs.

"Zachary, be serious." I shake my head.

"Fine ... And what if there is something in your hair?"

"Excuses," I roll my eyes.

"Fine."

"Fine?"

He nods. "Just one more thing." He reaches for his inside pocket, and brings something that looks like a ring. "You didn't say anything against gifts, so here's something I got for you earlier."

He reaches for my hand and slides the ring on my little finger.

"I swear it's your birthday today, not mine," I say, admiring the tiny pearls on the ring.

I'm about to say thank you to Zachary when suddenly, the door opens. I snatch my hand from Zachary's and turn to the door.

A woman wearing a radiant smile walks in. She looks heavenly in a sheer, silk-organza dress with a flared crochet hem. Her loose, brown curls bounce all the way to her waist. Behind her is a dark-haired man dressed in Van-Bailey All-Black designer suit with three gold stripes on the shoulders and the hem of the sleeves.

"Is this Alexandra?" The woman smiles, her eyes widening with delight.

The man smiles, too. There's a slight cheekiness to his smile similar to Zachary's.

"Yes," Zachary answers and turns to me. "Alex, meet Alexandra Van-Bailey—my mother."

I pause, frowning. "Alexandra?" I stare back at Zachary and he nods, smirking.

"Finally, we see this amazing girl you have been talking about all the time." Alexandra ignores my extended hand and pulls me over for a hug. She wears the sweetest perfume ever.

"She's lying," Zachary says to me as he rolls his eyes at his mother.

Alexandra places her arm around my waist, directing me to the dark-haired man. "This is Oliver Van-Bailey, Zachary's uncle."

While I shake hands with Oliver, exchanging a few "nice meeting you" words, Zachary seems lost in his mom. The two of them whisper to each other and laugh as if they haven't seen each other in years.

Still chuckling, Zachary reaches for my waist. "Okay, Mom, Alex and I are going to get a drink before you start telling her about those constant dreams I have about her," Zachary says and pulls me away.

"Congratulations on the partnership, Alexandra, honey," she calls as we walk away.

I turn back to her, but Zachary keeps pulling me away. "Thank you!" I wave.

"Dreams?" I ask Zachary as we turn toward the grand stairs. "What dreams?"

"All the time ... every night." Zachary laughs with his eyes on mine and rushes over as the orchestra plays a happy-birthday rhythm.

"Zandra!" Maxx raises his hand to help me down the stairs.

"My second-best." I kiss his cheek as he kisses mine.

In a plum outfit similar to Zachary, with a matching mask marked on his face, Maxx looks dashing.

"I see you've already received a peace token from my brother."

"Thanks to my second-best, I think we've reached a mutual understanding. Not exactly what I hoped for, but I'll survive."

"You have nothing to fear. Where the ring lies, there will his heart be."

"Do you ever run out of things to say?"

He pauses for longer than a while, then eyes me with a smug face. "I just did." He nudges me, and we laugh.

We stand aside, among the crowd, watching the band performing. "Did you see Sean or my best friend anywhere?" I ask.

"Sean is in the trial chamber, where the prosecutor, judge and the jury are one and the same person."

"What's that supposed to mean?"

"He's in my father's library, probably discussing his relationship with you."

"Is he in trouble?"

"Nah. I'd say getting a lecture about the dangers of engaging dainties who might end up as witches."

"He doesn't like witches either? Your father?"

Maxx shoots a suspicious look at me. "I see my brother has finally told you about my father's true feelings toward dainties."

I nod, and he smiles.

"Hybrids are forbidden. Dainties and witches, he loathes. Marshall John De Luca is the only living hybrid, and the only reason he's still alive is because of his gift. He can identify hybrids and witches just by looking into their eyes. He probably told my father how human you are."

John De Luca is a hybrid? I almost gasp, but hold my breath, hoping the shock has not masked my face.

"Don't worry too much about my father." Maxx side smiles. "He'll love you when he sees how you distract Zachary from his lost love."

I'm still absorbing Maxx's words, still processing the shock that John De Luca is a hybrid when Maxx puts his arm around my shoulder, chuckling. "See what I did there?" He points at Emily.

She stands with a dark skinned boy in a dark olive suit. He wears a multicolored mask, so it's impossible to see his face.

He whispers at Emily and she almost closes her eyes, laughing. My heart warms at how she seems to be enjoying his company.

"That's Tristan Devereux, a perfect match for Emily," Maxx whispers.

"How would you know he's a perfect match?"

Maxx chuckles. "Let's just say, I know more than anyone in this room."

"There you are, gorgeous!" Sean appears and takes me to the dance floor.

Three hours later, the masquerade ball is over. After freshening up in a guestroom, Emily and I change into our after-party outfits. Off-white, plunge V-neck dress for Emily, and a black and gold tutu bandeau dress, with a matching pair of high-heeled sandals for me.

Tristan comes for Emily, and the two, with selected guests, leave for the beach house, where the after-party is taking place. Sean, who I've been dancing with for most of the time during the masquerade, asks me to join him; he's about to show his present to Zachary. I follow him to Zachary's bedroom, where I was in earlier, but the room is empty.

"Where is he?" I ask as Sean and I sit by the dining table on the balcony.

"Family meeting," Sean answers. "I don't know why he's taking so long."

"Family meeting during his birthday party?"

"It's complicated, Alex." Sean scratches his head and sighs.

With Sean's constant pacing, it seems a long wait, but Zachary returns.

On entering, Zachary looks to me like a dead man walking. His brown irises that always glisten, no longer hold the sparkle. This time, they carry a sadness that seems like a gray cloud, loaded and waiting to drop that one drop of water, just that tear that would make everything all right.

As Sean speaks to him, I think I see his eyes tear up. His hand is too quick to his eyes, wiping away what I suppose to be tears.

For a moment, I feel his sadness, but soon after he smiles and it all seems like a dream. *Is he crying? I swear he is.*

"Zach?" I ask.

"Um, give me a second." He clears his throat and smiles, but not the beam I know.

As if he has lost his soul, Zachary walks to his bathroom. Ten minutes later, he's out, heads for the walk-in closet and comes out dressed in a pair of vanilla chinos, a waffle jersey T-shirt under a black leather jacket.

"Why are you two so silent?" Zachary says. I see he's trying to lighten the mood, but it's not working. "Let's go," he says, and Sean and I follow him, making our way downstairs.

At the door, Zachary pulls it open, but freezes on the spot. It's almost as if someone has sucked the spirit out of him.

With unflinching eyes and a tight jaw, Zachary senior stands by the door, blocking our way.

Sean pulls me toward the back door, where we pause and watch father and son glaring at each other.

I can't read Zachary senior's true emotions, but it's his chest that fails him, rising and falling unevenly as he and Zachary hiss at each other. I can't hear what they are saying, but soon they are yelling.

"What do you think this is, Dad?" Zachary shows he lacks the strong temperament that his father seems to hold. "Over my dead body!" he cries, almost choking out of breath as he forces himself past his father.

Wrath is written all over his face as he walks away from his father.

"Zachary." Zachary senior's voice is calm, but chilling. It sends a shiver down my spine.

Sean, perhaps sensing the fear in me, pulls me to his chest and holds me tight.

"Come back here!" Zachary senior roars. "Come back here, or—"

Zachary senior doesn't finish his sentence as Zachary turns, charging back to his father with blazing eyes.

"Or what?" he screams, then positions his face inches from his father's. "You will kill me?" He moves closer. "Oh, wait. I forgot you already tried that a moment ago!"

I didn't realize my mouth was open until a strangled breath escapes.

Catching a tear before it falls on his cheek, Zachary stares at Sean and I but says nothing. He picks up the pace, heading toward the garage.

I want to run and comfort him, but I can't, not with his father's eyes on me. Tears form in my eyes, but Sean's hand on my waist drags me out of the house.

"Let's go after him, Sean," I whisper as he leads me to a bench in the courtyard garden.

"Not now," Sean answers with a cracking voice. "Give him a minute."

XVI

THE AFTER-PARTY

"**I** love you, man!" Zachary cries out.

No more green trees, but a white, sandy shore. I smell the salty breeze and hear the beach waves as they break into a roar.

The dark sky is decorated by a bright moon and clustered stars shine down on Zachary's beach house.

With a distinctive sloping roof, the house, sits on a higher level, allowing the best views of the ocean.

The walls are nothing, but glass all around. The triple doors from the large entertainment area lead outside to the pool. Beyond that is a garage. It's here that Sean unveils the devil of a machine.

It's best of the best with everything considered, and that includes comfort, design, sound, but most of all, speed. Not just the horsepower, but also time. It is near impossible to buy the time it takes to get on the waiting list of that machine. However, Sean is a Deschanel. He must have pushed his dad to get it ready for Zachary's birthday.

Zetra Omni Scorpii, super sport, the best of a Theta Scorpii and a Zetra Zeus. If asked to pick a day I saw Zachary most sad and most happy, it would be today.

As I stare at that red car, I conclude Sean couldn't have given Zachary a better birthday present. I'm forced to reconsider my previous statement—what can one get for someone who seems to have everything. Seems is the key word. He seems to have it all until I saw this.

"Marry me, Sean Nicholas!" Zachary grabs Sean for a fifth hug, pulling him so tight; Sean is almost choking. They scream and laugh as if drunk on joy.

"Alexandra!" Zachary lets go of Sean, and comes to give me a tight hug. "If ever I forget, remind me how much I love this man." He laughs, handing me to Sean before jumping into the car.

While Sean leans in to give me a peck and a hug, Zachary roars the engine, and my heart warms to its alluring sound.

"Where is Mimi?" Zachary asks.

"She wasn't feeling well, so she left," I tell him.

"She was ill, and she didn't tell me?" Zachary frowns.

Not wanting to add any more lies, I shrug.

Inside the house, the party atmosphere has heightened, boosted by a deafening sound system. There's a wide range of alcoholic drinks and food.

Sean and I are on the dance floor. My hands encircle his neck while his wrap around me as he leans forward to whisper in my ear.

"You didn't tell me, you and Zachary are partners."

"Um ..." His question catches me unaware. I have no idea what Zachary must have told him. "I didn't think ..."

"It's fine. " Sean interrupts my vague response. I know why he did it. He's trying to get you closer to me, but I would never want you to feel pressured into a relationship with me. You believe me, right?"

My heart tightens, and guilt pushes me to kiss his cheek. "Of course, I believe you," I say, looking into his blue eyes.

He returns the kiss and pulls me closer to rest my head by his shoulder. We dance to the tune of the music.

Across the room, my eyes meet Zachary's who stands by the glass doors with one hand in his pocket while the other holds a glass of cocktail. As he drops his gaze, he tilts his head up and guzzles the cocktail. Sean swirls me around. When I stare back toward the glass doors, Zachary is gone.

A few minutes later, Sean checks his watch. "It's time," he whispers. "Find Zachary and take him to sit by the throne."

I find him outside by the pool talking to Megan. It only takes a smile from me to pull him away from her and take him to the throne-like seat positioned on the platform.

A happy-birthday rhythm begins to play, followed by the crowd singing, voices coming out weird but adding to the fun.

Three macho boys walk in with the giant, round cake, big enough to feed a small town.

My heart warms as I look at a grinning Zachary, knowing he has no idea what's coming. With a signal from Sean, the crowd goes silent.

From the corner of the room, Emily, in Tristan's arms, blows a kiss at me, and I do likewise.

Sean tells Zachary to blow out the giant candle on top of the cake. Smiling, Zachary steps forward and tries to pull the candle out, but the cake pops open. A dazzling Madeline springs out of it, wearing a revealing Latin dress embellished with tassels and sequins. The crowd screams, cheering and whistling.

With a grin, Zachary watches Madeline dancing for him as she slithers out of the cake. She moves her hips up and down and twirls in rapid and slow seductive moves, drawing closer to Zachary. The noise increases as she swirls around him, her arms pulling him tighter. When she stops, her lips are on his.

I swallow as Zachary's arms glide to Madeline's, his lips anticipating hers. While they kiss, I look away and find Emily cheering with the crowd. When she sees me staring at her, she stops, giving me a fake sad look.

I roll my eyes at her, and shake my head before walking outside, just to bump into Sean hanging up on a call. He gasps as he stares at me, pulls me into his arms and swirls me around with joy.

"What happened? Did you win the lottery?" I tease.

"It's Ashton. He called to say happy birthday to Zachary, and he's' coming home. My brother is coming home, Alex!" Sean embraces me again, trying to kiss me on the lips, but I stop him. He kisses my cheek instead.

I smile and look into his eyes. "When? When is he coming?"

"Soon, I think." Sean sighs. "He asked for the address of our new home … I can't believe this." Sean dabs the corners of his eyes. "I must find Vee." He plants another kiss on my cheeks and surges through the crowd toward the stair way.

I gaze around for Zachary and Madeline, but I see neither. The sound of the music and the crowd singing are in contrast with the outside. I sneak out for a moment of peace. Through the glass walls, Emily's eyes scan everywhere. I assume she's looking for me, so I turn to the pool to hide from her, and there I find Zachary.

With his legs in the water, Zachary sits at the edge of the pool with one hand over his face while the other holds a glass with a red cocktail. He sits in the shadows where no one can see him easily.

As I get closer to him, he raises his head a little and turns to me with exaggerated slowness.

"Zachary Van-Bailey, alone?" I stop behind him.

He chuckles, shaking his head as I continue.

"I thought you loved company."

"I enjoy my own company sometimes," Zachary replies, kicking at his reflection in the pool.

I step closer, consider sitting beside him, but hesitate, thinking of my VEGA vintage shoes. "Do you like my company?" I ask, my eyes meeting his as he looks up.

"Love," Zachary emphasizes, intertwining his fingers with mine. "I love your company."

My heart drums, a burning tingle shooting through my arms to my chest. I'm always ready for it when we touch, but it takes me by surprise every time.

I let out a short breath, and from the way Zachary squeezes my hand, I know he feels it too.

He pulls me down until our eyes are level. In silence, we stare at each other for a while.

"Stay with me," Zachary whispers.

"Where's Madeline?"

"She's gone to clean up."

I don't want to remove my shoes, so I sit across from him, my feet almost touching Zachary. He shifts closer to me, placing my legs over his lap. While I speak, he helps unbuckle the straps of my heels. Hesitating at first, he removes them, rubs my feet before releasing them into the pool.

Zachary drops his head again. I wait for him to look up, but he doesn't. I cough, and still he keeps his head down.

"What are you hiding?" I hold his face up.

"What am I *hiding*?" Zachary's eyes pause on my lips.

"You can't even look at me." I frown, trying to figure out, what's bothering him.

"I don't want to hurt you." He lifts his hand, reaching for my face, withdrawing before he touches me. Chuckling in defeat, he says, "You're beautiful, you know."

My heart responds to his words with a loud thudding. "No, I don't, but do you want to tell me?" I tease.

"I can't." He gazes at me for a second, before looking down. "I'm really trying right now, and I don't want to mess this up. I don't want to mess things up like I normally do."

"Mess what up?" I shuffle closer to him.

"Mess us up." Zachary looks into my eyes this time.

"Don't worry, I won't let you." I want to touch his face, to kiss him, and keep him close, but I know I can't.

"But the thing is ..." Zachary raises his hand, and this time he touches my cheek.

My chest rises as I fail to prevent my lips from trembling.

"I'm a sucker for those lips." He searches my eyes and sighs. "I really, really, really want to kiss you. But I can't because we are friends now, aren't we?"

Forcing a smile, I swallow the anticipated kiss. "We are."

"I can't kiss my friend, can I?" He nods. "Not even if she is you."

I look away. This time it's my turn to kick at my reflection in the water. His eyes are on my face when I look back at him. "You want to tell me what happened with your father back at the Stills?" I ask.

Jaw clenched, Zachary's face stiffens. "I don't think you want to know."

"I do." I face him, trying to reach for his hand, but stop myself, my hand resting on the ground. "I had no idea you could get so …" I trail off.

"So scary? I'm sorry if I terrified you."

"I was going to say, so furious. And I was more scared of what you and your father were going to do to each other." I sigh, remembering the scene. "There was so much bitterness."

Lips pressed together, he looks away. "That's my father; he brings out the worst in me. I guess he thinks the same of me."

"So what happened? Why were you fighting?"

"He doesn't want me to go to Dacia."

"You're going to Dacia?"

"I need to find her, Alex." He gazes into my eyes, helplessly. "She's a hybrid, and with all my father's laws, I'll never find her here. I have to go out there and look for her."

"Madeline and I are not enough for you?" I tease.

He smiles. "You remind me of her … a lot. Now that I can't be with you, I feel the need to find her."

"For the sake of your sanity, I want you to find her, but I don't … I can't think of Autumn Reigns without a father."

He grins and shakes his head. "That won't happen."

"She's going to kill you, isn't she?"

He looks down for a moment and back at my face. "I believe if I remind her who I am and what we were, she won't have the courage to destroy me."

I sigh, wondering what it is exactly that this Jo had that he can't get over. "Is it true what you said about your father trying to kill you?"

He nods. "It's true, but that's a different story, nothing to do with Jo."

"Do you want to talk about it?"

"Maybe when I'm back," he says in a low voice. "Will you wait for me?"

A smile spreads on my face. "If you ask me nicely."

He gives me a sideway glance.

"You are going alone?" My heartbeat races in anticipation of his answer. He lets out a deep breath. "With Madeline."

I shouldn't have asked. I nod, then drop my gaze, and keep a straight face. I can't let him see how that hurts.

"I thought you loved my company?"

"She asked me if she could come with me, and I couldn't refuse."

"Can I come too?"

The corners of his lips rise slightly. "What happens to Autumn Reigns?" He rubs the nape of his neck.

I shake my head, laughing. "You don't have to leave because of me, you know."

"I think I do. Maybe by the time I come back my jealous eyes would have died out."

"Jealous eyes?"

"You and Sean. He's not giving up, is he?"

"How long will you be gone?" I ignore his comment about Sean.

"It takes six weeks to kill an infatuation. Didn't you know?" He breathes a laugh.

"You're going away for six weeks?" I face him fully. "How will I ... Well, I can't ..."

"You can't what?" Zachary smiles.

"Autumn Reigns." I sigh. "I can't deal with those workers by myself."

He laughs. "You deal with them better than I do most times, beautiful."

"So, you won't be around for my birthday?"

"What do you want me to do, Alexandra?" Zachary runs his fingers through his hair. "You're not making things easy for me," he says.

Our eyes meet, and for a moment, I forget where we are.

Zachary raises his hand and with the tips of his fingers, traces my arm from the shoulder all the way to my fingers.

A thrilling shiver runs through me, competing with a warm woozy sensation that floods my belly. I move my hand to hold his, but Zachary vanishes at vampire speed.

I spend a few minutes by the pool, putting on my shoes before walking back inside.

There's no one in the entertainment room. It's quiet, except for the sound of a guitar. I follow the sound of the music. It leads me to a sunken living room where I see familiar faces snuggling on the white sofas. Sean on a stool with his guitar smiles at me.

"I was beginning to think you've abandoned me." He extends his hand for me to draw closer.

I step toward him, and he circles his arms around my waist, looking at the other faces. "I'm singing this for you," he whispers and directs me to sit next to Maxx, who's already removing cushions to make room for me.

With a smug face, Maxx shifts to the side, leaving me no choice, but to sit next to Zachary, who's cuddling Madeline to his right.

It's difficult for me to relax with Zachary and Madeline next to me. I feel as if my hand would just move subconsciously and entwine with his.

With eyes closed, Sean strums the guitar strings. "I do not own the lyrics, but I own the voice." He grins, clearing his throat and thrashing the strings louder.

The melody is tantalizing, with a hint of melancholy. Sean's raspy voice croons a soulful and passionate tune. I'm lost in the sound of his voice until Maxx nudges me.

"Are you listening or are you lost in Sean?"

"I'm listening." I frown at Maxx, who laughs quietly.

I look back at Sean, and this time I give my full attention to the lyrics.

Kisses in the rain,
She gave me a new heart,
Forgive me if I say she speaks like my love,
Her laughter reminds me of a love I once knew,
It must be infatuation
The kiss in the rain,
The wars I've won, the blood on my hands,
The secrets I never tell, desires that rule my life, and
the promises I break,
Thunder and lightning, I swear to bring upon her,
It's too soon. Too insane,
Is must be lust;
The kiss in the rain,
My words aren't as sweet as her lips, but they sure burn
like her passion,
Will she see my bleeding heart, the sadness coating my
smile?
The venom I carry, the love I lost, the future I can't
give her,
Will she run?

A cloud of sadness befalls me as I contemplate on the meaning behind the lyrics. I want to believe Zachary wrote the song for me, yet at the same time, I can't be so sure. I have to be careful of seeing and believing what I desire to be real.

The shrinking gap between Zachary and me steals my attention. He glances at me briefly before lifting his hand to brush Madeline's hair.

Sean is still singing when Zachary plants a kiss on Madeline's cheek, stands, walking toward the doorway. Madeline grimaces as she rises from her seat, hurrying after Zachary.

Like everyone else, I watch them walking toward the back door. I turn my eyes to Sean, who smiles as he continues singing.

```
     To think that I have seen her, felt the lifeline burn,
       through the palms of our hands just to give her away,
         I hate my soul that makes me hunger for her,
           My heart for flattering at her every move,
     And my fingers for urging my feet to draw nearer, closer
                          to her skin,
                 Is it lust, infatuation, or love?
                Is it nothing but a kiss in the rain?
     If it's nothing then forgive me if I say, I'm in love
                     with the kisses in the rain.
```

Sean plays the last note, and while others applaud and cheer, I stand and kiss both his cheek. "That was amazing, thank you," I say before excusing myself.

I have to know if Zachary wrote this song for me. If he did, I'm going to tell him I'm not entirely human.

Going after Zachary, I rush through the doorway and come outside. I find Madeline and Zachary in an embrace. I pause for a moment, giving them time, and when they don't part, I turn, walking back inside.

"Alexandra!" Zachary calls.

I shut my eyes briefly and turn around to face them.

"Are you looking for me?" He raises his brow.

I nod, but my lips say, "No. I wanted some air, but ..." I sigh and turn my eyes to Madeline. "Could I please have a moment with Zachary?"

Madeline nods. "Sure," she says and kisses Zachary's cheek before walking inside the house.

Zachary takes two steps closer to me and stares at me with anxious eyes. "Hey." He runs his fingers through his hair.

"Hey." I cuddle myself and sigh, gauging the unusual gap between us.

"What's wrong?" his voice comes out stifled.

"Did you write that song for me?" I move toward him, but he steps back.

Puzzled, I pause, frowning at his screwed face. "What's wrong?"

Creases form on his forehead. He moves his hands to his waist and nods. "I wrote it for you, but as I said before, you and I can never be more than what we—"

"Zachary, I have to tell you something—"

"Alexandra, please." His fingers tremble as he raises his hand to his forehead. "You need to stop while I still have the strength to do the right thing. You could die, do you understand that?"

"I think I could be something more than human."

"What do you mean?" He comes closer.

"Zach!" Madeline calls.

Zachary plants a kiss on my cheek and whispers. "I'll call you when I get to Dacia."

XVII

I Want To Hear You Say It

I can't do this. I can't look at his face and lie.

Inhaling and exhaling for the fifth time. I step toward my cheval mirror and try to stand with confidence. The loose fit, blouson sleeve, wrap dress feels comfortable enough for a liar. The soft smoky eye shadow makes my eyes look more innocent, and my hair falls free over my shoulders.

Don't sweat again, Alexandra; there are no more demure outfits left.

I step out of my room and breathe in the smell of cappuccino that tempts me to go downstairs where Marie is preparing breakfast. Mozart playing from Mother's room reminds me of a mission I have to accomplish.

A faint knock on her door and I walk in. Mother is in the shower. I rush to her handbag, fumbling through the pockets for her cell phone. It's not there. After a quick scan of the room, I find it next to her pillow.

"Lexie, is that you?" Mother calls from the bathroom, just as I pick up her phone.

The shower goes quiet.

"Morning, Mom," I call back. "I was just borrowing your sunglasses."

"Remember to check the meaning of borrow. Last I checked it meant taking with the intent of returning." Her voice sounds light and sarcastic.

"Invest in the revised version of the dictionary, Mom. Borrow now means to take and keep for as long as the owner doesn't notice what's missing."

I smile as she laughs, switching her cell off. About to walk out, I remember the glasses and grab them from her dresser.

Half an hour later, we are sitting for breakfast in the sunroom. Mother hasn't asked about her cell, so I assume she hasn't noticed it's missing.

Her pager beeps and my nerves vibrate. For that second, I thought it was her phone.

"I'm off, sweetheart." Mother stands and leans in to plant a kiss on my temple. "I see you have one of your favorite dresses on. Is Zachary back yet?"

"Don't know, Mother." I clear my throat, trying not to show any pain. "I'm not his girlfriend. You should try to remember that."

"I was only asking. I didn't mean to upset you." She winks, disappearing into the hallway.

The front door shuts, followed by the car door. The engine hums while the intercom beeps. She is gone.

I hurry back to my room and pull out the cell from under my pillow. I begin texting.

John, she knows. Please come home.

I don't wait for a response before I switch the cell off. I'm afraid he might decide to call back. *If he tries to call and gets no response, will he ignore the message?* I let out a deep breath, and make my way to the living room, to sit and wait.

Five cups of black coffee and I hurry to empty my bladder. I'm starting to think he's not coming, and each time I imagine him coming through the door, my stomach turns. I'm tempted to switch the cell on again.

Releasing my clenched fist, I flex my fingers as I pace to the windows and come back to take a seat.

A faint beep from the intercom and I rise to my feet. My heart is drumming as I glance at the intercom. The flashing green light tells me he's here—or at least someone is here. Suddenly, my knees weaken.

You weren't at the top of drama class, but surely, you can't be the worst performer in the world, Alexandra.

I have spent two weeks preparing for this moment, chiseling the questions I need to ask him. I've practiced the way I would pause in front of him, the smile, tone of voice, and the perfect embrace.

"Hello, Marie." My heart skips at John's voice. From the quick movement of his footsteps, I can tell he's not waiting to talk to Marie.

"She's in the living room," Marie calls out.

I take one more deep breath and wait.

The French doors open. John walks in. His black cargo outfit looks gallant on him, but makes him appear austere. For a moment, we stand in silence staring at each other.

His gray eyes blink as if in apprehension. "Alexandra, where's your mother?"

As I planned earlier, the corners of my lips curl to form a smile. However, something unexpected happens. The thought that I could be right, overwhelms me, but not as strongly as the lingering feeling that I could also be wrong. *What if John is not my father?* Being a hybrid doesn't make him my father.

His eyes seem to stare more like mine, now that I scrutinize them. And ears that stick to his head.

John's lips spread to form a smile, and that's all I need to give me courage. Warmth spreads over my chest as I draw in another breath. With teary eyes, I rush and give him a tight hug.

"Dad," I breathe.

John's voice is husky when he answers. "Hey, honey ..." His arms around me tighten as he kisses my hair.

"Are you really my father?" I pull off to steal the truth in his eyes, but all I see is a cloud forming. A slight crease marks his forehead. His chest appears so still compared to mine. I wish I could stop my heart from drumming so I can hear my thoughts.

My hands in his, I begin rumbling. "I mean, you are my father, right? All this time ... your eyes ... the nose, and um ... I always wondered if I got my nose from my ...."

"Your father," John finishes the sentence for me. Veins protruding on his temples, he cups my face, and I hold my breath as he parts his lips again. "You got the nose from me ... yeah, I see that." He smiles. "That's what you wanted, right? To call me dad?"

Failing to stop the rapid breathing, I suck in a jagged breath and sink into his arms. He pulls me closer, wrapping me so tightly. It's as if he's trying to compensate for all the time he couldn't. My head by his chest, I breathe in his scent, and tell myself this is not John DeLuca's scent, but my father's.

"Say it." I look into his eyes again.

"Say what?"

"I want to hear you say, Alexandra, I'm your father."

He chuckles and with exaggerated slowness, takes my face in his hands. "Alexandra Joanne De Luca, I'm your father." Tears well up in his eyes just as mine fall on my cheek. He pulls me into his arms. "You're my only child, my daughter."

We remain like that for a while until John's trembling arms shake me out of the moment.

"I love you, Alexandra." John sniffs.

Then I start laughing.

"What's funny?"

"Nothing." I keep laughing; hands on my waist at first, skipping to my hair, then rest on my face.

My body trembles and the laughter turn into sobs. "I'm your daughter." I laugh through the tears. "That makes me a hybrid, right? Except, I hoped I would turn out to be a vampire. How could I go from the most loathed to the forbidden?"

"Unlike me, you are a unique hybrid. Did your mother tell—?"

Unexpectedly, John grabs me by the waist. At a supernatural speed, he swings away from an object flying toward him. I tense at the sound of a ceramic object breaking against the wall. On the dark, wooden floor, pieces of a broken vase, colorful orchids and water creates a perfect painting of anger. John pulls me closer, our eyes turning toward the doorway.

Mother stands still, her pale face screwing up as she glares at John. "How dare you!"

"Anne?" John steps toward her.

"Don't! Don't come near me," she hisses at him. "You just had to be the one to tell her, didn't you?"

"What?" John grimaces. "I don't under—"

"I told you they found the Ring and all you thought of was to be the first to tell her she is a hybrid, huh?"

"Anne, you're not making sense. "You told me she knew, asked me to come and now…" He shrugs. "I thought this was what you wanted me to do—to talk to her."

"Jesus John!" Mother's face flashes. "You—"

"Enough!" I step between them. "I did it. I sent the text to John from your cell, Mom."

"You, what?" Mother frowns, her voice now composed, but her eyes wider. "Alexandra?" She stares back at John.

A renewed shock changes the expression on John's face.

"Well." Swallowing my apology, I move my gaze between them. "Alexandra De Luca fits me, don't you think?" I cross toward the door, heading down the hallway.

"Alex, wait!"

I pause at Mother's voice, and wait as she steps toward me. "You are not going out, are you, sweetheart? Because—"

"Of course, I'm not, Mother," I tell her.

Her face looks confused.

"There's nowhere I'd rather be than here with my parents telling me the story of my life." I take another step ahead.

"You're not angry with me?" Mother holds her breath, waiting for my answer.

"I'm tired of being angry with you, Mother." My lips stretch into a tight smile. "I'll bring coffee."

John, with a glass of whiskey in his hand, strolls past the potted butterfly palm as he comes in my direction.

I'm by the window seat, resting on a bed of cushions. I love this living room. With the bright sunlight shining through the high windows, the two cream sofas casually placed, wide coffee table set on the African rug, and a couple of potted butterfly palms on either side, the room feels as if the outside is inside.

For the last hour, John and Mother have been outside by the porch, arguing in whispers. They don't want to tell me anything. Mother said something about my past life getting mingled with my present; something to do with me experiencing extreme migraines, flash backs and thirst. All these will cause me to transform into a full hybrid. Losing my humanity sounds scary, but all I need right now is to know who I really am. I've refused to respond to any statement or question that does not involve me knowing who I am.

My eyes on the waterfall in the garden, I pretend I can't see John coming.

"Your mother and I planned that if we had a son we would call him Alexander," John says.

Placing his glass by the windowsill, he cuddles me as he sits by my side. "If we had a daughter, we said we would call her Joanne; a combination of my name, John, and your mother, Maryanne. In the end, you became everything; Alexandra Joanne." He lets out a soft laugh, his hand brushing the hair by my ear.

"Here you are, sweetheart." Mother appears and hands me a fresh mug of cappuccino.

"Thank you." I clear my throat.

Now changed into a dusky pink pencil dress, she sits in front of me, by the window seat. Watching John and me, she takes another sip from her favorite China teacup. She sets the cup aside, on the hand-painted end table, and draws nearer to sandwich me between herself and John.

"You have a past life, Alexandra." She begins.

My heart swells with anxiety. "Past life as in reincarnation?"

The two of them cuddle me as if I'm a newborn. I love the attention, especially from my new dad. However, I wish somebody else was massaging my feet like this.

"Something like that." Mother inhales. "Your last life was cut short because of an angel, the Cursed Angel."

"And who is the Cursed Angel?"

"The Alpha-hybrid." Mother speaks so softly, it's as if she doesn't want the palm next to her to hear. "The strangest being ever found on earth. A child born of an angel and a vampire. The Vangel, we called him."

I raise my head from John's chest to stare into his eyes. "A vampire and an angel? How did that happen?"

"A question I wished someone could answer," John says.

"And why did he kill me? What did I do?" I sit up, so I don't miss any reaction from their faces.

Mother turns to John. "Do you mind taking over from here?"

"It's not as if you've said anything, Anne." John chuckles at Mother.

"You father will tell you the whole story, sweetheart." Mother's smile remains fixed on John.

"Now, where do I begin?" John shifts, sitting up in a more comfortable position. He then takes my hand and entwines it with his.

"More than a century ago and before its destruction, the highest mountain used to be the Stills Mountain. The mountain stood in the middle of three cities, Pannonia, for the vampires, Dacia, for humans and werewolves, and Ashbourne for the angels. We—"

"Wait." I squeeze John's hand. "I thought Ashbourne was founded by the Van-Baileys?"

"That's correct. The Van-Baileys were the first to make a home here after the angels."

I nod. I'm curious about the angels, but I'm more anxious to hear more about myself.

I bend to pick up my mug, but Mother stands and hands it to me before sitting across from John and me.

"We called it the Empyreal Ashbourne." John's smile grows wider as he continues. "The angels held numerous games in the city, performing wonders with water, wind, fire, clouds … everything that nature provided for them." John searches my eyes. It's as if he's measuring the curiosity in me.

I eye Mother and turn to John again. It's not only what he's saying that fascinates me, but also the way he speaks. I'm noticing how his smiles kind of disappear and the way he steals glances at Mother. It's as if he's telling her the story too.

"It gets better." John grins. "The games took place in the night while during the day the angels taught humans the crafts of music. They showed us how to make swords, build ships and planes ..."

Mother looks at John, her head slightly tilted. "Joe, honey, you're now diverting from the story."

He laughs softly as if remembering something exciting. "Anyway, back to the mountain. Set on top of Stills Mountain was the home of the twelve immortals called the keepers, six men and six women. Your mother was one of them." John glances at Mother who nods slightly. "Fortified by the archangels, the keepers gained immortality together with special powers."

Mother clears her throat and draws my attention. "Though most people group us with witches, we are not witches. Our job was to keep the unity among the cities, negotiating on trades between vampires and humans."

"What do vampires have to negotiate with humans?" I ask.

"Vampires need blood, and so humans traded blood for weapons, and vampire labor."

"Hmm, sounds clever and fair to me." I sigh. "I'm thinking how fascinating your job must have been, Mother."

"Yes, it was, until I met your father." She looks at John, who's already staring at her, and they smile at each other.

I wait until she's ready to continue.

"Hybrids were a taboo, just as they are today. Often our job included eliminating hybrids." She clears her throat. "I was assigned to get rid of your father, but I failed. From the moment I saw him, I ..."She shakes her head, smiling.

"Love at first sight," John says, and I sense a slight tease in his voice.

"There is no such thing as love at first sight," Mother argues, a smile sneaking out to her lips. "I was attracted to you, at first, then I grew to love you."

"My God, Anne." John chuckles. "It's been a century, and still you won't admit it. You loved me from the first time you set your eyes on me. She still does," John whispers into my ear, loud enough so Mom can hear.

Mother stares at him for a few silent seconds and throws a cushion at him.

I hold a giggle. "I could leave you two if you want time alone, but you haven't finished the story yet."

Mother chuckles at John once again before turning to me. "It was easy keeping your father a secret until I got pregnant with you. I had to break away from the circle of the keepers. As a result, I lost my powers. We ran to hide in Dacia, with your grandfather."

John squeezes my hand, and we both turn, looking at Mother. The smile on her face has vanished, and she seems to have drowned in the past.

"Mom?"

She blinks back to the present. "Carrying you in my womb was the most exciting thing I ever did, but I worried—we worried. We knew what we had done and wondered what the future held for you. You were born on the eleventh of June 1892."

XVIII

Who Am I?

"1892?" My eyes widen. "And June eleven? Just like my birthday, at the present?"

"We didn't plan for it to happen as it did, but it's wonderful, isn't it?" Mother squeezes my hand gently.

"Oh, my God." I hold my chest with realization. "How did I look like before? Do you have any photos of us? How did I ... how was I born again? Did I—?"

"Slow down, Alex." John laughs, holding my hands.

"Lachey." Mother stares at me. "The woman you saw that time you had an accident?"

I nod. "Yeah."

"She helped bring your soul back to us. As for how it happened, that's another story for another day."

"Tell me now, please."

Mother shakes her head, smiling. "It's either I tell you about that, or go back to the original story."

My shoulders slump, and with a sigh, I relax my back on the cushions. "Go on. Tell me what happened after you gave birth to me."

John's hand reaches for my hair, brushing it back softly. "The happiest moment of my life was the day your mother gave you to me. The day I carried you in my arms." His eyes glitter as he continues. "You were so adorable. We couldn't take our eyes off you."

Mother exhales as she takes her gaze away from John to me. "Trouble came when we realized you were growing too fast," she says. "We heard gossip about the child who grew into a young adult within a year. We knew it would reach the keepers, eventually. We considered running, but we had nowhere to go.

The day the keepers came for us, we were coming from Ashbourne, and we had crossed the border into Dacia when they confronted us. Even the new skills we learned from the angels in Ashbourne were not enough to protect us. We were outnumbered. It was after they succeeded trapping us, we realized they didn't want to kill us, but they made us an offer."

I stare at her with increased concentration. "What kind of offer?"

"They claimed a witch told them you were the only one who could defeat the Vangel."

A shiver runs through me. I frown, about to ask why, when Mother adds, "Unlike your father, you were born and not turned. You were, and still are the one and only three-way cross hybrid. A cross between silver-werewolf, vampire, and an immortal keeper."

I smile; the title sounds flattering but confusing. "Wait," I turn to John. "Does that mean you're a cross between a silver-werewolf and a vampire?"

He nods.

I turn to Mother. "And you're an immortal keeper, right?"

"Correct," they chorus.

"And what's the silver in the silver-werewolves?"

"Silver-werewolves are resistant to silver, but vulnerable to wolfsbane," Mother explains. "However, you're more than a silver-werewolf, sweetheart. You've been endowed with immortality. Your blood is not only poisonous to vampires, but also lethal to the Vangel."

"Really? The Vangel who caused my death in my past life?"

Mother nods. "Now back to the story. Where were we?"

"The keepers saying I was the one to defeat the Vangel?" I bite my bottom lip.

"I see you are paying attention." She smiles and continues. "So the keepers wanted to use your blood to poison the Vangel. In exchange, they offered to protect you and disregard the kind of species you are. And also take me back into their circle."

My eyes widen. "I guess you agreed?"

Mother looks up at John. Creases form on his forehead. He drops his gaze, shaking his head.

"Why are you shaking your head?" I grab John's hand, pleading with him. "What happened?"

"I don't know if it was the right decision, but I would have done anything to give you hope. And that's what the keepers were offering." John pauses, lips parting as tears well up in his eyes.

"Dad?" I say it out loud before I realize it's the first time, I've called him, "dad".

"Honey." Squeezing my hand, Mother draws my attention away from John. "Your father and I wanted to find the Vangel, and to destroy him so you would have a life."

"I take it that's not what happened, is it?"

"We found the Vangel during the Empyreal Ashbourne Games. That was after several months of trying. We used to take you to the games every month to train. Your passion was to fight with swords. That's what the angels taught you. One day, you came home excited. You had an idea of how we could poison the Vangel."

I sit up straighter, eager to hear about the idea.

"You told me the Vangel was in love with you. You were so sure that you arranged for him to come home and meet us. 'The trick was for him to bite you as a show of affection,' you said. At first, I wasn't sure if it would work, but after I had seen the way he looked at you, I was sure he was in love with you."

"Wasn't he?" I'm more curious, this time.

"Maybe. You be the judge of that after you hear this."

I shift, taking a sip of my cold coffee to quench my sudden thirst. I put the mug on the coffee table and breathe in, facing Mother again.

"On the day you planned to poison him, we suggested you meet at the keeper's estate by the mountain, just as the keepers wanted. An hour after you left, we got a visit from a vampire. I remember seeing his face and wondering who had wounded his heart.

'Hurry! Go help her, help your daughter. He wants to kill her!' Those were his words.

He had such a soothing voice; it took a moment for me to realize you were in danger. He explained how the Vangel was only interested in knowing how to kill you. He told us to hurry and that an army of vampires was coming after us.

And for sure, within minutes vampires invaded Dacia. On the mountain, the werewolves fought against the vampires. Your father and I reached the circle of the keepers within minutes to find all the keepers massacred. You and the Vangel, however, were battling with the swords.

We tried to get to you, but a mass of vampires blocked our way. Angels from Ashbourne arrived to stop the war, but they couldn't do much. They broke the mountain into pieces. It fell, and water took its place.

I lost your father in the waters, and thought I lost you too until I saw you and the Vangel up on the small part of the mountain that remained standing, continuing to battle with the swords.

On a small island, the two of you fought for hours, days. Vampires hid from the sun during the day, and at night, they would come out to continue with the battle. Rain poured with lighting and thunder. Unexpectedly, darkness covered the skies. I never slept for all that time. I kept my eyes on you. It hurt me that I couldn't get any nearer.

When the sun appeared, I saw your sword and that of the Vangel, embedded into the ground. You and the Vangel stood in the middle fighting a different war. Intertwined, you were kissing with as much passion as—"

"Kissing? How did that happen?"

Mother shrugs. "I hope one day when you remember it all, you'll explain to us how it happened." She smiles.

"Wow." Staring at my trembling hands, I take in a deep breath. For a moment, I felt as if I remember everything.

Mother brushes strands of hair from my face and tucks them behind my ear.

"Did you find Dad?"

Her lips form into a faint smile. "That's another story for another time, honey."

"So how did I die? You said because of the Vangel, my life was cut short." I turn to John. "Dad, you've gone quiet."

He reaches for my hand, lacing our fingers together. "It's the memories. All this talk brings it all back."

He muses, then stares at me as he sits up, ready to pick up the story from where Mother left off. "The sun went down, and the vampires, under the orders of the Van-Baileys, crossed over the waters and attacked you. The Vangel rose to fight, and defended you. The vampires felt betrayed by the Vangel. They ripped your heart out. One by one, they dropped dead to the ground just as you did. You fell into the Vangel's arms.

The vampires turned their angry fangs on the Vangel. It took a while, but they got him to his knees in the end. Bleeding white blood as the vampires savaged on him, the Vangel screamed, 'Sun,', and it rose, breaking through the darkness.

Vampires ran to hide from the sun, but before long they realized the sun no longer had any effect on them. The white blood from the Vangel made them immune to the sun, and they healed quicker than ever. The vampires who drank from his blood became the White Bloods. They tried to kill the Vangel, but soon they discovered whatever they did to him, happened to them, as well.

With the chaos going on, I seized the moment and ran to you, but a sword surged through my chest before I could reach you. The last thing I remembered was falling into the deep waters."

"You died?"

"It took me a century to know he didn't die that day." Mother stretches to hold John's hand. Soon she lets go, taking my hands into hers. "You, however, died in the Vangel's arms. I hated what he did to you. I was so angry with him, and I wanted to take you, so I could hold you in my arms for that last time. But there was something in the way he held you closer to his chest as if you were the only thing that mattered to him. His cry pierced through clouds, and it began to rain again. Then he vanished."

"He didn't kill me." I shift my gaze between them. "He fought for me. He loved me."

"It was his fault. I believe that's what he wanted, to destroy you, and he did."

It's hard for me to understand when I don't remember anything. "What happened? Did he die?" I ask.

"No one knows exactly what happened to him." John relaxes on his seat. "Some people say, he compelled all of us to forget him, so we wouldn't recognize him."

"Do you think it's true? Do you remember how he looked?" I look at his eyes.

"It's frustrating that I remember him, but I can't seem to remember his face. Each time I try, I see him, but it's all like a dream, where you feel and know who is around, but can't see their face."

"Mother, you don't remember?"

She shakes her head. "I don't remember anything that happened after that. Your grandfather explained to me how I lost consciousness."

There must be a way for me to remember what happened.

Breathing in, I glance at John, then at Mother. "So how was I born again?"

Mother's lips part and for a moment nothing comes out of her mouth. Eyebrows arched, she cast her eyes down. "After almost a century of looking for your father, he found me. I wanted you back so much that I did the forbidden." She pauses, inhaling a deep breath as she looks into my eyes. "You have to understand I felt so guilty for not protecting you the first time. I wanted you back so I can make things right. I just wanted a second chance at being your mother."

"What did you do?"

John clears his throat. "She summoned the power of the great witch, Lynette Lachey, to have you back as our daughter. This angered the keepers.

Before your first birthday, three of the keepers appeared to us, and after binding us within their supernatural circle, they decreed the curse of nemesis on your father and me and the curse of the lifeline on you and the Vangel."

"What does that mean?"

"The curse of a lifeline means it is impossible for you and the Vangel to live in this world at the same time. One of you must die. You will certainly meet at some point, but you can't be lovers. The keepers will always thwart your relationship until one of you dies. They wrote your past and future in the keepers' book of curses—Cursed. You have to find the Vangel and destroy him before he finds you."

I shoot a look of disbelief at them and shake my head. "I have never killed a fly in my life, and now you want me to kill the most powerful being on earth? Someone who loved me enough to fight for my life? I don't think I can do that."

Mother shakes her head. "First, he is powerful and yet vulnerable to you. Your blood is the only weapon that can kill him. He betrayed you in your past life. I can tell you wherever he is, he is plotting the same. If he's the first to find you, he won't hesitate to kill you."

"I don't believe he will." I almost shout, but turn, staring at John then at Mother. "He fought to protect me. You said it yourself, Mom."

"I don't believe the vampire who came to warn us, was lying." John rubs my arms. "The Vangel can't be trusted."

"Even so, He will never find me. Mother, you have powers to hide my scent, so no one can identify me, right?"

"Alexandra." Mother takes my hand. "The powers I possess are not my own. They come from the sleeping Keepers. It's all part of the curse. They want you destroy the Vangel. It's because of their powers that I'm able to hide our identity. We're all shielded by them. If you don't destroy the Vangel, they will use me to destroy us."

"Why do they hate the Vangel so much? What did he do?"

"Their lives depend on his death. Their job was to make sure he doesn't exist. His existence means vampires can walk under the sun, eat, and procreate like humans."

"Vampires can have children?"

"Yes, those that drank from the Vangel."

I frown deeper. "How does that work? Do they grow old too, like humans do?"

"They grow naturally, up to the human age twenty-one." John explains. Once twenty-one, growth can only be triggered by procreation. The more children they have, the older they get." He sighs. "Even so, their degree of growth is only a fraction compared to that of humans. When they stop reproducing, aging stops too. Destroying the Vangel means nature will be restored. The keepers will be able to live again."

"You mean they will rise from the dead?"

"Like I said, they are not dead, but asleep."

"Where are they sleeping?"

"Under the sea—the Stills."

"How will they use you to destroy us?"

"We're not going to let that happen, so there's no need to talk about that."

A rage swells on my chest. I feel I need to escape from my life, from the creature that I am.

I rise and make my way to the open French doors, and lean by the doorway, taking in the fresh wind blowing from the waterfall.

From the corner of my eye, I see Mother coming toward me.

I don't move when she places her hand by my shoulder. "There's nothing wrong in you getting rid of the Vangel. It's the best thing for everyone. No more White Bloods, vampires will be vampires. Besides you'll retain your immortality."

"It's not as if they are harming anyone, Mom." My voice comes out weak. "And what about me? Are you forgetting I'm a vampire too? I look forward to having children, some day."

"The vampire and werewolf in you are not transformed yet, so you can still have children," Mothers says.

"And when I'm fully transformed?"

"You won't." John says. "We have everything under control."

Mother takes my hands into hers, rubbing them gently. "I have nothing against vampires or any other species. I just want you to live, Alexandra. I'll do whatever it takes to keep you alive. I want you to do the same. If not for you, at least live for me. I can't lose you again." A cloud forms in her eyes, and soon tears well up in my eyes.

She inhales a long breath and tilts her head slightly, staring at me. "You are worrying about Zachary and Sean, aren't you?"

I wipe my eyes. "I worry about Chan, if he's also a vampire? What if he's the Vangel? His family, Sean's family, Emily's Tristan and, yes, I worry about Zachary."

"I need to talk to you about that." John steps closer. "About young Zachary…"

I scoff. "Let me guess. I should stay away from him, especially from his father?"

"No." John smiles faintly. "We want you to stay on his good side."

"What?" I move my gaze between Mother and John. "Why?"

"Zachary senior keeps the book, Cursed, in his library. It's locked behind a security door that pricks a finger to identify the individual before allowing access."

"You didn't tell me the Van-Baileys had the book. And what are we trying to get from the book again?"

"The book holds record the events of your story; your past and your future. It has the list of those who became White Bloods, the Sleeping Keepers, and witches. It carries all the list of the curses, some cures, and most importantly, the name of the Vangel—the Cursed Angel."

"Now I'm confused." I run my fingers through my hair. "Why would the Van-Baileys have a book that holds my past and future?"

"Like I said, it also holds names of White Bloods—they are healers, and witches. Anyone who has the book holds power in his or her hands."

I shake my head, feeling a bit dizzy. "You want me to trick Zachary and his family, so I can sneak into the home of the man who hates humans and kills hybrids, to get a book that would make you powerful?"

"I'm not after power, Alexandra. Can't you see?" John voices, his tone saddened. "I have spent the last ten years hunting for this book. Finding the Vangel and destroying him will give you life. That's all I want; a happy immortal life for you."

"You're close to Zachary's father, can't you ask him?"

"He knows I'm a hybrid. As close as we might be, he would never talk to me about the book of curses."

My mouth screws up and I shake my head. "And if I don't find him? Or if I refuse to destroy him?"

John stands and adds more whiskey to his glass. "Once you're fully transformed, you'll turn into ashes and never exist again, leaving the Vangel to freely live an immortal life."

My heart stops beating for a second. "What?"

"You have lived life as an immortal before; you can only have another by eliminating the Vangel. That's your curse."

My throat tightens. "You mean I'm dying?"

"Not exactly."

"Not exactly?" I scoff. "Mother this is one of those questions that require a yes or no answer, remember? I'm transforming every day, which means each day I'm getting closer to my death. And you two are just telling me now?"

"Sweetheart—"

"Don't!" I shrug Mother's hand of my shoulder. "I thought you said you have everything under control?"

They both reach for my hands. "We do," Mother says, desperately. "We are waiting for the Ring. It will help stop your transformation. If there's no trouble on the way, we should have it by the end of the month."

My face still screwed up, I turn my eyes to John.

"The Rings buys us a little over a year before it expires," he explains. "I believe if you do as I say and follow my plan, we will find and destroy the Vangel within six months."

The two of them stand in front of me like two cops trying to persuade a witness to testify in court. I sigh and turn my back to them.

John steps in front of me. "Wherever the Vangel is, he's thinking and planning just as we are. If he is as smart as I know he could be, he will have an army of vampires, vampires who are not willing to live in the shadows hiding from the sun. Once you destroy him, the curse will be broken. All the vampires walking in daylight will burn in the sun." He pauses, making sure I'm still listening. "Vampires don't want that life anymore. If they know you are a threat to that, they will find you and take your life without thinking twice. Do you understand me?" John's chest rises unevenly.

I nod my answer while from behind me, Mother rubs my arms.

"And that goes for your vampire friends, too." John adds. "You need to convince Zachary not to pursue the hybrid he's obsessed with. You do that, and human or not, his father will treat you like a god." John's words echo Maxx's.

"I'm guessing you've already worked it out that I'm not his hybrid."

John nods. "A small part of me wondered if there was a connection between the Vangel and Zachary's curse of the hybrid. But when you two met, and we didn't experience the total eclipse, I got my answer."

I inhale before turning and throwing myself on the armchair closest to the French doors. "I think I liked it better when I didn't know who I really am."

"Alex." Mother takes a few deliberate steps toward me.

She looks at John, whose face has hardened again. He tightens his jaw before giving Mother a quick nod.

I sit up, wondering if there could be anything worse than what I've already heard.

"I knew all this would be hard for you to accept, and that's one reason I didn't tell you sooner, but that's not the main reason."

"What is it?" I ask. "Please, tell me it gets better?"

"There is something you must do as soon as possible."

I swallow hard, my heart still as I give her my full attention.

"You now have knowledge of your first life. Your present and previous lives have, therefore, intertwined. You will have flashbacks of your other life, and this will come with severe side effects, like nose bleeding, unconsciousness, severe migraines and most of all, thirst. These will not stop until you drink from a white-blooded vampire."

"No, no, no. I can't do this. Why didn't you tell me before—?"

"We did," they chorus.

"You didn't want to believe me, Alexandra." Mother's voice is pained. "You thought I didn't want tell you who you are."

I shake my head. "I just can't do this! You can't tell me all these things and expect me, suddenly, to switch into a monster and rip someone's neck open!"

"You don't have to rip anyone's neck, sweetheart."

"So how do I get the white blood?"

Mother sighs, her hand holding on to John's. "Zachary is white-blooded."

XIX

THIRST

"I'll be spending the night next door ... with Sean." Standing by the mirror in my bedroom, I slip my head through my sheer, sea pearl, and sequin dress.

As the dress falls and settles in the shape of my curves, I see Mother's deep frown reflected in my mirror.

"With ...?" She blinks, and the frown disappears. "It's your birthday tomorrow. Since you refused a party, your father and I thought it would be nice if we could have breakfast together."

Mother has her hair down tonight. In fact, it's been like that since John has been coming to see me for the last two weeks. With her hair over the shoulders, we look more alike.

Though I now regret wanting to know the truth about me, I think it was the right thing for her; she seems happier. Even her outfits are less severe, and more to the romantic side like the cream, beaded bodice dress she wears tonight.

Keeping a calm face, I continue applying faint eye shadow while Mother zips my dress. "If I stay in for breakfast tomorrow, will you tell me why you and John ... Dad can't be together?" I ask.

She sighs as she places her hands on my shoulders. "Where did you say Sean is taking you tonight?"

"Club Flash. Just so you know, changing the subject will not work." I set the make-up brush down, pick up my beaded clutch and turn to face her. "You still haven't told me why you and Dad are not together. It's obvious he adores you, and I hardly recognize you when you're around him. You still blush at his silly comments."

I steal a look at her and find her cheeks a deep pink.

"Your father thinks it's all too much for you to take in at once, and I agree." Mother reaches for my hands. "We'll tell you when it's time." She tucks in a strand of hair behind her ear, and pauses as if to revise her thoughts. "The Ring is coming before the end of next week, I think. Once you have it on your finger, we'll tell you about that, and about your father and me, too."

I study the sincerity in her eyes and nod as she smiles. "Fine, I'll wait."

Mother leans forward to kiss my cheeks. "It's not long anymore."

After a deep sigh, I turn my wrist to check the time. Ten past eleven, Sean will be here in five minutes. I rush to my closet and grab my long-line coat. I pick my laptop from my bed, and find Mother still standing by the doorway. This time an expression of concern covers her face.

Hanging the coat over my arm, I hesitate and observe her expression. "Mom? Are you alright?"

"Yeah." Her lips curl into a half smile. "I was just wondering if you've experienced any flashbacks, headaches or maybe—"

I shake my head. "You've asked me this several times now. Like I said, if I do, you'll be the first to know. Stop worrying." I move forward, plant a kiss on her cheek and let out a soft laugh. "You smell of Dad."

"Call him John." She sneaks in an apologetic smile. "I don't want you to end up calling him Dad in the wrong places."

I nod and head for the door, just to stop at the sound of her voice calling again.

"I really have to go, Mom. Sean will be here any minute."

Her shoulders rise an inch. "Are you and Sean a couple now?"

"No." I grimace. "No, we are not. Why do you ask?"

Her eyes waver. "Are you sleeping together?"

Now I realize this is what she wanted to ask.

I cough to drown out a laugh. "No. Not really."

"Honey…" Mother draws nearer, her eyes pleading with me like the good cop. "This is one of those questions that require a yes or no answer. I thought you and Zachary were—"

"Well, you thought wrong." My chest rises at the mention of Zachary. Zachary who left me six weeks ago and did not call or text—not even to check how I was coping with the racetrack. "Zachary is in Dacia with his girlfriend. If you think I've changed my mind about begging for his blood. I haven't and never will."

"Sweetheart." Mother sighs. "I'm only worried about the amount of paperwork you seem to be handling since Zachary left. You haven't slept for—"

"I don't sleep because I don't feel like sleeping. What's wrong with that? You and Dad told me, vampires can stay awake for at least three days, so two days for a hybrid ... that's nothing, right?"

"You are not fully transformed, honey, remember that." She sighs, rubbing my arms tenderly. "Did you call Zachary to find out when he's coming back?"

"Why should I do that? If he can be so wrapped up with Madeline that he can forget to check on me, why should I care about him?"

Mother's brow rises. "And so you think it's best to get busy with his best friend?"

"Why not? Sean likes me. I like him. He's cute, has a good personality, and he's the only person who doesn't seem to want to escape from me."

"You're not thinking clearly. That boy is in love with you. If you hurt him, you will risk losing Zachary, too."

I scoff and shake my head. "I can only lose what I already have, Mother. Besides Sean is a grown man. I'm sure he can take care of himself."

"You're sleeping with Sean to get back at Zachary?"

"I'm not sleeping with Sean, Mother, but I intend to."

Worry is etched on Mother's face. "I could call Zachary if you want me—"

"Mom!" I pause to calm my rising voice then take a step closer to whisper in her face. "Stop pushing me to Zachary. I'm not begging for his blood." *Is the hold that he seems to have on me not enough?*

"Red?" Sean shouts from his closet.

I move closer and stop by the door. "Any other color apart from red."

We are in Sean's bedroom, a spacious room, with high ceilings and lots of light flooding through square windows.

In the center and surrounded by parrot gray walls, is a black scroll bed with carved legs touching an aged oak floor. Resting by the wall closer to the doorway is a large display unit with two double glass doors locking in a variety of music trophies.

"What do you think of this? Come see." Sean calls again.

I slide the closet door to the side, and with my mouth open, I freeze, watching him naked. "Jesus, Sean!" I find my voice again and shut the door in the split of a second. I close my eyes as heat covers my face.

Sean's laughter is so loud I shake my head with annoyance.

"How could you do that to me? That's not fair," I grumble.

The image of him naked refuses to leave my mind. I hate to be thinking about this, but I must admit. He has it all.

He's still laughing when he answers, "I forgot I had nothing on. I'm sorry," he says, but his voice carries no regret.

I try not to think of him naked, and walk around the wooden floor toward the black display unit closer to the doorway. I take a moment to admire its contents, and rest my eyes on a photo of Zachary and Sean grinning at each other.

Looking at Zachary's eyes, I close my eyes and tell myself to ignore the warmth that spreads across my chest. I smile at the cheekiness in their eyes, and move on to admire the model sport cars lined on the top shelves. It seems it's a whole collection of the Deschanel Luxury Cars.

"Hey, Sean," I call out again.

"Yes, gorgeous?"

"That was an awesome machine you got Zachary for his birthday." I'm hoping this will kill the awkward moment.

"It's a special car. I know," Sean shouts. "Did you see how he melted with excitement like a little girl?"

"Not that I've known him for long, but I've never seen him that happy."

"He loved the bracelet you got him too," Sean adds after a silent moment.

"Oh, really." I move closer to the closet door. "Did he tell you that?"

"Yeah. Apparently, you and Mimi got him the same bracelet."

I shut my eyes. *Unbelievable.*

Sean continues. "He loves anything Madeline gives him, so don't let it bother you when you don't see your bracelet on his wrist."

I take a moment, making sure my voice comes out right. "He loves her, doesn't he?" I hold my breath.

"They love each other," Sean answers, his tone nonchalant.

A few seconds later, he stands before me in a maroon shirt with a matching waistcoat, briefs and nothing else.

"Did he have any girlfriends before Madeline?" I ask.

"Nah." Sean screws up his face. "Just boyfriends, until he discovered he was straight."

My mouth opens. "*What?*"

"Ha-ha!" Sean laughs. "You should have seen your face." He chuckles again.

"It's not funny!" I pick a cushion from the couch and use it to hit his head.

"You won't get an answer if you keep hitting me," he voices.

I pause and wait to hear what he has to say.

"Zachary, Mimi, and I were the inseparable trio until the two decided to have sex," Sean explains. "She was our friend, and I confess, until you came along, I was kind of jealous..."

"Jealous of Zachary?"

"Before they were a couple, she was our friend. I could kiss her on the cheek whenever I wanted. I'd spent some nights out partying with her. But now ... there are limits, you see."

"Were you in love with her?"

Sean displays a closed-lip smile. "At the time, she and Zach became a couple, yes. To some extent, I felt I was in love with her. Then again, there's a thin line between thinking you're in love and being jealous."

"So Madeline is the only girl Zachary has ever been with?"

"Hmm ... we could say that. All the kisses from the other girls always lead back to Mimi," Sean explains. "She helped him get over this girl he lost a long time ago, so for that, I guess she'll always be close to his heart."

He turns back to his outfit. "How about this? Not bad, huh? And not red, either."

I look down and quickly look up to see his face. "I don't really know where to look," I giggle.

"Come on, Lexie." Hands on my waist, he pulls me to the mirror and holds me in dancing pose. "Now imagine you and me dancing like crazy, with all eyes on us." He swings me around before kissing me on the cheek.

I can't resist laughing while he stares at me with a mischievous smile. "What?" He molds his mouth as if to contain a laugh. "Don't you think this is perfect?"

"You're so unbelievable." We stumble as I push him back in the closet. "All I can imagine is you naked."

"That's a good start," Sean shouts. "What about yellow?"

"I'm not going out with you in a yellow suit, Sean."

"But yellow is your favorite."

"My favorite, not favorite on you." I shake my head, laughing.

We were quiet for some time when I decided to ask a question that's been lingering in my mind for a while. "Nicholas."

Sean laughs. "Should I be panicking? Why do you call me by my middle name?"

I stay silent, trying to rephrase the question in my mind.

"Alex, are you still there?" Sean sounds concerned.

"I'm here." I push the question to my tongue. "I was wondering when you're going to tell me what happened between Zachary and his father. You promised to tell me last week, remember?"

Sean doesn't answer right away, but when he speaks, it's not to answer my question.

"I need help with my tie. Do you mind coming in and—?"

"No!" I close my eyes, annoyed that he's changed the subject again.

He laughs for a moment, clears his throat and slides the door open. Wrapped in his robe, he leans by the doorway and makes sure he has my attention.

"For a very long time, Zachary's father somehow believed Zachary was not his son."

"Not his son?" I frown. "Zachary's almost a spitting image of his father."

"I know." Sean scratches his head. "He wanted to prove Zach was not his son, so he did something that would have killed Zach if he wasn't his biological son."

I stare at Sean with my mouth open. "My God. What did he do? How could he be so heartless? And to choose his birthday out of all the days. How dare he?"

"Alex—"

"No!" My chest rises. "How could Alexandra let him get away with that?"

"Calm down!" Sean grabs my arms, and stares into my eyes. "It's fine. Nothing happened."

"Uhm." *Thirst.* I take a deep breath. *I feel thirsty.* "I'm sorry. I've been so stressed lately. Perhaps after tonight, I'll feel better."

"I told you, you needed a break." He smiles before raising his eyebrow. "Keep that between us, right?"

I nod. "Of course."

He disappears behind the closet door, and when he comes out again, I stand speechless as I stare at him. It's the jet-black fake mustache I notice first, then the outfit; a pair of blue silk breeches with a matching waistcoat embroidered in gold, and by his neck is a white cravat. On top of the statement attire is a knee-length coat embellished with satin stripes and beaded trims.

"My God, Sean!" I laugh. "Wherever did you find that?"

"You remember when you said I should dress like I'm from the eighteenth century? So here I am." He laughs and poses in front of me with open arms. "How do you like me now?"

"I think you look perfect." I giggle as I step forward to adjust his cravat. "And all this time you've been teasing me, huh?"

He glances at his watch and with a brilliant smile, he rushes to scoop me off my feet, and swirls me around before putting me down again. "Happy birthday, Alexandra," he whispers.

"Midnight, already?" I check my wrist.

"Wait right there." Sean speeds to his dresser and brings out a small jewelry box tied with a red ribbon.

In front of me, he opens the box and reveals a pair of pear-shaped diamond earrings.

I smile as he inserts them into my ears, one after the other.

"What do you think?" Sean's voice sounds anxious.

I turn to the mirror by the wall near the door, and smile, dazzled as I admire the dangling earrings. "I love them." I peek at them again, and turn to kiss his cheeks. "They are absolutely beautiful. Thank you."

"Anything looks beautiful on you, Alex." Sean breathes, staring at me through the reflection of the mirror.

We gaze at each other for a moment. A familiar look in his eyes makes me feel at ease.

He reaches for my cheek, brushes it with the tips of his fingers and leans in, aiming for my lips. Before his lips touch mine, I move in to bury my head by his neck.

I can sense the disappointment in his arms as he holds me tighter, and drops the kiss he intended for my lips by my ear.

Club Flash, in the middle of the cavorting crowd, Sean and I are holding hands, smiling and laughing as we dance to the beguiling sound of drums and guitars.

An hour earlier, Sean convinced the crowd to sing a happy-birthday to me. Then we drank shots, enough to spell the letters that form my first name and surname.

Now the colorful lights from the ceiling are making me dizzy. My knees are weak, but it's nothing compared to the buzz traveling through my blood. I just want to dance and have more of Sean's crazy shots.

Holding our hands up, I swing and turn under his arm. A couple more joyful spins, and I come back to rest on Sean's chest. We laugh and extend our arms to dance again.

"Are you …?" Sean is trying to say something, but I can't hear him. The music is too loud.

"What was that?" I lean in by his ear.

"I think we should go home now," he says. "Your mother—"

I shake my head once, but stop; it feels heavy. "No." I raise my head to look him in the eye. "I want more of that … what was it again?"

"Viper. And no, you've had enough."

"But I'm thirsty." I leave him on the dance floor, heading for the bar. "Double viper, please." I smile at the bartender.

"No more drinks for her, Charlie." Sean grabs the spilling shot glass.

"What do you think you're doing? You're my mother, now? I hate my mother, so you better not be. My dad is cool, though." I laugh, moving my lips inches closer to his.

"Alex, we should leave." Sean doesn't wait for me to answer before he pulls me by the hand.

We sway through the crowd, heading for the steel doors marked exit. The letters are in bold, blurry red, or possibly my eyes are fuzzy.

A few feet from the door, my senses ignore the sweet floral and virile fragrances I had been breathing in all the while. They choose to focus on a different scent. I smell something that makes my throat dry, something that calls the whole of me to surrender without shame. My glands, throat, and veins celebrate the birth of a new kind of desire. A hunger and a thirst I've never quenched before.

"What's wrong?" Sean asks as we approach the doors.

"I want that …" I take in a lungful of the scent and snatch my hand from Sean.

I speed to the left by the bar, where a woman is drinking what seems to be a red cocktail.

"This is it." My mouth waters as I stare at the red liquid in the glass. I try to stop my throbbing throat. As if I'm out of control, I take the woman's drink, gulping the entire liquid at once. I hate that it's cold; that's all I think about as I wipe my mouth.

Sean apologizes on my behalf while I hunt for another drink.

"Alex—"

"I want more." I shiver, my body coiling and aching from a premature pleasure. "Sean, please, I just need one mo—"

"I said, no, Alexandra!" Sean loses it this time. His stern face somewhat shakes the alcohol out of me, but not the desire for that cocktail.

I yank my arm out of his grasp and rush to snatch a glass from a man sitting on a stool closer to the exit. I swallow half of the contents before the glass vanishes from my hands.

"Enough, I said!" Sean hisses.

"Why?" I scream. The music swallows the volume of my anger. "I hate you! Why are you doing this to me? Why can't—?"

"Because it's blood, Alex!"

"*Wha ... what?*" I blink once and twice.

Sean grabs me by the arm and pulls me toward the exit again. This time, I don't resist. I ignore the inquisitive stares as we sneak past the doors into a brisk breeze.

It seems quieter than normal now that I'm out of the club. The moon and the stars shine as if to show me off to the world. My mind is processing Sean's words as we cross to his car at the far end of the parking lot. There are low lying branches next to the car.

Holding me close to his chest, Sean opens the passenger door for me to get in. I hesitate, responding to a motion of heat rising from my stomach. Salty saliva floods my mouth. I tense up, my hand on the stomach, hoping to calm the waves of heat swirling inside. I break away from Sean's arm, rushing to the nearest tree. Bending over, I begin retching.

"Alex?" Sean rushes after me. Crouching beside me and holding my hair off while I spew, rejecting all that I drank. I struggle to breathe.

"Think of something you like. It helps," Sean whispers, his gentle hand rubbing my back.

It's all over in another moment. Sean holds me by the waist and helps me back to the car. With bloodstains on my dress, I look like a victim of a car crash. Once on the passenger seat, Sean secures my seat belt before hurrying to the driver's seat. He hands me a box of Kleenex.

The drive home is silent. I'm still trying to figure out how I ended up drinking blood. I can't wait to take this bloody dress off, not because the blood is repulsive, but because it's making me hungry.

"Your house or mine?" Sean asks as we turn into Vine Lane.

"Yours."

"Are you sure?"

I nod.

A minute later, he's driving through the gate of his house, and down a paved driveway lined with bright floor lights.

He parks by the entrance and leads me inside and upstairs to a guestroom situated opposite his room.

It looks too clean. Everything's white apart from the floral curtains. The floor appears a shade darker than the winter white walls, matching the sleigh bed with textured bedding. There's a large sofa near the TV and a blanket box in the middle, serving as a table.

I'm thinking a shower will make me clean enough for the white bed.

"Need help undressing?" Sean teases as I head for the bathroom.

"No, silly."

"Great. I see you're feeling better now." He kisses my cheek. "I'll get you something. Is there anything in particular, you'd like to eat?"

Blood is the first thing that comes to mind. "Cappuccino?"

Sean smiles. "Not good for this time of the night, but if that's what you want …"

I nod. "That's what I want."

"Feel free to use anything you find from the wardrobes, and you'll find clean towels, toothbrush—"

"I'll be fine, Sean, thank you."

I wait until he shuts the door before making my way to the shower. I'm hoping the warm water will reduce my cravings, but that's just a wish. Fifteen minutes later, I come out of the shower, still hungry. There are a range of colorful shirts in the wardrobe. I choose a white one.

The clock on the wall reads 3:30 AM, yet I desire no sleep. I know there's something wrong with me. I'm starting to think my need for blood is keeping me awake.

After a gentle knock, Sean walks in with a mug of cappuccino in his hand. He looks fresh and classy in the soft, cream sleepwear. His hair neatly brushed back and the fake mustache now off.

We sit on the couch watching TV. He says he's waiting for me to fall asleep, to make sure I'm okay before he goes to his room. That makes me feel relaxed. I don't want him to go, at least not now.

I take two sips of my cappuccino and instantly know that's far from what I need. I place the mug on the side table, and cross my legs, nestling next to Sean. "I'm sorry for messing up tonight."

"Don't be. It's your birthday. You're allowed to mess up. Besides, I'm the one who should apologize. I didn't know you were a vampire."

I tense up, not only at the truth that I'm a creature who desires human blood, but also at his assumption that I'm a vampire. "I didn't know that either." I sigh.

"If you're still trying to find your identity, we can work together. You and I can go to Dacia; there's a witch who can help you if you want to try."

"I can't. I don't think I want to know anymore."

Sean nudges me playfully. "Alexandra is chickening out?"

"It's not what we are, but who we are that matters," I say, in a tired voice.

A moment passes.

"Are you not attracted to me, Alexandra?"

My hearts skips at Sean's question. Before I can think of an answer, he continues. "The first time we met, I was sure we connected somehow, but you kind of faded away, and left me wondering where I stand."

I swallow, and a sudden craving cuts through my throat. "I am," I tell him. "But I'm emotionally involved with someone."

"Who is that someone? Your ex?"

I remain silent.

"If it's your ex, I could be what you need to move on." He rubs my arm gently. "Tell me about him."

"There's nothing to say. He left. They all leave me." I let out a soft laugh. "He gave the goodbye letter to my mother and disappeared." I pause remembering that day Chan left. "'Your world and mine are different,' he said."

"Was he your first?" Sean asks.

I smile as my face warms up. "Yeah, yeah he was." For a moment, Chan's closed-lip smile distracts my thoughts.

"And the other?"

"The other?" I grimace.

"You said they all leave you."

"Oh, um ..." I shut my eyes for a bit and add, "He was never my boyfriend, really."

"What do you mean?"

"We were more like what you're asking you and me to be. It was fine at the time until I discovered he'd decided to go back to his beautiful girlfriend."

"What happened?"

"Nothing happened. He just decided it was time to leave me."

"Were you in love with either of them?"

"I don't even know the meaning of that anymore, but what does it matter, hey? Be it love, infatuation, lust or whatever one calls it, what matters is what one feels in the end, right?" I pause, controlling my breathing. "It hurts, especially when there's no one to blame."

Sean squeezes my hand, pulling me closer. "I'm sorry."

"I just don't want to hurt you. I know once we cross that friendship line, everything gets complicated, and you'll run away like the rest of them."

"I can look after myself, Alex." Sean studies my expression. "And whatever happens, I want you to know we will always be friends."

I give Sean a faint nod, and he pulls me closer to rest my head on his chest. After a long while, I hear a light snoring. I raise my head and find Sean's eyes shut. He's fast asleep.

"Sean," I whisper. "Sean, wake up."

"Hmm ..."

"Wake up," I whisper again.

"No, I'm good." He moans in a sleepy voice and turns, burying his face in the corner of the sofa. "I'm ... um. I love you," he mumbles.

I pause and smile, watching his tousled hair. "I love you too, but not in the same way; not the way you deserve." I lean in and plant a gentle kiss on his cheek.

He opens his eyes, a little confused at first, then smiles.

"Look who's been waiting for me to fall asleep?" I tease.

"I'm sorry." He yawns and stretches as he stands, then extends his arms to me, to help me up. "Let's get you to bed," he says.

I hug him as I rise to my feet. He tries to pull away, but I pull him closer. His scent is satisfying part of my cravings. I bring my hands down to his chest, and lightly press my lips on his cheek. "Night."

"It's morning." He stifles a laugh and hesitates for a minute, looking at me. Then he grabs me by the waist and plants a quick kiss on my lips. "Get some sleep, your eyes look tired."

After tucking me in, Sean kisses me on the forehead before heading for the door.

The light from the breaking dawn is already sneaking through the curtains when I snuggle in the strange bed, trying to fall asleep, but the craving won't let me sleep.

Browsing through new emails, I smile at one from Grandpa Henry, and click it open.

My Immortal butterfly,

With so much time gone without us talking, I find myself thinking you are in love. Then again, since young Chan is not with you, it brings me to wonder who may have taken his place. Falling in love is like taking a trip to Venus. If you are lucky, you will find a lover wise enough to remind you to come back to earth, back to places like Viennamo where your grandfather sits in anticipation of your visit."

Happy birthday, butterfly.

Love, Grandpa.

It's a few minutes after six. The birds sing in the trees as if to report to the world that I'm still thirsty. I'm determined to hold it down. Though I haven't slept since coming back from Flash, I'm still in bed, sitting up with my back against the pillows.

I pick up my phone and read happy-birthday messages from a few people, including Emily, John, Mother and hilarious messages from Maxx Van-Bailey. I'm replying to a text message from Maxx when I hear a call alert beeping from my laptop.

I open it, and my heart skips.

"Happy birthday, beautiful," Zachary says, twirling in his executive leather chair.

"Hey, knight," I smile back, dazzled by his beaming eyes.

It has been long since seeing him. I want to be angry with him, but the rage seems to have dissipated.

Zachary's smile disappears. "Have you been crying because you miss me?"

I roll my eyes. "Don't flatter yourself, Zachary."

"It's just your eyes. They look different—tired."

"Perhaps it's your eyes." I force a smile. "You look yummy tanned. Don't get too orange, though."

He's wearing a silk robe, wine colored, same as his drink in the wine glass set in front of him. He takes a sip before running his fingers through his messy hair. "Wait until you see me in person. You will know it wasn't a coincidence God made me the way I am." He smirks.

"Hmm." I lean back on my pillows and sarcastically I say, "Speaking of coincidence; I haven't heard from you for the past six weeks. Not that it matters, but—"

Zachary snorts.

I close my eyes briefly before continuing. "Yeah—not that it matters, but considering we're dream partners, I thought it odd that you just forgot me like you did. The day after my mother asks me about you, you suddenly call me as if you care. I understand if I'm not important to you, but—,"

"No, no, no, Alex." He tries to explain.

I refuse to give in. Instead, I raise my voice. "But we do have a child together, remember? Kids pick up on these things. I'm sure you're aware of how important Autumn Reigns is to us, or at least to me."

Zachary shakes his head. "Alex—"

"So, Zachary, I was hoping you would make me like you again by telling me this is all just a coincidence. You, calling me is your own choice, and not my mother's."

Zachary shuts his eyes for a moment and stares at me with a mischievous smile. "Finally, it worked," he says.

I grimace. "What worked?"

"You don't know how I've worked day and night to make you hate me." He snickers, perhaps enjoying my annoyed face.

His arrogant attitude infuriates me this time. In annoyance, I put my laptop aside, stand and lean toward the screen with both hands on the bed. "Zachary, in case you haven't been paying attention, this is serious. Look at my face. Unlike you, I'm not smiling."

"I love it when you're really angry. You should see how kissable your lips are, pursed like so." Zachary chuckles.

Hearing his laughter again, I almost smile, but in the end, I succeed in maintaining my composed expression.

I stare back at him. Our eyes meet. "Do you mind telling me what's so funny?" I narrow my gaze.

He mimics my frown and I turn away, hiding my smile. Walking around, I pretend to tidy up the room. Zachary begins to hum a song. I find a T-shirt and throw it on the screen at Zachary's face. Then I sit back down on the bed.

Zachary crosses a leg, swirls in the chair for a moment, looking back at me with a straight face.

"Come here." He stares at me in a different way this time, and my heart flutters. "Come closer. Is that my shirt you're wearing?"

"You're unbelievable." I almost yell. "It's Sean's," I say with confidence.

"No, that one is definitely mine." Zachary insists. Check the label. He must have stolen it from my house."

I sit back on the bed, pull up the collar and look at the label. Zachary's name is printed in gold. I stare back at his smug face and sigh before forcing my lips apart.

"Okay. It's yours." I avoid his eyes, but he waits until I look up at him.

He begins to laugh again.

"Zachary, if I had known, I wouldn't have worn it," I add.

"As if ..." Zachary's snort makes me want to scream. "Now take it off," he orders.

"What?" I whimper. "300 miles away? What will you do if I don't?"

"I'll fly over first thing tomorrow, before sunrise, and take it off you in style."

"I dare you." I bite my bottom lip.

Zachary muffles a laugh, and when our eyes meet again, the smile on his face disappears. So does mine.

We remain quiet staring at each other.

"I've always loved your hair messy like that." Zachary breaks the silence.

I spread a faint smile. "I added highlights. Did you notice?"

"It's beautiful," he says with a serious face.

"How is Madeline?" I ask after another moment of silence.

"Still gorgeous." Zachary drops his gaze, playing with his fingers. "She's in the shower."

"So ... you two are totally back together?" I ask.

"Yes." A crease forms on his forehead as he swallows. "I see it didn't take you long to hook up with Sean."

I swallow. "Isn't it what you hoped for?"

He nods first but quickly shakes his head. "No. That's what I feared."

"What do you mean?" I frown. "You are the one who pushed me to Sean, remember?"

"I thought, deep down, somewhere in your subconscious you preferred him to me."

"Why?" I grimace. "Why would you think that?"

"You kissed him first, yet we met first."

"Zachary ..." I sigh, but say nothing more.

We go silent again. Zachary opens his mouth to speak, but pauses, jaw tight as he looks into my eyes. "Are you sleeping with him?"

I resist the urge to scoff. "Are you sleeping with Madeline?"

He remains silent.

Realizing he wasn't going to say more, I decided to tell him my thoughts. "There's something I wanted to discuss with you."

"What is it? Don't tell me you're in love with Sean?" He chuckles, but I don't laugh with him.

"I don't think we should be friends anymore." I put on a strong face, staring at his furrowed brow. "I want to buy you out of Autumn Reigns."

"Wait," He sits up straighter, eyebrows knit together as he lets out a short breath. "You're talking about our partnership, as well? Does this mean you don't want to see me again?"

"It means I want to avoid being around you as much as possible."

"By buying me out?" His voice comes out harsh. "What if I don't want to leave?"

"Then I'll be forced to sell my share to Emily. I'm sure you two will have fun working together."

"Alex, why are you doing this to me? Is this because of Madeline?"

"I just think it's the best thing for you, me, and everyone around us."

He blinks once and stares at me with parted lips, hand almost touching the screen. "Alexandra, you can't just cut me out of your life as if—"

"Yes, I can. I just did."

"Stop and think about this for a moment," Zachary lowers his voice. Do you really think you can forget about me? Because I've tried to ignore you for past six weeks and failed."

"It's my turn. This is my way of killing an infatuation."

He breathes in anger. "Sounds like revenge to me."

"Not everything is about you, Zachary." *I won't let you rule my life.*

"What's wrong with you, Alexandra?"

"You know what's wrong with me," I hiss.

"Alex?" The door opens after a quick knock, startling me. "Are you alright? Sean walks in with a frown. In his hand is a blue cooler bag. "I thought I heard you talking."

I smile but say nothing.

He comes closer, puts the cooler bag by the side table and settles down beside me, his eyes on my laptop.

Zachary raises his hand to greet Sean.

"I see someone remembered your birthday." Sean grins as he and Zachary salute each other.

Without warning, I reach for Sean's face and kiss him on the lips. He hesitates, but only for a second before he grabs my waist, and takes control of the kiss.

As my lips mingle with Sean's, the visions come back. This time it's different. It's clear.

Inside an ancient room with large square windows, I stand in front of a huge fireplace. I'm anxious.

The fire is warm. I remove the shawl wrapped around my shoulders. At vampire speed, I fly to the window. Outside, the darkness shadows the pouring rain. There are no lights, apart from the one provided at the mercy of the moon. The stars are scattered around the sky.

Lightning flashes and I try harder to use its light to see if he's here. It seems I'm expecting someone, someone important enough to make me nervous.

The sound of my heels on the block of wood is becoming part of my heartbeat. I smile because I'm familiar with the knock, pausing to take a deep breath before dashing down the stairs. The pouring rain makes me worry for him. The door creaks as I pull it open. It doesn't matter because the person who stands before me seems to have gotten all my attention.

I watch the rain dripping from his hair onto his heavy dark coat.

He blows water off his lips first before speaking. "May I come in? Or perhaps you delight in watching me soak?"

I recognize the voice, but I can't put a face to it. It's dark, and I need to see his face. My eyes are almost there, closer to meeting his.

"Alex?" Sean backs away, bringing me back to the present. His hands on my face, he stares at me with such tenderness it moves my heart. "Please tell me this is not another of your mistakes before I go insane."

"Uhm ..." I blink, trying to compare his voice to the one I heard in the vision.

What have I done? I turn to my laptop, remembering Zachary, but the screen is black now.

My heart aches as I stare at Sean, who's waiting for an answer. "I'm sorry I got carried away and did that in front of your friend."

Sean grins. "You are worried you kissed me in front of Zach?" He chuckles as he pulls me closer to him, giving me a hug. "I was worried you were going to change your mind again."

I smile. *I can't bear to hurt his feelings again.*

"Sorry about last night, I fell asleep." Sean takes my hands into his.

"You sleep like a baby." I let go of his hand and sit on the reclining chair next to the windows. I stare outside at the morning sun, and try hard to ignore a thirst lingering in my throat.

Sean, with the cooler bag I saw earlier, steps closer and crouches beside me. He stares at me with curious eyes and unzips the bag.

"Judging from what happened last night, I thought maybe we could try something." He brings out three bottles marked *Red.* "We call this *Red.* Yes, it's human blood."

A few weeks ago, the idea of drinking blood, human, animal or mine, seemed repulsive. However, since last night, and now as I watch Sean placing the pints on the table in front of me, my veins throb with a need to drink.

"We have both minus and plus. A, B, AB, and O. You can have a taste of each; see which one goes down best."

"No, I can't. It made me sick last night." I tense up.

"What made you sick was the combination of two types, plus alcohol."

"How do you know all this? Are you a vampire, too?"

"We're talking about you, not me." He smiles. "So what do you say? You want to give it a try?"

I want to, but I'm terrified of puking again. I'm not sure if it's a combination of two types as Sean says that made me vomit, or the fact that I can only drink white blood as Mother said.

I shake my head. "No, I can't, Sean, but thank you."

"Alex, I know you haven't slept for days and what you need is just a few sips of blood, and you'll sleep like a baby."

"How do you know I haven't slept?"

"Your eyes." Sean tilts his head. "When vampires don't drink or sleep the lining of their irises turns blue like yours. You either sleep or drink. Vampires can't sleep if they are hungry or thirsty, just so you know."

I take a moment to consider Sean's words before giving in and swallowing a hesitant sip of each type. I come back for A plus. It's still not perfect, but I force it down just so I can sleep.

Sean was right. Not long after a few sips, I feel my eyes getting heavy. It's as if they carry all the sleep I missed for the past two days.

I stretch to give him a hug. "Thank you."

He smiles. "You're welcome."

The morning sun beams across the room, as Sean helps me to bed. The last thing I remember is him shutting the curtains.

Six hours later, I'm leaving Sean's house, heading home. The cravings woke me up. I hate that the thirst makes me unsure of myself. Sean insisted on walking me home.

The door opens, and Mother appears in her crimson pencil dress. I don't know if it's the color of her dress, but a unique, hunger-calling scent travels down my throat to sit at the bottom of my stomach. Hunger calls.

Mother smiles, thanking Sean for taking me home. She receives my laptop and a small bag carrying my blood-stained clothes.

I give Sean another hug, holding him tighter. My eyes close. I dread the hunger tingling in my veins.

The unique, fresh scent passes through my nose again, making my mouth flood with saliva. A burning sensation travels up from my feet to my chest. Each time it moves an inch, it triggers every hungry fiber in me. The craving vibrates through my veins, burning through my blood. When I swallow, my jaw stretches. I think my fangs want to flash out.

"Call me if you need anything," Sean whispers.

I nod and wave as he walks away.

"Are you alright?" Mother asks after shutting the door.

"Yeah," I sigh, but shake my head. "Not really."

I'm waiting for Mother to ask why when I see her eyes scrutinizing the shirt I'm wearing, and the white shorts I got from Megan. "I didn't sleep with him, Mom." I answer her unspoken question.

"I didn't say anything."

"But your eyes did."

She smiles but soon a serious look replaces the smile. "So what happened?"

"I wish I can tell you everything, but I'm really thirsty." I lean closer and whisper in her ears. "I need blood, Mom."

"Come here." Mother embraces me. "Someone's here to see you," she says.

I pull back and stare into her eyes with a frown. "Who? Emily?" I ask, but it's that scent again. "Something smells delicious. Is it possible for you to get me white blood from somewhere? I really—"

She shakes her head. "Upstairs. He's waiting in your room. He's been here since eight in the morning. I told him you were next door, but he—"

Who? I don't wait for her to finish before rushing toward the stairs. My heart drums, my mind thinking of two people who can surprise me on my birthday, but it is almost impossible for either of them to be here, today—now.

Outside my door, I pause adjusting to a whiff of a mouthwatering scent. My glands are screaming for a drink, and not any drink, but the one I smell in this room.

My chest rises and falls as if in conflict with the beating of my heart. I hold the handle down, and push the door open, walking inside.

A short breath escapes my lips.

In a pair of camel, slim fit pants and a matching shirt protruding from a winter white shawl, collared cardigan, he runs his fingers through his flowing locks and stares at me with anxious eyes.

Ignoring the happy-birthday balloons floating up to the ceiling, I glance at the long box of lilies tied up in a thick, yellow ribbon. The pastel-colored box of cupcakes draws my attention, but only for a second.

I lock my eyes with his, and a shiver runs through me. His presence talks to me in a way that only my body understands. Fighting the urge to run and hug him, I force myself to remain still.

Then I breathe. "Zachary?"

A line forms on his forehead as he parts his lips. "Hey, beautiful."

XX

We Usually Fix Things Better In Silence …

Zachary stands with arms by his sides. He stares at me with questioning eyes that seem to ask where I've put *his* Alexandra.

I'm not *his* Alexandra. I don't owe anyone an explanation, especially him. I choose what to say to whom, and when. Right now, I'm not speaking to him.

As if to unlock the door to my thoughts, Zachary tilts his head. The look on his face is somewhere between a frown and a smile. With deliberate slowness, he takes a step toward me, and another, then pauses.

He walks and my pulse races, my nerves trembling at the veiled emotion on his face. All of a sudden, he rushes toward me. I expect that he'll pull me in his arms and tell me that he missed me. Kiss me, perhaps. My pulse races faster and faster. There's a tingle of desire in my fingers; an ache to touch him. My lips quiver for the kiss I expect. Only he stops an inch from my face.

My stomach tightens, and a wave of heat washes over my face. I bite my lips to prevent them from quivering. I'm not sure if it's the unfulfilled desires—both for him and for his blood, but right now, as I stare into his smug eyes, I want to break his bones.

I breathe, absorbing his scent, and swallow the relief I imagine his blood would give me. Staring down at our almost touching fingers, I raise my little finger to touch his. He lets out a stifled exhale. I withdraw my finger and stare up to his eyes again.

He steps nearer, closing the small gap between us. I lean forward, my nose almost touching his. He tilts his head slightly, and parts his lips, aiming for mine. As soon as his eyes shut, I smile and step aside to stand behind him.

With eyes still shut, he inhales and turns to face me again. Shoulders high, he begins to move sideways, circling me as if to wait for my moment of weakness.

My eyes never flinching at his daring gaze, I remain silent. He wants to prove something, maybe. I follow his gaze as he goes around me in a circle before he disappears behind me. He pauses, leaning closer to breathe in my ear. I hold my breath, my chest up; waiting for him to speak, for his hands to reach for my waist, but all I hear is his chuckle. Goose bumps spread all over me.

I can do it; I can forget him, get over him and be with Sean.

I fix my eyes on Zachary, shaking my head as I skip to the balcony. With mouth open, Zachary takes a step to follow me, but stops as I shut the balcony doors.

Gazing at the waterfall, I count ten breaths before turning back at Zachary. He stands still, but this time with a pained expression on his face. His chest rises as his mouth opens, but nothing comes out. He runs his fingers through his hair, drops his hand to his waist, and without looking back, heads for the door, slamming it on his way out.

I run back in and follow him. At the stairs, I pause, listening to him saying goodbye to Mother.

"Did you and Alex talk things out?" Mother asks. "Did she tell you anything?"

"Um, no. Was she supposed to tell me something? Is something wrong wi—?"

"No, no," Mother voices. "Nothing like that. She seemed angry with you. I expected she would be screaming at you, but hey ... whatever you said must have worked."

"We usually fix things better in silence." Zachary laughs, but the laughter sounds forced.

"You should come join us for lunch next weekend—if you're not busy," Mother says.

I shut my eyes, annoyed.

"I could never be too busy for you, Maryanne." *Maryanne?* I frown at Zachary's comment. When did Mother become Maryanne to Zachary?

"Actually, I think you and my mother will get on very well," Zachary adds. "Why don't you and Alex come join us for dinner on Friday?"

"Hmm." Mother pauses. I assume she's thinking over her schedule. "Not unless you make it Sunday?" she speaks again.

"Sunday is fine," Zachary answers without hesitation. "I'll tell Mother to call you."

My shoulders drop, and I march back to my room in frustration, pick up my phone and dial five then wait for an answer.

"Hey, beautiful ..."

I frown. That's not the person I called. "Zachary?"

"Gotcha!"

"Maxx, that wasn't funny!"

"Can't blame a guy for trying." He laughs. "Anyway, guess who's nineteen today?" Maxx adds with delight.

"Nineteen and pissed," I grumble. "I've never met anyone in my entire life, anyone, who makes me as furious as your brother does!"

"Tell me about it," Maxx chuckles. "He makes me feel that way, too. Sometimes I wonder if I was your brother in a past life." He sighs before adding, "I'm sorry, but all I can do is apologize on his behalf. What did he do, Zandra?"

"I don't want anything to do with your brother anymore, Maxx. Just make sure you keep him away from me."

"What happened?" His voice is serious this time.

"He spends six weeks away with Madeline and now he comes back behaving as if he owns me. I'm not his Zetra Omni Scorpii. Just remind him that."

"He cares about you too much. I know he didn't mean to hurt you."

"Well, he has a funny way of showing it." I pause to control my breathing.

"Did you two have an argument?"

"Well, kind of. He didn't say anything. It's his ... his, um ..."

"Face?"

"Yes, his face." I sigh. At last, someone understands me. "And these facial expressions. He does this annoying thing with his ..."

"Cheeks," Maxx and I say in chorus and laugh.

Then Maxx asks, "Did he do that stupid chuckle?"

"He did. My God, Maxx," I cry. "I just want him to leave me alone. He doesn't care about my feelings. Why is he doing this?"

"I don't know what you want me to say, Zandra. What exactly did he do?"

"Everything he does is just confusing. I can't take it anymore."

"He had a choice to come for you or go and do a spell to find the location of his hybrid, and he chose to come to you; that doesn't sound like a joke to me."

"What?" I ask. "Did he—?"

There is a knock at the door, and Mother walks in.

"I'll talk to you later, Maxx." I hang up and turn to Mother, whose face carries a stern expression. "What's wrong, Mom?"

"How could you let him go without—?"

"Don't start on Zachary and the blood, please." I squeeze my forehead.

"Fine, but I want to know why you remain so adamant about not getting blood from him."

I pause, my hand brushing my hair back as I take a seat by the edge of my bed, next to the box of lilies.

"I'm scared I might kill him, Mom. If I stay near him, I don't think I'd be able to control myself. One day, I will jump for his neck."

Mother frowns and takes a seat beside me. "There's no way you can kill him unless that's your intention, sweetheart."

"You don't know that," I say, looking down at my fingers. "Fangs flashed out my mouth earlier. Guess who they scared the most? Me." I glance at her smiling face. "That's how terrified I am right now."

"There's no need to worry." With a gentle touch, Mother squeezes my hand. "No matter how deep you bite, you will not release venom unless you intend to, and only if you feel threatened."

I shift position, giving her my full attention.

"Hybrids are blessed with a natural reaction that matches their feelings," Mother continues. "When hungry, they will draw blood. Threatened, they will release venom naturally, and the same goes for other emotions."

"What other emotions?" I stare at her playful eyes.

"Um ..." She smirks and shrugs her shoulders. "Like sexual feelings."

I suppress a smile, but the sparkle in her eyes is hard to resist. "What do you mean?"

"Vampires, including you, can express their feelings with or without intent, through neck bites. It's as intimate as sex."

My lips curl into a brilliant smile. "Tell me more."

"Perhaps another time, honey." She gives me a wistful gaze, then sighs. "So, you still don't want to try Zachary's blood?"

"You are a *bad, bad* mother." I shake my head, laughing.

She laughs with me, and we stare at each other, smiling. "So?" She raises her eyebrow.

I sigh. "Seriously, Mom, Zachary and I are not in a good place right now. Is there any other way?"

She exhales and changes her beaming expression with a serious, doctor one. "Your father and I are working on that, but still I fear you might have a few days before you begin to react to the sun, and we are not able to get blood until next week."

"I can survive with the normal blood." I tell her about the blood I got from Sean and how it reduced my cravings. "I will get used to it, Mother."

Adamant, she shakes her head. "This is just the beginning, sweetheart. It will get worse in a few weeks or even less. I'm meeting your father in Eastbourne. We're going to talk to someone who might help us with white blood."

"Who's that?"

"No one you should know, honey. He's a blood dealer."

"There are blood dealers?"

"We've never done this, sweetheart," she says in a low voice. "Don't say this to anyone. I'll be back after the weekend. Marie has agreed to sleep over while I'm gone. If you feel anything out of the ordinary, even a slight headache, Alexandra, call me. Remember to stay away from the sun as much as possible. We can't afford anything that would trigger transformation."

"You're leaving today?"

She nods. "Tonight. You can call Emily or Sean to keep you company if you want."

Smiling, she brushes a strand of hair off my face, then stretches to pick the box of lilies and pulls the ribbon off. "Guess who invited us for dinner next week Saturday?"

I roll my eyes but make sure she doesn't see me.

Later that night, after hugging and kissing Mother goodbye, I call Emily.

Tristan drops her over to my house and gives me a hug before driving away. After giving Emily an update on what happened with Zachary, we spend the night talking about her and Tristan.

She tells me how they're planning to visit the Great Pannonia Cave. According to Tristan, the milky white walls of the cave are the dry tears of the angels, and if lovers feed on the powder, they will love each other forever.

"Is Tristan a vampire?" I ask.

Emily doesn't answer. When I turn to look at her, I realize she has fallen asleep.

Sean looks smart in his tennis whites, his blond hair gleaming against the sunshine. The sunglasses have deprived me of the chance to appreciate his blue eyes.

We walk off the court to rest by the shaded seats. "Should we go for another set?" Sean asks.

I laugh breathlessly. "Winning two sets is not enough for you?"

"You seem distracted today." He throws a towel at me.

I catch it in the air before it lands on my head, wipe the sweat off my face and take a seat. There's a small fridge behind me, and I grab a bottle of cold water.

"They are taking too long to give us permission for the racetrack to run over the two hills."

"It's only a matter of time, which I'm sure you and Zach have plenty of it." Sean circles his arm over my shoulder.

I force a smile, laying my head on his shoulder.

"How's the craving going?"

"Thanks to you, I feel better today."

My cravings are far away and for the first time in a long while, I can focus on my feelings without the hunger and thirst taking control of me.

It happened after I drank from the pint Sean brought for me this morning. Though the blood still carried the harsh, tangy, and briny taste, it covered my throat with a sweet lining that killed my hunger altogether. When I asked Sean what it was that made this pint different, he confessed that he added some white blood, but refused to tell me where he got it.

"So can we move on to number six?" I ask.

In the first half, Sean was telling me stories about his former girlfriends and said he'd continue after the match.

"Number six was Emma," Sean says, smiling. "She was crazy about me. I liked her, but I wasn't as madly in love with her as she was with me." He laughs softly. "She tattooed my name on her boobs."

I elbow him, laughing. "I see you liked that."

Sean laughs some more and takes a couple of sips from the water bottle before turning his eyes back to me. "Yeah, I liked that ... I really liked that." He looks at me as if to study my face. "It was mostly the thrill. Each time I saw my name sticking out in her chest. The black ink—"

"Enough," I say and he laughs. "Let's move on to number seven."

"Seven?" Sean draws in a huge breath. "It's not that easy for me to talk about number seven," he says.

I sit up straighter, wanting to hear more. This feels like the story I have been waiting for, the one with the drama and the passion.

"Come on, Sean, tell me." I take his hand into mine.

He looks at me with a huge grin and shakes his head. "I'll tell you if you kiss me."

"That's not fair," I moan.

"Well." He shrugs. "Life is not fair. That's the deal, take it or leave it." He stands, adjusting his sunglasses before bending to pack his bag.

I remain seated for a few more seconds, taking in some more water. "Okay, tell me." I grab his hand and stand. "The kiss comes after you tell."

Sean wraps his arms around my waist and smiles. "Seven." He breathes. "Now, that's different. The most beautiful girl I've ever seen. From the moment I saw her, I never stopped thinking about her. At first, I thought the feelings would go away, but they never did." Sean's lips pucker and he sighs, staring into my eyes. "I don't know, but I think words won't do her justice."

My heart aches at his words. "So what did you do to scare her off? You cheated?"

"No." Sean shakes his head, a smile clashing with the frown already on his face. "I did nothing. She's right here in front of me," he whispers. "And she has no idea I would give up who I am just to be with her."

My cheeks flush, and I smile, gazing into his eyes.

"I wish she knew how I feel. How she has changed my way of thinking," Sean continues. "How good it feels to have her right here with to me. I just wish she could see that."

"I think she sees that now," I say, raising my hands to encircle his neck.

"She does?" He reaches for my waist and draws me closer.

I nod. "Yes, she does." My hands trail from his neck to his chest.

"I've waited so long to hear that." Sean leans in and presses a tender kiss on my lips.

Our lips move in unison, just to stop at the sound of hands clapping. I turn in the direction of the applause.

Zachary and Madeline stand in tennis whites.

XXI

I Did All For Me ...

My heart pounds as I lay my eyes on him.

"It's Zachary." Sean grins as he releases his hand from my waist. "Look who's back!" He flings a tennis ball toward Zachary, who catches it, and laughs before throwing it back to Sean.

There's something about Zachary that defeats my being, an aura that erases my beliefs, prevails over my willpower. I hate that he makes me feel that way.

Nevertheless, I'm stronger now, I tell myself, watching him and Madeline approaching. He grins; his hand on Madeline's waist, he pulls her closer and kisses her cheeks.

I force my lips to curl, trying to conceal my irritation. Madeline smiles back at me; she probably thinks I'm smiling at her. Her skin once ivory now looks almost bronze - evenly tanned, and glowing in the sun.

"Alexandra." Zachary bites his lips and pulls me closer for a hug.

He's behaving as if we didn't see each other yesterday, using the hug as an excuse to lay his hands on me. As if we parted on good terms. We barely exchanged words, but we said it all somewhere in the silence.

"So sorry, my ... I should be saying yours actually; the bracelet you bought for me got stuck in your hair."

He catches my hair clip before it drops on the ground.

"Sure it did," I murmur into his ear.

Madeline shakes her head at Zachary. "You're such an idiot," she says and opens her arms to give Sean a hug and a kiss. "How do you remove a hair clip like that?"

"Don't worry, I'll put it back in for you," Zachary whispers on the nape of my neck.

His breath on my skin sends shivers down my spine. The smell of his blood is so appealing; I wish I didn't have to let him go. *It's either I'm not as stronger as I thought, or he's just tougher than I thought.*

Zachary chuckles as my arms hold him tighter. He plants a quick kiss on my cheek before sneaking behind me. His fingers in my hair, he takes his time clipping my hair back. A flash of heat travels from the roots of my hair to the soles of my feet.

"Thanks," my voice comes out soft.

I walk back to sink into Sean's arms.

"Careful, Mimi, Sean is taken." Zachary smiles at me.

I know him well enough to recognize that isn't a genuine smile.

I rest my head on Sean's shoulder. He pulls me over for a kiss.

"Slow down, Alex," Zachary comments while I intensified the kiss. "It almost looks as if you're trying too hard."

He smirks and makes a quick turn, to Madeline. He cups her face and presses his lips on hers.

Hot-air spreads across my chest. "What's wrong, Zachary? Jealous?" I glare at his hands sliding to Madeline's waist.

"Oh. Is that what you were trying to do yesterday?" He puffs out a sarcastic laugh. "Cute you should think that."

How dare he? Speaking to me like that? My eyes lock on to Zachary's. I snatch my hand from Sean and step toward Zachary.

Sean pulls me back. "What's going on here?"

I ignore Sean and voice at Zachary breathlessly. "You can talk now, hey? I see you've grown wings now that you have your girlfriend around."

"Hey, hey." Sean moves between Zachary and me.

Zachary glares at me. "Don't speak to me like that, Alexandra."

"I can speak to you anyhow I want." I yank my arm from Sean. "You have no idea what I'm capable of, Zachary."

"Guys, calm down." Mimi holds Zachary back as Sean restrains me.

"No, I won't calm down." I fume. "Why don't you tell them exactly what's bothering you, Zachary? Spit it out!"

"What is it?" Madeline stares at Zachary.

"Zach?" Sean asks.

"I'm just watching out for Sean, my best friend." Zachary opens his arms wide, yelling. "Hopefully, you don't ask him to sell out your newly formed relationship."

"Zach, watch what you're saying." Sean's voice is deep and firm. He tightens his grasp on my waist as I try to escape his hold.

"No, let me go!" I pull off Sean. "He can't stand that you're happy. Just because I want out of the stupid racetrack, he wants to take it out on you."

"Is this true?" Sean frowns at Zachary.

"Of course I am upset about that," Zachary breathes in anger. "That's why I want to prevent you from getting involved with such an unreliable person."

"What?" I scoff. *Unreliable now because I kissed Sean if his face?* I charge toward Zachary. Madeline blocks my way and Sean again tries to pull me back. "You are such a child, Zachary. Why don't you just fuck off?"

"Come on, Alex! What are you going to do? Beat me out of our partnership?" Zachary laughs sarcastically.

"Honey, you need to calm down," Mimi whispers at Zachary.

"Why are you trying to ruin my happiness?" Sean steps in front of Zachary. "You have Mimi; you can't have it all, Zach," he screams. "Just let me make my own mistakes."

"I don't want it all," Zachary shouts at Sean. "Weren't you listening to me?"

Anger flush onto Sean's face, his eyes blazing as he closes in on Zachary. "For fuck sake, Zachary! Five years, five years you two have been dating, and I never said a thing. You took her from my life. All of a sudden you set these limits and shit!" Sean rages. "You didn't even ask if I was okay with that—either of you!"

He turns to Madeline before coming back to Zachary, standing inches from his face. "I still stood there, and every time she let you down I was by your side. I picked up all your little, fucking pieces, no matter how sharp they were. I swear, my heart would bleed because we seemed to share the pain. Funny, because we didn't even share the girl. And, guess what? I'm going to be right by your side when Mimi leaves you again next month."

"Shut the fuck up, Sean." Mimi rushes to Zachary's side. "Why would you even say that?"

"Because I can, and I will." Sean glares at Madeline. "You don't want to hear the truth, do you, Mims?" Sean turns to Zachary again. "No one asked me to do all that for you Zach. No one. All I want is a relationship with Alex without your interference, your advice, and your whatever it is!"

Zachary's chest rises. "We are brothers. I'm looking out for you now." Zachary rolls his eyes. "Can't you see that?"

"You know what, Zach? You just don't get it." Sean waves Zachary off and turns from him, pulling me along as he goes to pick up our bags.

"Sean, I'm trying!" Zachary calls after us, but we ignore him and continue walking.

"How do you know she loves you?" Zachary spits.

I pause, so does Sean. We turn our eyes back at Zachary.

How dare he to tell me how I feel about anyone? Who does he think he is?

"You are punishing Sean because of what I did to you?" I shake my head at Zachary. "You know what? Maybe this is why your dad did what he did to you on your birthday." I say it out before I realize.

My words hit Zachary like a double-edged sword would strike a knight. He staggers and Madeline, who stares at me with mouth open, hurries to catch him.

Silence takes over. I feel like a soldier on the wrong side. It looks like I have used a forbidden weapon.

Zachary stares at me with mouth open, his eyes blank. He seems drained as if I have swallowed his soul. I can't bear to look at him. My heart aches to think I have caused him so much pain. *What is happening to me?*

Shaking my head, I turn to Sean. "I'm sorry." I rush off the court.

"Alex, wait!" Sean calls.

I don't stop. My bag on my back, I rush out of the court through the dressing rooms and out to the parking lot. I find Sean's car and get in, waiting for him to take me home. It's not long before Sean arrives. He takes the driver's seat and shuts the door with more force than necessary.

"I don't know what came over me, Sean. I'm sorry. I shouldn't have said—"

"Hey." Sean reaches for my hand and waits until our eyes meet. "It's not your fault. I don't want you to worry about Zach. He's my friend. We'll fix things. We always do."

"Did you see his face?" I shake my head, fighting tears. "I didn't mean to cause him so much pain. I just wanted him to stop." I sniff.

"And he did." Sean rubs my arms then cups my face. "Everything will be all right, I promise."

⁂

Back at my house, Sean cooks lunch, and serves my share with a glass of Red laced with a hint of white blood. This time, he shows me the tiny vial with a thick, opaque, white liquid.

He's more playful than usual. I'm not sure if it's because he feels like it, or maybe he's trying to take my mind off what happened earlier.

In the kitchen, Sean is loading the dishes in the washer when I receive a call from Mother. She is checking to see how I'm coping with the cravings. I assure her everything is fine. I talk to John, who gives me another speech about how much he adores me.

As soon as I hang up, Sean smirks, drying his hands with a dishtowel. I tilt my head, staring at him with a frown. I'm still admiring how his hair always seems tousled in a perfect style, when he moves at vampire speed, scoots me off the breakfast stool and into the living room to set me on the large sofa.

I gasp, staring at Sean as he stoops beside me, his hands grasping mine as if scared I would run away.

"I'm tired of not being myself around you."

My mouth opens. I'm not shocked that he is a vampire, but I'm curious why he didn't tell me earlier.

"I knew you were a vampire." I smile as he rises to sit close to me—too close. "But is that all you are?" I think he could be a White Blood.

He looks down and entwines our hands. "I'm something more, definitely. Just as you are and like you, I'm not ready to tell." He stares into my eyes again.

We remain silent, smiling at each other until Sean's smile disappears. He leans in, aiming for my lips.

I return his kiss with the same tenderness. For the first time, my stomach flutters at his touch. Our lips mingling, Sean's hands move from my neck, sliding to my waist, and laying me down on the cushions.

I grab his face and kiss him deeper. He pulls my hands down, his lips tender as our tongues mingle. My hands grasp on his T-shirt, ready to pull it off, but Zachary invades my mind. I pause.

"What's wrong?"

"Nothing," I pull him down to my lips again. As his lips nibble on mine, the scent changes. All I can smell is Zachary. I try to go on, but it's Zachary that I see now. My pulse races faster, my hunger increases, and a shiver of excitement runs down my spine. I kiss him deeper. He unhooks my bra, my lips frantic as they move in unison with his. I moan, but this time it's out of frustration. I'm not getting the satisfaction I need.

"Sean, stop."

"What is it?"

"I can't do this."

"What's wrong? Is it something I did?"

I shake my head. "You did nothing wrong. It's just ... I keep thinking of
..."

"What are you thinking?"

"I don't want to hurt you." I stare into his eyes.

"Let me worry about that. I know you don't feel the same, but you feel
something. I can feel it. That feeling will grow in time. I'll make you forget
him."

"Him?"

"He, that is making you hold back."

He kisses my neck, breathing over my now naked shoulder. A surge of
excitement rushes over me. I gasp, my hands slipping under his T-shirt and
pulling it over his head. He brings his lips back to mine. Hands on his bare
chest, I pause at the sound of the intercom, followed by my phone ringing.

Sean shuts his eyes briefly. "Leave it," he whispers.

I hesitate, but when his lips brush my neck again, I give in to him.

The intercom keeps ringing and so does my phone. This time we both
give up, and I stretch to answer it. My heart drums as I stare at the caller ID.
It's Zachary.

Sean opens his mouth to speak, but stops at the sound of a knock at the
door.

"Alexandra!" Zachary calls. "Alex, come on, I need to talk to you."

"I don't want to talk to him, Sean." I pick my dress and fix my hair into
a rough ponytail.

"I'll tell him where to go." Sean starts for the door.

I grab his hand. "Don't fight, please."

He nods. I cross my arms, walking toward the French doors. I don't
want hear Zachary's voice. I stare out at the garden, but I can't stay still.
Pacing in front of the doors, my mind takes me back to the tennis court.
Zachary's face haunts me. I should talk to him. *I should apologize.*

In haste, I turn to run for the door. I falter when I see Sean in front of
me, with Zachary behind.

"He says he wants to apologize." Sean clenches his jaw, staring at
Zachary.

I inhale, my eyes avoiding Zachary's.

Sean gives Zachary a sideways glare. "Don't mess this up again." He
turns to leave.

"No!" I call Sean back. "Don't leave me. I'm sure Zachary can apologize
with you here."

Zachary's jaw tightens as he stares at me. "Alexandra." He swallows hard
and takes a step toward me, stirring the beating of my heart. "I'm sorry for

what happened, and all that I said. I was angry, and I handled my frustration in the wrong way."

My eyes well up and I turn my back, blinking tears away.

"I agree to sell my share to you on one condition," he says.

I take a swift turn to face him. "And what's that?"

"Dinner tonight, so you can hear me out. If you still feel the same, I'll sign out with no arguments."

I search Zachary's eyes for a moment, then stare at Sean.

He scratches his head a little. "If it means you two can come to an agreement, and we can all stop fighting, then I think you should hear him out."

I nod and stare back at Zachary.

He raises his brow. "Nine o'clock?"

"Eight o'clock at the Nair?" I say.

A soft smile spreads on his face. "Allow me to pick you up."

I nod.

"Uhm ..." Zachary widens his eyes, staring at me as if contemplating.

"What is it, Zachary?" I ask.

My chest almost explodes as he rushes to me and leans forward to whisper in my ear. "Your dress is inside out."

❋❋❋

Fastening my caramel locks into an intricate chignon, I dress my ears with a pair of teardrop pearls. I sigh, examining the formfitting teal dress designed with a delicate lace. Knee-length with cape-style shoulder design, the dress appears more conservative than flirtatious. I don't want Zachary to turn this dinner into more than what it is. *If he thinks he will get a hug or hold my hand, he's in for a shock.*

My heart skips a beat at the sound of the intercom. I pick up my vintage-style clutch, slide my feet into silver heels and make my way to get the door.

"Alexandra." In slim jeans and a long-sleeved T-shirt under the famous Van-Bailey blazer, Zachary smiles.

"Zachary." I return the smile.

The detail on his blazer screams unique and expensive; gold chess and horse symbols with shoulder epaulets to match the design to the buttons and the sleeves.

We walk toward his Zetra Omni Scorpii. He starts the engine and drives away. We smile at each other but don't say a word. Even in silence, it almost seems as if our thoughts are in a conversation.

Halfway through the journey, I'm almost frustrated with the absence of spoken words. With him so close, it's easy to drift into the buried desires. His scent reminds me of the things I miss. Suddenly, all I want is to hear him speak, to hear him chuckle. I long to see his eyebrows rise and his side smile, calling in those fluttering butterflies that I feel whenever we touch.

Zachary brakes at the light. I gaze out the window. Apart from the bright streetlights fighting to overcome the darkness, there's nothing new to admire. However, I prefer to stare at nothing than to face Zachary's questioning eyes.

Without warning, he takes my hand. I gasp softly, turning to eye him. He doesn't smile as I expect, but threads his fingers with mine, using our hands to shift the gears.

Letting go, he slows down and turns on to a country lane. After going another mile, he pulls over to the middle of a forest landscape. The engine dies, and my eyes search his, waiting for an explanation.

"I know you'll never admit that you missed me." Zachary pushes his door, gets down, and walks over to my side. He opens my door and gives me his hand. "I'm going to be the bigger person here, and actually admit it." My hand in his, he rubs it gently while helping me get out. "I missed you."

I snatch my hand from his. "Zachary, what I want to know right now is what we're doing in the middle of nowhere. I thought you said dinner at the Nair."

"I said dinner and you said at the Nair."

I roll my eyes.

He grins and gestures with his head for me to follow him. Through the hidden pathway beneath moss-draped live oaks, I follow him.

It's dark, but I don't have a problem seeing. The chilly breeze makes me want to cling on to Zachary. Five minutes of walking and I stop.

Zachary pauses, turning around to face me with a frown. "What's wrong?"

I sigh, staring down at my heels. "I really don't appreciate my heels digging into the dirt."

"I could carry you."

I shake my head. *He's not touching me.*

Zachary tilts his head, holding my gaze. "I know what you're going through. I do the same; telling myself I won't let my eyes linger on her. I will resist her touch and deny the way she makes me feel." He shakes his head. "It doesn't work, beautiful. Here, let me—"

"Don't touch me." I back away.

"Do you hate me that much, or you're scared that my hands might remind you there's a fine line between hate and love?"

I take in a deep breath and gaze into his eyes. "Yes, I hate you that much."

His smile disappears and he turns, walking ahead. I still can't see any sign of a building in front of us. After another silent minute, I spot streaks of light through the tree branches. Zachary stops, waiting for me to reach his side. He takes my hand and leads me past a small gate between hedgerows. Then, I see it.

"Wow!" I gasp.

I have seen many outdoor cinemas, but this is different. The giant screen is nestled in a most rare private setting surrounded by oaks, dogwoods, redwoods and magnolias.

A short distance from the screen sits an open roof vintage motor, but something else draws my attention. In the center of everything else, the green grass, towering trees, and the lush landscape, is a round table for two on a deck covered with white rose petals. The milky linen dressing the table matches the nearby dogwood.

Zachary studies my face with a faint frown. "I know it is not enough to say I'm sorry, but maybe it will ..."

In a swift turn, I throw my arms around his neck. He hesitates for a second before enfolding his arms around me, groaning while clasping me to his chest. As if reading each other's thoughts, we change places. Zachary's arms shift above while I bury mine under his, my head finding comfort by his shoulder. I sink deeper into his arms, my nose taking in his scent while his broken breaths fill my eyes with tears. It seems this—the hug—is what I was fighting for all along. All the frustration, the anger, and resentment have vanished.

The smell of his blood makes my mouth water. I try to break away from his embrace, but Zachary restrains me. We exchange kisses on the cheek as his arms circle tighter around me. Gradually, his lips brush my cheek, moving to my lips, but end up by my nose. Zachary takes a long breath then kisses my cheek. A shiver of excitement overwhelms me.

I pull away in panic. "Friends don't hug for more than three seconds."

Zachary chuckles. "Let's see." He leans in, nuzzling my neck. "Three seconds times seven days times six weeks. I think I'm still within limits."

We laugh and step back to gaze at each other. Zachary takes my hand and entwines it with his. We then take a stroll to the table.

"Thank you," I say as we take our seats on padded dining chairs. "This is amazing."

"The pleasure is mine," Zachary says.

As he raises his hand, a waiter appears with a trolley of silver sets. With a smile and a pleasant greeting, he sets the food on the table. Soon Zachary takes over, and the waiter leaves, heading toward the bright lights I see shining not far from us.

"Sea bass?" I bite my bottom lip, smiling at the food on my plate. I look up at Zachary.

His lips curl into a smile. "Your favorite."

Sitting on top of bean sprouts, shitake mushrooms, and a few potatoes, the fillet looks delicious.

For a moment, our eyes lock. I cast my gaze down, digging into the food.

"How's Sean?" Zachary asks after a moment of silence.

I take a sip of my white wine, frowning.

"I mean, how are you two doing? As a couple?"

I study his face, but it's difficult to read. "We are fine, I guess."

He looks down and picks a piece of his fish, raising it to his mouth. He then places it back on his plate.

I shoot a suspicious glance at him. He smiles, eating again.

We eat in silence. I'm expecting Zachary to start the conversation on recent events, but halfway through the meal, I realize he isn't intending to discuss the racetrack any time soon.

"What did you and Sean do for your birthday?"

"Uhm, I kind of messed things up," I say in a low voice, then smile as I remember what Sean did to me. "You want to know the funniest thing that happened before my birthday?" My voice comes out a little too excited.

Zachary lets out a soft laugh. "Do I have a choice?"

"Yes you do, but I'll tell you, anyway." I smile and continue. "So it's a few days before my birthday, and here I am in my room when Sean appears, saying he has something for me. We sit and talk for a moment when he stands about to leave. I ask about the something he wanted to give me."

"Hmm," Zachary is already smiling.

"Then he pauses, dazed for a moment before he says, 'give me a minute', skipping out of the room ..."

"Don't tell me he forgot?" Zachary's smile grows wider.

I shake my head. "No, listen first." I put my fork down. "A few minutes later, he's back. This time he hands me a rectangular box wrapped nicely in gold with white ribbons. He tries to leave again, but I demand he stays until I open the present. I'm expecting something out of the universe, but what I see is a book titled *Top Hundred Things To Do Before You Turn Nineteen* ..."

Zachary chuckles, his eyes bringing out the delight of the moment. "Nineteen or twenty?"

"Nineteen." I voice. "I mean... what is that? Besides, I was turning nineteen, so the book was of no use to me, right?" I laugh.

Zachary is laughing harder. "That was a prank, right?"

"He absolutely got me." I nod, and then realize something. "Wait, you know?"

Zachary nods, still smiling. "I can't believe he played that one on you!" He tilts his head and stares at me with his chin resting on his fist. "What did he get you for your birthday?"

"A pair of diamond earrings, but my favorite was the chess set, made of vampire-like models. You should see it. It's fascinating. When I saw the vampire knight, I thought of you."

"What did you think? That I'm a vampire?" Zachary raises his brow.

"No, silly." I wipe the corners of my lips with a napkin. "I mean a knight."

He smiles, more to himself and goes quiet again. His plate is only half empty.

"Are you going to eat anything?"

He shakes his head slowly. "I don't really have the appetite."

"You're not sick, are you?"

"Of course, I'm sick." He searches my eyes and quickly drops his gaze as I stare at him with concern. "I'm lovesick." He laughs through his nose.

I pause, waiting for him to look up and when he does, he adds, "This usually happens when I'm around you."

Heat splatters across my chest. "I make you sick?" I tease.

"Alex, you know what I mean." He smiles and extends his hand to me as he stands. "Come and see what used to be my favorite movie." Zachary holds my hand, and we wander toward the vintage car in front of the big screen.

A moment later, I'm resting my head on Zachary's shoulder. With his head touching mine, and arms around me, I feel at home until Zachary decides to wake me out of it.

"So, talk to me," he says. "Do you still want me out of Autumn Reigns?"

I frown, lift my head from his shoulders and stare into his eyes. "Are you telling me you thought planning a romantic dinner with me would make me change my mind?"

"No, Alex. That's not what I mean."

"What do you mean, then?"

"I thought you might have changed your mind from the time I apologized to now."

"You're unbelievable," I scoff, bend to fix my shoes and get out of the car.

244 of MANTISSA CREED

I'm not planning to leave yet. I just don't want to get angry and end up biting him.

"And what makes you think I would have changed my mind?" I watch Zachary stepping out of the car. "What changed from then to now? Apart from your well-planned dinner and—"

"Will you just stop, Alexandra!" He speeds in front of me.

One hand on his waist, he yells. "I did this because I wanted to!" His eyes widen. He turns his back to me, just to turn around and face me again. "In fact, it wasn't for you. I did this for me. I wanted to see the look on your face, to see that frown melting away from your face and to watch the light in your eyes when you look at me. I wanted you to hug me like you just did a moment ago." He breathes in deeply. "See now. It was for me. I did it all for me because I ..."He closes his mouth.

"Because what?" I take a step closer to him. "You're a rich, spoiled, self-centered good-looking boy?"

His face tightens as he looks up to meet my eyes. "Can't you see, Alexandra?"

"See what?" I cough.

He stares at me for a moment, steps back and holds my hands to his chest. "How did we get here? You and I hurting each other. Take me back." He cups my face. "Tell me where it all started so we can go back and fix it."

"You left," I whisper and turn my back to him, hiding my teary eyes. "You messed up when you left me to deal with Autumn Reigns by myself."

Zachary steps behind me, and gets close enough to speak in my ears. "I thought you were fine with that. You didn't—"

"No!" I spin to face him again. "I wanted you to call, to show that you care, but ..." I shake my head, choking from a lump forming in my throat.

"To show I care for the track or for you?" At last, Zachary gets it. "Because if this is about us, you know I care for you more than I should," he says.

A warm sensation flows through my veins. "So why didn't you call me? Six weeks, Zachary."

"Because I can't do this anymore, Alexandra! It's easier if I don't see you. See what happened when I called to wish you a happy birthday? What do you want me to do, hey? What would you do if you were in my shoes?"

"I would leave Madeline for me." I say it out as my chest rises.

It takes another second for me to process what I've just said, and how I've left my heart at his mercy.

Zachary stares at me without blinking. His face blank as if he is watching a ghost of a girl he loved and murdered.

He shakes his head. "I can't. My father will—"

I hurry to cup his face, to force him to look into my eyes and see the creature in me. "If I told you, right now that I'm not human, but a vampire, would you? Would you leave Madeline for me?"

He hesitates, and in his eyes, I read a book about rejection and despair. Too late to wipe a tear from my left eye, I brush it from my cheek.

"Alexandra." Zachary tries to hug me.

"No, don't." I step back. "I don't know why I continue to have any hope about you."

Zachary's face tightens. "Are you telling me you are a vampire?"

"Answer my question, first."

He takes a deep breath. "I don't know. What I feel about you and what I have to do are not the same."

"Ha!" I scoff. "So all the excuses about your dad are nothing, but just that—excuses. It's always going to be Madeline, right?"

"Alex, it's not that straightforward. Madeline is not the problem. My father will kill you. The minute Madeline leaves me; he will know it's you."

Staring at his arched eyebrows, I wrap my arms around myself. "Remember before you left, I wanted to tell you something. You promised to call when you reach Dacia, but you never did."

Sadness is etched in Zachary's eyes. His eyes turn glassy as if clouded with tears. "Do you want to know why I didn't call you all that time? Because I knew it was the right thing to do. Funny, how I counted days, waited for your birthday, for a reason to call." He tries to smile, but it comes out wrong, almost like a sneer. "In Dacia, I wanted to see a witch, to find Jo. Instead, I spent most of my days thinking of ways to make us work. There's no way, but to be friends."

"That's not working, Zachary, can't you see?" My breathing increases.

Zachary's drops his shoulders. "I need you alive. I have enough blood on my hands to add yours." His hand escapes to his hair.

I move closer to stand inches from him, and lean forward to press my lips next to his mouth. "We can't work together anymore. Neither can we be friends," I whisper. "Take me home."

His jaw clenches. "Not only do I lose Autumn Reigns, I lose you, too?"

"Losing Autumn Reigns, my doing, but you, losing me, that's your choice, so don't even think of blaming me."

In anger, I spin over to the table, pick up my clutch, and head toward the pathway. With Zachary behind, I make my way to the place we left the car.

As the engine roars, I turn away from Zachary and look outside my window. Except, I'm not concentrating on anything; my thoughts are with Zachary.

"I'm sorry, I upset you," Zachary says, driving us home. "This isn't the way I intended to end the night."

I say nothing and close my eyes. I don't want to look at him. It seems there's something in his eyes, each time I look in his eyes I end up forgiving him. For the rest of the journey, I keep my eyes closed and my mouth shut.

When I get home, Sean is sleeping on the sofa in my room where I told him to wait for me. I kiss his cheek and make my way to the bathroom for my night shower. I think of Zachary as I shower, and the thoughts of him leave me feeling exhausted.

When I'm done, I walk out of the bathroom and find Sean awake.

"You're back." He yawns and opens his arms, inviting me over. I was beginning to feel awkward, here alone in your room."

I gaze at him, and I can't explain why I feel so emotional. With a faint smile, I tighten my robe and walk over to sit on his lap.

"What took you so long?" he asks, raising his hand and reaching for my cheek.

"Nothing." I run my fingers through his hair and plant a kiss by his temple. He smells good—a strong fresh scent carrying a hint of lavender. "You know Zachary; he talks too much." I shower kisses on his forehead, moving to his cheeks and his lips.

"What time is it?" Sean nibbles on my lips.

"It's late." I smile and lean forward to whisper in his ears. "How about you make me forget, like you offered earlier."

He raises his eyebrows. His approach changes as soon as he absorbs my words. He kisses me with a different kind of need. His hold stronger, and with intent, he slides his hands up my robe to my waist. While he carries me over to my bed, I circle my arms around his neck, and kiss his lips, moving to his neck and his chest.

"Wait." Sean pauses as he lays me on the bed. "What does this mean?"

"Um ... I don't know... me, luring you to my bed?"

He laughs. "Damn, how did I let this happen?" He reaches for my stomach, rubbing it gently before kissing it. "Could I become more than just a distraction?"

"Maybe we should discuss that in the morning." I smile, reaching out for his chest. I remove his shirt as our tongues touch, and we continue through the night.

I open my eyes the next morning to a very bright day. The sun's rays stream onto my face. To avoid the sun from blinding me, I shift, facing Sean, who's still fast asleep. I rub my eyes and stare at him. He looks at peace, with his body coiled up like a baby, and his palm under his cheek.

I smile at how he looks so different with his blue eyes closed. I raise my head to kiss his eyes, but stop when I feel the vibration of my phone.

It's Zachary again. I shut my eyes ignoring call number twenty-one.

The buzzer rings and I jump off the bed, grabbing my robe on my way downstairs to tell Marie not to answer it if it's Zachary. Before I get to Marie, I hear the sound of the intercom. I sigh, knowing she has opened the gate already.

I meet her in the hallway; her eyes filled with worry. Instead of heading toward the door, she rushes toward me.

"I'm sorry; I didn't know what to do. No one told me he was com—"

"It's fine, Marie." I display a faint smile. "I'll deal with him."

Preparing my line, I walk toward the entrance, take a deep breath and pull the door open.

"You need to—Jesus!" I gasp. "Chan?"

XXII

I'M SORRY, WRONG HOUSE

At the door, Channing hands me a white rose. "For you."

My eyes never leaving his, I hold it to my unsteady chest. I appreciate the sweet smell of the rose, but it's his scent my senses desires more.

"I know you adore calla lilies. Did you know a white rose symbolizes pure love, absolute faithfulness and loyalty, wavered by neither time nor distance?"

Flashing images of the day he left take over my mind. I blink into the moment again, staring at him. If there's a smile on his face, it must be hiding behind the visible anxiety.

As always, he looks fresh and clean. The rich cream jeans and the matching Ashbourne polo perfectly trace his gracious build. He appears taller than I remember—and older. It's possibly the light stubble look complementing his slick haircut; shorter on the sides with smooth top layers. Like before, his hair is brown, much lighter than Zachary's dark-brown, but not blond, either.

I come back to his eyes, to study the face I have seen so many times in my dreams. The face that almost faded in my memory, and yet my heart never forgot.

I hoped one day I would see his face again; see his blue eyes, and the grin. Now that day is here, and this is the moment.

Perhaps I'm dreaming again.

Hoping to calm my pounding heart, I raise my hand to meet the other on my chest.

His slight grin drops as he stares back at me, possibly wondering why I haven't jumped in his arms yet.

Of course, my eyes have bear witness to his presence, but my heart is yet to acknowledge him.

Channing's face appears more worried than confused. "Are you all right?"

"I'm not dreaming, right?"

Slowly, Channing steps closer, removes the rose from my hand and places it on the table below the mirror.

He comes back to stand in front of me. As if he's afraid he'll break me, he hesitates then raises his hand to my face. His fingers glide to my hair, brushing it backwards before tracing my face. Drawing in a deep breath, he trails his fingers past my neck to my arms, all the way to my hands before raising them to his lips.

"You're not dreaming," he whispers, pulling me into his arms. He muffles a laugh as he kisses the top of my head. "Not unless I'm dreaming, too."

Quietly, I gasp at the sound of his laughter and wrap my arms around him, remembering his warm embrace, his scent, the smooth texture of his hair through my fingers, and remembering him – the whole of him.

He pulls away, turns and shuts the door. This time when he faces me again, I rush to embrace him; arms tight around his neck, the way I've always seen myself doing in my dreams.

He laughs. Holding me with the confident touch I remember, he kisses my cheeks and moves down my neck. His scent takes me back, reminding me who he is; the boy I fell in love with, never having fallen out of love with him.

In breathless anticipation, I hold him closer, tears now flowing down my cheeks. His lips move to press on mine.

Sean.

Then I realize this isn't a dream. It isn't one of my fantasies, nor is it one of those faraway places where I can kiss him all I want without a care of what would happen. This is reality, and in the real world, actions always carry consequences.

"No, don't," I say, pushing him away.

He frowns as he studies my expression and spreads a strained smile. "I know there are many reasons you would push me away, but that one makes me tremble."

He raises my hand to kiss it again, but I snatch it back and pull his hand, leading him to the living room.

As if he's never left, he relaxes on the sofa, leaning on his elbow as he faces me. The normal way would have been me, nestling in his arms, but this time I sit next to him, close, but not too close.

"I'm too late, aren't I?" he asks after a moment of silence.

I open my mouth, but nothing comes out. I have so much to say, to ask, but my mind seems frozen.

"Jo?" The softness of his voice reminds me of the comfort it carries.

"I thought one day I would find you, but never did it cross my mind you would come back to me." I laugh through happy tears.

It's sinking in now that he's here; right next to me.

Chan dries my tears and pulls me to his chest, back to our usual sitting position. "You don't know how much I missed you."

"I missed you more." I embrace him again.

He squeezes me closer as he breathes out. "I thought leaving you, was hard, but living without you was harder."

I pull out of the embrace and search his eyes.

"I'm glad to find you well. You look more beautiful than I remember." He reaches for my blushing cheek and smiles. "Tell me. How have you been?"

"Trying to adapt to a life without you." My mind drifts to Zachary, and I force a smile.

Chan raises his eyebrows. "So no one took my place in your heart?"

Zachary crosses my mind again. I gave his place to Zachary, but he refused it. "No." I drop my head, but gaze up to his eyes again. "But someone almost did."

A smile forms on his face. "Am I allowed to know whom, or why 'almost'?"

I open my mouth, but shut it when I hear Sean. "Alex!"

I stand up in haste; stare at Chan once more before rushing out of the room and down the hallway.

"Oh, there you are." Sean pauses with a smile and brushes his locks back. Playfully, he rushes over and sweeps me off the ground.

"Sean, wait." I laugh as he tickles me.

I try to stop him, but he pins me to the wall. "Tell me why you left the bed so early?" He leans over to my neck. "I was going to make you breakfast, but ..." He pauses, a deep frown embracing his face. "Is someone here?"

He doesn't wait for me to answer, marching toward the living room with me behind him.

"Ash?" Sean gasps, staring at Channing as if he had seen a ghost.

Channing stands up with a smile, but there seem to be a deep crease on his forehead.

Sean rushes to embrace him. "I don't believe this!"

Then it hits me. *Ashton?* I frown, watching as they embrace, laughing and exchanging complex hugs. Sean is doing most of the hugging and teasing while Channing or Ashton is a bit overwhelmed.

"What are you doing here? When did you get home?" Sean's hand is now around Channing's shoulders.

Should I say please, don't tell me they are brothers even though I see now that they are?

They seem to have forgotten me as they continue chatting. Now that they stand together, I can see the resemblance in the way they brush their hair and their smiles. Their posture reflects pride, except Channing, like their father, is softer in his looks and gentler when he speaks.

A thought crosses my mind. I tense at a feeling in the center of my chest. A storm of rage is coming on.

"I haven't been home yet." Channing's eyes move from Sean to me.

His gaze is almost like gasoline on my burning anger. I hold it back, trying not to purse my lips. I want to give Sean the joy due to him.

Playfully, Sean snorts at Channing. "What do you mean you haven't been home? Who told you I was here?"

Channing glances at me for a moment, and I cross my arms and stare back at him. I dare him to lie.

My chest rises as he turns his gaze back to Sean.

"I didn't expect to see you here either. I'm here to see Jo."

Sean moves his lips, but falters. With a puckered brow, he turns to me then to Channing. "You came to see … Alex? You two know each other?"

Channing nods, and I lose myself. "No, I don't know him." I struggle to calm my fury. "So you're Ashton?" I move closer to Chan.

His jaw tightens. "I prefer my first name, Channing."

I shoot him an incredulous look. "Just like you prefer Carter to Deschanel, huh? Or—"

"Jo, I know what you're thinking—"

"Don't," I hiss as he tries to come near me. "You don't know what I'm thinking, and I doubt if you will ever know." I shudder, my anger overflowing. "Don't ever, ever say you know what I'm thinking."

"Hey." Sean reaches over to hold my trembling hands. "What's going on?" His eyes shift between Channing and I.

"Ask your brother." I gasp for air. "How could you do this to me?"

"Jo, I'm—"

"I want you to leave, Chan." My blood goes cold. I feel the shield forming to protect my heart; to show no emotions and to receive none.

"Alex, calm down." Sean circles his arms around my waist. "He's my brother."

"I trusted you!" I step nearer to Chan, close enough to breathe his scent, and resist it. "If you can lie about who you are, I don't know if I can trust you. You and I; the only thing I thought to be true, and you ..." I hold a knot in my stomach. "Just leave."

"I know you don't mean that," Channing whispers, his voice defying the weight of my words.

I stretch a tight smile, but fail to hold it. "To hell with you Channing, Ashton, Carter, Deschanel, or whatever your name is!"

"Man, what did you do to her?" Sean asks before forcing me into his arms.

I rest my head on his chest, my mind repentant of what I did last night. Not that I regret the actual sex, but I hate myself for being so carnally weak.

Channing clears his throat. "I should leave now. I'm sorry, Jo." He gives me a slight bow and heads for the door.

I hear his footsteps as he walks away, and my heart stops beating for a second. Raising my head from Sean's chest, I watch Chan disappear down the hallway. Suddenly, a wave of emotion constricts my throat, and I push Sean off, gasping for air.

"God, Alex, what's going on?" Sean pulls me in for another hug. "What did he say to you?"

"He's my ex," I sniff. "Your brother is my ex," I add and step aside to stare out at the garden.

"Ashton?" Sean's voice faint as if he's asking himself. "Uhm ... I don't know what to say." With a sigh, he places his hand on my shoulder, but I shrug him off.

"I just want to be alone right now."

"Do you want me to leave?" Sean tries to hold my gaze, but I nod, and keep my head down.

He leans closer. "Why do I feel like you're upset with me, too?"

"For goodness' sake, Sean! Can't you give me just a moment to breathe?"

Sean stares at me for a moment and swallows. "I love you." He kisses my cheek.

As he walks away, he mutters, "You're not getting away with this, brother."

"Sean?" I try to call him back.

He's gone.

Once the door shuts, I make my way up to my room and find Marie waiting by my bedroom door. In her eyes, I see a reflection of my pain. As soon as she opens her arms, I rush in and sob.

A sound of tires screeching forces me to jump. I rush straight to my balcony to look outside.

In his car, Sean speeds through the gate and down the driveway, heading to his house. There's the sound of a loud squeal.

My thoughts wander to Channing, Ashton or whoever he is. I think Sean's temper is not going to stay in the car, but he might take it out on his brother. I'm thinking of Channing again, at the door that moment when I saw him. Thoughts of Zachary interrupt me. *How did I put myself in this situation?*

I take a seat on my chaise, and dial Emily's number; she's not answering. I try five times before calling Mother.

"Lexie? Are you all right?"

My eyes well up at the sound of her voice. "Chan is back, Mom." She remains silent, but I can hear her breathing. "Mom?"

"Uhm ..." Mother's voice breaks.

"Are you crying?"

She laughs, still sniffling. "I'm just *so* happy, honey; so happy he's back."

I pause, frowning as I try to understand her emotions. "Um ..." I break off, thinking of how she would feel knowing who Channing truly is—a liar. "He lied to me, Mom. I just found out he's Sean's brother. I can't believe all that time I ..."

"Sweetheart, why don't we discuss Chan when I get back? We're leaving tonight; we should be there by tomorrow morning."

I can't believe she just said that. "Did you hear what I said?"

"I heard you. I think you should give him a chance to explain things."

"Is that all you have to say?"

"We can't discuss this over the phone."

"Really?" I gibe. "You don't sound surprised at all, Mother. That tells me you knew all along. Here, I was thinking we are finally telling each other the truth, and you still hide things that matter to me."

"Alex, you have to listen to me."

"Listen to what exactly, Mother? You let me get close to Sean, yet you knew he was Channing's brother?"

"I didn't know he was a Deschanel," She voices. "I never did until he called me a moment ago. He deceived me too, honey."

"It doesn't sound as if you were deceived, Mom. You seem happier than upset. To think you're encouraging me to listen to more of his lies. What is wrong with you? He lied to me, to you, and you're not bothered?"

"Because I can't," she voices. "As much as I want to be upset with him, I can't."

"Why? Did he threaten you?"

Mother exhales before saying, "Alex, Channing went to the Great Vaults, and risked his life to get the Ring for you. He has the Ring, honey. That, to me, is more important than him lying about who he is."

My mouth opens, but nothing comes out. *Channing got the Ring.* I take in a sharp breath. "Chan is the vampire you said is bringing the Ring from Pannonia?"

"I could have sworn …" Now she sounds surprised. "I don't think I told you about Pannonia, did I?"

I ignore her question. "Is this why he left? You hid it from me?"

"Honey, he didn't know if he would live. He didn't want you to hope, and blame yourself if things didn't work out."

"If he died, you mean?" I wipe tears from the corners of my eyes. "So, you and Chan plan my life and make decisions for me behind my back. You thought if he died because of me, and without my knowledge that would be okay? Really?"

"Alexandra, I have to go," she whispers as if she has unexpected company. "Promise you won't do anything rash."

"See you tomorrow, Mother." I hang up.

Rising from the bed, I start to pace. My thoughts going back to the first time I heard about the Ring. I remember my mother's words to John.

He knows the angel—the Cursed Angel and promises to do all he can, making sure the angel never gets close to Alexandra.

I didn't know she was talking about Chan at the time.

If Chan knows who the Vangel is, I could convince him to tell me. Moreover, I won't need to get the book from Zachary.

An hour later, after a cool shower, I put on one of my favorite jumpsuits, mocha, with a cross over V neck. It's not too casual and not too formal, comfortable enough for a ride on my Black Mamba. A ride would relax my stiff bones.

There's an ache lingering in my forehead; I think it's to do with the stress, the shock of seeing Channing, maybe.

I try calling Emily again, but still can't reach her. Staring at Channing's number on my phone, I'm tempted to press call, but in the end, I dial Sean instead.

He doesn't answer either, and now I'm worried. I call his sister, Megan. She seems to be upset as she explains to me about the row between Channing and Sean. According to her, they were quarreling about me before Chan packed his bags and left.

My body goes cold at the thought of him gone again. I'm still pondering on what to do when I receive a call from Zachary.

"It's Sean. I think you should come over," he says. "I've tried talking to him, but he won't listen."

I waste no time, grabbing the keys for my Black Mamba and heading toward Van-Bailey Stills.

I ring the bell and wait. It's not Alexandra Van-Bailey, I fear, but her eyes. The way she stares at me makes me nervous.

The door opens, and yes; it is a woeful day. My prayer angel has taken a break, probably enjoying the sun in heaven while I wait here to face the death eyes of Zachary senior.

He stares at me with a tight face. "Yes?"

I fail to move my tongue as my eyes behold him. He stands in white trousers with a Classic Van-Bailey Blue cashmere jersey, loosely styled in a way that gives him a pristine look. Even the softness of the cashmere is not enough to tone down his harsh expression.

"Um … I." I remember what Emily said about looking into his eyes, so I drop my gaze, but soon I look up again. "I'm sorry, wrong house." I turn to make my way back to my bike. *Why must the great Zachary the third answer the door?*

Considering the closest house is at least a mile away, "could I use your bathroom" might have been a better excuse. I have now shortlisted this moment into the top five most embarrassing and ridiculous moments of my life.

It isn't just that I'm petrified of Zachary senior, but also I wasn't prepared to meet him.

"Alex!"

I turn at Alexandra Van-Bailey's voice. She gestures for me to come back. I'm torn between running back home and obeying Alexandra's call, and face Zachary senior again.

"Mrs. Van-Bailey, I—"

"Now, don't make me come and get you." She steps out of the door, barefoot, and extends her arm toward me.

She looks at me with the usual brilliant Zachary-like smile. Her conspicuous eyes carry comfort as if to say everything will be fine. The curls of her extra-long hair flow past her waist. The light-brown shade complements the bronze cap sleeve, chiffon dress she wears, covered in delicate resin shard embroidery.

"There." Alexandra smiles as she reaches for my hand. She leads me inside and shuts the door behind us. "And I'd love it if you'd be kind enough to call me Alexandra."

"Sure, Alexandra." That feels awkward, saying my name.

My eyes glance around for Zachary senior, but I don't see him.

"Don't worry about my husband. It takes time to get used to him." She studies my eyes before taking me through the foyer down to the inner hallway.

"I'm sorry about walking away from the door. I just—"

She shakes her head. "There's nothing to be sorry about, honey. Even my husband thought you were brave, turning away as you did. Now..." She pauses, her eyes staring toward the kitchen. "I think Madeline's in the kitchen, and the boys, upstairs."

I thank her, grateful for the absence of Zachary senior. Alexandra puts her hands together, returning my smile before turning back.

I take a few more steps ahead, and there she is, Madeline Cruz, the bane of my happiness. As I approach the kitchen door, she sees me through the glass wall. She smiles, flipping her hair back before pulling the sleeves of her long, cream jumper. "Hey, Alex."

"Hey." I lean by the doorway with my hands in the pockets of my jumpsuit. I watch her, filling two mugs with espresso.

"I heard what happened." She stares at me thoughtfully. "I can't imagine how you're feeling."

I wonder what she heard. My mind drifts and I see Zachary's hands on her, his lips touching hers. I imagine him undressing her, and my eyes shut as if to block the thoughts out of my mind. Then, I think of Channing, and the thoughts take me back to the reason I'm here. Sean.

"Coffee?" Madeline asks.

"No." I blink back to her bare face; she must have slept here ... with him. "Thanks." I force a smile. "I don't think I can swallow anything right now."

With two steaming mugs in her hands, she hugs me, careful not to spill the drinks while I peck her cheek.

"Come. The boys are upstairs." She leads the way. "I had to tell them to move to the terrace. The noise was too much."

"Were they fighting? Is Sean all right?"

"Not physically, but yes, they were fighting. Sean is really mad. Zach tried to stop him, but I don't know ... something is wrong with Zach. He seems ..." Madeline pauses on the stairs and stares at me with a thoughtful look. "He's not himself. That's all I can say."

"Maybe it's the racetrack; the thoughts of leaving could be depressing him."

She gives me a faint smile. "You could be right." She continues up the stairs. "But my gut tells me he's drifting into his old self again. Especially after what the witch in Dacia told us."

Old self? I skip a step to get closer to her. "What did the witch say?"

Madeline shakes her head this time, but continues walking. "'He gave his heart away, but not to you'. Those were her words to me."

"And what did Zachary say to that?"

"He said he didn't know what the witch was talking about."

I think of Zachary's hybrid; Madeline knows about her, so maybe that's what the witch meant. "Witch or no witch, I know he loves you very much." That feels awkward coming out of my lips, but it feels good to say it out without wanting to punch her face. "So much that I admit I'm sometimes jealous of you."

"Jealous?" She gives me a sideways glance. "Are you falling for my boyfriend?"

"Yes, I'm in love with your boyfriend."

Madeline swings around to face me, her face pale. "What?"

I stifle a laugh. "It's a joke, Mimi." I take that back; I think we have enough fight for today.

She frowns. "Too harsh, Alex, dilute your jokes a little next time."

"I'm sorry, I—."

"It's not you. It's ..." she takes in a deep breath. "It's just the way he looks at you."

My heart skips a beat. "What do you mean?"

"He stares at you with this 'forever dancing in the rain' look."

I laugh. "I've never heard of that. How does that look like?"

"Like you're dancing in the rain, naked, and he's watching."

My cheeks flush. Wow, she's brave to tell me this, unless she's trying to force a confession out of me. Well, I kind of confessed. She turned pale on me.

I wish I could tell her how he speaks of her as if she's the strongest of all pillars of the world. But I won't. I don't want to make her any stronger than she already seems.

She glances at me again. "Sometimes, it makes me wonder ... makes me think—"

"Zachary?" Mimi and I call at the same time as we reach the top of the stairs. We find Zachary standing there with his hand resting on his chest. As soon as he sees us, he drops it to his side.

Mimi hands the mugs to me and steps closer to Zachary. "Are you alright?" She places her hand on his chest.

This time it's not Zachary's movements controlling my emotions; it's hers. The way her hand is rubbing his chest and how she looks into his eyes. It's as if she wants to take him back to that perfect moment where she's the only one that matters in his life.

Zachary coughs lightly and turns to smile at me. "Just on time, Alex. Those two brothers are ready to kill each other ... and me." He breathes out a sarcastic laugh.

"What happened?" I pass him one of the mugs, and stare at his chest.

He glances at me with the mug to his lips. "I should be asking you."

I frown, my eyes growing wider. "No, I mean what happened to you? You don't look well."

Zachary eyes me as if to doubt my concern. "Forget me. I'll be fine." He takes another sip and continues down the stairs.

I hand Madeline her coffee and she follows Zachary while I continue ahead, walking down the hallway the terrace at the end.

Dreading to see the two brothers, I stop by a mirror on the landing to breathe, catching my breath. At the door, in contrast to what Zachary said, I hear nothing, but silence.

My heart skips as I reach for the handle of the wooden, double doors. I pause when I hear Channing speaking, his voice as calm as always.

"No, it's not fair to her," he says.

"I'm just making sure you know where we stand." Sean's voice sounds spiteful. "You left her; you don't deserve her. You can't—"

"I didn't just leave without a reason, without a purpose. When I left her, it was the right thing to do. Now I'm back."

"You want her back?" Sean asks.

"It would be a lie to say I don't, but I respect that she's with you now."

"If you respect that, then you should leave and go back to Pannonia."

"I can't do that," Channing answers without hesitation.

"So what do you want, huh?" Sean's voice is low, but harsh. "Answer me, Ash!"

"All I want is a chance to explain to Jo why I left, and—"

"And try to win her back?"

"No, brother, she's with you. Unless she—"

"No, she won't!" Sean screams. "You broke her heart! What do you think this is? Respect your elders and give them your girlfriend?"

"It's about her; her choice, her happiness, and not you or me. Of course, since you said you two are not exclusive, if she decides she wants me back, I admit that would be the happiest day of my life," Chan says.

My heart jumps at the sound of Sean's fury. "That's not going to happen, Ash! It won't happen. Do you hear me? It won't—"

I push the door open and see Sean standing inches from Channing.

Sean breathes, backing away from Channing. "Alex?"

I stare at Sean. "What's going on?"

Chan steps forward. "Jo, I—"

"I'm not talking to you, Chan."

"At least allow me to explain before you shut me out." Chan moves to stand in front of me.

"No, let me do that for you, brother." Sean pushes Chan off, laughing sarcastically before turning to me. "He left us to look for a witch. Found your mother. Pretended he was in love with you to get close to her. My guess is he got what he wanted and left, leaving you heartbroken."

"What?" I first grimace at Sean, before I turn to Channing. "Is this true?"

A crease forms on Channing's forehead. "There is truth in what he said, but he missed the part where I fell in love with you. Everything I did, I did for you, Jo. You should—"

"You're a manipulative liar, aren't you, brother?" Sean taunts. "Did you wake Mother from the dead? Judging from her absence, I'm guessing you failed. Now you come back for Alex?"

"I never denied I'm back to work things out with Jo, but like I said. It's her choice." Channing sighs. He motions to me. "Can we talk in private?"

Anger flashes on Sean's face. "Fuck choice and fuck you, Ashton! She's going nowhere with you. If you have something to say, say it here, now."

"Mind your language, Nicholas," Chan warns.

A renewed rage embraces Sean and gives birth to a war of words between them. Their faces flash with pain, intense fury, hatred, and resentment flying from one person to the other. Eyes red with anger, burning with utter revulsion, they fight to conceal the truth hidden somewhere in their hearts, the truth that beside me, they love each other.

It's all my fault, I conclude, before revising my statement. No, it's Channing's fault. If only he had been truthful, I wouldn't have been in this mess. Except it doesn't feel right to blame him.

"Stop!" I rush over to separate them, pulling Sean to stand beside me. I turn to Channing. "You need to leave."

Channing remains silent for a few seconds, letting out a painful laugh as he stares back at me. His eyes seem to be hunting for that hold he knows he has on me, but in all the time he has been away. I learned to hide it. If he's looking for a sign that I still care, he isn't going to find it.

"Hear me out," he whispers.

"Ash, you heard her." Sean stands beside me with his arm around my waist. "Leave."

"Is that right, Jo?" Channing's voice comes out tired. "Is that what you really want?"

I remain silent, my heart pounding as I imagine him gone, but I refuse to show it.

"Tell me there's no part of you that still loves me, and I promise I'll leave. You won't have me around to cause you any trouble."

Blood rushes through me, stirring my desires. My mind and heart battle against each other. I stare at Channing, and my stomach tightens; the sadness in his eyes tangles my tongue, and I can't speak.

"Don't let him play the sympathy card on you, Alex," Sean comments. "Tell him what you want."

I can't find the courage to part my lips. The stillness in Channing's eyes ties my tongue for the moment.

"I need to hear you say you don't want me anymore." Channing steps closer, and stops midway while Sean's arm around my waist tightens.

I remain silent. *Do I love him? Do I love Zachary? Then again, what is it that I feel for Sean?*

Well, Grandpa Henry once told me that when asked a question, it is always wise to find the meaning of words I don't understand, before coming up with an answer. In this instance, it seems I don't know the difference between love, lust, and infatuation.

It is possible to lust after the one you are in love with, is it not? Also, possible for that someone you are in love with to be the object of your infatuation, and to lust over the object of your infatuation, which might be the love of your life. Is it not also true that these three things can exist separately? Lust for one person, infatuated by the other or be in love with another?

Time is the only factor to distinguish between lust, infatuation and love, Grandpa Henry once explained to me.

As time goes by, lust will evaporate like a puddle fighting against the midday sun. Infatuation will fade like dry petals blown to bits by the wind. However, love – true love will not only grow stronger, but deeper.

Those were his words. Still, that isn't the subject here. Right now, it's all about doing the right thing.

"Alex?" Sean rubs my waist.

I open my mouth and in that instant, the doors open. Zachary walks in with Madeline.

Staring at me, he says, "Can I have a moment?"

Sean grimaces at Zachary. "You do realize we were in the middle of a conversation, right?"

Zachary takes two confident steps toward Sean and I. With eyebrows furrowed, he laughs. "Some conversation; you are literally suffocating her."

"Zach." Madeline signals for him to come back.

Zachary turns and follows Madeline. I see them whispering by the doorway.

Chan stares at me for a moment before heading for the door, following Zachary and Madeline.

My mind goes to the Ring. I'm tempted to call him back, but I think of Sean and stop.

With the two of us left in the room, I lift my head to face Sean and catch his questioning eyes on me. I know the question he wants to ask, and I know I don't have an answer to it, at least not yet.

I try to hide from Sean's gaze by stepping to the glass walls, but his hand clutches me by my waist.

"You still love him."

That sounds more like a statement than a question, and so I remain silent.

He pulls me closer. "Okay, maybe you never fell out of love with him, but …" He pauses, steeples his fingers and taps them gently on his lips. "You want him back?" he asks through his fingers.

"I didn't say I want him back." I finally find my voice.

"But you are thinking it?"

"I don't know what I'm thinking right now."

Sean shakes his head. "It's not that you want him back that hurts me. It's that you can't be honest enough to tell me you want him. Because if you cared for my feelings one bit, Alexandra, you would have told him to fuck off."

"It's more than that, Sean, please."

He puffs a mocking laugh and starts for the door.

"Sean, wait!"

He doesn't stop, disappearing at vampire speed. I rush after him, skipping down the stairs and passing through the living room. Zachary and Madeline are sitting and listening to Chan, who appears to be telling a story.

"Alex?" Zachary calls at the same time as Channing says, "Jo."

I ignore them and breathe a sigh of relief when I don't see Alexandra Van-Bailey, or Zachary senior. I rush for the door.

I step outside just in time to catch a glimpse of Sean's car, disappearing out of the main gate and onto Stills Lane. Without hesitation, I rush for the driveway and jump on my bike, fire the engine, and like a flash of lighting, I speed after him.

The gate is closing as I approach it, but I don't wait. I fly through the small opening before it shuts.

Tires squall as I cut into the curb. I turn onto Ashbourne Highway, and shift into a comfortable position as I stare ahead at the long road. The wind blows through my hair and for a second, I think it's causing my head to ache, but the pain disappears as I see Sean's car ahead.

I honk my horn, trying to stop Sean. He keeps going. The row of palm trees seems blurry now as I increase the speed, but the blazing sun hitting on the center of my helmet-less head, forces me to slow down. With the heat boiling through my veins, I can only wish for rain. But it appears the clear, blue skies are not in the mood for pregnant, gray clouds. However, I welcome the breeze carrying the freshwater scent from the river that's running along the highway.

Apart from a car far ahead of Sean, we are the only ones on the road. I pick up speed and close the distance between us. Maintaining my speed, I beep the horn again. Sean finally pulls over. I stop behind him and park my motorcycle on the stony pavement. Sean slams the door as he storms out of his car. I slide off my bike.

My stomach heaves, but it's not because of Sean. It's a sting of heat embracing my spine. I remember the pain very well, the battle of hot and cold. It happened the day Channing left, and it's happening now. In vibrating movements, heat travels through my back, coming to my chest, and now it sits by my throat as if waiting for my tongue to dance and bring in the oxygen.

Sean stands impatiently. "Why are you following me?"

"Where are you going?" I'm relieved when no heat moves past my throat.

"I don't know." Sean places his hand by his waist. "I just want to go as far away as possible."

"Faraway from …?"

He averts his eyes and sighs. "From you."

I don't know if it's the army of pain marching in my head or a reaction to his words, but I feel lightheaded.

I wait for him to look up. "Remember, you promised you wouldn't run from me."

His face screws up as if he's sucked a lemon. "I just need to breathe." He laughs painfully, a smile similar to Channing's. "I know I have no right …

we are not a couple, but you can't blame me for hoping." His jaw tightens. "I can't lose you now. It's not fair; I just found you."

"I'm not going anywhere. You're the one running." It's as if my voice is echoing my words.

"Tell me the truth, Alex." Sean takes a step toward me, but stops short. "Do you still love him?"

"Um," I search my heart, but find no answer. "I have loved him, and I love … I've loved him alone for a very long time."

"He lied to you." Sean roars. "And broke your heart. What more do you want him to do before you realize he's no good for you?"

"I know, but—"

"But what? Did I not meet to your expectations last night?"

"Sean, please."

"Please is not an answer, Alex."

I look up, and our eyes meet. "Of course, you did. You know you did."

His eyes soften, but he stares at me with a slight frown. "But not better than him?"

"Come on, Sean. That's not fair."

"Then why? Why do you want him to stay?"

"It's complicated," I sigh.

"You gave him more than a year of your life. All I'm asking is you give me half of that—without any interference from him. I'll prove to you; I'm a better man."

"He's your brother. If I tell him to leave, imagine what that would do to your father. He just got him back."

"Excuses, excuses, Alex," Sean sings, shaking his head. "I'm going to get in my car and drive away. Please, don't follow me."

I step to reach out and stop him, but pause at the sound of my phone ringing. I pull it out of my jacket pocket and place it by my ear. "Zachary?" I answer.

Unexpectedly, a few drops of blood fall from my nose to my chest. "Crap!" I reach for tissues from my pocket. My heart is beating faster. I fear what that what happened before might be happening again.

"Are you all right?" Zachary asks.

Hot blood teases my nerves as it circulates all over me. My head raised, with soft tissue on my nose, I try to answer Zachary, but my voice chokes.

"Alex?" Zachary's voice rises. "Are you crying?"

I pause, listening to Channing in the background; he's saying something to Zachary.

"No, Ash, you stay here for now, please," Zachary says to him, then switches back to me. "Lexie, are you there?"

"I'm … I'm fine." I try standing still to stop whatever is happening inside of me.

"You don't sound fine. Where are you? Let me come get you."

"Arggh!" I hold my stomach.

"Alex?" Zachary calls while Sean speeds toward me and grabs the phone.

"What happened? Are you alright?" Sean places the phone back in my pocket.

"Yeah." I try to breathe through my mouth, but it seems to be cutting into my throat. "I think I'm fine now."

"Let me have a look at that." He reaches for my bleeding nose. "Tilt your head back," he adds. "Now, lean forward."

I follow his instructions, but close my eyes at the hot air blowing out of my ears. I don't hear what Sean says as it rings like a high-pitched tone. The noise if everywhere, especially the sound of the river; it's so much clearer.

Sean tightly squeezes my nose with his fingers and tells me to use my mouth to breathe. I can't open my mouth; I'm scared I won't be able to control my tight jaw.

I part my lips slightly, but shut them at the sound of tires skidding. Zachary veers his Zetra Omni Scorpii and snappily brings it to a halt.

Leaving the engine running, he slams the door as he gets down and dashes toward us at vampire speed, depriving me of the expression on his face. It's when he grabs Sean by the collar that I notice the anger printed on his face.

"Are you out of your mind?" Zachary hisses.

I stare at him with confusion. Not only because of his rage, but I hear something like a huge fan, or maybe wing flapping. I screw up my eyes, my gaze switching between Sean and Zachary. I can't see any wings.

Zachary drags his friend to the edge of Sean's car, away from me. He looks straight into his eyes. "I thought you were better than this."

"Better than what? What are you going on about?" Sean seems just as baffled as I am.

"Zachary, what's wrong?" I step closer to them. He yells for me to stop.

"What's your problem, man?" Sean tries shaking off Zachary's hold.

Zachary grabs Sean by the collar and moves closer to him. "Tell me you didn't?" he breathes.

Sean frowns, about to say something when Zachary shouts, "Just tell me you didn't hit her."

"What?" Sean grabs Zachary's arms and tugs him off furiously. "How could you think that?" Sean cries out. "I love her. And since when have I been hitting girls?"

Zachary's face drops, his eyes blink in confusion as he studies Sean's face. He turns to me.

I gaze at his suspicious eyebrows. "It's just a nosebleed, that's all. Sean was only helping me."

Zach sighs and turns to Sean with apologetic eyes.

Sean, adjusting his shirt, shoots a glance at Zachary. "If I didn't know you better, I would say you have a thing for Alex."

"I'm sorry." Zachary scratches his head, his eyes pleading with Sean.

Sean shakes his head.

"Uhm ..." Zachary stammers.

"What?" Sean's forehead creases as he stares at Zachary. "I see you're on Ashton's side now. You think I don't deserve her, don't you?"

Zachary shifts his weight to one side. "I didn't realize we are now taking sides."

"Tell Ash to stay out of my way." Sean heads for his car, glances at me once more before ducking into the driver's seat and driving off.

Zachary turns to me, taking two steps closer, but stops midway. "And you have the audacity to tell me you're okay?" He sounds annoyed.

"I was okay." A sharp pain strikes my forehead. I look down and keep still.

"And now?"

Another pain arrests my spine. I keep calm and wait for it to pass, but it spreads from my pelvis to my ribs, and my chest. Zachary's still talking, but I can't hear what he's saying; it's too noisy. The wind, trees, and the birds, it's all too loud.

"Alex?"

"Arrgh!" I place my hands on my ears to stop his voice. It's now sounding shrill in my ears.

Zachary hurries to me. I don't want to him near me. Every step he takes is making me hotter.

"Are you all right?"

"Get your hands off me!" I gasp for air, but this time the air is not as cool as it was a moment ago. "You are burning me. Just go away."

He steps back, but I still feel hot. With arms open wide, it seems he wants me to fall into them. I'm more interested in his eyes; his pupils seem crystal-like. I see the fine lining around them.

He's saying something, but it sounds too loud. I can't make out his words. He comes closer, and I stumble on a rock as I step back. The heat reaches my feet, burning my toes while my fingers throb in pain.

"Alex?" Zachary's voice seems kinder to my ears now. "It's me," he says in an alluring tone. "What's wrong? Tell me. I can help you."

I want his blood. My jaw is expanding, and I can't stop it. Every cell in my body is pushing me to Zachary. I hear his pulse; strong, thick and steady. Saliva surges through my mouth.

"No, don't come closer," I cry.

Zachary obeys and I pause, brushing my hair away from my face. With caution not to disturb the heat that feels like a dormant volcano within me, I pull my feet out of my shoes.

Relief comes only for a moment before I scream with pain. The heat penetrating through the soles of my feet is unbearable. I pause to breathe, and it only takes me a second to realize the cold air, icy air puffing out of me, and another to know death is here.

Broken screams come out of me as the sun sets me alight. Fire overcomes me. Amid the scorching heat, I hear Zachary's loud bellow. "No!"

XXIII

THE BLOOD

I'm on fire; burning. The sun has turned against me, scorching me as if we were never friends.

The smell of my burning flesh reminds me that I'm still human.

My knees fall to the ground. I could cry for mercy from the sun if not for my lips, which are now sealed.

Before my back hits the ground, a pair of arms scoops me up. Now, I remember—Zachary.

At vampire speed, he flies through the trees down to the valley and jumps into the river with me in his arms.

"No!" I force my lips apart as the water covers my head. I can't breathe for long underwater. Forcing my head up, I scream and sink back, hiding from the sun's burning rays.

As I struggle to breathe, Zachary grabs me from behind. With his arm tight around my waist, he forces his bleeding wrist into my mouth. I swallow once, and gag as the earthy, bitter-root taste of his blood goes down my throat. I release his wrist from my mouth and choke on gulps of water.

My legs and arms feel light and detached as if they are no longer mine. Zachary lifts me out of the water. Gasping for air, I cling to him. I cringe expecting burns from the sun only to realize it's raining. Heavy clouds have swallowed the sun, and now rain pours on us.

I circle my legs around Zachary's waist and my arms around his neck while he secures me to his chest. His arms tight on my back, he carries me out of the water toward one of the leafy trees along the riverbank.

Under the tree, he rests my back on the trunk. A rush of prickling movements tells me my skin is healing. I'm no longer in pain.

The rain has turned to a drizzle, and water drips from Zachary's hair. As I shiver from the cold, Zachary pulls me into his arms, my back to his chest.

"You need more of my blood," he whispers.

It's bitter. I realize my lips did not part. No words came out.

"Alex?"

"You smell of fresh calla lilies." I quiver as I inhale the skin of his arms. "I always wondered about your scent. Now I know ... a masculine calla lily ... if there's such a thing." I shiver from the water dripping from my hair.

Zachary rubs my arms before reaching out for my trembling hands. "There's only one other person who said the same thing to me."

"Who?" I rub my eyes, but my vision remains blurry.

"Are you still in pain?" Zachary asks.

I can't see clearly. It's as if the trees are moving. My eyes switch between seeing complete darkness and a growing light. I'm drawn to the light even though it's making me sleepy. "I think I'm dying."

"No." Zachary holds me tighter. "You're not dying. You just need more blood before the sun comes back."

"I should call my mother."

My mind drifts to Sean, then Channing. Zachary raises his wrist to me. In an instant, I see Channing on Zachary's balcony with Madeline. He's pacing with a phone to his ear.

"Come on, Zachary, pick up," he mutters.

"Chan?" I rise to my feet, only to find my knees too weak. I fall back into Zachary's arms.

"He's not here." Zachary secures his arms tighter around my waist. "You're starving, and that causes you to hallucinate."

"I ... I need to talk ..." I need the Ring.

"Shh ... you will talk to him, but not now."

Zachary's whisper sends shivers all over me, and his hands—the heat that I always feel when we touch—makes me feel not only warm, but alert and amorous.

A vibration of heat blossoms in my chest and radiates throughout my body. Zachary's light gasp makes me think he feels the same. Abruptly, he turns me around and embraces me.

My mouth waters as my lips brush against the skin of his neck. I don't know if I want to kiss him or bite him. As his arms encircle my waist, a burning tingle, a sudden strength builds up in my thighs. I raise my head to look at his eyes, but I find them closed. Then, they open. We stare at each other for a moment, and without warning, darkness covers my eyes again. Soon the light appears. It's making me feel as if I'm drowning.

"Alex?"

I gasp, and open my eyes to see Zachary's brown eyes. Once again, I'm in his arms, and he's resting on the same tree we were leaning against before I blanked out. He's still wet; so I don't think I was out for long.

"Zachary, you're here?"

Stroking my cheek, he smiles and whispers, "Where else would I be?"

I reach out for his wet cheek and smile. "Alexandra's knight."

He lets out a quiet chuckle. "Am I allowed to call you my beautiful Alexandra?"

"You and I." I swallow. "I wonder if I could ever refuse you anything."

"I'll hold you to that." Zachary's words are almost a whisper. "You need blood to make you heal faster." He raises his wrist to my mouth.

"Wait, I have to tell you something." Not one thing, I have a number of things to tell him. "I think, I'm …"

"You think what?"

"Nothing."

"Come on, tell me. Is there anything you want? I can get it for you. Anything."

My lips curl. I sit up and bury my head into his neck. "Don't leave me, please."

Zachary pulls me closer. "I won't. I'm here," he whispers.

We stay silent for a moment, Zachary's hand in my wet hair, while the other rubs my back. He pulls away and stares into my eyes. "The sun will be out soon. You really should feed."

I nod, already fighting not to show how much I desire his blood. My heart drumming, I sit up straighter. The more I fight the urge, the faster my pulse races.

Zachary stands and sits back down. This time he positions himself behind me, pulling my back to his chest as I sit between his legs. He raises his wrist to my mouth. "Here."

My fangs show no patience for my indecisive mind as they thrust my jaw wide, flashing out and piercing into Zachary's veins. I pause as the bitter taste coats my throat. I let go of his hand, but Zachary forces it back.

"Keep drinking, the bitterness will go away in a minute."

His hand on my waist squeezes me tight, sending a fluttering sensation in my stomach. It distracts me from the unpleasant taste. I keep sucking. Gradually, the sharp taste disappears, replaced by a burst of flavors.

The taste of Zachary's blood is liberating. It's not only the racy acidic taste overpowering the sweetness or the rich, smooth aftertaste that coats my throat as it goes down, but there's a complex note—a burning sweetness—right after I swallow that ruptures, exploding through my senses.

I feel his blood cleaving through my veins. Its soul-quenching taste heats up my chest, stimulating my breasts before spreading all over me.

I drink one more mouthful and pant, reaching to clasp his wrist and draw some more. It's no longer the hunger driving me to drink more, but the way his blood makes me feel.

"Enough, Alex," Zachary groans.

I ignore him and put his hand back on my waist. I'm losing the battle with the longing to feel his hands on me. A few more seconds and I'll stop.

"Alexandra," Zachary grunts, burying his head on my neck as he slides his hand up to pause just below my breast. "If you don't stop, you're going to ..." He kisses my ear. "Stop."

I pause and linger on his wrist for a few seconds before I wipe my mouth and look up to his face. The warmth in his eyes steals the strength in me.

There's a crease on Zachary's forehead, and he swallows hard. "I'm sorry," he sighs. "I had to stop you."

Wiping blood off my chin, he continues. "Sharing blood is usually a two-way thing, mostly done by partners. Right now, it's one-way, and it gets to a point where I can't control myself, especially when I feel the way I feel about you."

How do you feel about me? I study his face but find no trace of a smile.

"It's just ... I mean... it's sexually arousing; you, drinking my blood."

"Uhm." I think I should apologize, but he doesn't look as if he needs an apology. "I had no idea. My mother told me that on the neck—"

"I know." Zachary reaches for my blushing cheek. "That's why I gave you my wrist, but when it comes to you, everything seems ... amplified. Every nerve, every emotion is just intense; nothing like I've ever felt for a century." He lets out a hopeless laugh. "I guess I become too sensitive with you around."

I let out a muffled, weary laugh and lean forward, evading his lips to kiss his eyebrows.

"Zachary?" I look into his eyes again.

"Yes."

"Why do I feel so sleepy? I can barely keep my eyes open."

"Your body is adjusting to my blood," he says and places my head on his chest. "Sleep. I'll take you home when you're strong enough to resist the sun. It won't be long now."

"I don't trust you, watching over me while I'm asleep." I smile, still fighting with my eyelids.

"What do you think I could do to you?" Zachary's chuckle vibrates through his chest to my head.

"Feed me love potion, so I'll fall in love with you."

"Is that what you did to me?" he asks.

I laugh weakly. "Are you in love with me?"

"What does it matter now? It's too late; Ashton is here to stay."

"I can't hear you; I'm sleeping." I smile and breathe in his scent again. After a moment, I turn, adjusting my head on his chest. "Knight?"

He laughs softly. "I thought you were now asleep."

"You know what I said about leaving Madeline?"

Zachary tenses. "Yes."

"Don't. I was wrong to make you choose."

His hand on my back rubs me gently. "What made you change your mind? Is it Ashton?"

"It's everything. Madeline worries you don't love her anymore."

"Did she tell you that?"

I nod. "You don't have to leave Autumn Reigns either. It's unnatural— Autumn Reigns without you, just as it is for you and me to fight."

Zachary kisses the top of my head. "Why do I feel as if you have given up on us? And before you answer that, I know what you're going to say; 'what is it you want, Zachary?'"

We both chuckle before he continues. "I want what I don't deserve, what I can't have. I need more time, time that you can ..."

Zachary's voice fades as I slip into my dreams, and cross over to what I believe to be my past, back to the same ancient mansion. It seems I'm seeing the same vision as earlier.

"Perhaps you delight in watching me soak?" The same male figure speaks to me.

I hoped to see his face, but it's impossible. He must be the Vangel.

"You're already soaking," I tease, and watch as he shakes his feet on the doormat.

He turns and shuts the door, sliding the latch at the top to the side.

"You needeth not come tonight." I step behind to help him remove his coat. "With all the rain, you risk catching a cold."

"I couldn't sleep without knowing you're well ..." He accepts a towel from me and uses it to dry his face. I hand to him. From his coat pocket, he brings out a bottle of red wine.

I thank him with a smile and lead him to the living room upstairs, where I put the wine on the table next to the fireplace.

I reach for his shirt, unbuttoning it carefully. The shirt drops to the floor while my hands reach for his abdomen. He groans with pleasure as my fingers trace the tattoo on his chest. It's a large black sword with fading, white wings.

"You will never know how good that feels." He shuts his eyes, smiling. "I know how good this feels." I kiss his abdomen, on the center of the tattoo. It comes to life, illuminating white light rays. I inhale; it's calming, warm, and fluttering. "The light is brighter than last night," I say. "I healed my brother a while ago," he says, bending to remove his boots.

Afterwards, he sits on the rug with me, combing his hair with his fingers. I kiss his cheeks, and as always, wrap a small blanket around him. I sink in his arms, and we both stare at the burning fire. With my head by his shoulder, I whisper, "I rather you come not if the weather is unfriendly as it is." "I fought against the urge to see you, and I'm not ashamed to say I failed." He kisses my hair. "It's only I couldn't bear losing you to pneumonia. What will I do—?"

"Forgive me for interrupting." He cuddles me with a desperate need. "We don't die where I come from."

"You keep saying, but I must tell you, I believe you not."

He laughs, forcing kisses all over me. "Come now," he whispers. "Feed my ears with all the news of the day. How was your day? Did any gentleman offer you fine wine?"

My eyes skip to his curled lips. "Must I answer that?"

"Yes, you must." His smile grows wider.

Mischievously, I shift, moving to his lap. I push him to lie down on the rug, and move on top of him. He places his hands on my waist. The light from the fire brightens his face.

"A handsome gentleman with the face of an angel," I begin with my eyes on his. "Eyes radiant, and as clear as a newborn child's. His hair more lustrous than that of a lady, and his scent ..." I breathe, rubbing my nose with his, and look into his eyes again. "His scent enthralling, enticing if not seductive, and surely—" I gasp as his hands slide up my waist to my chest.

He sits up with me in his arms and kisses me softly on the neck. "Surely?"

I giggle, running my fingers through his hair. "Surely, something I shan't forget, not now, nor even in my next life." I finish with a tender kiss on his lips.

He kisses me back, shifts at a supernatural speed and lays me on the rug, where he moves on top of me. Kissing my neck first, his lips across my chest—lingering on my breasts—as his hands work on the laces of my corset. I can hardly breathe as he goes lower. His hand grabbing my thigh, he brings his lips back to mine and glides down again. I let out a loud moan as he plants soft kisses on my inner thigh. He moves his hand further, and I gasp, blinking my eyes open, to find I'm back in the real world.

I'm in my bed. Cool air blows through the half-open balcony doors. Outside, it's neither dark nor bright, and from the fading light, I think I just missed the sunset.

My God. My eyes widen with realization. The tattoo; I saw the Vangel's tattoo. A sword with wings. I sit up in haste. I can hardly contain my excitement. "I saw his face. I saw the Vangel's face." I gasp quietly, smiling.

I brush my hair back, and pause, focusing on the dream again. My smile disappears. Nothing about his face comes back to my memory.

"I swear I saw him," I whisper desperately. "I kissed him." I drop my shoulders. I remember everything, except his face. I throw my head back on the pillow, gutted.

The smell chicken, mushrooms, and coconut fills my nostrils, but the aroma is not as appetizing as it should be.

Someone laughs; the sound comes from the garden. I hear Madeline's voice and sit up again. Marie and Zachary are with her, I think. I rise from my bed and walk cross to stand by the balcony doors.

"Zach," Madeline calls. "Zachary?"

"Hmm?" he answers. "Are you all right?"

"I'm fine," he says. "I'll go check on Alex."

"Wait." She raises her voice. "Why is Sean or Ash not here yet? Didn't you call them?"

"I called Maryanne. She'll be here soon," Zachary replies. "The last thing Alex needs is those two brothers here, fighting."

"Would you like some more coffee?" I hear Marie say.

"No, thanks, Marie." Madeline's tone is edgy.

Quietly, I hurry back into bed and lie down with my back to the balcony doors. My heart pounding, I close my eyes and wait for Zachary.

I smell his scent, and in another minute, the door opens. I keep my eyes shut, listening to his footsteps as he walks in. He takes in a deep breath, and I feel him getting closer to the side where I'm facing. Weight on the bed, he sighs.

He says nothing for a while, then I feel his hand on mine. Gently, he rubs my fingers and plants a tender kiss on the back of my hand. Overwhelming warmth shoots through my arm, straight to my chest; I almost open my eyes to look at him.

"Alex," he whispers; it's as if he doesn't want me to hear him.

I remain silent.

"You and I, it seems we're always in a silent war." I sense him rising off the bed. "I can't hurt you," he says. From his sighs and his soft, silent laughs, I conclude he's talking to himself. He's quiet again, but I sense the words he's still to say hanging in the air.

Exhaling, he adds, "I need you far away from me yet you keep getting closer. At times, I kneel down to pray for fortitude, but you rise and pin me down." He's back on the bed, and this time he whispers, "I know I make you cry, and I know sometimes you feel like giving up on me, but I make you laugh too, remember that, Alexandra. One day, I'll show you how much I—"

The door opens, and Zachary rises in haste. "Hey."

"Hey," Madeline answers. "She's still asleep?"

"Yeah, I hoped she would be awake by now, but ..."

"We could go home." Madeline sighs. "I'm sure Marie will keep an eye on Alex until Maryanne arrives."

"You go ahead; I'll follow soon. I should wait for Maryanne, so I can explain what happened."

"I'm going home to my father, not to your house." Madeline's voice sounds cold. "I thought you wanted to spend the night with me. What happened?"

"I don't know, Zachary." She hesitates. "Is it me or ...?"

"Or what?"

"Are you in love with Alex now?"

The beating of my heart almost causes me to jump, but I remain in sleeping mode, trying hard to maintain my breathing.

Zachary doesn't answer.

"Zach, I asked you a question."

"Come, we—"

"Don't touch me." Madeline hisses. "Answer my question."

"Outside, Mimi. I don't want to wake Alex."

The door shuts, and I open my eyes. I can still hear them.

"So, what is it?" Madeline says. "She's gotten into your head too?"

"It's all in your head, Mimi," Zachary says in a tired tone.

"You don't have any feelings for Alex?"

"Of course, I have feelings for Alex." Zachary raises his voice. "She's my friend, my business partner, my best friend's girl, Ashton's ex, and your friend."

Madeline scoffs. "Don't mess with me, Zach."

"Why wouldn't I mess with you when you're accusing me of falling for my best friend's girl? You want to cause a fight between me and Sean, huh?"

"How dare you twist this on me?" Madeline's breathing increases. "I see the way you look at her. We've been here for hours, and you can't sit with me for five minutes. You keep flying up here just to sit and watch her sleeping. Do you know how sick that makes me feel?"

"Mimi, Alex needs me right now. I promised her I'd be here when she wakes."

"Remember what that witch in Dacia said about us?"

"And you remember what I said to you." His voice is now soft. "It's you ... you know it's you. It's always going to be you. I love you." He sighs.

I love you. I repeat his words to myself. He *loves her.* I take in three, deep breaths, melting the lump forming in my throat.

"My dad needs me home," Madeline says faintly. From the sound of their breathing, it seems she's kissing him. "I'll see you tonight."

"I'll come get you if you don't come back," Zachary teases.

Their voices grow fainter, and silence follows.

I take a deep breath and sit up, thinking of having a shower. The instant I think it, I rise at vampire speed.

"Whoa." I feel as if my body is too fast for me, and too light, yet strong.

Careful this time, I take a step forward. I feel human again. Now I see why Sean prefers the vampire state; it's lighter.

I make my way to the bathroom and step to the mirror just to scream at the girl I see looking back at me. It takes me a few seconds to realize the girl in the mirror is me.

I stare at myself again. My face is firmer than usual, and so is my whole body. My hands glide down my natural linen dress, pressing my abdomen, waist, and hips. My hair, a little longer than yesterday, looks radiant. The whole of me is more defined and firmer.

I smile at my new glowing skin, but the smile doesn't last as I remember something important. *How could I forget?* Now I hate myself. Fighting tears, I open the door and walk over to my bed. Before I climb into bed, I sense him outside my door.

He knocks. "Alex, are you all right?"

I open the door and walk rush into his arms. "I think I've lost it. The one human thing I ever wanted."

Zachary steps back to look me in the eye. "What have you lost?"

"Look at me. I've fully transformed I can never have any kids, can I?"

Zachary stares at me with a blank face.

"I'm sorry," I sigh. "This is all too much for you, right?"

He frowns, tilting his head slightly. "Every vampire in Ashbourne can reproduce, and that includes hybrids like you."

He knows. My heart skips a beat, my tongue tied.

"You're neither a human nor a vampire. Are you, Alexandra?"

I stare at him, not knowing what to say. "Uhm, I wanted to tell you—"

"Come here." He steps forward and embraces me. "My father should never know what you are. Never tell anyone, do you hear me? No one. Not Ashton, not Sean and not me."

I nod and hug him for another moment before crossing to my cheval mirror.

"If you think the changes in your appearance are because you have transformed, there's a chance you could be wrong."

"What do you mean?" I stare at his reflection in the mirror.

He comes up behind me, hugging me with his arms tight around my chest. "Usually my blood, tend to change people's appearance, temporarily."

With my hands on Zachary's, I stare at our reflection in the mirror, and tilt my head to touch his, nestled into my neck. "How did you know I'm …?" I trail off.

He raises his head, staring into the mirror. "On your first bite, my blood tasted bitter to you, and when you bit me, I sensed that instead of a set of fangs on each side, you have only one on each side. Only hybrids are like that."

I turn around to face him, my hands on his chest. "Except I'm not your hybrid?"

"No." His brow furrows. "Yet, it feels like you are." He gazes at me for a moment and reaches for my hands on his chest, kissing them lightly. "It's written that day we meet, for a moment, the moon will pass through the sun and earth. It will conceal the sun, bringing total darkness on earth. If not for that, I would have sworn it's you."

"That sounds amazing; a total eclipse."

"Not as amazing as your desire to have kids someday." Zachary's eyes lock on mine. "I thought you would be satisfied with the one we already have."

I copy his smile. "Autumn Reigns is the child of my dreams and ambitions. However, I do desire to see the blood of my blood, a mini me, one day."

I inhale, take his hand into mine and exhale. "Don't you ever imagine a mini Zachary? In maybe ten, twenty years? A little boy with a head full of your brown locks, and tiny toes on tiny feet?"

Zachary laughs and bites his bottom lip. "I do. Probably more than I should, considering I've lived for more than a century." His voice fades, as if drowning in melancholy.

He evades my eyes as I try to identify his emotions, but when he looks up, the expression on his face is somewhere between sadness and wistful.

"What are you thinking?"

His face beams, and he brushes his hair back before saying, "I was just imagining a little Alexandra, frowning as she pauses, dressed in a miniature yellow robe." He pauses to chuckle. "She opens the door with very, very tousled hair, and whispers, 'knight'."

Fighting a smile, I grimace and advance toward him, aiming to give him a playful punch.

"See, just like that." He backs away, laughing. "That's the frown I'm talking about."

I take a step toward him and pause; a sharp pain runs across my forehead.

Zachary rushes to hold my hand. "Are you all right?"

I nod, and with a smile, I grab a cushion from the couch and charge after him. We run in circles, laughing. Unexpectedly, I switch into vampire speed and pounce on Zachary, dropping him to the ground.

My hands on his chest, I open my eyes wide. "Are you all right?"

"Better than all right." He laughs, placing his hands on my waist.

I try to stand, but my muscle stiffens. I don't want Zachary to worry, so I remain still and give him a faint smile.

There is a knock at the door. "Miss Lexie, can I come in?"

At supernatural speed, I rise and fly to open the door.

"Goodness!" Marie widens her eyes. "Um, I have never seen you more beautiful."

"It's only temporary."

"Aah …" It seems she's still admiring my looks. "Just to let you know Mr. Deschanel is on his way."

"Sean?"

She shakes her head. "Channing, Ashton... I'm not sure what name—"

"Channing. Call him Channing. And thank you, Marie."

As Marie walks off, I leave the door ajar and turn to smile at Zachary. "Did you tell him what happened?" My head feels heavy, and my vision blurred.

Zachary shakes his head. "I didn't know if you wanted me to, but I called Maryanne."

"Sean?" I ask.

"What about Sean?"

"Did you tell Sean?"

He shakes his head again.

I step closer to him. "It's okay if you didn't want to share me with anyone else." I tease. "I feel that way about you, sometimes."

He laughs.

From downstairs, I hear Channing's call.

"Jo!" His voice sounds urgent.

Zachary and I stare at each other, frowning.

"Jo?" I sense Channing at my bedroom door before he walks in.

"Holy …!" Channing pauses, looking at me first, then Zachary. When he turns his gaze at me again, all I can read in his face is pain and anxiety.

Zachary shoots a worried look at him. "Ash?"

He remains silent.

"Chan, what's wrong?" I hurry toward him, but he vanishes at vampire speed, whizzing toward Zachary.

In haste, I turn to Channing; my gaze following his speed, but I'm too late. In the blink of an eye, he flings a wooden stake and stabs Zachary through the heart.

A sharp breath escapes my mouth. I can't see clearly. In my imagination, I run and help Zachary, push Channing off, and pull the stake out so I can hold him in my arms, but that's in my mind. Right now, I stand frozen to the spot.

Zachary grunts and struggles in Chan's grip for a second before his body gives up.

Chan lets go of him, and I watch as Zachary's knees plunge to the ground. Hand on his chest, he falls face down on the rug.

The moment the stake punctured Zachary, it's as if it stabbed me, too. My body feels numb. It's like my blood has stopped flowing.

"I'm sorry I had to do that." Chan's voice echoes in my ears. There are two of him; two faces. Maybe it's my vision.

He's coming closer to me, but I'm going down. He catches me before I touch the floor, and I cringe at his murderous hands. I shake him off and drag myself across the floor. I crawl over to a motionless Zachary.

Struggling to find my voice, I heave for air. "Zachary? Zachary, get up."

XXIV

THE RING

"No, no. Leave me alone." I rise in a flash and speed toward the doorway, but Channing gets to the door before I do.

In a swift supernatural turn, he slams the door shut, and grabs my arms. "I'm not going to hurt you," he says.

"Take your filthy hands off me." I shake him off and back away at lightning speed, just to slam my back on the wall across from him.

"Jo?" he rushes to me again.

My breathing quickens and with my back against the wall, I slide to the ground, sobbing. "You ... you killed him, Chan." I tremble, crying. "You killed Zachary. Why?"

My knees and palms on the rug, I crawl to Zachary, who's still motionless. "Knight," I whisper, holding Zachary's face. "I'm so sorry..." I grab the stake with both hands and prepare to pull it out.

Channing pushes my hands away. "No!"

I shoot him a puzzled look.

"We don't have time. Come on, get up." He pulls Zachary away from my arms and carries his motionless body onto the couch. He then comes to lay his hand by my shoulder. "He's not dead."

"What?" I sniff, looking at his eyes. "But you ... he's there, look at him. He's—"

"The stake will only demobilize him for a while." Chan stands next to me, disregarding my puzzled look. He pulls off his polo shirt and heads to the bathroom.

I stare at Zachary for a bit and rush to kneel by the couch. My eyes stare at the stake in his chest, and then glance toward the bathroom door. My hands on the stake, I hold it tight, about to pull it. In a flash, Chan appears and grabs me by the waist, snatching me away from Zachary.

He releases me in the bathroom, gently resting my back against the wall "Vampires from Pannonia are here in Ashbourne." He breathes on my face. "They have been looking for me, looking for the Ring. They have a tracker who will find the Ring soon if you don't wear it now. So, please." He puts my face between his hands. "Will you trust me and calm down, so we can do this."

I nod with understanding, slowly and wrap my arms around his neck, just pull away in a rush, staring at him with wide eyes. "Are they coming after you? What happens if they find you?"

"You don't have to worry about that. Once the Ring is fortified, and you wear it, they won't be able to track it down." He steps aside, standing in front of the mirror. "That's why I have to do this now before they find us."

Out of his jeans' pocket, he pulls out a pen. He flips it open to reveal a blade and raises his arm, directing the blade into the side of his body, just above the ribs. With caution, he makes a small incision.

I wince at the sight of the open wound. "What are you doing?"

He digs two fingers through the opening, lets out a low grunt as he brings out a small object. I can't see what it is as it is covered in blood, white blood.

White blood? "Are you a White Blood?"

He turns to me. "You'll need to put this on immediately, but that's after I've fortified it."

"Is that the Ring?"

He nods and I follow him to the sink. He turns the tap on to wash the blood off the Ring.

"Chan, you need to explain to me what's going on, and especially, why you hurt Zachary?"

He remains silent, focusing on the Ring.

"Chan?"

"In a minute, Jo."

From the back of his jeans pocket, he brings out a white handkerchief and places the Ring in the center of it. The rustic silver ring is crafted with a leaf patterned band. I scrutinize the heart-shaped stone on the bezel of the Ring and grimace.

"It's moving. The stone is pulsating, can you see that?" I look up at Chan then drop my gaze to the Ring again.

The stone seems not to be a stone at all. But rather, it acts like a heart; it pumps the white liquid through the pattern of the Ring.

"It's the blood. The Ring needs white blood to work and will feed on your veins." Channing's fingers, under the handkerchief, rub the Ring with caution before placing it in my hands. "Hold it tight. I have something to show you."

With his hand on my waist, Channing moves to stand behind me. His hands skip to my face and gently pull my hair back. We stare at our reflection in the mirror. "What color are your eyes?"

"Gray," I answer without hesitation.

"Look again."

I stare at them again, and this time they flash from gray to green, amber, and back to gray. And, there are black veins protruding from the side of my neck. "What's happening to me?"

"You're phasing, but don't panic. Once you have the Ring on, it stops you from transforming, and you'll forever preserve the part of you that is still human."

"You mean I haven't transformed yet?"

"The actual transformation is happening inside you, Jo. What you see outside is the result of overindulgence of Zachary's blood. His blood enhances your looks." He steps in front of me. "Did he feed you from the neck or wrist?"

"Wrist," I say, examining my smooth jaw and remembering how pleasurable it felt to draw fresh, warm blood.

"Good." Chan takes my hand. He leads me out of the bathroom and into my living space.

Zachary lies still on the couch. I glance at him for a moment and rush to take a small fleece to cover him.

"Stop worrying, Jo." Channing's lips spread into a faint smile. "He's stronger than you think," he adds, advancing into the area where my bed is.

On the phone, Channing talks with my mother. It seems he's getting instructions on what to do. Then he passes the phone to me.

"Lexie?"

"Mom? I thought you would be here by now," I say.

"We're just ten minutes away, honey. Do as Chan says. I'll lead him through the fortification process. Everything will be fine. How are you feeling?"

"I'm okay." I breathe softly and ask about John before I say goodbye.

I give the phone back to Chan. With the phone by his ear, Chan tells me to lie on my back on the bed. He places the Ring precisely on my belly button.

"This should be pain-free. You're free to move your arms as long as your abdomen keeps still." He listens to my mother on the phone and recites her words, beginning the incantation.

"Nuante. Citrato. Nai-nai
Uplato. Grantua. Nai-nai
Northiay Nai-nai, Southiay Nai-nai
East twa West Nai-nai … Nai-nai Nai-nai Nai-nai …"

As he repeats the strange words, the Ring rises, floating in the air in parallel to my belly button. It spins, continuously drawing my energy and pushing it back. Each time it pushes it back, I feel stronger. The rhythm of my heart now sounds heavier and thicker than before.

"This will take about five minutes, then it'll be ready for your finger," Chan says.

"What happens when I wear it? Is it painful?"

"We'll have to wait and see." He turns his wrist and checks the time. "You should know the Ring will only be visible when you're thirsty, so remember to feed when you need to."

He sits on the floor next to my bed, his eyes moving between mine and the Ring still floating. "I'm sorry about what happened to you out there. It's good you had Zachary with you."

"I still can't believe I was on fire. Zachary was incredible."

"I know he cares about you, but his family is known throughout the four corners of the world. It's dangerous for him to know who you truly are."

"He already knows I'm a hybrid."

"That's all he should know. He can't know you are the Nersii."

"Nersii?"

"The inescapable. That's what the vampires call you. The Ring is missing from Pannonia, so a few vampires must now be aware of your existence. It won't be long before everyone else does, and they will be on alert, looking for you."

"You think Zachary will betray me if he knows what I am?"

"I don't doubt his loyalty to you, but I worry more about how you could burden him, knowing who you are and trying to hide it from his father, his family. Besides all that, he has an uncle who can read minds."

"And what about you? How are you able to keep the secret?"

"I have a gift. No one can read my mind."

I stare into his eyes and smile.

"Do you know who the Vangel is?"

Channing pauses, staring at me, then swallows. "Yes, I do," he says. Then he goes silent.

"Aren't you going to tell me?"

"I can't. I wouldn't betray my kind, just as I won't betray you. My agreement with Doc was that I keep the Vangel away and get the Ring for you. The Vangel never finds you, and you never find him. Doc will fulfill her promise to help me with a spell. I need it to wake my mother. Thereafter, I'll ask you to marry me." At that, he grins.

I ignore his last statement, and after another silent moment, I turn to him again. "How do I know you're not the Vangel?"

He chuckles. "I might have been in Pannonia for a while, but I haven't forgotten how your mind works, Jo. Let's not play the game of elimination, because I still won't give away any clues. And, hey, if I am, I could never hurt you, so you have nothing to worry about."

"The day you left, I overheard my mother saying you told her the Vangel was in Pannonia, and you were going to keep him away from me."

"True, I said that. ..."

"But?"

Chan opens his mouth to answer me, but shuts it, rising to his feet as the Ring drops back on my belly button.

He tries to pick it up, but backs away in a quick movement. "It burns." His face tightens then relaxes as he turns, looking at me. "It's not burning you?"

"No." I grimace, extend my hand and take the Ring from my belly. With Channing's approval, I slide it onto the middle finger of my right hand. It settles into a perfect fit.

I sit and gaze at it, vibrating, and transmitting little sparks of what feels like an electric current. Its starts slowly, moving through my fingers, then to my hand. Before I glance at Channing's anxious face, my body is jerking.

I can't speak, can't stop the movements. Chan draws me into his arms, only to grunt. He let go of me for a few seconds before pulling me close again. The jerking stops and I feel as if I have been on a roller coaster. The movements slow down and gradually I sink deeper into darkness.

❦

Bright light flashes on my face and suddenly I'm conscious. The first emotions to greet me are hunger and thirst. Since they said the Ring freezes my transformation, I hoped it would stop the thirst too, but I guess I was wrong. I'm frozen in the state of thirst and the need to satisfy the Ring.

It only takes a second for me to realize I'm in my room, on my bed. After a couple of blinks, I smile at the person sitting on the armchair beside me.

"Hey," I whisper, reaching for Sean's hand.

"Hey, gorgeous. You're back." He leans toward me and claps my hand between his hands. "How are you feeling?"

"Like I haven't seen you in years."

Sean stifles a laugh. "Years without seeing me? I won't let you off that easy. It's been a long three days, however."

"Three whole days?" My eyes widen.

"I was really worried especially after how we parted the last time." He helps me sit up. "I'm sorry for leaving you on the road, like I did. If Zach wasn't there, you could have died, and—"

"Sean, don't." I raise my right hand to reach for his arm as I sit up, but quickly withdraw it. Deep black veins are showing on the finger where I have the Ring; a confirmation of my need to feed. "You know what?" I cross my arms over my chest.

Sean grimaces, staring at me with raised eyebrows. "What?"

"You are my favorite vampire."

His frown turns into a smile.

I tighten my arms on my chest and sigh. "I might not know how I feel about anything or anyone. One thing I do know is that your words are worth more than silver and gold. You, unlike me, or anyone else, are always truthful."

Sean smiles and raises his hand to brush his hair back. "Were you dreaming of me? Or did you just think of that now to make me feel better?"

"I think about it all the time. When the sun almost burned me to ashes, I wondered why I never told you before."

"You were thinking of me?"

"Of everyone … everything."

He pauses; his eyes seem to measure the truth in mine. "Come give me a hug." He pulls me up as he stands, wrapping his warm arms around me. "I'm so glad you are okay. Now I feel terrible; I should have never said some of the things I said to you before the accident."

"Don't be. You were right about me beating around the bush when it comes to you and your brother." I inhale and exhale, finding a way to make my words less hurtful. "I've decided the right thing to do is to let the two of you go. You are brothers, and it kills me to think I've sandwiched myself between you two."

Sean drops his head and shakes it. "I'm sorry, but I think I'm beginning to resent my brother for coming back." He stares at me and shakes his head again. "No." He reaches for my arms, rubbing then gently. "You and I had an agreement, remember?"

"Sean, I—"

"You said I should make you forget him."

"He's your brother," I stress.

There's a soft knock and the door opens.

My heart delights at the sight of the traditional side parted, silver hair with matching full beard. "Grandpa?"

"My immortal butterfly." He grins, and steps gallantly toward me with open arms.

I run to him with more speed than I'd intended, and jump on him, my hands circling his neck. "Can't believe you're really here, Grandpa?"

"I'm here. You feel those strong arms?" He hugs me tight, chuckling. "It's been too long." He looks into my eyes, grabs me by the waist and swings me around. "You're no longer in pain, are you?"

I shake my head, smiling.

Laughing as he sets me back on my feet. I swallow, trying to ignore the thirst itching on my throat.

"I better leave you two to catch up." Sean smiles at us and comes nearer to plant a kiss on my cheek. "Good to have you back, gorgeous." He turns to Grandpa. "Henry, I'll see you soon."

I frown, staring at Sean and Grandpa. "I see you too are already friends?"

"You bring people together, butterfly, don't you?" Grandpa winks.

With both hands, Grandpa pats Sean's cheeks. "Soon. Don't forget to bring me the new album. Maybe I might persuade her to forget your brother."

Sean laughs. "Yes Sir." He grabs his coat from the couch and smiles at us before shutting the door on his way out.

My throat burns, but I don't get the chance to think about it. Grandpa holds me in a dance position, ready to dance as he sings our usual song.

He grimaces. "Are you sure you're feeling all right?"

I nod. "Sure. I feel so thirsty."

"Of course, you must be thirsty," he says, stepping back to the doorway. "It's a good thing you are now frozen in this state, which gives us a year to find the Vangel." He pulls the door open and calls out, "Maria."

I know he means Marie. We all have corrected him so many times, but he still calls her Maria. *Thank God Marie doesn't mind.*

"Tell John, she's awake." He says, shutting the door and walking back to me with a smile. "Look how beautiful you've grown." He pulls me over to sit by the chaise lounge.

"I don't trust your vision, Grandpa; it's always biased. Besides, you're getting old."

"Two brothers fighting over you? Good heavens, I say my vision has never been clearer."

I roll my eyes.

"And there's that intriguing young Zachary." He rolls his eyes sarcastically. "He doesn't look as if he's into fishing."

I giggle. "I see you only looking for a fishing companion."

"Those who don't fish often find it hard to understand the skill and—"

"Yes, I know, Grandpa. You've told me many times."

We smile at each other.

He stares at me silently, his eyes skipping above mine. "I'm loving the hair," he says. "What's the style? Growing wild?"

I brush it back, smiling and look at him again, remembering his square-shaped face, the enchanting violet eyes, and the beautifully molded chin that stands out whenever he smiles.

"I'm glad you're here, Grandpa." I lean forward and hug him again.

"I couldn't miss the drama, could I?"

"Thank God for dramas. Otherwise, you'd never have left Viennamo; I know how your ranch is your sanctuary. How's Dana?"

"She wanted to come, but I couldn't leave the ranch unattended."

"And Martyr?"

"I retired Martyr from the racing last summer, and I think he's getting depressed."

My stomach rumbles. Heat, emerging from the Ring on my finger, sends a need for blood ripping my throat apart.

Grandpa frowns. "Are you alright?"

I push strands of hair behind my ear. "I'm just wondering if Zachary is all right."

"Young Van-Bailey?"

I nod. "The last I remember he was unconscious."

"He must be all right. He was here last night."

"Is he all right."

He eyes me teasingly. "It's more than just business with him, isn't it?"

"I don't know, Grandpa." I shake my head. "He confuses me."

"It's a good thing you're aware of your confusion," he teases.

The door opens, and Grandpa and I turn, looking.

"Alex?" John rushes over to hug me. "Thank God. I was beginning to worry. Are you feeling okay?"

"I'm good," I say, and a hunger pang tightens my stomach. "I'm just hungry."

"Tell you what? Why don't you freshen up while I make you something to eat ... and drink?"

"White blood?" A shiver runs through me as I think of Zachary's wrist on my mouth. A twinge holds my jaw together while I indulge in the memory of my fangs in his veins.

"Are you alright, Butterfly?" Grandpa asks.

John frowns at me. "Let me get your mother—"

"No." I almost shout. "I just need a moment to myself. I'll come down in a minute."

John and Grandpa Henry stare at each other before looking back at me. "Okay," John says as he starts for the door. "We'll be down in the living room."

I nod, and fold my arms across my chest to hide my trembling hands.

The door shuts and I turn back to my bed. I'm looking for my phone when I remember the fire. Frustration makes me go faster as I pace about the room.

There's an envelope on the bedside table. I pick it up and tear it open. From the handwriting, I'm guessing it's from Zachary.

If you wake to find you need a friend to talk to, or feed on, you know where to find me.

Smiling, I rush to the bathroom. The shower pouring over me is not helping. It's making me thirstier. Ten minutes pass, and I'm out.

Starting to lose my patience, I change into a pair of black skinny jeans and a matching tight-fitting Ashbourne polo. My hands are shaking as I close my door. I feel my feet attempting to speed, but I try harder and walk in human mode.

Approaching the stairs, I spot Mother pacing at the bottom. She sees me and sighs, placing her hands on her chest. "Alexandra, honey, it's so good to have you back." She extends her arms and embraces me as I reach her.

After examining my eyes and showering me with kisses, she links her arm with mine, leading me into the living room, where I find Grandpa sitting in an armchair. John stands by the French doors. He smiles at me, excuses himself and leaves the room, heading toward the kitchen. I sit down for a few seconds but rise again; the hot blood in me wants me to do something, to run maybe.

John walks back in. "Here." He hands me a cool pint of blood.

I groan with desire and struggle, opening the pint in a rush. John holds my hands and helps me unscrew the top. Before he's done, the pint is already on the way to my mouth. I squeeze it and gulp down the blood. Then I stop, choking.

I turn to John. "This is not white blood, is it?"

"What do you mean? That's the best of all the whites. I requested and tasted it, especially for you." John steps forward and takes the pint from me, then tastes it himself.

"It's good," he says to mother and Grandpa, who stares at him in anticipation. "Maybe you still need a day or so to adjust to your taste buds."

John hands the pints back to me but even with my pressing hunger, I shake my head. "I can't."

"You have no choice, honey." Mother takes the pint from John and forces it into my hand. "Come sit with me. We need to explain—"

"I can't!" Hands on my waist, I pace with frustration. "You don't understand. I can't sit down. I'm hungry."

"Then drink this." Mother extends her hand with a fresh pint. It looks the same as before.

"No." I tuck my hair behind my ears. "Can I borrow your phone?" I step toward the leather couch and pick up my mother's phone.

As soon as I hold it, the phone drops from my shaking hands. Heat from the Ring spreads over my hand and up to my shoulder. As I stoop to the ground to pick up the phone, I drop my knees to the solid wood.

A hand touches my shoulder, and I spin in defense, ready to fight. They all scream for me to stop. I pause, realizing it's my mother. I then cross over to stand close to Grandpa.

"You can't use supernatural powers; you're draining your energy." Grandpa takes my hand. "That will make you hungrier."

"But I am already hungrier." I yell. "I need him!"

"Who?" They all stare at me with confused faces.

Familiar scent brushes past my nose. That's him. Marie walks in to announce the visitor, but I already know who it is.

"Excuse me, Dr. Watson," Marie says. "Mr. Zachary is here."

Without wasting time, I disappear in rapid motion, out of the living room. I continue down the hallway and stop a short distance from Zachary. He's waiting by the entrance door.

The black outfit he wears matches his gloomy face. "Zachary?"

"Hey, beautiful," he says in a tired voice.

I rush to embrace him, my hand tight around his neck. "You came. Thank you."

He rubs my back as he squeezes me tight, then releases me. He steps back, holding my hands. As he drops his gaze to my hands, my heart pounds; *I forgot about the Ring.*

"You're shaking." Zachary shoots a wry look at me.

My eyes averting his, I snatch my hands from him and fold them over my chest.

"Are you thirsty?" he whispers. "You should have told me if you needed blood. I left a note—"

"I know." I stare at him but say nothing more.

The crease on his forehead melts away as he looks over my shoulder. I follow his gaze, and at this exact moment, Mother, Grandpa Henry and John appear.

I give Zachary a moment to say his hellos before leading him upstairs to my room.

He shuts the door. I take quick steps, and place my hands around his waist, resting my head on his chest. "I thought you died," I whisper.

"Me or you?" Zachary chuckles. He reaches for my face, and I try not to stare at the throbbing vein in his neck.

He's not the usual Zachary. I'm wondering if he's still recovering from the effects of the stake.

"Your eyes." He quickly rolls up the sleeve of his shirt and pulls me to sit on the chaise lounge next to the window.

My back against his chest, Zachary raises his wrist to my mouth. "Here," he says and his free hand rubs my back.

My lips part slightly, my mouth flooding with moisture as I stare at his veins. With trembling hands and a pounding heart, I grab his wrist and raise it to my lips. Snappy and crunchy, my fangs sink into his vein. This time I'm not ashamed of the desire I have for his blood. The bitterness flows down my throat. I swallow in haste, knowing the reward will soon come.

"Aaah." I sigh with satisfaction, pulling my fangs out and looking at Zachary. He nods slightly, and I raise his wrist to my mouth again.

My fangs pierce his veins once more, and this time he groans, his forehead dropping to rest on my back. I quiver and draw more blood, faster and deeper.

Zachary's head moves to my neck while his free hand reaches for my left hand, and we thread our fingers together. The heat from the Ring disappears, replaced by a tingling sensation surging from Zachary's hand to mine.

A deluge of desire burns in my blood and forces me to spring to my feet, Zachary responding likewise. I let go of his hand and cup his face, my lips aiming for his. Inches from sealing our lips, I pause, my blood boiling as I listen to his racing pulse.

In a flash, my jaw opens wide, ready to bite on Zachary's neck, but he's faster. He swerves to the side, swirling me in his arms before flinging his wrist back to my mouth. I curl up in his arms again and obey the sound of his broken breath. In silence, we both pause breathlessly.

"Zachary?" My voice is almost a whisper.

He doesn't answer. Neither does he complain, so I drink some more. His hand rubs my waist and moves up to my chest. A fluttering sensation fills my stomach, just as a fuzzy heat spreads all over me.

As Zachary tightens his grip, his lips brush my collar bone. I sense a different kind of desire building up. This time it's my skin that's hungry, craving for Zachary's touch. I let go of his bleeding hand, and immediately, he turns me around to face him. Like I'd done previously, his hands cup my face with tenderness. In his eyes, I see a look I've never seen before.

He hesitates as his head leans closer, and just as I open my lips to receive his, he embraces me instead, his hands holding me tight to his chest.

"I should go," he whispers, and pulls away to look into my eyes. "Um …" His thumb rubs the corner of my lips.

My need for him to tell me what he has to say forces my lips to part. For a dreamy second, I thought his words would be coming out of my mouth.

"Why do you look so sad? Are you still in pain because of what Chan did to you?"

He stares at me and looks away. It's as if the sight of me is causing him discomfort. "Hurt, but not because of that."

"What is it? What's wrong?" I lift my hand to reach for his lips. He vanishes in the blink of an eye, leaving me baffled.

Now that I'm full, I remember I wanted to ask how he's been, what happened when he woke up from the stake Channing forced into his chest a few days ago.

With a quick intake of breath, I cross over to the mirror. I wipe a dash of white blood off my lips. Licking it, I study my gray eyes, my hair, which looks glossier than normal.

Perhaps Zachary, like his father, now resent the creature I've become.

XXV

IT'S NOT ABOUT PROMISES, IT'S ABOUT HOPE

"**I** suspect one of your boyfriends, is the Vangel," Mother says.

We are sitting outside by the porch. John and Grandpa have left to find out why I'm rejecting the white blood. Mother thinks they got the plastic-white, the fake white blood, but John disagrees. The blood is vital as it feeds the Ring, that's according to John.

For the past hour, Mother has been quiet, watching the waterfall. Now I know why; she has been thinking of the Vangel.

"Is it a gut instinct, or you have facts, Mother?"

She sighs, glancing at me. "A bit of both."

Part of me wants to hear her facts, and the other if afraid her words might make sense. My worst nightmare would be finding out Channing, Zachary or Sean is the Vangel.

"Can I hear the facts?" I ask.

"I'm still gathering the key points. I'll tell you when I'm ready."

I breathe a sigh of relief. "You said we only have a year to find the Vangel?"

"The Ring only keeps you frozen for a year or so." She stares at me a little longer than usual. Her eyes cloud again. "It would put me at ease if you could put more effort in finding the Vangel."

"Chan said I can live with the Ring without the need to kill the Vangel."

"Chan thinks it's possible for him to take the Ring back to the Great Vaults and renew its strength, but I don't think we should take such risk. The trackers are already looking for the Ring. I'm sure they will have people waiting at the Vaults. You should remember Channing is a vampire too. He doesn't want the Vangel to die. That's if he's not the Vangel himself."

"Come on, Mom, even after risking his life to get me the Ring, you still don't trust him?"

"My motto; never trust anyone, especially someone who knows the Vangel, but won't say whom he is."

"Let's agree to disagree. I believe the Vangel is in Pannonia, not in Ashbourne." I kiss her on the cheek as I stand. "Can I go now?"

"You're an hour late; I thought you weren't going to Autumn Reigns today."

"I'm waiting for Emily, and I still need to talk to Chan."

"Remember, the more you hang around supernatural beings, the more blood you'll need."

I shake my head. "I should probably get new friends, don't you think?" I don't wait for her answer as I make my way back inside.

Taking one step after the other on the marble stairs, I frown. I'm frustrated because with all the power that I possess, I still have to use human energy to climb. I push the door open and feel someone is behind me. In a vampire flash, I turn, grabbing the intruder by the neck and carrying him over to the wall. Then I look up to see the face.

"Vampire skills, huh?"

"For goodness sake, Millie. What are you doing?" I let go of her, and wait to see if she's hurt.

"I came to see a friend who almost died, and now she wants to kill me."

"Lesson number two; never sneak up on a hybrid."

She stares at me with a grin. "Hybrid, huh? Look who's showing off."

"How did you get in here?"

"Marie let me in. She told me you were talking to Maryanne, and I decided not to disturb you two." Emily sighs, her eyes staring at me from my feet to my hair. Her eyes ultimately rest on my eyes. "Look at you." She places her hands on her waist. "I know this sound insane, but I would go through all that happened to you if its means I would look as glorious as you do right now."

"I thought this time, maybe I would escape from your dramatic performance, but you never change, do you, darling?" I open my arms for a hug.

"Is that not why you love me?" She hurries over to hug me.

We bath in each other's fondness for a moment. She pulls away to look at me. "I thought you were gonna die, Lexie," she says, and with a cracking voice, she adds, "I've never been so afraid in my life."

I laugh. "You have, actually. Remember when Clive fell from the bridge?"

She laughs, wiping tears from her eyes. "I missed you. All these days away, I almost forgot how good it feels to be around you."

"Does it feel as good as it feels with Tristan Deveraux?"

She looks down, smiling.

"Are you blushing?" I laugh as she rolls her eyes. "Wait. You're in love with Tristan, aren't you? You two have been spending too much time under the sheets. Is that why you've been ignoring my calls?"

"Can we leave Tristan and talk about the return of Prince Channing?" She sits down on the chaise lounge and crosses her legs, her back against the cushions. "So tell me. Is the infatuation with Zach Van-B finished now that Chan is back?"

"I slept with Sean."

"What?" She sits up. "You slept with Sean, and you didn't call to tell me?"

"I did, and you didn't answer. Like I said, you've been avoiding me, and you seem to have no explanation."

"Sean? My God." Emily shakes her head. "I didn't think you would go that far to make Zachary jealous."

"At first, that's what I intended to do, but that's not how it happened. I like Sean and all I can say is that it was a moment of weakness."

"A moment of weakness." Emily bursts out laughing. "So how was he?"

Tongue in my cheek, I give her a sideways glance. "Great."

"Your tone isn't telling anything. Was it better than Chan?"

"Different. Then again, it's not about performance, but how I feel about each of them that determines the outcome, if that makes sense."

"Give me a break from your philosophy, and tell me his size, plea—ese."

I hold a laugh. "A great size."

"How great is great?"

I force a frown. "Well, forgive me because I forgot to take a tape measure to bed."

"What happened to us telling each other everything?"

"Tristan happened. Tell me about him."

Emily puckers her lips. "What do you want to know?"

"And your eyes light up again." I take a seat next to her. "Are you going to tell me where you've been when I needed you most?"

She folds her arms. "Tristan and I visited the Great Pannonia Cave."

"You went to Pannonia without me?"

"It was …" she sighs. "We ate from the angels' tears. It was amazing."

"I don't get you. You two feeding on the white walls mean you will love each other forever. That's what you said, so unless you don't believe it, I don't understand why you would allow Tristan to take you there."

"I know." She grabs a cushion and hugs it to her chest. "He ..." She seems to be hiding her arms or hands, maybe.

"What did he do?"

She stares at me without blinking.

"Remember you have a hybrid as your best friend. If anyone talks any shit to you, they'll have to answer to me."

"Emily laughs. " 'Shit' from your lips, kind of loses its meaning. After-effects of one night with Sean, I guess."

I repress a smile. "I'm still waiting for an answer."

Emily's smile disappears. She looks down before looking up to my eyes again. "Uhm ..." she trails.

"You broke up with Tristan?"

She turns her head to look out the window, smiling. I breathe in, relieved it's nothing serious since she's smiling.

"Millie?"

"I'm engaged, Lexie! I'm getting married!" She extends her hand toward me, showing off a ring carrying a whopping diamond.

While I'm still staring at the ring, Emily throws her arms around me. I remain silent and return her hug with no enthusiasm.

She pulls away from the hug. "Which is it? You are too stunned or not happy for me?"

My lips part, but nothing comes out. I lean forward and reposition the red tulip almost falling from her hair.

Her forehead creases, her lips tight. "This is what you always do, Lexie." She stands in anger, and advances toward the balcony.

I hesitate before following her to stand a few steps behind her. "Millie."

She turns to me with fury. "I support you in all your stupid moves, Lexie; your senseless infatuation with Zachary, your insane relationship with Chan, and the last one." She looks me in the eye. "The one with the sweetest boy you don't love. I'm there for you. But, what do you do when it's your turn to be a loyal friend? You get jealous."

"Ha?" I grimace. "I'm not jealous. I just think it's ridiculous."

"Ridiculous? How dare you?"

"I'm your best friend, the only thing close to a sister to you, yet I don't know this boy you're now engaged to. Not once have we sat down for dinner. I don't know where he lives. I'm a stranger to him, yet my best friend is marrying him?"

"How would you know him, Lexie when you're so wrapped up in two brothers and a Van-Bailey, who doesn't love you?"

I grimace and open my mouth, but she speaks before I do.

"Should I stop my life because you're obsessed with three boys? I'm not immortal like you."

"What the hell is wrong with you?"

"What's the hell is wrong with *you*, Lexie? I love Tristan, and he loves me. Is that not what's important?"

"Of course, it is," My voice softens.

I take her hands in mine. "Look what I found out about Channing after all that time. Besides, you're still in college—you're eighteen …"

"Nineteen in two months."

I sigh. "Still … come on. We still have so many hot guys to date."

"No. You do, not me."

"I guess your dad will agree with me."

Emily shakes her head as if disgusted. "I thought, for once, you would be a friend and not my mother." She picks her purse and heads for the door.

"Millie, come on. Where are you going?" I follow her, and quickly open the door she just shut violently. "Emily," I call, coming down the stairs. She ignores me.

Then I see Chan coming in. He smiles at me at first, but pauses for a few seconds to look as Emily rushes out.

Chan steps closer to me. "Is she alright?"

"I don't know, Chan. I'd rather not talk about it right now."

"How are you?" He stares at me as if to study me.

"Good." I smile.

"You look better than good."

"Where have you been?"

"Did you miss me?" He grins.

"I wanted to thank you. I really—"

"You don't have to thank me. I—"

"No, look at me." I cup his face and force him to look into my eyes. "Thank you for the Ring and for everything."

"Does that mean you forgive me for not telling you I'm a Deschanel?"

"Only if you tell me why you lied."

"Come, let's take a walk in the garden, and I'll tell you all you need to know."

Chan takes my hand into his, and we head toward the French doors. Mother is no longer sitting outside as we walk past the porch to the garden.

We stroll side by side, and it almost feels like he never left.

"What happened when you removed the stake from Zachary's chest?" I ask after a moment of silence. "He must have been upset with you."

"He was." Channing displays a slight smile.

"What excuse did you give him?"

"That I was jealous when I saw you glowing from his blood and concluded he allowed you to feed from his neck."

"Did he believe you?"

"Of course not." Channing grimaces. "He began rummaging on about how strange it was that I moved around with a stake in my pocket, waiting for jealousy to possess me."

I laugh as Channing smiles.

"He's still determined to know the truth. He probably will ask you about it." Channing raises his hand to tuck a strand of hair behind my ear.

He takes a deep sigh. "How did you end up choosing my brother over Zachary?"

"Maybe, I saw you in him."

"So, Zachary was also an option?"

"I didn't say he was."

"You don't need to. I see it all over his face and yours, too." He stares into my eyes, but I drop my gaze. "I guess that's why Madeline left."

"Madeline left Zachary? Oh, my God."

"Come." Channing ignores my surprised face and takes my hand, leading me past the bed of roses to our favorite bench.

We sit in our usual position; facing each other with our elbows resting on the back of the bench. "I didn't mean to lie to you about my name," Channing begins. "When I left Pannonia, I didn't want my father to find me. I enrolled for college in Milbourne, gave them the right name of course, but chose to be known by a different name—which we always do to avoid the media. I used my mother's purple crystal to find Doc."

"What does the purple crystal do?"

"Before she died, my mother told me only an immortal keeper would be able to do a spell that would give her life again."

"Give her life, where is she?"

"Her body lies in our family vault, in Pannonia."

"So what happened when you found my mother?"

"She panicked at first, but after a few months of pleading, she agreed to help me on the condition that I don't tell anyone she's an immortal keeper. When I settled in Milbourne, I met you that day at the assembly. You introduced me to Doc the following week. I had no idea you were her daughter, but she never believed me. She thought I wanted to use you to get what I wanted from her. Then I overheard her and John talking about you, the real you. I confronted her the next day, and she denied ever talking to John until I offered to go to Pannonia to get the Ring for you."

"And you didn't think to tell me?"

"Now be honest, Jo." He eyes me with intent. "If I had told you, would you have agreed for me to leave?"

I drop my gaze, shaking my head.

"I didn't think so."

I look up at his eyes again. "Did you stop to think that perhaps in your selfless way you were being selfish? Denying me the right to adore you for your courage and to mourn you if you had died?"

"That's what I didn't want you to do, spending your days mourning. You deserve to be happy."

"I still mourned when you left me."

"But you had hope." His voice is convincing. "Hope makes people go on."

"If you are aiming to keep me happy every day of my immortal life, you're in for a huge disappointment. Grief, sorrow, and pain are all part of nature. We can never know happiness without them."

"Did I tell you I still love you? Because I never stopped."

We stare at each other for a silent moment. His gaze takes me back to the first kiss, and my heart responds with a buzz.

"Um ... tell me how it was in Pannonia. What did you spend your time doing? Who did you spend your Christmas with last year?"

"There isn't anything compelling enough to say. I had to change into this person I don't like to remember."

"Do you want to tell me about this person?"

He shakes his head. "Maybe some other time."

"And Christmas?" I ask after he remains silent. "You can tell me about Christmas."

"Christmas." He shifts and pulls me into his arms, resting his chin on top of my head. "Well, I was alone because my friends left me; they were fed up with me talking about Joanne."

"And what did you tell them that got them so fed up?"

He takes my hand to play with my fingers. "I can't remember, but it's probably what I missed most, like the smell of your skin, and how it helps me to fall asleep." He lets out a soft laugh. "And maybe how I laid awake the last night we were together, watching you sleeping and wishing there was any way to keep you with me forever." He breathes out and kisses my hair.

"I would leave you too if I had to hear you lament over a strange girl."

"It's funny, the things I missed; my eyes peering through your hair. You know how you stare at me while you're reading a book …"

I close my eyes, smiling and adjust my head on his chest.

"And I missed tennis with you. Saturdays were the worst, especially after the last Saturday we spent together."

I smile. "We played a lot of tennis that day, didn't we?"

He chortles. "We sure did."

"Were they as depressing as they were for me? The Saturdays?"

"There are no words to describe the feeling, but it's like a continuous pain without a cure. I would lose appetite, lose sleep and at times, I'd think I've lost my mind. I'd find that corner at the collar of my shirt. It was a place where I could still smell a bit of Jo, so I held on to that. I'd think the scent would bring me comfort, but no; it only called on a hunger that turned into a desperate need, a yearning to have you in my arms. Still, what hurt most was the possibility that it might never happen again. I might never hold you like this." He wraps his arms tight around me, squeezing me to his chest.

I raise my head and stare into his eyes. "I should have waited for you," I whisper.

"No, you did the right thing. I wanted you alive, happy, and safe. You are now, and that's all that matters."

"Don't know about happy, but alive and safe." I lean in and rest my head on his shoulder.

"What do you need to make you happy? I'll do my best to make it happen."

I shake my head as I look into his eyes. "Not even you can fix this, Chan."

His brow creases as he waits for me to continue.

"I don't want to hurt Sean, but it feels like either way, no matter what I choose to do, I'll still break his heart."

"Sean is my brother, and I love him. If you want to be with him, I'll stay away. It'll be hard, but I'll try—"

"No, listen to me." I stop his hand before it reaches my face. My eyes pierce into his, hoping to find his soul—to make him see, make him understand.

"What?"

"I can't be with you. Neither can I be with Sean. It's not only because he's your brother. I love you. I've always loved you. And I'm afraid I always will. Being with Sean while you're around is near impossible."

"You want me to leave Ashbourne?"

"No." I sigh and reach for his hand. "Of course not. I just need you to understand for the sake of your brother, you and I can't be together."

"Jo, this is silly. We could live in Pannonia, if you—"

"I'm not changing my mind Chan."

Staring at me in silence, Chan tightens his jaw. "I have no one to blame but myself."

"I'm sorry." I feel a lump forming in my throat, and his pained eyes give me no comfort. "I wish I could go back in time and ..." I break off, wiping tears as I catch a breath.

Channing pulls me in for a hug. "Don't cry. These things always have a way to fix themselves."

"It's just the choices I made ... I made many mistakes, and now I don't know how I feel anymore. I don't even know how I feel about you. That one thing I used to be so sure about and now ..."

"Listen to me." Chan cups my face as I sniff. "So much has happened, especially to you. Your emotions are possibly all over the place. I'll give you time to think about what you want. I'll be in Milbourne. If you need me, want a game of tennis or chess, call or write me a letter."

"A letter." I chuckle. "A letter would be brilliant, yes." I throw my arms around his neck. "You remember when I said I didn't need you?"

Channing chuckles. "I know you didn't mean it."

"I meant it, but I was wrong." I raise my head from his shoulder. My eyes on his and his on my lips, our faces get closer. Gently, he cups my face and leans in, touching his forehead with mine. He breathes. "I love you, Jo," he whispers, sending my heart on a race. "You said you made mistakes. Don't make another, trying to make my brother happy. That will only make you miserable."

Chan stands and helps me up as he says goodbye. He turns to leave, but stops midway, stepping back in a rush to hold me tightly. He brings his lips close to mine then, whispers, "Since I couldn't kiss you goodbye when I left, hello, when I came back, can I at least kiss you now?"

I stare at his eyes, then cast my gaze down to his lips. I want to kiss him, if not to satisfy my own selfish desires, at least to thank him for sacrificing his life for me. His scent is inviting me to give in to him. He kisses my cheek as if to remind me he's still waiting for my answer.

"I can't." I hastily kiss the side of his lips and circle my arms around his neck. "I can't hurt him. I know how it feels not to be chosen."

Channing pulls away and frowns at me. "What do you mean, not to be chosen? I've never—"

I place a finger on his lips. "I know," I say, staring into his eyes. "I know you've never put me second. We need to give Sean some time. It's you, I love, and it will always be you."

Channing leans forward, his lips directed to mine. I'm still contemplating stopping him when Sean appears in vampire mode, spinning Chan from my front. He pauses and shoots a jab at his face. "Fuck you, Ashton!"

Chan staggers backwards, his hands touching the ground before he rises. "In front of Jo, that's so gentlemanly of you, brother."

His hand on his bloody nose, Channing stares back at a furious Sean.

"I don't remember telling her I'm a gentleman." Sean steps toward Chan. "And why don't you call her Alex like everyone else? Or do you think calling her Jo will make you special?"

I move between them, facing Sean. "It's not what it looks like."

"What is it then, Lexie?" He holds my gaze. "All you had to do was tell me before you started making out with him."

"I didn't. It was a goodbye kiss. That's all."

"Oh yeah? It sure looks like it," he utters sarcastically. "And how come I don't get these goodbye kisses. Maybe I should jump in and get mine too, huh? Or perhaps we can have a goodbye fuck, too. How about that?"

"Sean, I—"

Sean shakes his head. "All I've ever been with you was honest from the very start."

"Can you at least trust me this once?" I yell.

"It will always be him, you said." Sean shakes his head. "I heard everything, Lexie."

"I never promised you anything, Sean, remember?" My eyes well up with tears.

Sean's jaw tightens. "It's not about promises, it's about hope." He starts to leave.

"Sean!" I run after him as he walks away.

Chan grabs my arm. "I'll go talk to him and explain everything if you let me."

I nod, and Channing squeezes my hand gently before going after Sean.

XXVI

ARE YOU IN LOVE WITH MY SON?

The orange shades from the setting sun are almost fading as I fire up the engine of my Black Mamba, speeding home. With Emily refusing to answer my calls, no calls from Channing, Sean, or Zachary, I dedicated the last two days to Autumn Reigns. According to the project manager, the tracks won't be complete for another six months, and since Christmas is in four, my dream of racing on Christmas day will not come true. I need to talk to Zachary.

Vine Lane is silent as I drive down it. The bright streetlights remind me of the day Channing left when I almost felt like I was dying.

As I arrive at the gate, I glance next door and recall recent events. At the front entrance, I push my bike into the garage, remove my helmet and head for the door.

Dinner smells like roast beef. I don't feel hungry. Nor do I feel thirsty.

"Miss Lexie."

"Ms. Marie Montress." I smirk at her as she removes her apron.

"Your mother has just left for work, and Grandpa Henry left with John. They tried to call you."

"I know. I was busy when they called." I wash my hands before picking up a slice of garlic bread from the tray and take a bite. "How are you? I like the new earrings."

"George bought them for our anniversary last week."

"My God. How could I forget? Happy belated anniversary. Did you enjoy your night?"

Laughter bursts out from her, followed by a deep sigh. "Phoebe is back with that abusive boyfriend of hers."

I frown. "You want me to talk to her?"

Marie shakes her head and drops her gaze.

"The track will be open soon, and if you allow her to join, I can keep an eye on her."

"Miss Lexie, you know I can't afford—"

"Miss Marie, what do you take me for that I should make you pay? Phoebe is like a sister to me, just as you are my second mother."

She stares at me for a moment then rushes to embrace me, stepping back to hold my hands. "You are a good girl, you know," she says in a passionate voice. "Don't ever let anyone tell you otherwise."

"Thank you." I fight tears back. After the recent events, I truly needed to hear that.

"And please stop calling me Miss Marie."

"Only if you do the same." I chuckle, walking out of the kitchen to my room.

I pick up my phone to call Zachary. The phone goes straight to voicemail.

Hey, knight. It's been a week, and I haven't seen you at Autumn Reigns. We are doing a test run on the first-half tomorrow, and I was hoping you would be there with me.

I hang up and pause for a second, staring into the screen of my new phone; I'm still getting used to it. John surprised me with the phone a week after the drama with Channing and Sean.

My fingers rest on the name Sean, my mind contemplating a call and ask him if he knows where Zachary is. In the end, I decide not to. After refusing to talk to me for the last two days, last night Sean answered my call. I apologized. He accepted, and that was it. I believe he's still not ready to forgive me.

After taking a shower, I pace on my balcony talking to Chan, who tells me he hasn't seen or spoken to Zachary for three days.

"If you want him for a feed, I suggest you stop depending on him because you could get addicted to feeding from the vein; warm blood is addictive."

"I don't need a drink, Chan. I'll need him for the track tomorrow; I hate making decisions without him."

"Is that all you want from him?"

"What else did you think I want?"

"I don't know. Maybe you miss his company."

I pause to consider his statement. "Are you still in Milbourne?"

"As I promised, yes, but I was home last night with my father and Megan."

"Have you spoken to Sean lately? How is he?"

"Good as he can be. He misses you. You should call him."

I nod as if Chan could see me. Hanging up, I step back inside and head straight to my closet.

From my designer collection, I choose a cream pencil dress with a lace overlay. My hair hangs over my shoulders, and on my ears, I insert jade earrings. Before making my way downstairs, I wear my silver heels and grab my keys to the Theta Scorpii. I tell Marie I'm going out and head for the garage.

In the car, I put on my favorite music and drive away. I take the back road, past the cinema where Zachary and I had dinner the other evening. The thoughts of our conversation haunt me as I change gears and pick up speed, heading for Stills Lane. It takes me another ten minutes before I arrive at the Van-Bailey Stills.

"Miss Watson." Thomas, one of the security officers saluted as I wait for him to open the first gate. "Good to see you again."

"Is the knight still living in his palace?" I tease.

Thomas smiles. "Haven't seen him for a while, but I was off-duty yesterday."

"Thank you, Thomas." I smile at him as the gate opens.

"Goodnight."

"Night." I wave as I drive away.

After five minutes of deep breaths and speed, I slow down. I turn into the Van-Bailey driveway, finding a space to park next to a black SUV in the visitor's area.

I inhale as I approach the heavy, wooden double doors, and press the thumb shaped doorbell. The door opens.

"Alexandra?" Zachary senior raises his brow.

I try to open my mouth, but he shuts the door in my face. My jaw drops, but before I could gasp, the door opens again.

"Sorry, wrong Zach." He laughs.

I feel I should laugh too, but I'm utterly taken aback, surprised that he can not only smile, but also joke. "Hello, Mr. Van-Bailey."

"Zach-Louis." He extends his hand to shake mine and lets me in before shutting the door. "Long time no knocking on the wrong house, huh?"

My face warms up as I recall what happened the last time we met at this door, but the nerves vanish when I notice a warm smile on his face, similar to Zachary's.

I breathe in a delicious smell of something baking as Zachary senior leads me out of the brightly lit, grand foyer and down to the inner hallway. The lights are dim, warm and cozy. The silence makes me uneasy. I don't feel comfortable being here alone with Zachary senior, especially with his sudden pleasantness.

"Mr. Van—"

"Zach-Louis." He pauses and smiles at me. "I would like you to call me Zach-Louis. Everybody does."

"Zach-Louis, I'm not staying long. I was hoping to see—"

"That day." He ignores me as if he didn't hear me speak, and continues walking, glancing back at me. "You looked at me and said wrong house."

My heart pounds as I wonder what he's about to say.

He shakes his head. "I spent the whole day playing the scene in my head over and over again."

Weird. "Uhm ... I'm sorry. I know that was silly—"

"No, it wasn't," He rubs his chin with his thumb. "I thought that was a bold move. You challenged me to run after you. If my Alex hadn't, I'm sure I would have." He laughs again.

Still baffled, I force a smile. Here is a man I thought incapable of a civil conversation, who now seems to be just as warm as Zachary, the knight is. I realize I'm frowning and relax my face.

Zach-Louis stops by the white double doors and gestures with his hand for me to go inside.

Stepping on the untreated floorboards, my eyes skip to three bright chandeliers hanging from the ceiling. The white walls are almost the same shade as the large sofas dressed with patterned cushions. The designs on the cushions carry a combination of the colors in the room, camel, pastel-green, brown and gray.

Waiting for Zach-Louis to offer me a seat, I step aside and admire a portrait of him on the wall above the neo-gothic style fireplace.

"Alex?" Alexandra startles me as she hurries over and embraces me.

I suppress a sigh of relief as her sweet smell of roses fills my nostrils.

"I thought it was you." She steps back to look at me before taking my hand and directing me to sit on the large sofa. "I was so looking forward to seeing you and Maryanne for dinner the other day, but she called to tell me you had food poisoning. Poor you. How are you feeling now?"

"I'm better now, thank you." I nod, smiling.

She stares at me as if to examine my expression and nods slowly. I don't see Zach-Louis, and though I wonder where he went, I'm pleased he's gone.

"I'm sorry for visiting so late. I thought Zach—"

"Don't apologize." Alexandra relaxes her back on the sofa. "You're free to visit anytime you want."

"You are so kind, Alexandra," I say and almost roll my eyes as Zach-Louis walks back into the room. In his hand is a glass of blood, 'A' positive; I can smell it, and two mugs of cappuccino.

He hands a cappuccino to his wife and pulls her close, planting a quick kiss on her lips. He then passes a steaming mug to me. "My wife's favorite. I hope you like it, too."

"Thank you." I accept with a smile, and hesitate to take a sip; I don't trust him. Mother warned me of the dangers of the Lucca-viper, a scentless poison lethal to hybrids.

Zach-Louis grabs a thick book from a built-in bookshelf. He crosses his legs as he sits on a leather armchair, closer to the fireplace. After placing his glass of blood on the end table, he holds the book open and begins reading from a marked page.

Nersii, The Inescapable. My heart skips as I read the title.

"Alex, are you alright?" Alexandra reaches for my hand.

I nod and force a smile.

There's an awkward silence as I stare at the cappuccino. I raise it to my lips and take a reluctant sip. When I look up, Zach-Louis's eyes are on me while Alexandra watches her husband.

"Is Zachary or Maxx home?" I direct my question to Alexandra.

She shakes her head. "Zachary left home a week ago," she says as she shrugs, hugging her mug before she takes another sip. "Don't worry; he called to tell me he's fine."

"Is he at the beach house?"

"Yes, but he told me not to tell you ..."

"He doesn't want me to know? I frown. "Why?"

Zach-Louis scoffs. I turn and look at him; he's smiling, but his eyes are on his book.

"I think I should leave now." I prepare to stand.

Alexandra takes my hand and tilts her head. "Why so soon? Is it because Zachary is not here?" She raises her eyebrows.

"No, it's just that ..." I try to stand, but Alexandra pulls me down.

"Give me five minutes." She stands. "I have a special pie in the oven, and I want you to take some for Maryanne."

She rushes out of the room before I could argue.

Zach-Louis flips over to the next page and remains focused on his book while I wait for his wife. I steal a look and study his resemblance to Zachary, wondering how a man like him would want to kill his own son.

"Instead of staring at me, Alexandra, you can ask me anything you want." He shuts his book and stares into my eyes. "You have any questions for me?"

"No … yes. Is Maxx with Zachary?"

"I thought you would never ask." He gives me a weak side smile. "Scarlett, my only daughter is with her Grandpa in Pannonia. We're expecting her back next week."

I grimace. "I asked if Maxx was with Zachary."

"I heard you." Zach-Louis folds his arms across his chest. "Is Maxx in love with you, too?"

"I'm sorry?" I blink in confusion.

"I thought it your style to seduce brothers." He raises his eyebrow.

"What?"

"What do you want from my sons?"

My chest swells with fury. "Are you saying what I think you are saying?"

Zach-Louis gulps down the remainder of his drink and rises to his feet, his empty glass hanging too loose in his hands as if he wants to smash it on my face.

He stands in front of me, weight on one side. "You are okay financially. You've managed to seduce my son into a partnership. I do not know what you offered him that made him give away half his dream to you."

"Give away?" My breathing increases, I rise, stepping away from him. With shaking hands, I place my mug on the coffee table and turn, standing behind him. "I paid for what I own."

He steps around and faces me. "The question is the currency you used. What was it? Dollars? Sterling? Japanese yen? Or was it carnal delights?"

Something moves inside of me. Perhaps, it's the strength of what I am, the Nersii. I feel energy pushing through my veins. Then, I remember I have to pretend to be nothing more than a human being.

"How dare you?" I battle to control my trembling hands. My eyes challenge his intense glare. "I respect you as Zachary's father. I know you scare and intimidate the world, but I must tell you I'm not the world. I am Alexandra. I take no insults from any souls, and that includes yours. You think—"

"Hold your tongue, child." He grabs me by the chin, raises it up as he leans into my face "I know you're neither ignorant nor stupid. Did you truly believe my son could not afford to pay for the track?"

My chest rises with fury. The strength of his hand on my jaw makes me want to spin and pin his head under my elbow. But I hold my temper and breathe in as his masculine scent fills my nostrils.

Freeing my jaw from his hold, I glare into his eyes. "How about you ask your son?" I hiss.

"For a girl, you have guts and too big a mouth for a human. Which makes me wonder; why is it you don't smell like a human? Are you a witch?"

I let out a short gasp as he swings at me and grabs my neck, pinning me to the wall.

"Argh." I grunt.

"Are you in love with my son?" he whispers. "Answer me."

"Which one?" I taunt. "Maxx?"

His fingers still on my neck, he presses tighter. "I could kill you right now, right here."

"I'm surprised you haven't, considering you almost killed your son the other day." My voice comes out strangled.

In an instant, Zach-Louis lets go of my neck. Like young Zachary at the tennis court the other day, Zach-Louis stares at me with a stone face. Hands by his side, he clenches his fists. My bones suddenly stiffen as he scowls at me.

I'm not sure if it's my fear or his mind beginning to destroy me. My heart beats louder and faster while I struggle for breath. I fight to stop a nauseating vibration at my temples.

"Zachary, don't!" Alexandra panics as she walks in. "You're hurting her." She rushes to hold his face as I choke. "Let her go. If not for your son, forgive her for me."

"Get her out of my sight." He flings up his hand carelessly, and I fall to my knees.

Alexandra hurries and helps me up. She carries me to the sofa and disappears. Zach-Louis appears again. This time he looks at me and falters, turning in the direction he came from. He pays no attention to Alexandra, who's walking in with a glass of water.

"Here, drink some." She places the glass to my mouth. I take a few sips, and hand back the glass to her. After examining my neck, she pulls me into her arms.

"I'm sorry," I moan quietly.

"Shh," She says, brushing my hair back. "I shouldn't have left you with him."

After a moment in her arms, I raise my head. "I want to go home," I sigh.

"I'll drive you." Alexandra says. Before I can shake my head, she adds, "I insist. The least I could do is making sure you get home safely."

"What were you thinking, Alexandra?" John yells.

Because of what I did last night, I took my Black Mamba for a ride earlier than usual this morning. I thought I could come back early, sit in the sunny breakfast room and eat in peace while everyone was still sleeping. But, after taking a bite of my sandwich, John rang the bell. I dreaded explaining what happened with Zach-Louis to Mother, but I overlooked the relationship between my father and Zach-Louis.

Now John stands before me with hands on his waist, anger printed all over his face. "Fighting Zach-Louis? What is wrong with you?"

He did most of the fighting. "You should have heard what he said to me," I argue.

"I don't care what he said. You don't get yourself in an argument with Zach-Louis, Alexandra. You could have died!"

"But I didn't."

Hands on the wooden table, he leans in, so his eyes are level with mine. "You're lucky to be alive after what you said to him. What if you failed to control yourself and revealed the hybrid in you? Did you think of the consequences?"

"He has no right to insult me like that. 'I thought it your style to seduce brothers.' Why does everyone blame me? Channing lied to me about having no family, and I ended up with Sean. I didn't go after Sean. On the contrary, he seduced me. I told him I wasn't over my ex, but he kept pushing and pushing. He even stripped naked in front of me. No one says anything about that. What if it was the other way round; if I was the one who took off my clothes and flashed myself in front of him? It would be my fault too, I guess. I am human you know ..."

John chuckles, then I realize my mistake.

"Well, at least I'm part human."

"So what's the story with young Zachary?"

"He's not a child; he knows what he wants. And, guess what? He deceived me, too. He said nothing about Madeline until she showed up from nowhere. Now his father insults me. Why? Is it because he thinks I'm human? Or maybe everything comes down to the fact that I'm female? Tell me, which is it, Dad?"

"So out of all the people in your life, you chose to put your frustration on Zach-Louis?"

"I didn't choose to. He started it."

"You did when you decided to visit his home. Instead of getting him to like you, you start a war with him?"

"You taught me to stand up for myself, Dad, remember? 'Fight back,' you said."

"It's clear you forgot the simple rule; if the opponent is more powerful than you are, you use your brains."

"Dad—"

"You need to go back there and apologize."

"*Apologize?* I'm not—"

"Oh yes you are, honey. Even if it means—"

"Whoa!" Grandpa enters. "Enough, John." He comes toward me and kisses my cheeks.

"Morning, Grandpa." I return his kisses.

"What's this roar I hear tarnishing this blessed morning? You two are more alike than you know." He stares at John.

John shakes his head as he opens the fridge. "She wants to get herself killed. After all that we've been through." He brings out a pint of Red and stares at me while he unscrews the cap.

I look away, resisting the urge to roll my eyes.

Grandpa walks over to open the refrigerator, brings out a cooler bag and places it on the table in front of me. "The younger Van-Bailey brought this for you while you were out."

I push my mug aside, drag the bag closer and unzip the cover. It's full of fresh pints of white blood.

John grimaces. "Young Zachary brought blood for Alex?"

Grandpa shakes his head, waving his hand from side to side as he takes a seat opposite me. "I know young Zachary well enough not to mistake him for any other person. It was the one who was born with a cheeky smile; the seer."

"The seer?" I ask.

"He's talking about Maxx," John says.

"Maxx is a seer?"

"Grandpa moves his eyes back to John. "Did you not tell her?"

John shakes his head, crossing his arms over his chest.

Grandpa pauses as if to try to remember. "He showed his talent the other year at the Supernatural Summer Games, held at the arh ...What's that place again, John?"

"They changed the games a few years ago, Henry." John scratches his head a little and folds his hands again. "They are now called Hurricane

Games. Membership starts at a million dollars. It's clear that's a deterrent for ordinary people—humans."

"So what does Maxx do? How is he a seer?" I stare at Grandpa with curiosity.

"He sees not only relationship types, but their strengths. That's why you, your father, and your mother should never be in the same room if he's present."

"You mean he will know John is my father?"

Grandpa nods.

I wait for him to swallow before he speaks again. "Not only that, but also because John is actually in love with your mother and not—"

"Henry, not now," John voices.

I stifled a laugh, gazing at John. "It's obvious, Dad. Stop trying to hide it."

John sighs, staring at the cooler bag. "You should have told me you were feeding on Zachary." His voice turns harsh. "Drinking from the vein can be addic—"

"Dad. I know." I stand and grab the cooler bag. "Chan told me." I glance at him and find him grinning. "What's funny?"

"Nothing." He hugs himself. "It's just you calling me dad. I'm still getting used to that."

I smile, and grab a pint from the cooler bag, then put the bag in the refrigerator.

As I step away from John, his hand clutches around my waist and pulls me back for a tight hug. "I love you," he whispers.

"Love you too, Dad." I kiss his cheek, smile at Grandpa, winking at me, and walk out of the room.

"Apologize to Zach-Louis, Alexandra," John calls. "Apologize."

Do I have to? I roll my eyes.

❧❦❧

About fifteen minutes later, Mother arrives from work. I'm in my room, and I dread seeing her; I know she'll have something to say about what I did last night. I know I'll have to face her eventually, but right now, I just want some peace of mind.

I tie my hair into a loose bun and sit my work desk. I open my laptop, and that's when I hear a knock on my door.

Marie walks in. "Miss Lexie, your mother wants you."

I sigh before rising to my feet.

"How is she?" I whisper, following Marie as she walks out of the room.

She glances at me. "Your name in every sentence. And yes, full names."

Arriving in the breakfast room, I'm relieved to find Grandpa still sitting around at the breakfast table. My mother sits next to him, and John is brewing coffee. Mother stands to receive a steaming mug from John, then pauses, staring at me. Despite spending the night working, she looks stunning in a simple black dress. Only her eyes are a little dull, possibly the lack of sleep.

"Mom." With exaggerated excitement, I rush and kiss her cheek. Avoiding the mug in her hands, I give her a hug. "Did Dad tell you how I stood up for myself last night at the Van-Baileys?"

"I know what you're trying to do Alexandra." She returns my kiss and sits down. "I heard what you did, and I agree with your father you have to apologize, but that's not why I called you."

I frown at her stern face as we join Jon and Grandpa at the table. "What happened? Why did you call me?"

"Your mother thinks one of your friends is the Vangel."

My heart pounds, *I don't want to hear this*. I'm not ready. I rise to my feet. "Can we do this another time?"

"Alexandra, sit down." Grandpa calls me by my name; this is bad. I sit back down and try to ignore the heat at the bottom of my stomach. "We need some information about the boys, Channing, Sean and Zachary."

"What kind of information?"

"Characteristics," Mothers says. "First off, the Vangel is white-blooded. Zachary is a White Blood, so that makes him a suspect. I don't know about Sean and Channing." She stares at me with raised eyebrows.

"Well ... I don't know either. I've never seen Sean's blood."

"And Channing?"

I frown, remembering the Ring. "I can't remember. My eyes were blurred the time I saw it."

"Alexandra?" Mother shoots a warning look at me.

I sigh. "White."

Grandpa's forehead creases. He stares at Mother. "If he's a White Blood, why did he feel the need, finding white blood for the Ring?"

John clears his throat. "Maybe because his blood is poisonous to Alex just as Alex's blood is to him."

"Is it, really?" I turn to John. "Is the Vangel's blood poisonous to me?" If it is, it means Zachary is not the Vangel. Then again, Channing or Sean turning out to be the Vangel will not make me happy.

"That's just my theory," John answers.

"If Channing is white-blooded," Grandpa begins. "And since him and Sean are brothers, it brings us to the conclusion that they are both White Bloods."

"Which means any of them is possibly the Vangel."

"Why did you just pick on my friends?" I stare at my mother. "Why didn't you start searching in Pannonia?"

"Have you forgotten I'm an immortal keeper? I have extra senses, and I suspect one of your friends to be the Vangel." She directs her eyes to Grandpa. "Dad, you mentioned something about the effects of the Ring on the Vangel."

"Yes." Grandpa sits up. "It is said that if the Vangel gets in contact with the Ring, he might burn, almost like he's holding hot ashes."

My mind goes to Chan and my pulse races. *What if it's he? What do I do?*

"Since Channing carried the Ring from Pannonia, we can conclude it didn't have any effect on him," John says.

"I agree," I say, hiding my relief.

Mother remains silent for a moment before she says, "Zachary is white-blooded. Alex feeds on his blood, so that makes him less likely to be the Vangel, right?"

"Only if my theory of the Vangel's blood being poisonous to Alex is true," John says. "Chan carried the Ring from Pannonia without burning from it and would have hurt Alex from the day he knew whom she was, but he didn't."

"Maybe he's waiting for Maryanne to help him with the spell that will raise his mother from the dead before showing his true colors." Grandpa says to John. "And why did he not offer Alex his blood?"

For a moment, we all look at each other, silently.

"I guess that leaves us with Sean," Mother leans forward, her shifting among us. "I think Sean is the Vangel."

I grimace, shaking my head. "What?"

"We don't know anything about him." Mother shrugs. "He seems in love with Alex, just like the Vangel in her past life."

"Chan loves me too, remember?"

"Chan before he left for Pannonia, he told me the Vangel was in Pannonia." She continues, looking directly at me. "He promised he would do all he can, keeping him away from you. Sean came from Pannonia. Chan refuses to tell us who the Vangel is because it's his brother. Remember, I had to force him to wash his hands in the welcoming bowl. Moreover, he has characteristics closer to an angel; finding it hard to lie. Sean is the—"

"No!" I rise. "You're wrong, Mother."

"Alex, calm down." Mother stands.

I stare at her with pleading eyes. "Everything is just circumstantial, Mom. I don't want to hear it anymore." I start for the door.

"Butterfly, before you leave," Grandpa calls. I pause, turning around to look at him.

He stands, coming over to me. Reaching for my hands, he sighs. "You're right when you say none of the points raised is a fact, but they are all possibilities. I know you don't want any of your friends to be the Vangel. If you think none of them is the Vangel, you can help us find proof. All we want to do is eliminate the possibility of any of them turning out to be the Vangel."

I cast my eyes down for a moment. Then, I nod, reluctantly. "Okay, I'll do all I can." I stare at Mother. "Is that all?"

"I have more to discuss with you, but I think you need time to understand what your grandfather has just explained to you." She raises her hands and cups my face, then kisses my forehead. "By the way, has anyone asked to take you to Pannonia?"

"Yes." I frown. "Chan did. Why?"

Mother takes in a deep breath. "There's a hill in Pannonia. If you go on it, your true nature will be exposed. You will phase into a werewolf, regardless of the Ring you wear. And it is very easy for the Vangel to kill you when you're in wolf form. That's why I never wanted you to go there." Mother hesitates before adding, "I hope Chan is not planning to take you on the hill."

"I turned him down, Mother." I answer her silent question. "You don't need to worry."

Without warning, tears well up in my eyes. "After all Chan did for me, you still think he wants to hurt me? I shake my head and turn for the door.

EPILOGUE

Zachary, I think I messed up with your father last night. I'm sorry. It's been a week now, and I'm ... I'll postpone the track test until I hear from you. Please call me back.

I wait for Zachary's response for the entire day, sleep, wake up the next day, and still no messages. After putting on a pair of jeans and a polo shirt, I stand in front of the mirror in my room and fix my hair into a ponytail. I'm ready for my morning ride.

I couldn't sleep last night, thinking of Zachary. The track test is tomorrow afternoon, and I'm beginning to feel like I have no partner.

I pick up my phone and walk out to the balcony. There's one person who will tell me what's going on.

"Zandra, it's 6 a.m. ... I'm still in bed," Maxx answers.

"Why is Zachary avoiding me?" I ask.

"What?"

"You heard me. Don't even pretend you don't know what I'm talking about."

"He just wants to be alone," Maxx says in a sleepy voice.

"Alone is different from ignoring me." I sigh. "I know you know why, Maxx. Just tell me, please."

He exhales. "It's somewhere between Madeline leaving, you, with Ashton, but I think more to do with him finding out that you and Sean, um ... took the relationship to another level."

"*What?* Who told him about that? Can't I keep anything private?"

"Next time, tell Sean to keep things private."

"In any case, I don't see why that should upset him. I'm not his girlfriend."

There's a long silence before Maxx speaks. When he does, his voice is sober. "Who you are to him is defined by how he feels about you, and how he reacts to what happens in your life. The same applies to him, too. You hurt him, Alex."

I pause for a minute, thinking over Maxx's words. I know Zachary has no right to be upset with me, but I still feel guilty. Maybe Maxx is right. I know I'm right too, but that doesn't make me innocent.

We say our goodbyes, and as I hang up, I dial Zachary's number. The call goes through to the answering machine. I leave yet another message.

Well, I thought of color changes; changing my bedroom color to yellow. Then again, that's too bright. I thought of the color of your room. Not that I want to be rude, but your colors are just too dull. I guess they are contributing to your sorrows. In any case, I have this brilliant idea to mix your colors with mine; your creams, browns with my whites would be lovely, I think. Call me as soon as you can.

I hang up and grab my keys to the Black Mamba. Careful not to wake my mother, I make my way downstairs. I really don't want to talk about the Vangel early this morning. In the hallway, closer to the kitchen, I pull my phone out again. This time I dial Emily's number.

Nothing has changed. The answering machine has now become my close friend. In spite of Emily ignoring my last message, I still leave another.

Emily, I know you hate me right now, but maybe we can meet halfway; how about two-year engagement before you can get married? Don't roll your eyes. I still love you.

I take a deep sigh, shoving my phone back in my pocket and stepping into the kitchen.

"Problems everywhere, huh?"

My heart skips a beat before I realize who it is. "Grandpa you startled me."

"It's a good morning, did you notice?" He shuts the book in front of him and crosses his arms. He's sitting on one of the bar stools surrounding the center island.

I grab a pint of white blood and kiss his cheek before taking a sit next to him. "What good is a morning if my friends refuse to speak to me?"

"Tell me more?" He looks at me with a slight frown.

"It's Emily." I take a sip from my drink, and suddenly the taste, the scent, and everything in it takes me back to Zachary.

"What about Emily?" Grandpa asks.

"She's getting married. Can you believe that?"

"And you think she's rushing things."

"I *know* she's rushing things."

"Sometimes it is best to allow people to make their own mistakes. If you stop her marrying whomever she wishes to marry, you risk her resenting you for how things might turn out in her future. Be her friend, be honest with your opinions, but don't let that stop you from being there for her."

I stare at him silently, and shake my head as tears fill my eyes. "I've been a terrible friend, haven't I?"

He puts his arms around my shoulders. "You've lost most of your humanity, so some of these emotions don't come naturally. You have to work harder to find them deep inside of you. You do that by avoiding hasty decisions. You have an immortal life ahead of you, there's no need to rush."

"Except I have to find the Vangel, right?"

"We have a solid plan. You'll find the Vangel in no time."

I jump at a text. *It's not Zachary.*

Chan: Tennis 8 p.m. same place. If you win, I'll agree to a race tomorrow at the Van-Bailey Speedway.

I smile and text back.

Me: Deal. You better get ready for the track.

"So who are you going to pick?" Grandpa's gaze moves from my phone to my eyes.

I shoot him a baffled look. "What do you mean?"

"Is it gonna be music and romance, suits, balls and fine wine, or is it fast cars, food and fashion? Who is fast and tactful enough to win the heart of the Nersii?"

I smile with understanding, my cheeks warming up as I look up at his eyes. "Or maybe he doesn't need to be fast or tactful; he only needs to be himself."

"Perhaps he just has to be the one you're in love with." Grandpa's eyebrows rise.

I stand. "Grandpa, I think it's time for my ride now."

"I'm just trying to help."

With a soft chuckle, I kiss his cheek. "I love you," I say and make my way to the front door.

"Butterfly," Grandpa calls.

I ignore him as I hear him chuckle.

He calls again. "I put my money on ..."

My hand on the door handle, I pause to listen.

"I put my money on you, following your heart. Don't pick a fight with your heart. You'll never win."

"I'll see you soon, Grandpa." I smile, pulling the door open. I step out and hurry to the garage.

⁂

In my Black Mamba, I speed out, ready for my morning ride. Vine Lane is quiet as I fly past the leafy trees. Onto the highway, I look back in time and frown at the things I didn't know. My frown grows deeper when I imagine things that I'm still to know.

I lean in, preparing for the corner ahead. I'm thankful for the overhanging branches. As much as I enjoy the sun, I still fear its burning rays.

Past the sharp turn, I ride uphill. Once on top, I slam on the brakes and shut the engine. Instead of gazing at the river below like I always do, I look ahead, past the dense forest to the top of the tallest hill in Ashbourne. I smile, marveling at the Van-Bailey Stills. It feels less haunting than the first time I saw it from here.

Obnoxious Zachary, I smile remembering my words to Emily and my mother. I pull out my phone from my pocket and dial three.

Zachary, I heard you and Madeline arguing the other day when I was sleeping. I can't help but feel I'm to blame for her leaving, at least to a certain extent. I'm sorry she left. If you want, I'm ready to go to Thracia with you, and I'll explain to her that nothing is going on between us.

By the way, I have something serious to discuss with you. I think I might be a serial bloodsucker. You must have read the stories back in sixth grade, about the vampires who never stopped killing humans. If you didn't, well I did, and I'll tell you all about it. I know by now you must be terrified of my fangs. Don't worry, I don't feel hungry or thirsty this week, so I won't bite you."

I laugh nervously.

"Please call me. We need to talk. Or rather, I need to talk to you. And, um … I miss you.

I could almost hear his amused chuckle after that last line. Fist clenched he would celebrate, "*Yes; she admitted she missed me.*"

At least, that's one-way of seeing the outcome. The worst would be Zachary refusing to talk to me.

It's downhill time; time to play with the wind. I start the engine again, ready to go. My head buzzes as I await the thrill. I roll the throttle for speed. My heart is thrashing hard now, excitement rushing through my veins. Adrenaline flashes down my spine, my cheeks numb to the strong air current. I pull out a smile. Staring on the road ahead, I don't look at the speedometer. I remember the giant dog, but it's not here this time. I speed along, sighing as pass the spot I crashed last time. Thoughts of the Vangel visit me again.

I don't know if I have the courage to destroy the Vangel. Nevertheless, I will find him, if not for my life, at least for my desire to see his face.

I hope he will be as selfish as I am. It makes things easier.

Alexandra Joanne Deluca. I smile. *Watson never sounded right to me.*

THE STORY CONTINUES IN

The Vangel

BOOK TWO OF CURSED.

MANTISSA CREED

READ A PREVIEW OF CURSED: THE VANGEL

I

"DID YOU SAY YOU LOVE ME?"

Zachary is not healing. Maxx's words keep ringing in my head.

Another day ends. The sun sets while Mother and I say goodbye to Grandpa at the airport; he's going back to Viennamo. The plane takes off, and on my way home, I drop off Mother at the hospital for her night shift.

He's not human. Why is he not healing?

Arriving home, I rush to my room and reach for my laptop. For the past weeks, I've been busy at Autumn Reigns. It's frustrating to know that I don't have control over time. Stretching a day to forty-eight hours would be helpful. I need to find a way to get the track finished before Christmas.

I'm in the middle of emailing John for ideas when I hear a video call alert. My finger pauses on the answer key, pushing it down carefully.

"Hey, Beautiful." Zachary smirks.

"Knight?" My heart swells up as I look at him. It's been too long.

He seems to be at the back of a moving vehicle. From the executive leather seats, I assume it's one of those chauffeur-driven cars.

We both sigh at the same time and chuckle a little. Then the smiles disappear.

"I remember that look from the first time I saw you," Zachary whispers.

"I'm surprised you still remember me."

"You remind me of a beautiful girl I lost three weeks ago."

"I'll take that as a chat up line," I say, smiling.

He widens his eyes. "No, I'm serious."

"You are?" I frown.

"Hmm." He nods tentatively. "I miss her."

My mind goes to Madeline. "What happened to her?"

His lips pressed together again. "It's a long story."

"Too long for me?"

Zachary drops his gaze. "Well, she called me to say she had become a serial bloodsucker that feeds on human blood. I wanted to imagine her hunting as I know a vampire would do, but I couldn't."

"Maybe she just wanted your attention."

"I know she did, and I wanted to call back and tell her how angry I was with her. How she evoked some emotions that I never knew I had. I wanted to look her in the eye and tell her how she hurt me, but I saw her lips parting to say, 'you have no right, Zachary.' So I chose to drown in my sorrows."

"She hurt you? How?"

"I never thought it would hurt. Maybe because I blocked my mind from thinking about it, but when my best friend told me what happened, I couldn't erase the image from my mind. Like I said, I have no right, but then again, why do I feel like I do?"

Staring into his eyes, I take a deep sigh. "I'm sorry. I'm sure she didn't mean to hurt you. The time it happened, it was more for her than hurting you. She wanted to feel something for someone else."

Zachary swallows, a line forming on his forehead. "Did that work?"

I drop my gaze. "I thought it did, but then Chan came back."

"Do you still ..." He looks down, then back to my eyes. "Are you in love with him?"

"I don't know." I shrug. "I think I am, yes."

Zachary presses his lips together and nods gently, but says nothing.

"What happened with Madeline?"

"She left. She said she was giving me time."

"Time for what?"

"She thinks I'm in love with you."

Are you? I stare into his eyes, but decide not to ask. Yes, or No, I don't think I'm ready to hear his answer. Moreover, I don't want him to throw the same question at me.

We remain silent, staring at each other. Then Zachary places his hand on his forehead. "I was about to tell her," he breathes.

"Tell her ...?"

"The day Chan came, I was about to tell her that I ... it's you. I was going to break up with her, but things got complicated."

I stare at his furrowed brow and sigh. "I heard you telling her it will always be her." Struggling to hide the pain in my voice, I continue. "That you will always love her and her alone."

With a serious face, Zachary stares into my eyes. "I think I was trying to convince myself that's the case, but you ..." He breathes in, then mumbles. "God, why is it so hard to talk about you?"

"Try singing."

He laughs. "It's easier to touch you."

We gaze at each other again, smiling.

"Does your father know Madeline left you?"

"Yes he does. You have nothing to worry about. He won't give you a hard time anymore."

"Why? What did you tell him?"

"Nothing much. We just came to an agreement." He says casually.

I know he's hiding the truth from me because two days ago, Maxx told me a little about what that happened.

"Maxx said you had an argument with your father," I say.

He frowns, avoiding my gaze. "What exactly did Maxx tell you?"

"For once, Zachary, tell me what happened." I voice, then pause, controlling my voice. "Do I have to ask everyone around you before knowing what's going on with you?"

A smile melts the frown on his face, soon to be followed by a stern look. "He asked me to get rid of you." Zachary's eyes narrow. "To cut you out of Autumn Reigns and out of my life."

I'm aware Zach-Louis hates me, but I never thought he would consider taking Zachary from me.

Swallowing hard, I stare at Zachary. "Is that why you were ignoring my calls?"

"I tried. Thinking of you with Sean helped, but only for a few days." He smiles to himself. "So, I presented my father with an offer he couldn't refuse."

My chest rises. "What was that?"

He looks into my eyes and smiles. "I get to have you in my life, for as long as I don't pursue my desire to find Jo."

My eyes widen. Then I blink. "You gave up your Jo for me?"

"I want you to know you don't have to fear my father anymore." Zachary's voice is strained. "He promised to treat you better."

"You did that for me?"

He shakes his head. "When will you ever see that when it comes to you, everything I do, I do it for me?"

We remain silent, gazing at each other. I almost forget he's in a car until he orders the chauffeur to stop. My heart pounds as I dread hearing him saying goodbye. I breathe in as he shifts into a relaxed position, his back resting on the long seat.

"That feels much better," he says, running his fingers through his locks.

"Thanks for the pints." I stare down at my fingers and look up again. "I thought maybe you were terrified of my fangs, so you decided I feed from the pints instead."

He grins. "Of course your little fangs terrify me."

"The little fangs must have traumatized you, huh?"

"I'm shaking right now." Zachary drops his gaze, perhaps to hide the smile on his face, but it's clear even with his head down. "That's why I'm leaving for Pannonia right now."

My mouth opens. "What?"

"To get some counseling," he adds.

I'm not sure if this is part of a joke or not. Is he truly leaving for Pannonia?

I stare at him with a frown. "Seriously, are you going to Pannonia?"

"I'm visiting my grandfather for a while."

"Maxx told me you were not healing? What happened?"

"That boy needs a loyalty check. Which part of not telling you anything did he not understand? Now he should come and see your worried face. Maybe that will teach him a lesson."

"So is it serious?"

"It's nothing to worry about. That's why I'm going to meet my grandfather. He knows what to do."

"When did that start?"

"I'm not sure. Probably, the time Ashton came back from Pannonia."

"So you didn't want to tell me?"

"Well I did." He rolls his eyes. "I'm telling you now."

I gaze at him in disbelief. I then raise my hands and begin to fan my face.

"What are you doing?" He grimaces.

"Well, I'm obviously traumatized, and maybe I could do with some counseling, too."

A deep chuckle cracks from his chest. I struggle to keep a straight face, watching him laughing some more.

"You're traumatized because I told you, I was leaving for Pannonia?" He's still smiling as he shakes his head.

"I don't see why you should laugh. It's not funny." I bite my bottom lip, holding a laugh. "And you didn't say goodbye."

CURSED: THE VANGEL ⚓ 5

He grimaces as if disagreeing with my statement, but before he speaks, I quickly add, "At least say goodbye in person."

He drops his head, laughing again, and I use the opportunity to make him feel guiltier.

"Some people have died from sudden news like this, don't you know?" I raise my voice to emphasize my point.

As he raises his head, our eyes meet, and I can't help but return his brilliant   smile.

"I expected you to come and tell me in person or perhaps over lunch or something like that. Besides I have something I wanted to discuss with you, something important."

Slowly blinking, Zachary gazes at me, his eyes glistening. "Can't that wait until I come back?"

"When will you be back?" I don't wait for his answer before adding. "This is serious. I might die before you come back. You don't know."

He laughs again. "You really love me, don't you?"

My face warms. "Did you say you love me?"

Zachary chuckles. "I should be back in a month, maybe two."

"Jesus, Zachary! Won't you miss me, at all?"

He throws his head back on the headrest. "Is that your way of telling me you'll miss me?" His eyebrows rise, one higher than the other.

"Well," I said slowly. "I won't miss you at all. I'll just miss you, missing me; that's all."

"Since Ash came back, you only miss me when you need my blood."

"What?" I gasp. "How could you think that? Are you jealous?"

"Of course not," he snorts

I smile as he stares at me, and for a second, my mind wanders back to the first time I met him. "You're still full of it, Zachary. And to think I was going to kiss you goodbye. But since you're already gone, well …"

"Damn. When does that kiss expire? Can you freeze it for me until I come back?"

"Nope. It will never taste the same."

"Then I shall forever whip myself for missing out on that kiss."

I snigger, and we stare at each other in silence.

"I'm sorry I spoke to your father the way I did. I was frustrated looking for you, and I took my anger on him. Don't ask me why."

"It's okay. I take it out on him too when I don't see you."

"He wanted to kill me."

"He almost killed me." Zachary smirks.

We laugh.

"I'm really sorry, though. I was out of line. I should have walked out."

"It doesn't work. I've walked out so many times."

I laugh, and again, we exchange gazes. "Bring me something special when you come back."

"That's easy. I'll bring you myself. Goodbye, beautiful," Zachary whispers. Immediately, my screen goes black before I could respond.

"Goodbye, Zachary," I murmur to myself.

A blanket of sadness wraps over me. I try to continue with my email to John, but my mind keeps drifting to Zachary.

I think of Channing, then end up comparing him to Zachary. *I can't do this.*

I rise, heading for the bathroom and take my night shower. Now Emily, Sean and Zach-Louis intrude upon my thoughts again. My mind flashes back to that moment we argued, and how I still need to apologize. What excuse will I give him?

I'm a Gemini, and so I tend to have two personalities sometimes, so that was my bad side.

I laugh at how silly that sounds.

Coming out of the bathroom, I change into my caramel nighty and take a seat by the dresser. This is something I rarely do. I begin brushing my hair.

There's a knock at my door. I hesitate, and gently place the hairbrush down on the table. Another knock and I rise. As I turn around to face the door, I stumble and stop, my mind flashing back to what I see as the past. I hear the same knock, the same rhythm, and I rush to open the door. *Sean?*

The vision ends, and I realize I still haven't answered the door.

"Come in," I call and sit back down.

Slowly, the door opens, and I see a reflection of the visitor's face in the mirror.

"Zachary?" I gasp and spring up with my hands on my chest. "My God, I ..." I rush toward him and jump into his open arms, my arms around his neck and my legs around his waist.

"Hey," Zachary tightens his arms around me. "Now how's that for a surprise?"

"You're insane, you know that?" Still in his arms, I punch him playfully.

As he shuts the door with his foot, Zachary laughs, planting kisses on my cheeks. Grinning as his eyes meet mine, he comments, "It's far better than me actually telling you I was coming, right?"

"Right." I breathe in, and wipe my eyes as Zachary places me back on my feet.

"Are you crying?" he teases, wiping my cheeks.

I roll my eyes at him, take his hand, and lead him to the couch. We sit close together, facing each other, and I tie my hair into a bun before Zachary unties it and grabs my hand, entwining it with his.

I stare into his eyes. "I swear you were on your way to the airport."

He holds my gaze, then answers, "I know," tucking a loose strand of hair behind my ear. "Did you really think I would leave without seeing you? Without saying a proper goodbye? ... Plus I need that goodbye kiss."

"Uhm ..." I close my eyes for a second to hide from his penetrating gaze. "About the kiss, I didn't—"

"Don't tell me you were kidding. Not after I drove all this way." With a smirk, Zachary slowly leans toward me. My heart is on fire as he pauses inches from my face. He reaches for my blushing cheek.

"Zach, I can't—"

"Close your eyes," he whispers.

"What?"

"I said, close your eyes." He comes an inch closer, and now I give in to his scent. I smell his breath, and it's as if I'm falling into his arms.

Reluctantly, I shut my eyes and in that same instance, the speed of my heart beat increases. His nose brushes mine, and I fail to stop my lips from parting. His breath by my lips causes me to let out a quiet puff. I fight to stop myself from closing the tiny space between our lips. Then he moves away, and I swallow.

"Keep them closed." I hear his voice again.

I obey. After a brief moment, I hear my door opening and shutting, all happening within a moment. He's next to me again, close as before.

"I smell cappuccino," I whisper.

He chuckles. "Don't spoil the surprise," he says and asks me to open my mouth. He feeds me with a piece of a red velvet cupcake. Halfway through chewing, I open my eyes to meet his on me.

"Did anybody ever tell you how painfully unselfish you are?" I ask.

"No, but I always hear them saying it to Ashton."

"He's like an angel, isn't he?" I breathe out.

"And I can't compete with that, can I?"

"Who said there's a competition?" I smile, picking up a cupcake. I feed him and watch him eat. As he swallows, I can see he can't wait to speak.

"By the way, I actually walked into the Nair Saif, straight to the kitchen, and with my uncle making the cupcake, I was preparing you a cappuccino. So, I created that with these hands." He flexes his fingers. "It's far from commercial, just so you know."

"Thank you, I know you love me." I kiss his cheeks.

"Ewww, take those crumbs off my cheek, please," he teases, turning his cheek to me.

I shift closer and slowly brush the tiny remains of the cupcake off his face.

"I think you should use your lips instead." He smirks. "They're gentler."

I laugh bust still, I lean closer and used my lips to touch his cheek.

He pinches a cupcake and puts the bit on his lips. "Look, they're over here, too," he mumbles, pointing at his lips.

Laughing, I lean in toward his lips, but stop before my lips touch his, just as he closes his eyes. We both laugh as I lean back on the couch.

He wipes his face with serviettes. When he's done, he puts his head on my lap.

I kiss his forehead before moving my fingers through his locks.

"You will tell me what you're thinking about Madeline, won't you?" I ask after a moment of silence, my eyes on his, which are closed.

Zachary doesn't answer immediately, but blinks his eyes open a moment later. "You said there's nothing going on between us."

"I think I can talk to Madeline. I'm sure she will understand if I explain it to her."

Zachary's eyes remain closed. "But that would be a lie."

My hand in his hair pauses. "What do you mean?"

He opens his eyes and sits up, gazing with conviction as he looks at me. "That there's nothing going on between us. Is this nothing?" He takes my hands into his and weaves his fingers with mine, creating an explosion of heat that spreads all over me.

I indulge in the fluttering sensation for a moment, then stand and pace toward the balcony doors.

Zachary follows. "Not talking about our feelings doesn't make them disappear, Alexandra." He breathes behind me, sending my heart racing as he hugs me from behind.

A shiver runs through me, and I coil into his arms.

He sighs. "Because I don't say how I feel about you, doesn't mean the feelings are not there. Usually what we don't hear, we feel, and what we feel deep inside is what we fail to talk about."

I remain quiet. He turns me around to face him. "So what do you say we talk about us? Not the track nor the partnership, but you and me."

I stare into his eyes and shake my head. I'm not ready; I was just getting used to being on my own.

Before I can think of what to say, He slides his hand in his jacket pocket, fishing out a blue velvet ring box. My mouth opens as he goes on one knee.

"Zachary, what are you doing?" My heart skips a beat, heat spreading all over me. *He can't do this.* I'm not ...

"Alexandra Joanne Watson. You've become part of my life and my dreams. Accept this and make me the happiest man in the world."

The box flips open.

"What?" I frown at a set of keys carved with the Zetra Omni Scorpii logo. "I could kill you right now." I shoot him an annoyed look.

As he chuckles, I drop my knees to join his on the wood. Our eyes level; we smile at each other, entwining our hands together.

"The car is yours to race with me to Pannonia." He places the keys in my palm and holds my hands between his and to his chest. "One week on the road, just you and I," he whispers.

"Pannonia is 7000 miles away, Zachary."

Zachary lowers his head, kissing my cheek before bringing his forehead to touch mine. "I want you to meet my grandfather, Zachary the second," he pleads. "Come to Pannonia with me."

CURSED

THE VANGEL
BOOK II

THE CURSE
BOOK III

FOR EXCLUSIVE CONTENT AND THE LATEST UPDATES:

WWW.CURSEDTHESAGA.COM

Your eyes staring into my eyes,
Who am I but a guy with two eyes on the prize,
And the prize in my eyes is 10 times
The surprise in your eyes as I kiss you goodnight.

Your smile is the fire that rocks my soul
Gonna remember it until I grow old,
'Cause life is too short we gotta do things right,
So baby let's just party toni-ght.
Baby let's just party toni-ght.

We've come out on top, we're in front of the line,
We're here to rock out and have a good time,
'Cause the past is the past and the future is bright,

So baby let's just party toni-ght.
Baby let's just party toni-ght.

Mordecai and Rigby - "Party Tonight"
The Regular Show
Episode "Mordecai and the Rigbys"

22796528R00200

Made in the USA
Charleston, SC
01 October 2013